PRAISE FOR
OPENING NIGHTS

"A fine and complex novel, a comedy and then some."—*The New Yorker*

"Exhilarating . . . Vivid and precise . . . Burroway, who has been in the theater, is superb on the molding of a production through its rehearsals, and on the fever lines that work through a theater cast that finds itself in a strange town, its life condensed into its work on stage."—*Los Angeles Times*

"Burroway's hallmark is her honest, ironic portrayal of characters who fall into their own traps and are then surprised to find the simplest truths in the unlikeliest of places. And this is achieved in chapters of gem-like completeness, all of which stand on their own like short plays."—*Kirkus Reviews*

"Not only does this book thrive on its author's sure knowledge of stagecraft and costume design, but it also intimately reflects the nuances of difficult relationships through the personalities and thought patterns of the protagonists. They are complex and instantly recognizable, a warm and lively bunch whose selves, to use the author's words, are not 'too well hidden to be mined.' "—*Publishers Weekly*

BANTAM BOOKS BY JANET BURROWAY

OPENING NIGHTS
RAW SILK

OPENING NIGHTS

Janet Burroway

BANTAM BOOKS

TORONTO · NEW YORK · LONDON · SYDNEY · AUCKLAND

Passages from The Nuns (les Nonnes) *by Eduardo Manet, translated by Robert Baldick, reprinted by permission of the author, Editions Gallimard, and John Calder (Publishers) Ltd., London.*

Lyrics from "Handy Man," words and music by Jimmy Jones and Otis Blackwell, copyright © 1959, 1984 by CBS Catalogue Partnership. All rights throughout the world controlled and administered by CBS Unart Catalog Inc. All rights reserved. International Copyright secured. Used by permission.

"The Pardon" by Richard Wilbur from Ceremony and Other Poems, *copyright 1950, © 1978 by Richard Wilbur. Reprinted by permission of Harcourt Brace Jovanovich, Inc.*

"Love Calls Us to the Things of This World," by Richard Wilbur from Things of This World, *copyright © 1956 by Richard Wilbur. Reprinted by permission of Harcourt Brace Jovanovich, Inc.*

*This low-priced Bantam Book
has been completely reset in a type face
designed for easy reading, and was printed
from new plates. It contains the complete
text of the original hard-cover edition.*
NOT ONE WORD HAS BEEN OMITTED.

OPENING NIGHTS

*A Bantam Book / published by arrangement with
Atheneum Publishers*

PRINTING HISTORY
Atheneum edition published June 1985

Bantam edition / June 1986

ISBN 0-553-25892-3

Published simultaneously in the United States and Canada

PRINTED IN THE UNITED STATES OF AMERICA

KR 0 9 8 7 6 5 4 3 2 1

For The Freen

Bring them down from the ruddy gallows;
Let there be clean linen for the backs of thieves;
Let lovers go fresh and sweet to be undone,
And the heaviest nuns walk in a pure floating
Of dark habits,
              keeping their difficult balance.

"Love Calls Us to the Things of This World"
Richard Wilbur

CONTENTS

OPENING NIGHTS

1. *A True Eye*

Henry got hit about six A.M. The squeal of tires waked her, and Shaara was half up by the time the first cry came, racing through the rec room in bare feet with her gauze nightshift and her red hair flying, banging out the kitchen door, her stomach knotted. He had dragged himself ten feet up the drive, and he stumbled there, raised his head for one long complaining moan, dropped it, was already dead by the time she squatted and pressed a hand on his side. Then it was the fat woman out of the Ford van howling: "I'm so sorry! I wouldn't for the world . . . he just ran right out!" The bristled ruff was warm but his long Shepherd legs stuck straight out with unnatural formality. There was no mistaking he was dead. Shaara thought she could handle Henry but that she could not handle the woman, who was high-pitched and wringing her hands, clearly trapped. Maybe she would already be gone if Shaara hadn't come outside so quick. Hit and run, Shaara would have advised her. But aloud she mumbled reassurances, tucked her shift between her knees, stroked Henry's feathery tail, and waited out the woman's angry innocence.

Now at six forty-five she stood in shorts and sneakers, calf-deep in a red clay grave in a Memorial Day dawn. It wasn't all that bad. The mist was hanging in the hanging moss, translucent yellow where the light spun through. The ground broke luminous and eddied up an underground smell of immaculate decay. Henry lay with lumpish grace in the wheelbarrow, the flow of tail protruding from the Indian bedspread they'd used as a beach blanket ever since he puppy-chewed a hole in it four years ago. Whatever burst had been internal; no blood. The blood was in the color of the Georgia earth. He could have the blanket.

What she had to do was to dig until she could stand to the depth of her shorts cuff, deep enough to discourage possums and other dogs. If she kept at it she could have it filled and tamped before Kevin waked. She hacked at a pecan root with the axe, squinting, measuring the straightness of her grave sides. She had a true eye, and could scissor a hemline through $14.98-a-yard Lurex without chalking it. The ground, which was probably worth more than that, she sliced with the same accuracy. The muscles of her upper arm were singing little tremolos. She suffered a mild attack of tachycardia from the exertion. She lifted the axe over her head and brought it down with such clean force that the split root lifted like an arm, and drops of sweat scattered in the damp earth.

Then she slung the axe out and reached for the shovel again. It was not that she couldn't handle it, god knows, or that she didn't know what she had to do. It was that, having psyched herself for this particular day, having accepted that it would be grim and long, it seemed unfair to add this task to the front end of it. There was a tedious Sex Equity Review meeting to get through this afternoon, and then in half a dozen or a dozen hours—he had not bothered to let her know which—she would be facing Boyd, whom she had not seen since the divorce five years ago. She had already noticed it was Memorial Day without reckoning she'd be digging any graves herself. Things come at you from whatever direction you aren't looking. Last night she had washed her hair and shaved her legs, even treated herself to an overdue pedicure, not because she gave a shit how she looked for Boyd but because clean hair and glossy legs made her feel sexy, and feeling sexy raised her general level of competence. Now her scalp was frying and her toes were gritty inside her sneakers. She should've put on socks. When she flung the shovelful her eyes did a blurred scan of her territory: a Pizza Hut of a house, cedar fences around a modest quarter-acre that immodestly burgeoned with tropical fronds, pine, palm, pecan and figs. She did not want Boyd blundering into it, snapping twigs under his toes. She put a foot on the shovel and drove it home, laying her claim three inches in the ground. And now, finally, she was crying. Not about the dog.

Shaara Soole had a tendency to self-torture. Big-boned, lanky, melon-breasted, her best feature was a head of rusty-barbed-wire hair that she tried to control with a wardrobe of scarves and headband things. Like most costume designers, she dressed with more originality than taste, usually on the Oriental or Polynesian side, sometimes with voluminous loops of thong and matte metal over an ordinary shirt. This was somewhat eccentric in Hubbard, Georgia, but Shaara was oblivious of her eccentricity, being so concerned to keep her essential foolishness in check. Her personality was not streaked with sentimentality, but marbled with it, like a fine Chateaubriand. She wept at television appeals for Save the Children Federation, and got misty-eyed when somebody let her into a traffic lane.

Nevertheless she had carved out a life for herself and Kevin in this cracker-academic backwash, a pit-stop just off the Interstate on the route from Atlanta to Florida, so that at any given moment its population (40,000) was a quarter transient, student or tourist according to the season. She had raised her son to a normal, hungry, and so far cheerful adolescence (Kevin kept an iguana named Bette Davis, but this was not considered eccentric in Hubbard, Georgia). She had got herself promoted, tenured and salaried at $18,000 in the Theater Department of Magoor College for the Liberal Arts. She liked to say that it had done her good to be elevated from a scatty woman to an absent-minded professor. When Dean Dimbleton praised her in committee as a "shit cutter," she liked to reply that she had studied cutting under Bevan at Yale.

But in the fifth year her foolishness had betrayed her. During a phone call to arrange Kevin's Christmas vacation in New York, Shaara had mentioned to her former husband that Magoor was looking for a director for the opening production of its new grant-funded theater. It was not a slip of the tongue, exactly. Boyd was a director, but not the sort of director anyone would expect to want a semi-pro in the rural South. He worked mainly in New York and the Northeast, sometimes L.A. if it paid expenses. She was astounded when she found out he'd applied. She was speechless when Joe Dimbleton announced the appointment, as if congratulating her for bringing it off herself, being clever enough to have the lure of Boyd Soole's son in Hubbard. Thinking about it made her anger overflow again, and she tried to redirect it into the force of her shoveling. Somehow or other, which would have to be some other how than it used to be, they would have to work together. They would have to present some sort of composite attitude to Kevin, who had got quite comfortably used to seeing them separately. They would have to get through one of those enervating opening nights where, everything being quite adequate including her costumes and his directing, everyone would feel bound to announce a theatrical turning point, an apocalypse of the avant-garde. Made worse this time by a clutch of benevolent officials—they'd been promised a Swedish consul, a black senator, and by some fluke of luck (the whole damn project was charmed) Burt Reynolds—who would congratulate them on the spreading of the professional arts to the boondocks.

The clay was wet and hard and she had to fork each layer first, axing the roots she snagged up, then scraping the lumps up in the shovel and tossing them out, higher every layer, so that it got harder the tireder she got. She was barely up to her knees and if she didn't get it finished by seven-thirty Kevin would catch her here.

Nevertheless she propped herself against the clay for a minute, wiping her lashes, and the tickling sweat out of her cleavage, with a damp Kleenex, and registering the fact that among the dignitaries due for opening night there was one she nervously wanted to meet. There was one who inspired in her the same self-conscious greed she'd felt when, as an apprentice designer, she had struggled through gawky peers to shake the hand of Samuel Beckett. She had, on that occasion, ached for words at once simple and profound, to make Mr. Beckett understand that she understood him. But she was wearing purple shoes. She had not thought that Mr. Beckett would be capable of recognizing empathy from someone in red hair and purple shoes, and she had experienced a sharp irritation against Mr. Beckett for his failure. And yet it was more likely that she might have made friends with the taciturn absurdist than that she should be able to make contact, on opening night, with the second Mrs. Soole.

Shaara carried around with her a snapshot of her former husband's second wife. Kevin, thirteen, had dropped it out of his history book one morning in a scramble for the last bell. Shaara tucked it in the celluloid pocket behind her Exxon card, meaning to keep it for him. Now she encountered it whenever she gassed up the VW—once a week—and had it lying in her lap the whole time William "Bud" Rufus fiddled with her battery.

Wendy Soole showed a shy ridge of Kodachrome teeth before a deep-gray Cape Cod sea. She was very young and very slender, her pale hair fringed in a gamin cut around her ears. Whereas Shaara flailed and thrashed through life and always looked somehow caught out in a snapshot, Wendy Soole sat graceful and serene. In fact she had more Peter Pan than Wendy about her—a boneless boyish sexiness—and a look of scrubbed and shielded expectation that made Shaara want to say, "Poor dear!" Was that the point? Was that what Boyd had always wanted, somebody more patiently *protectable*?

She meant to give the photo back to Kevin, but she forgot. People, Shaara knew, actually rarely forget such things. She didn't run out of gas, for instance. Maybe she was waiting to see whether Kevin would miss it. Maybe she was subconsciously keeping it from him—this seemed the sort of thing the subconscious would do. Maybe her curiosity was jealousy in disguise. But Shaara did not believe it. What Shaara believed was that she liked the picture and liked looking at it among the emanations of axle grease and regular. What Shaara confusedly believed was that under the convolutions of appropriate response—curiosity, jealousy, rage, contempt—she shared an intricate empathy with the second Mrs. Soole.

The sun was getting higher and hotter, attracted to the arch of her nape. A redneck. And her breasts were in the way. They'd been in her way ever since they started ballooning in the sixth grade months ahead of anybody else's, and some precocious wit had nicknamed her Mother Nurture. She'd already had a reputation for eccentricity on account of the Heinzdorfer family's general reputation for eccentricity and on account of her unruly hair, but she'd never actually *done* anything so eccentric as to get breasts. In the seventh grade she tried cropping her hair, but it made her head look no bigger than either of her breasts, so she let it grow out again. Lately people had been complimenting her on her "Afro," but in the eighth grade they called her Frizzie Lizzie. In the eighth grade she took to crushing her books against her chest in folded arms; somebody thought up Tit-wit. These memories might have made her a radical feminist in the 'sixties if she had not been trying to stay married to Boyd Soole, and if she could manage without a bra. As it was, even with an underwire and stretch lace, she had pins and needles in the aureole from swinging over the grave. She needed all the support she could get.

Suddenly she'd had enough. The hole was only a couple of inches above her knee but her breasts were stinging and her biceps felt wrung out like a rag and she decided it would have to do. She set the tools apart and wheeled the barrow to the edge, started to tip it, and then out of some minimal sense of ceremony lifted the corners of the blanket instead, testing the dog's dead weight against her shuddering muscles. She twisted and dragged the bundle over her shoulder, staggering slightly as the corpse hit her hip, then swung it and lowered it, panting. She kneeled at the edge of the opening and leaned into the musty fragrance of hacked roots, tucked Henry's tail and arranged the blanket border over his long face. She lay a hand briefly on his still-warm hip, then stood quickly and began shoveling.

She'd liked Henry, even "loved" him, a goofy, sloppy sort of Shepherd with a kingly ruff and an endearing, if fatal, talent for opening the back porch door. But in her thirty-seven years she had buried enough dogs, enough kittens, turtles, rabbits, flushed enough goldfish, to know that you take death on. If you were going to own a dog, then at some point you would be cleaning shit out of the shag, and at some point fetching him back from the pound for a ten-dollar fine and a lecture on the leash law. At some point Mrs. Richard Healey would call, stentorian, to inform you that her back porch was ankle-deep in doo-doo, and you would commiserate, gritting your teeth; and eventually one morning you'd be waked before dawn by a screech and a yelp, and run out to the stranger in the Ford van, wringing her hands in the road, wailing, "He just ran right out. . . ."

That is, you get used to the ways things are. You put a Band-Aid on a bloody scrape, you bury a dog. You apply a one-night stand to a divorce, a bottle of Jim Beam to the one-night stand, and an Alka-Seltzer Gold to the hangover. Life is a long accident, and most accidents occur at home. You can sit and wait for them. You can sit on a Naugahyde couch in the seedy comfort of the Magoor faculty lounge eating Granola crumbs out of a vendor bag; you can fit yourself out in tenure and a cedar two-bedroom and take no more risks than an occasional

pair of stack-heeled shoes; and sooner or later the entire goddam Grumbacher Foundation for the Arts will single you out
for culture, and Boyd Soole will come leaping down out of the
Big Apple where he belongs, bringing in his train, on opening
night, the one person in all the world in whom you have the
greatest interest, and the one person in all the world whom
you have the least right to know: the second Mrs. Soole.

Shaara tamped the earth with sneaker treads and dumped
an armful of dry leaves.

2. *The Heavy*

Boyd Soole was in a bad place in his life, and already in the first couple of hours the bad place had taken on the atmosphere of Hubbard, Georgia.

He'd lumbered half a mile in the midday swelter lugging seven weeks' worth of shirts because he'd found out in advance that his motel was called the Campus Side, and that the Greyhound depot was right next to the campus, and had inferred that the motel was within walking distance without further postulating that the campus sides might be long, or that there would be two of them. They'd offered to meet him but he'd waved it away because he didn't want to set any precedent for chitchat with administrators and arts buffs. His air fare had been paid but he bused from Atlanta because he disliked small planes—the claustrophobic johns, the knee space, the wing shudder just before landing, and the notion of death generally.

The mistake disoriented him; neither of his wives would have made it. A trio of coeds in Levi cutoffs, and no more halter top than could've been made by one bandana among them, giggled when he stopped to mop his face. Boyd wasn't used to being giggled at, and that was a precedent he didn't care to set, either, in Hubbard, Georgia.

Boyd was a big man, a boiled missionary still sweating from the cannibals' pot. Sometimes he dreamed that he was being chased by his own body. He knew Delmore Schwartz's "The Heavy Bear Who Goes with Me . . ." by heart, and recited it to himself while waiting for planes or while walking along badly lit Lower East Side streets. He ought to have been ugly but the evidence was otherwise; men deferred to him and women scrambled for his praise. As a director he rarely needed to raise his voice because his presence was so intense; he created a wake. Clothes disliked him—he was the sort of person whose buttons pop—but he'd never had any trouble finding someone who wanted to put him in repair.

He turned on the air conditioning and opened the fake leather three-suiter that was Wendy's mother's idea of a copy of a Gucci. He took a bottle of Jack Daniels from one side and his directing script from the other, found a plastic tumbler in the bathroom, and settled himself at the kneehole dresser. He ought to make two phone calls, one to reassure Wendy he'd arrived safely and the other to say hello to Shaara and Kevin. But he was aware of a—what was it Capote called it?—a "floating anxiety," and his dislike of telephones was so profound that he decided to let himself off for a couple of hours. He toyed with the Act Two blocking for half the drink, then let himself off that too, knocked the rest back John Wayne style, and decided to take a nap.

But he couldn't sleep right away. The closed drape didn't make it so much dark as dirty-light. He thought he was a coward for not calling Wendy, who would probably be anxious. And thought he was a rotten so-and-so for not wanting to talk right away to his son. And he thought he was in a bad place in his life.

He was forty, the same age that his dad had started going to pieces, though Boyd hadn't known that at the time. He was a good director, and he had one of those resumés that made a prospective employer take a look, but he was forty and he hadn't made it. Unlike Shaara, he'd managed to avoid the academic route; he'd kept the freedom of the freelance and he did eke out a living. But he'd missed the big time and he had a feeling that the big time hadn't noticed. He did his eking in the Catskills, Off-Off Broadway, grant-funded projects like the present one. He had a feeling that his wave was cresting and that if he didn't catch it it would pass him by. In the meantime he had taken on a second wife who grew up in middle-class comfort that she didn't at the moment miss—but what would happen if she had to live year after year in this catch-as-catch-can existence? And now Wendy was probably pregnant. He couldn't deny so young a wife a family if she wanted one, but how could he keep his freedom and manage two families? Money was always tight, and some months he had trouble making child support for Kevin. Medical bills had to be humiliatingly put off. What did he think he was doing starting all over again? And what did he think he was doing in Hubbard, Georgia?

When he finally slept, his dream was the standard theatrical dream, every actor's version of being naked on a thoroughfare. The curtain opened on Act Two but there was no Act Two; he'd forgotten to do it. The company swarmed in the wings buzzing at him. Shaara was there, shaking her Medusa hair, and Kevin as a small boy, whining, and the three gigglers from the campus. His leading lady, Gunilla Lind, was got up in a Max Ernst outfit of owl feathers, aiming her beak and breasts at him. "*Gut ist mir*," she said darkly, or "Gutter smear," in an accent heavier than her own. There was smoke welling up between the backstage floorboards, enveloping the actors and the curtain ropes, and when the smoke broke over his ankles he woke up. He was sweating; the sweat turned instantly to surface chill in the air conditioning, and the sensation injured him with a memory of his father, whose dreams had had a different sort of subject matter but the same menacing and chilling atmosphere.

Boyd was driven by ambition, and it drove him through some funny territory for a competent professional. Some of the territory was inhabited by spiders the size of an International Harvester reaper; some by vampires that emerged in sticky embryo from little leaves opening on, say, an ordinary Midwestern window sill; some by malevolent diesel wheels or live electric wires that were, in fact, alive. On several occasions he had said to his mother, and then his wife, and then his other wife, "I had a weird dream last night." The point of telling the dream always turned out to be that it was particularly original, inventive, brilliant. The dream was diffused in the effect; praise laid the ghosts. He decided early to go into drama, and people said he was driven by ambition.

But his choice of medium was a little askew, and he was dismally aware of that now as he went for ice, refilled his plastic cup, fiddled with the air conditioner, and sat back down to the blocking copy, script pages neatly scissored and cemented in a black three-ring, of Eduardo Manet's *The Nuns*.

It was a case of the forest and the trees. Boyd had grown up in Hollywood, within cycling distance of the Grauman footprints at a time when fifty cents would get you in to see every murder, monster, black mass, vampire, zombie, werewolf and nuclear holocaust the day of its release. He'd probably seen every horror flick ever made, but he never took the trouble to remember them. It never occurred to him to *study* them, any more than he'd've studied "Fibber McGee and Molly." His grades and his glasses had marked him an intellectual from the time he was ten, so when it came to choosing a profession he went East and studied Ibsen. He was into his thirties before anybody started talking about Hitchcock as a great man or doing critical histories of the horror film. He should've been Roman Polanski, he should've been Bergman. But by the time the horror trade got legitimate enough for him he was into legitimate theater and it was too late to learn the trade. Not surprisingly, his thing was black comedy, and it was because black comedy (in the wake of the film) was now respectable enough for summer stock and regional semi-pro that he'd been able, just barely, to keep out of teaching.

The Magoor opening was important to him, and maybe more important than he wanted to admit, since, forcing himself to focus on the opening stage direction of Act Two (*The stage looks as if a tornado had hit it. Furniture is piled against the door on the left*), the image of Gunilla Lind in Ernst feathers still hung around the edges of his eyes. Already the image had begun to take on a celluloid clarity of definition, and whatever sickened in it attached itself to the dull pages before him, to the Act Two blocking that was not yet done. It didn't need to be done, he wouldn't use it for a week. But not to be prepared was the source of nightmare. If the blocking were not finished before he went into first reading tonight, he would carry with him the sense that he was lying to the actors, pretending a grasp that he didn't have. Then, effortfully, he would set himself to impress them. He would succeed, with an empty underlying sense of fraud because the blocking was not done and he didn't know where he wanted them to move in Act Two. If he told them that the blocking was not done, if he should say, "I never get the blocking done before rehearsals start and it always panics me," it wouldn't diminish his stature by a centimeter in anybody's eye. But he could no more do this than he could walk nude onstage and crack an ostrich egg over his head.

"Do you believe in the occult?" Gunilla Lind had asked him in their one interview.

"Only," Boyd said, "as a metaphor for the horrors of ordinary life."

She was impressed. She took the part. For a minute the thing that drove him (ambition, they said) lay still in his stomach.

But he was worried about Gunilla Lind. It was a triumph to have her—exactly the kind of triumph you'd better make good on. Colleagues in New York had twitted him about what he must've done to get a hot-stuff foreign starlet down to Georgia, but Boyd had known well enough what he was doing, and it had damn all to do with sex. Gunilla Lind, for all her film credits and her limpid image, had the European cast of mind that still thinks theater serious and film a toy. She prided herself on her social conscience, and considered theater in the provinces a moral issue. American actors think politics is the only step up from stardom, but the British and the Europeans are always looking for intellectual respectability. "I seduced her with my intelligence," Boyd told his fellow directors, and they guffawed as he intended. Now he wondered whether the Magoor College for the Liberal Arts was any place to convince Gunilla she'd acquired an academic link.

He wrote down on the margin of his script: *A metaphor for the horrors of ordinary life*.

Then he placed the red tiddledywink, representing the Mother Superior, downstage right on the stage plan.

The Mother Superior, her robes torn and filthy, her head shaven, is rummaging feverishly among the packing cases.

The Magoor people had told him he could have a free hand in picking his play, and Boyd had taken them at their word. *The Nuns* was a bold choice for a place like rural Georgia, but he could maneuver anybody into a you-and-me-against-the-Philistines stance when it suited him. He supposed there was pretension enough in any college town, including this one, to assume the intellectuals would be on his side. If a few Catholics were shocked enough to write the local press, so much the better.

And he'd been wanting to do this play. In Haiti during the first Negro revolt of 1804, three nuns lure a young noblewoman into an abandoned cellar on the pretext of saving her life. In the first act they rob and murder her. In the second act, trapped by the counterrevolution, they dig her up again, hoping to buy their way out. They lash the rotten body to a post and load it with the jewels. The unexplained thing about the script was that the nuns were to be played by men, with no attempt at passing for women, but no acknowledgment even among themselves that they were anything but nuns. It wasn't clear, ever, whether they were men characters disguised as nuns or male actors playing nuns, so it worked in a lot of directions at once.

Boyd wanted to work them all: the sexual ambiguity, the comedy, the dazzle and the rot; the voodoo drums in the background, the suspense in the first act and the horror in the second. He had a dark amorphous vision of the way the whole thing ought to be, which immediately disintegrated when he started pushing tiddledywinks around on the plan.

Sometimes Boyd could work and sometimes he could not. When he could work, his mind was the thread into a labyrinth; he had only to pull himself hand over hand after the felt certainty of his path, to arrive at the luminous center. When this happened, his physical surroundings were a matter of complete indifference. He could work in a bar with a lighted disco floor in front of him if necessary. He could work on a raft.

If he could not work (the condition was involuntary, like the obsessions that the ancient Greeks gave the names of gods), then the labyrinth was dark, the path blocked by rocks or mirrors, and his physical surroundings thwarted him. The dresser at the Campus Side was some four inches too narrow and three inches too low. If he set his feet on the floor, his knees would sit free of the dresser but would be awkwardly constricted left and right. If he crossed his legs, he could hook his right foot comfortably outside the left of the kneehole but would bruise his thigh at the drawer. If he shifted back, he was placed at an awkward distance from his script. And in this position he could not work.

Anybody—Wendy included—could understand that he'd taken the job in Hubbard to spend a summer with his son. But in the meantime it had taken on another importance for him, so childish that he wouldn't have admitted it to a kid half her age. When the Dimbleton person called him to say he'd got the job, and tell him (an odd combination of Dixie drawl and academic twitter) that Mr. Burt Reynolds had agreed to be present at the opening, Boyd had been cordially indifferent. But ever since, Reynolds had been turning up on talk shows, corn-pone sincere about the careers of "the young." Boyd began remembering that Reynolds was known to scout the South, half out of love of the South and half out of that same anxious social conscience Gunilla had. He began to think about the fact that the lively arts were all fleeing the sinking City, and that Reynolds owned the best professional theater in Florida at Jupiter Beach, where half of Hollywood moved in and out in starring roles. He'd begun to fantasize that the production would be good enough to catch Reynolds' eye, that he'd be asked to direct at Jupiter Beach, and that contracts there would lead to film . . . and the big time. Boyd was forty but he pipe-dreamed like a schoolboy. He was too well known in the city for anybody to make a discovery of him at this late date. But Reynolds? Florida? The flicks?

He filled his glass again, hung a few shirts from the open suitcase and sat in front of the phone until he'd pulled himself together enough to dial Wendy. The line was busy. Annoyed, he got out Shaara's number but arrested himself with his hand on the receiver, rolled his shoulders with resolve, and went back to the script again.

MOTHER SUPERIOR

All this trouble because she got everything ready! If we'd gone to sea it would have been just the same. Nothing to eat and rubbish galore. Rags and dolls . . . the stupid bitch.

He wanted it to be wonderful. He wanted it to knock Reynolds off his heels. He wanted it to get him out of New York.

3.   *Ingenue*

———◆———

"But, Mama, I like to be alone."

This sentence—a mistake—left New York, invaded Boston, and struck directly to the heart. Pauline Greton chuckled, which was the way she habitually received a wound, and drew breath for the counterattack. All of Wendy's adolescent door slammings hung between them on the wire.

"And of course I'm not alone," she added quickly. "I'm hoping to get the living room sanded and have the mess over with. I wouldn't trust them to do it without a little overseeing." Decor, and the incompetence of workmen, were always safe.

"I didn't mean for the whole time," Mrs. Greton said, audibly tight along the jaw. "But seven *weeks*. You're bound to get lonely. Why don't you just pop up for the weekend?"

It was raining in New York, and the apartment was brown with gloom. A warm gloom; Wendy liked it, and hoped the rain would keep up. She fingered the mail, still unopened beside the phone, propped the receiver on her shoulder, and slit a magazine ad.

"Oh, I can't this weekend. I've got an appointment with the gynecologist on Friday afternoon, and then I'm taking an evening train out to the Carsons' place in East Millstone." She did have an appointment; the country weekend was an invention. Wendy let the envelope and the ad flutter to the floor, scuffed them in the direction of the wastebasket.

"The gynecologist?" Mrs. Greton would not ask the real

question, which Wendy would not answer. Frustration rose between them. Pauline Greton would cheerfully have lashed herself to a railroad track for her daughter's sake, only, unfortunately, the occasion did not arise. In the meantime she'd done what she could and raised Wendy on a creed of avoidance: wet feet, dark alleys, public toilets, hard words, high places and low types. It had never been part of her intention that Wendy should avoid *her*.

"You'd be surprised how busy I am."

Mrs. Greton sighed, indicating that nothing in the way of being busy could surprise her. "Have you still got cockroaches?"

She had also preached the trinity Ajax, Borax, and Clorox, with the result that Wendy reached adulthood never having had mumps, pox, or any sort of measles. Mrs. Greton now learned from the women's pages that this was a maternal mistake, and was more afraid than ever that Wendy would find herself in the proximity of bacteria.

"Everybody's got cockroaches!" Wendy called gaily up to Boston, and dropped a Graphics Society brochure on top of the ad. "It's a constant battle. That's one reason I don't want to be away too long."

The bottom letter on the pile was from Shaara Soole. Wendy recognized the extravagant mauve envelope and the loopy handwriting. The loops were tall and full and faced the world on their own terms. Shaara Soole, she supposed, would never have to lie to her mother to avoid a weekend at home. Shaara Soole, she supposed, would have spoken quite freely of wanting to be alone, of being broke, of possible pregnancies.

"Well, I just want you to know you're welcome up here *anytime*."

"Next weekend, maybe," Wendy said. She pictured her mother at the hall phone in Boston, ankles crossed and upright on the tapestry-back chair. Her free hand would be lightly checking her upsweep at the ear and nape. Wendy clamped the receiver between jaw and shoulder and ran a fingernail under the fluted edge of Shaara's envelope.

"Next weekend," Mrs. Greton said tentatively. "Well, now, I believe your father has symphony tickets Saturday. Should we try to get you one?"

"Ummm," said Wendy, equally tentative. What a goddam confident handwriting Shaara had. She would like to be Shaara

Soole and have the guts to go around wearing mumus or caftans or whatever foreign sort of stuff she wore, organizing committees, directing crews.

Dear Wendy,
    Here's the final awful bill for Kevin's fracture. Naturally the insurance found a clause that let them out of most of it. K. has got the signed cast (it's filthy) in the iguana cage, and I think he's truly sorry to have it off.
    I am so looking forward to meeting you on opening night.
                                            Best,
                                                Shaara

"Wendy?" said Mrs. Greton. "Are you there?"
"I was just thinking, Mama." She was thinking about her mother's hairdo and the tapestry-back hall chair. *Wendy, are you there? I am so looking forward to meeting you on opening night.* She was thinking how very much she wanted not to be like her mother, and that she had married a man who had married a woman like Shaara Soole. Was that a psychological insight?
"Maybe I'd better let you know about the ticket," Wendy said.
"It's Mahler, I believe," said Mrs. Greton, "and Prokoviev. Although you know how your father gets about Prokoviev, and he'll probably be an old bear the rest of the evening. Did I tell you what a fuss he made the night they did John Cage?"
    There was a little more of this, then a few anticlimactic references to neighbors and products before Wendy could terminate and rock the phone back into its cradle. She hid the bill in the drawer and propped Shaara's note against the phone. She made herself a peanut butter sandwich and a Black Russian and dumped the knife in the sink on top of last night's dishes. Boyd had been gone less than twenty-four hours and already the place was a mess. Paper towels misaimed at the garbage, eggshells, too. Ordinarily she was obsessively neat, just like her mother. She always fell to pieces when Boyd went away. The trouble was that she liked falling to pieces. It made her feel reckless and interesting that the tabletop was crumby and the cushions were jumbled on the floor in front of the TV, which was on but soundless on account of Mrs. Greton's call. The Bionic Woman, slow motion and silent, was leaping across a field of autumn leaves in

pursuit of an international jewel thief. Wendy left it as it was and flipped on the radio.

You're just a mama's baby, Bay-bee . . .

Maybe she was wrong about Shaara's supposed candor. It was a peculiar way of wording a conventionality: "I am so looking forward to meeting you on opening night." I am so. Are not! Am so!

She lifted a bunch of dead daisies out of the vase and dumped them in the wastebasket but left the stagnant water where it was. Chewing peanut butter, she kicked off her slippers and settled into a rocker, then changed her mind and slid belly foremost onto the cushions. The cushion whoosh sent fluff off the end of the carpet toward the corners.

I want my peck of dirt before I die, thought Wendy, and began to cry, rather idly. Except for the idle crying she did not feel particularly pregnant; not sleepy, no nausea, her eating habits no odder than was usual when Boyd was away. Maybe she could just go on with it and take the whole thing in her stride.

Boyd had once surprised her by referring to her "Victorian temperament." Wendy was extremely interested in other people's judgments on her character, having so few of her own. She knew by hearsay, for instance, that she had been an "ethereally" beautiful child until she was about fourteen, when the late bloomers had begun to bloom and (she knew this by experience) her pallor had begun to seem a little pallid. At that point she had heard Mrs. Greton confide to a friend that her daughter was moody, and Wendy had taken advantage of, and a good deal of comfort in, this assessment until she got to Swarthmore and discovered that she was not moody at all. Rather genial, in fact. The moody ones broke windows, went on pot binges and spent weekends in the psych wards, where Wendy took them paperbacks and peanut brittle.

As Boyd's wife she had, apparently, a Victorian temperament. He seemed to mean it as a compliment. She turned the phrase over, applying it to herself, thinking not of drawing rooms but of Magwitch in a ditch, all those underscullery sorts that never changed their chemises, nits in the hair. You are doing this to yourself, she said, because she'd been a psychology major. Then that seemed okay. I like doing this to myself. What I would like to have is a bed that never gets made and never gets washed.

It's a quilt cocoon ready to wrap up in. I eat there and throw the crusts out on the floor.

She shook free of this. She stood, in order to shake free of it, went back to the desk, and shuffled in the drawer for the checkbook Boyd had left her. She scooped up the bills and did a few quick calculations. If she paid the rent, Con Edison, the insurance, MasterCharge, and Kevin's fracture, there would be no money left. *No* money. She propped the checkbook against the mauve envelope and understood in a sudden flash why the marriage of Boyd and Shaara had not worked out. Their handwriting was of the same size, had the same force. She reached for something in her own hand—a grocery list, it was—and compared the round schoolgirl control of her little letters. She had a sudden impulse to call Shaara and say: I know what was wrong between you!

The stupidity of this made her laugh, but she was quite capable of following through on a stupid fantasy. In that she had remained constant throughout her various phases. So while she made another drink she outfitted herself in a drooping beige felt hat and a chiffon scarf that trailed behind her shoulder, met Shaara in Atlanta and drew her into a dim corner of the airport lounge—are there any dim corners in Atlanta airport? And so, when the telephone rang she started guiltily, knowing it was Boyd—it was Boyd—and began on the wrong, defensive, note.

"It's nearly four o'clock. Weren't you getting there at noon?"

"I was bushed from the bus so I took a nap. I tried you before but the line was busy."

"Oh, yeah, that was Mother."

"This is a lousy place to think of spending seven weeks without you, baby."

She was contrite. She was also, she realized, a little drunk. "Well, the e-vi-dence," she said, mock professorial, "is that I miss you, too."

"How so?"

"I've been drinking all afternoon and letting the place go to pot. I even cried a little."

"Poor baby," he chuckled, and because she was a baby, because she was drunk and moody, this response, the one she sought, annoyed her. "How're *you* doing?" she asked.

"Usual stuff, terror over the blocking. You know."

What was wrong with her? He didn't feel "terror," of course. *Terror* was not what he felt, such as people feel in war, plague, famine and earthquake, but it was a perfectly acceptable conversational ploy. He had warned her from the very first that he was bad with telephones, cryptic and distant, long-distance. If she'd never got used to it that was her problem; there was no point being angry over it.

"*Talk* to me a little, Boyd," she demanded nevertheless.

So he told her about his dream, which appeared to be very clever and cinematic. Wendy liked to say that she had married her husband for his imagination. This was not the whole truth but it had enough truth about it to give it a certain glow. Her own imagination ran along conventional lines, thrills and adventure, Walter Mitty stuff, the stuff of prime time. Boyd's was dark and funny and original. She had met him in Provincetown when he was rehearsing *The Changeling* and she was doing research for her honors thesis on non-verbal communication in the theater. She was supposed to be observing how the actors used body language, but she ended up listening to Boyd more than watching the cast.

"I married him for his imagination," she would say, glibly to others, or sentimentally to herself. It made her feel good. Just as she was reassured by assessments of her own character, she was comforted by the naming of emotions that otherwise seemed vaporous, awash. As a student she had excelled at identifying symptoms: the woman in this case is suffering a separation trauma, this is a classic case of sibling rivalry, paranoia, penis envy. She got A's for it. "Put all things in their own peculiar place," her mother used to quote, "and know that order is the greatest grace."

"Listen, Boyd. I told Mama I was going to spend a couple of days with the Carsons, to get out of going up there, and it put the idea in my head."

"Good idea. Why don't you?"

"Well, for one thing," she said reasonably, "I got the bill for Kevin's fracture. If I pay the bills I won't have the fare."

"Then don't pay the bills," he said, also reasonably.

At one point—her junior year—she had become a passionate partisan of Transactional Analysis. Her background as a Bostonian and a Greton had made her particularly quick to identify the games people play. Then at some point it had struck her that there were games underneath the games, within and beyond the games, which no system was adequate to account for. Here was, clearly, a cordial "adult" conversation, in which a problem was being solved by the choice of a logical alternative. How was it that she knew, exactly, that Boyd knew she had avoided mentioning Shaara's name, and that he was both indulging and warning her: take a vacation but don't bug me about money.

"I should be getting paid here tomorrow," he said, "and I'll send you some." Then again, maybe she had imagined the whole thing. She had run amuck of her Transactional Analysis professor in the second term, and moved on to Body Language.

"I don't see why she sent me the bill when you're down there."

"Ah, she's just a bit flaky. I'll pay her directly, shall I?"

Flaky? Was that accurate, was that it? "Okay," she said. "Boyd—there's another thing." She wiped a space free in front of her on the desk. Some of the bills fell onto the floor with the discarded mail. "I was thinking maybe I'd like to see somebody else than Dr. Malspies. Maybe down in East Millstone."

"Why?"

Why. Because Dr. Malspies had impeccable credentials and a Victorian manner and called her "little lady." Because Dr. Malspies had been recommended by her mother on the recommendation of Dr. Todd in Boston. Because her mother would never have chosen a doctor that would be chosen by somebody like Shaara Soole. "I can't explain exactly. If the test is positive he'll be so damn . . . delighted. I just thought I'd rather talk to a stranger."

"Okay, but why?"

Why? said Mrs. Greton. Just because, said Wendy, swinging on the porch post. Mr. Greton said: I'll wash your mouth out with soap, and once he sat her in the basin and washed her while he spanked her, splashy slaps, for playing doctor with the neighborhood tough. When Aunt May came to stay she put Wendy in the bath and washed and washed what she called her "private parts," which were not so private when Aunt May was washing them. Why? *Because it's very important. Because germs. Just because.* Once she went out in the rose garden as soon as Aunt May had taken off for Maine and scooped dirt into her underpants with a garden trowel.

"The truth is that I'm having doubts about this," Wendy said.

"Of course you are! It's a big step!" His voice buoyed up from a deeper register. He was delighted she should have doubts. It was probably as delightful to have doubts as to have a baby. I am so looking forward to your having doubts.

"I mean real doubts, Boyd. I'm not sure *I'm* anybody, enough to . . . does that make sense?"

"Wendy, baby, you are not anybody; you are *everybody*."

Her real feeling was anger. But the moment you spoke of "real feelings" (she'd heard it over and over again in class), you implied some ennobling truth. "Real" was a justifying notion, and "feelings" were supposed to have some intuitive inside track to the heart of things. This was not the case, it was sentimental semantics. Real feelings were often stingy, perverse, self-serving. Her mother's martyrdom was a real feeling.

"You're sweet," she said. Frustration rose between them.

"Go on down to the Carsons and have a natter with Cass. I'll call you latish Sunday night. You'll only brood if you stay up there all alone."

"Oh, it's all right," Wendy said. "I like to be alone."

After she hung up she took out the New Jersey phone book and made an appointment with a stranger.

4. *Domestic Animals*

———◆———

Kevin took the dog's death oddly. School was out for Memorial Day, and after he'd made himself a breakfast of three easy-overs, grits and hashbrowns, he flung "I'll be at Bobby's" over his shoulder and took off on his bike. When he got back mid-afternoon, Shaara was dragging a dustrag desultorily round his room, waiting for the right moment. But after he'd downed a quart of milk and a couple of Zingers he went straight to the phone, hunkered down on the shag, and wandered a sneaker over the wall in a way that suggested he was settling in.

So she started more earnestly on the terrarium. Bette Davis the iguana drowsed on the knee of the split cast. She blinked through the glass and rolled her eyes suspiciously after the cloth. When the terrarium was done, the bookshelves. Not many books here but a whole trove of leavings and gleanings: spare model tank treads, sloughed bug skins, clock guts, a six-whorl snake rattle, a squirrel skull, a convincing pile of plastic vomit. Another snapshot of Wendy Soole, this time with Kevin and a bass, the two of them (not the bass) simperingly exultant, as if they were about to spring into the halcyon sky over never-neverland.

"What're you *doing*?" Kevin accosted. The phone call had evidently not gone well.

"I'm dusting." Meaning: obviously.

"Why're you doing it *now*?"

Meaning what? Shaara faced him and shoved a patch of hair off her forehead. His own, tousled, tumbled to the shoulder that he propped on the doorframe. Luckily he got his hair from his father, although for pallor and bonelessness he could equally well have been Wendy Soole's son. Or brother.

"I dust from time to time," said Shaara.

"But haven't you got a meeting?"

Ah. She did in fact have a meeting, of the Sex Equity Review Committee, but what he meant was: don't you have a meeting with dad?

"The cast doesn't get together until tonight. Listen, Kevin." She sat on his quilt and twisted the dustrag in her hands—as it might be a black-bordered handkerchief—not feeling at the moment any great sense of loss, but wanting to get it right. "Henry got hit by a car this morning. I'm sorry. I've already buried him."

He acquired a spine. He lifted himself off the doorframe, took in a breath, and ejaculated, "Oh, my *god!*"

She'd been prepared for grief or indifference—one never knows—but not for this, clearly, accusation. "I know, love," she murmured nevertheless, as if he had wept.

"Jesus Christ!" Kevin said. She had a notion he'd have flounced on the bed if she hadn't been sitting there. And yet he was a good-natured boy, a bit of a loner perhaps, but not given to snarl. Maybe she really had caught him at a bad time?

"Your timing's terrific," he cried.

Meaning to confirm this? "I don't think he suffered at all. He was dead before I got to him. I guess we"—a slight pause after the *we*—"forgot to lock the porch door last night. It always did worry me, that cute trick . . ."

"But couldn't you have done something?"

"I, ah, buried him."

"No, I mean, take him to the vet or something!"

"Kevin, he was *dead*. I'm sorry."

But for what? Clearly she should have waked him after all, let him shovel the red dirt, let him lift the dead weight. Don't children blame the dead for desertion? At what age do you believe in death? He perched now—clearly he would not sit beside her—on one corner of the terrarium. The metal frame creaked and Shaara winced, but she said nothing. Kevin was going through a phase that had something to do with his equilibrium. He would not acknowledge the functions of things. He stood on basketballs and radiator pipes, he did headstands on chairs, jumped on walls, sat on books and bureaus, read in the bathtub and slept on the floor.

"*Dad* gave me that dog," he came out with.

Explaining all. Henry had become so much a part of this land-scape that she'd forgotten his arrival, by Eastern Airlines in a vinyl cage, from the Maryland summer resort where Boyd had bought him. He was right: the timing was fairly rotten.

"Kevin, *I* didn't run over him," she suggested.

"But that's not the point."

No. Nor was it the point that Kevin was accusing her. The point was that Boyd might. Or might accuse him. They maintained a civilized and sensible broken home, which meant they flung far fewer accusations at each other than any family intact. But Kevin wasn't stupid. The stress of the next seven weeks took her again, a visceral knot of angst and anger into which she pressed the dustrag. Why did Boyd have to come *here*?

"The point is that your father is a perfectly reasonable man," she began, and was saved from any more of this. Kevin shifted his weight minutely on the corner of the terrarium. The glass cracked in one clean diagonal to the floor and in another from the crack to the side. He lifted and they watched; it seemed for a second that the glass would hold, then the metal groaned and the neat triangle shivered to the floor. Bette Davis gave one languid blink and was out. She zapped up the curtain and panted on the rod, throat muscle bloated and quivering.

"Quick, the window! No, freeze! Slow!" Kevin contradicted.

He advanced on the sill, reached stealthily for the crank while Shaara lifted her forearm to plug the space between the rod and the wall. Bette Davis regarded them heavy-lidded.

"Don't scare her."

They both held their breath while the crank squealed one revolution and another, another, the window arched grudgingly toward them. Shaara inched her free hand upward. The window and the hand closed in at once, and Shaara lifted the iguana down onto her bosom. By this time Bette was asleep.

Shaara stroked the shiny scales and they breathed relief at each other. "It's time we put the screens on, anyway," she said.

"Yeah," he son agreed. "We better."

Dean Joe Dimbleton was of the opinion that a sex equity adjustment could not be made for Ms. Una Pendleton of the Music Department unless one was also made for Ms. Ellen Chiesa of Italian. Harvey Nims pointed out, confirmingly, that the budget breakdown of Modern Languages showed an eight percent poorer record, sexwise, than Music. Oswald Link raised the issue of whether Ms. Chiesa's being half Sicilian put her in the minority category. Sam Whittle averred that she was not half Sicilian but married to a full Sicilian, which was not the same thing. Harvey opined that she was half Sicilian *and* married to a Sicilian. Sam evinced that if she were Sicilian she would be named Elena and not Ellen. Joe did not consider this conclusive. Harvey was appointed to look into it.

Magoor was a second-rate liberal arts college, converted from a women's normal in the 'forties, opted into the state funding system in the Baby Boom, and currently chafing as it dwindled, what with falling enrollments and a tax-haggard populace. It suffered generally from isolation, gothic architecture, and an illegal inability to find black staff; and at this juncture from a deep intellectual malaise. That is, of the two hundred thirteen faculty members, perhaps the unlucky thirteen believed that a college education was worth having and/or that the students were worth giving it to. Committee work had become very popular. From time to time Shaara envisioned herself tap-dancing the length of the president's conference table, toeing manila folders off left and right into the gentlemen's laps. This meeting was the more trying to her because, of the six male members of the seven-member Equity Review Committee, she had slept with three.

"What's very trying," she said, "is that we all know Una's a brilliant teacher, whereas Ellen is malicious, incompetent and alcoholic."

Oswald attested that, however this might be the impressionistic consensus of the committee, hard evidence was lacking. He stabbed the evaluation forms with a chunky forefinger. He was rather frisky in bed; hard evidence. Larry McElhaney, a squarish man with a surprisingly long and graceful cock, substantiated that Ms. Chiesa had four monographs to her credit over the past three years, whereas Ms. Pendleton had none. Emory Eliot, who had not yet roused himself to an opinion, had a peculiar configuration of black hair down his torso, like a single strip of arrows directed at his pubes. All three were now remarried.

"Una's a pianist," Shaara said. "She doesn't write monographs, she gives concerts."

That might be the case, but it was also to be considered, as regards public performance, that Ms. Chiesa regularly spoke for the Cerchio Italiano and the Rotary Club, and had attended a conference of international visibility on the works of Cesare Pavese. It was apparently not in the folder that she had, internationally visible, thrown a champagne bucket at a visiting scholar from Settignano. Emory now inferred from the record that Ms. Chiesa was more likely to pursue a grievance to the courts than Ms. Pendleton. Shaara sighed.

Larry enthusiastically certified that there was no more than a point three spread in the student ratings, which would make it ball's-ass difficult, pardon his Italian, to defend a divergent decision if it came to the courts. A romantic, he had stemmed a punnet of strawberries, eaten half of each one and fed the other half to her one morning when the dogwood was shedding. He was the only humanist she'd tried more than once. Somehow the second time both strawberries and dogwood were out of season.

Emory turned to ask Shaara for a clarification of her objection to an equal equity adjustment in both instances.

"Una's good and underpaid," she clarified. "Ellen isn't and isn't."

"Now, Shaara," said Dean Dimbleton. "Don't do your Andy Griffith on us. You know the HEW is breathing down our necks."

Joe Dimbleton was no fool. He'd done some spectacular plugging of the sinking ship. The Magoor Arts Theater, for instance. Why the Grumbacher Foundation had singled Magoor out for a professional theater was a matter of some speculation, and it was hinted here and there that Jimmy Carter had a hand in it personally. The truth was that Joe was as fine a hand at grant writing as the Southeast had produced; he could spin you a humanistic value out of a sow's ear. He could also plug into Trumanese when it suited his purpose.

"Emory's right. Ellen will take it to court if we give her a chance. She'll love it. She'll get a hotshot lawyer to do her up some charts with Affirmative Action written all over them. What are we going to take in there? Gossip? *Conviction*?"

"Aren't you guys making the payoff before you get black-mailed?"

"Leo could get three members of the department to testify she's incompetent," Harvey put in, "and then she'd get four to testify she should've been chairman instead of Leo."

"We could wiretap," Joe suggested.

"Couldn't you at least take it up with the academic vice president?"

"I tried. He's on a Role and Scope Retreat."

"You can dissent, Professor Soole," said Oswald. "Of course, it would look odd."

"Shaara," square Larry now shifted in his chair to face her squarely. "She drinks too much. So do I." He was too tactful to say: so do you. "Maybe she meets her eight o'clock hung over three days out of five. You've got to remember she's had a pretty rough time of it, with Sergio out of work and the kid in Harwood Center."

Bull's-eye? Did he infer, out of an aura of dogwood petals, that this first-stone argument was the one she could not refuse? It seemed to Shaara that it would be useful to know. It was commonly supposed to be men who did the mental undressing. It would be useful to know, for instance, which of the three was currently cognizant of the mole on her right pelvic bone, of which all had taken note. If she knew men were better than she was at blocking out past intimacy, it might give her some clue as to how to work with Boyd after eleven years of scrapped conjugality. Why did he have to come here?

She hesitated. "I don't want you guys to think you're doing any favors for feminism."

"All right," said Joe laconically.

Oswald quickly moved a twelve-hundred-across-the-board for Ms. Pendleton and Ms. Chiesa. Sam seconded. Joe asked if the committee were ready to take action.

"Affirmative," Shaara sighed.

Joe Dimbleton had a strong argument with the Grumbacher Foundation in the matter of a "physical plant," because Magoor had finally completed its new gymnasium, and the old one—a gloomy brick-and-stone affair almost buried under kudzu vine, originally intended for volleyball, modern dance and other female sports—could be converted at minimum expense into a theater.

The building had been cut into the contour of the hill, so that what you entered was actually its third floor, now offices and classrooms, and a palatial stone staircase ushered down toward the gym itself. This had been turned into an arena theater by shortening the rectangle with a cyclorama, stripping its wide fir floorboards, and replacing the bleachers with U-shaped tiers of armchair seats from a bankrupt movie house. The ceiling had been lowered and the walls painted deep dead plum. The effect was Depression 'Thirties, somewhere between cozy and sinister. Below this, half underground, the two dance studios had been "converted" into costume and scene shops by moving the Singers into one and the Black and Deckers into the other.

Shaara had never worked in so satisfactory a space. Her shop in the old theater—auditorium, really—had been dark and cramped; Education was welcome to it. Here she had a quarter of an acre, windowed on the downhill side, the other three sides mirrored so you could see any costume from any angle and distance you chose. There was thirty feet of trestle table for cutting, and the ballet barre offered display space for a couple of hundred bodices under construction.

Not that they'd ever have money for a big production. This show only asked for three nuns' habits, one dress, and a breakdown of each. A dull play to costume, in fact, except that it allowed her to work without an assistant and to concentrate on detailing the one spectacular Empire gown. She'd be able to make an exact replica and then break it down for the disinterred corpse, slashing it, sanding it, burning it, dragging it over the shop floor. Such leisure was a luxury.

She unwrapped the bolt and flung the fabric down the table, a stageworthy imitation of slipper silk, lemon yellow, with a widely scattered motif of embroidered day lilies in lavender and silver. It would startle, on entrance, by contrast with the nuns' dark habits. Gunilla Lind, who would be wearing it, wouldn't be averse to a startling entrance—Shaara didn't have to mention that she'd found it cheap at K-Mart. Curious that in Hubbard nobody would have worn it but a tart, whereas on a Caucasian noblewoman in nineteenth-century Haiti, it could be made to read wealth, innocence and doom. The vagaries of fashion.

She shook it into folds along the warp to watch how it draped in the mirrors. She'd got used to her own reflections and didn't mind them, the multiple giantess in batik and Bantu hair. Across the hall she could hear Gene Keyes whistling Country 'n' Western over the buzz saw. She organized the equipment, which she'd already organized twice, oiled the industrial Pfaff, shifted trim from one shelf to another, and looked for a place to store scrap as she turned it out.

Between the shops there was a laundry room with a hotplate, which she shared with Gene. She stepped across now to ask if he wanted coffee.

"Sho-ure," he called, but when she went to make it, it was

already perked. She poured a couple of mugs, sugared one and creamed the other, went in and sat on a flat. Gene snapped off the buzz saw and straddled a sawhorse.

He was forty-two, a widower with a face leathered by road construction, thick black hair a little tonsured, and a grin with the pilot light always on. He'd been hired as a Maintenance III, which meant top-level janitor. Theater had unethically come to assign him more stage construction than building repair. He could have gone into supervision, but he would stay where he was because, as he explained, he "preferred the making." He made very well. The set designer Tebo Harkey had thought it safe to leave him the *Nuns* sketch and take off to London for the summer. Shaara was supposed to oversee construction of the set, but she wouldn't have to. What she might have to do was explain to Boyd why a laborer had been left in charge.

He blew on the coffee and grinned over the rim. Gene had not, in Shaara's experience, ever initiated a conversation.

"Have you got time for a couple of extracurricular projects?"

"What d'you need?"

"Three or four scrap bins and about fifteen more foot of shelf. They could go on the right side between the door and the mirror."

"No problem. Is that all?"

"No. The other thing is moonlighting, for me—Kevin, actually. He sat on his iguana's terrarium this afternoon and broke one side of it."

" 'Course he did."

"I could replace it for about fifty dollars, but he's had this elaborate plan for a custom cage—slats of one-by-two cedar, different levels. It's very good, really, but if he drills the holes in the wrong place we'll have an expensive pile of firewood. Would you feel like helping him build it?"

"I'd like that a lot," he said, too quickly.

"I can't pay you much."

"Whatever."

This might turn out to be another folly. Shaara had three rules: no married men, no theater men, and no students. Gene was none of these, but he was a cracker, and he had a crush on her, which he'd betrayed a few weeks ago with the gift of a bird feeder made of teak much too fine for such a thing, too carefully sanded. Crushes were all right, an occupational hazard she'd learned to handle. The word "crush" itself was an aid; it indicated so lofty a gap between crusher and crushee that it didn't have to be dealt with.

But ever since Theater had moved into its new quarters at the end of winter term, and they'd been stationed together in this hall of mirrors, they'd taken to long easy talk over coffee. Shaara, with her easy impulse toward confession, might have told him more about her life than she'd meant to since, lately, out of the ease a tension had perversely budded. She did not want to start thinking of him as being in love with her. She also did not want to start thinking of the tension as anything so dreary as electricity. Electricity is for Black and Deckers. She wished, as a matter of fact, that he had the decency to work with his shirt on. He was, like Shaara, five foot ten, but built to some other scale. He had a narrow small-boned frame, underfed except for the shoulders that the Interstate had constructed. Where he sat hunched over the sawhorse his skin corrugated itself into ridges no wider than a pencil.

"Well, we'll see," she backtracked, fidgeting. "He doesn't get out of school till next week, and I'll have to figure out if I can afford the wood . . ."

"Just lemme know."

The anger stirred again, just under her lungs where it had been lodged ever since she leaned over the red grave in the morning mist. "Anything's all right with you, isn't it?" she flared.

"Most nearly anything."

Most nearly any fool would have left it at that, finished her coffee and gone back to make busywork until time for the reading. Shaara propped herself on an elbow. "The dog got killed this morning too."

"Oh, Jesus. Really?"

"The trouble being, that Boyd gave him the dog, and Kevin seems to feel it as, I don't know, a kind of snub against his dad. I didn't know he was so nervous about Boyd's coming, though I suppose I should have. I'm nervous enough. Do you plan to go to the reading?"

"Hadn't thought. Prob'ly not. Do you?"

"I'd like to. It's just the first of all those clutzy little things I'm going to have to deal with. Do I wait for Herr Director's invitation? And then if I don't get it and I don't show, does it look like I'm being a prima donna, or what?"

"Did you used to go to first readings, when you worked with him before?"

"Sometimes, depending how busy I was."

"How busy are you?"

"You know what I mean."

But there was no reason to suppose he did. He professed himself to have been wholly happy with his wife, Harriet, their only grief that she was barren. He'd spent most of his life contentedly in plastering, carpentry, construction; though when she died he said he'd gone "temp'rarily bats."

He showed Shaara a picture of Harriet once. It embarrassed her a little. She was a pretty, placid woman, who didn't look sickly except that her parchment skin and poodle-curled hair bespoke an older decade altogether. Childless, she looked more motherly than Shaara ever expected to achieve. She'd been two years younger than Shaara.

"The whole thing is so stupid," she pursued now. "Boyd talks as if it's some wonderful opportunity to develop a healthy relationship with his son, and it never crosses his mind he might open a batch of old wounds."

"Is he stupid?"

"How can I say that? I can't even say he's insensitive. He could give you an impromptu anytime, on the multiple motivations of Ophelia. It's just that somehow he's got the idea that anything *dramatic* belongs to the theater. Jealousy, pain, screaming grief—those are the things that *characters* feel. *People* are supposed to behave rationally. Do you know he even asked if we had a spare room to put him up? He thought it would be nice for Kevin. His wife sits up in New York doing god-knows-what, tatting doilies for his return, and we're supposed to give him home comforts in the meantime."

"You resent *her.*"

She looked up at him, hunched motionless over the sawhorse. She herself twisted her hair, pulled at her ear, turned wood scraps in her hands, shifted from side to side on the uncomfortable flat. Gene, like the dependable prewar appliances, had just two positions, on and off. When he was in motion he moved cleanly, an economy of line and energy. At rest he was motionless, plug pulled.

"No, I don't. It would probably be a lot more natural if I did. But I was done with Boyd and his affairs long before Wendy came along, and I'm mostly . . . curious about her. If I resent anything, it's Boyd's starting over again, with another innocent. I was twenty-one when I married him, and she was twenty-one when she married him, and I keep imagining that she's going through the same things I did, in the same order. Don't you see, I don't know a damn thing about her, probably never will. All the same I know what her life is like, minute by minute, meal after meal, better than I know anybody's life. I know how she has to fry the eggs and fold the socks. I know how *she* feels when *he's* lost a contract. I never did understand how he feels."

"You want to tell her how to handle him."

"Do I? Maybe."

"What advice'd you give her, if y'got the chance?"

"Oh, nothing spectacular. Nothing she couldn't pick up in a magazine. Don't be bullied, don't be awed. Figure out what she wants to do and then do it."

"Like, go along to the reading?"

"Come *on*, Gene," she complained. "You mean people should be rational."

"Well." He emptied the cup and swung off the sawhorse. "I think, f'r example, they should eat when they're hungry. D'you have to go home for supper?"

"No, Kevin's got a friend over. See, we don't know if Boyd expects to see him tonight, and it doesn't occur to the bastard that Kevin might want to have some kind of . . ."

"Pizza?" Gene suggested.

5.   *Monday-Night Frights*

There is something faintly ludicrous about stage-fright. Like fleas or hemorrhoids, it has no dignity. What, after all, is the worst thing that can happen? You fluff a line, you dry or stammer; you can make a fool of yourself but you can't die. Once Boyd had produced *Short Eyes* in a New Jersey prison. His lead was a six-and-a-half-foot arsonist who'd beaten or buggered everyone in his cell block into line, but when the play went on he sweated the dye out of his shirt and retched into a bucket backstage between scenes. The actors would be feeling it seven weeks hence, but tonight was Boyd's opening performance. He had to take one rising starlet, one Irish ham, one TV villain and one apprentice fag, and convince them into a cast. If he fluffed or dried they would pick, instinctively, another leader, and where the director does not control there is no show. He wouldn't fluff or dry and he had faced it often enough to know that; it made no difference. His focus kept spacing out and the smell of his body altered toward vinegar.

The cast and crew were to assemble at seven. Boyd came early enough to look over the theater, which was so right for the play that it rather unnerved him. It was something out of a Bela Lugosi fantasy, a mound of smothering creeper like an oversized vault, gothic arches picked out by moonlight. You descended into a catacombs, the work lights making a couple of pools in a purple hole. In the empty shops the mirrors threw back an eerie series of Boyd Sooles. Tomorrow he would love it but tonight he was travel-tired and jumpy, unready.

He decided to capitalize on the atmosphere—bull by the horns—and dragged a table from behind the cyclorama into the dim stage area. He was joined by a wiry black technician who knew where the chairs were, a high yellow of a stage manager, and a props person female, fat, and anxious to please. "Dor-a *Fish*-er," she announced officiously. A lighting man arrived who made it clear, carefully offhand, that he was not a student, before positioning a couple of spots. The Dimbleton person who'd got the grant wandered in and said what an honor this was for Magoor blah-blah, but didn't seem to expect an invitation, and wandered out again.

"Oh me gawd," boomed Wyman Path. His slightly nasal brogue came out of the floorboards somewhere. "I didn't know it was a *round*. Do we have to do the whole thing with our backs to them?"

"No, in their laps," Boyd said, sweating, smiling. "How are you, Wyman?"

Wyman dragged a hand along the velour seat backs, rolled on the balls of his feet. He had thick white hair and magnificent jellied jowls that lapped over his turtleneck. He could be difficult. He'd been trained at The Abbey in Dublin and imported in the 'sixties for a Circle in the Square revival of *The Iceman Cometh.* Like a handful of his compatriots and contemporaries, he'd never gone home again. He'd played most of the heavies in Synge, O'Casey, and O'Neill in the regionals, and he picked up minor film credits whenever the script called for a sentimental/temperamental Irish lush. But the casting was a little too close to type for comfort. His Abbey background gave him the discipline of a martinet in performance; backstage he'd fallen into a stage-Irish number among the other actors—truculent, sloppy about rehearsal times, and often drunk.

"I say, lads. We have a positive *parlor* to work in." Pretty Barnard Jones danced court around Wyman's bulk. It was instantly clear to Boyd that the boy would play novice nun to the Mother Superior offstage as well as on, and that alone would have made it worth hiring him. There were other reasons: he'd caught the critics' eye in three productions in a row at the WPA Theater off-Broadway, and *People* had featured

him in a one-page panegyric to "Androgyny in the Arts." He
had a thin camp voice that set Boyd's teeth on edge, but it
didn't matter because Sister Ines, the character he was to
play, was mute. And he had extraordinary presence for his
age, an arresting delicacy, light-catching eyes like some virgin
martyr out of a Florentine masterpiece. In any case he'd been
the choice of Wyman Path. Boyd wondered briefly if there
was something up between the two of them, but dismissed
it. Wyman was too fond of his reputation with women to make
the switch in middle age, and more likely to want a boy sy-
cophant than a boy lover.

"We have a creak here," Wyman announced, rolling his
foot on a floorboard. The technicians and the stage manager
ran to check.

It was Orme Sullivan, the malicious Sister Angela, who sat
quietly and arranged the flung scripts and pencils around the
table. Steady, lonely, almost professorially precise by nature,
he'd been making an equally steady living as hit man and
extortionist since the early days of "Hawaii Five-O." Over the
years he had blackmailed Mannix and tried to murder Barnaby
Jones, had been paired with Jack Palance and been invited
back five times to clip the jaw of James Garner. But, stuck on
the side of the bad guys, he'd never garnered a show of his
own, and when things were slow in the world of TV mayhem
he liked to get out of Hollywood and up on stage—not that it
got him out of playing bad guys. He had all the requisites of
villainy: emaciated height, heavy eyebrows, hatchet nose and
lantern jaw. His taut chin was always blue with shadow, a
wonder among makeup men at NBC. Boyd spread the ground
plan in front of Orme, specifically, and began a low-key explanation of the set to forestall Wyman's bitching.

Gunilla Lind arrived at seven-seven, late enough to be last
but not late enough to be at fault; her timing was impeccable.
She came unobtrusively through the arch, her body fluid, hesitant, in a long belted blouse of some shiny ivory stuff. Her
cheekbones found the light. She gave a nearsighted wandering
glance from under a lock of amber hair, raised a tentative hand
and stirred it into the shadow.

"Boyd?"

It was very tasteful, a calculated vulnerability, a riveting
desire to be invisible. Boyd rose to greet her: "Darling." Orme
and Barnard did the same. A very small laugh caught in her

throat, she gave an even smaller shake of her rich hair, her face broke into the beatific smile of one saved, and rather than lifting her cheek she offered her scented temple to be kissed. Obediently protective, Boyd drew her toward the table.

"So looking forward to working with you, how was your trip, I thought you were marvelous in such-and-such, where are you staying, don't you know my friend so-and-so?" Boyd was careful to include the crew in introductions but, like him, they stood back while the professionals small-talked themselves into acquaintance. He listened to the voices, trying to filter out Barnard's weedy tones, admiring the conglomeration of levels and accents: Wyman's volcanic resonance, Gunilla's range of gutturals and trills, Orme's oily monotone that had a threat behind it when he said so much as "It's a pleasure to know you." It was as good a cast as he had ever assembled, a coup to get them to this podunk town at barely Equity wage. He had risked the standard con, promising Wyman, Orme and Gunilla, each in turn, that the others had agreed to come. Once Gunilla actually signed they were easy enough to convince, having in any case reasons of their own.

For Barnard it was a break to be part of such an established company; Orme had been out of work for six months on account of a recent fad among TV directors for casting babyfaced boys as the psychopaths. Wyman, weary of O'Neill and Shaw, was truly dazzled by the play and the part of the Mother Superior, which was in fact the lead role, though people would come to see Gunilla play a corpse. And Wyman would know this. Boyd could see the alliances forming, the tensions budding in fifteen seconds of meaningless how-d'you-do's. Wyman began to underplay Gunilla, and when she praised his performance in a Central Park Shakespeare, failed to match it by mentioning one of her own. Boyd realized with a sick catch in his gut that he had not settled billing between them before he got them here.

So it was a relief when Shaara finally showed, someone among the strangers whose moods and priorities he knew, and knew that he could work with. She looked fine, leaner and looser than he remembered, hesitant in the arch with one hand lifted vaguely, like a parody of Gunilla. Only Shaara wouldn't have been late in order to make an entrance—she'd probably left a pot of milk boiling over somewhere.

"Shaara." She smelled of oregano.

"I wasn't sure if you meant me to be at first reading or not."

Slightly accusatory? And actually hung back, as if he might say no.

"Of course I mean you to be here. You look marvelous. Come and meet the cast."

Still she did not. She shifted her weight and wrung the tips of her fingers. "Did you, ah, call Kevin?"

"Yes, yes; I talked to him."

"What did he have to say?"

"Oh, you know Kevin. Not much for the telephone."

"Oh?"

"Was there anything he should have said?"

"I just wondered."

"I said I might come home with you."

"Tonight? To the house?"

"If you don't mind driving me back to the motel."

"He has school tomorrow."

"Yes, well, let's settle it after the reading, shall we?"

"Are you going to rent a car?" she persisted, still hanging back, still pressing her fingertips, her mouth a little pursed. And yet she was professional enough to know that this was not the right moment for domestic details. It occurred to him for the first time that *Shaara* might be tiresome, Shaara who could always be counted on for a backstage feather smoother, a fund of clumsy motherwit among the tantrums. And he was surprised by memories as elusive as the memory of a taste, of conversations dwindling, with Shaara, into a silence not so much pregnant as petulant. They had had, for two people with such drive, a curious ability to make each other limp, as if their energies, maybe wary of collision, had contained themselves at the level of a fidget.

Behind him Gunilla was singing the praises of arena theater. "Intimate rapport with the audience," he heard, and Wyman's marked silence. He couldn't afford to let that develop now. He ignored Shaara's question and clasped her hand in both his own.

"You've done a marvelous job with the theater. Manet himself would have chosen it. Come and meet the cast."

She followed a little stiffly, he thought, but she followed, and laughed with the rest when he introduced her archly, "Our costume designer Shaara Soole—no relation at the present time."

So they settled, and he called for silence by pressing both hands heavily on the open script. He wiped his mouth and rolled his head back, focusing on a purple patch behind the spot. Gunilla signaled her seriousness by donning a pair of granny glasses. Shaara scrabbled nervously in her bag for a pencil. Wyman, he thought, sulked.

"I want to do a very easy reading tonight," Boyd said, searching the wall, as if testing, discovering, that this was what he wanted, although in fact the speech was as good as memorized. "No performances. Except for Barnard—since you have nothing to *say*, you may *act*."

They laughed. So far so good. He had taken their attention, then broken the solemnity. Now he had them for a paragraph, which would have to generate conviction enough to earn him a second. And so forth. He supported himself on the table and forced his voice to languor.

"Just let it flow. What I mainly want to do tonight is to feel the shape, and before we begin I want briefly to suggest one way to see it. All of you have had a dream . . . in which you appear onstage without your lines. You don't know the plot. You're naked, or dressed for the wrong part in the wrong play. Am I right?"

A titter of recognition ran around the cast.

"*The Nuns* is a play about two dreams, and the wrong one of them comes true. The nuns have a vision of escape, to some civilized place where they will live in wealth and ease, like virtuous noblewomen. In order to enact this dream, the Mother Superior calls in the little Senora, and makes up a nightmare to frighten her. There are bad guys, she says. Blood, burning buildings, murder, looting, rape, revolution. The Mother Superior frightens herself a little in the process, but she knows it's just a story.

"And then it isn't.

"You see, we make things up and then they happen. Every invention begins as a fantasy, but so does every holocaust. Some shepherd boy in ancient Crete dreams of going to the moon, and sooner or later a Yank in a plastic suit will do it. But also, a second-rate Austrian art student dreams of burning Jews, and sooner or later they will burn." Boyd paused, swallowed, while the image of his mild father walked into his mind and out again. "Here, in the first act the Mother Superior invents a vicious mob that is out for the Senora's blood, and then in the second act the mob is real, but it's out for her *own*.

"Because the other thing is that danger is never exactly where you look for it. You protect your flank and get shot at from the rear. If the revolution don't get you, the counter-revolution will. In the Mother Superior's story it was the voodoo rebels that were going to break down the door; in the second act it turns out to be the loyal royalists.

"And then, of course, the trouble with any kind of dream come true, happily-ever-after or nightmare, is that you have to live with it every day. So all the glitter, the feasts, that glamour of horror itself, give way to the rasping annoyances of experience. They're hungry, they're dirty, the drums are pounding. The murder was not real to them, but the corpse stinks. And somebody is hammering at the door.

"Now, what we have to find over the next seven weeks is the reality that works for us, and if we find it the whole thing can have that awful logic that a dream has while you dream it. We don't want any camping from the men. Physically you are men, and as you take off your wimples and gird up your skirts to disinter the body, you become more blatantly masculine. But your minds are the minds of nuns. *You* know you're nuns, as you know it in a dream, no questions asked. As the stench and the drums and the flames close in, you become the innocent victims you have invented, and *that* is reality.

"All of this involves a lot of passion—greed, terror, so forth. But what I want you to read for tonight is the extreme reasonableness of it all, that dream-reasonableness in which you question nothing, consult nothing but your own conviction of your own normality. We'll find the points of passion later. Tonight, do it in the small. I'd rather you'd whine than shout. All right?"

While he read the opening stage directions he listened for the quality of their attention. He'd stopped sweating and could afford to run his handkerchief under his glasses, reach for his pipe. His stomach was calm and his focus on the script was normal. Everyone seemed intent; only Shaara's pencil scratched, making sketches in the margin. Orme began in the casual way he'd asked for:

You think everything will go all right?

* * *

But Wyman hit too loud and would be resonating, performing, by the time they reached Act Two.

Everything . . . fine.

You don't think there'll be any hitches?

No trouble at all.

Boyd muted his voice as a cue to Wyman. "Sister Angela takes a cigar out of her pocket, rolls it between her palms, bites off the end and puts it in her mouth."

SISTER ANGELA
You may think so, but I don't like it when things look too easy.

6. Creeper

Shaara's house sat in a red clay trough too abrupt to be a valley, too shallow to be a ravine, but wide and deep enough to trap the damp. Everything flourished willy-nilly in this neighborhood in the summer wet, children and the bacteria in their middle ears; pinworm, ringworm, impetigo; iron oaks and the wisteria that choked them, roses and the aphids gnawing at their leaves. Lush, moist, fecund—everything vegetable, reptile or six-legged indigenous to this lowland was a creeper. Gene Keyes, two-legged, was also creeping, along the twist from the highway where his truck was parked, away from the streetlamp on her side, on the crackling top of this year's leaves that lay over the rot of last year's.

He could say he was taking a walk. He was. But he had driven nine miles in a four-wheel-drive Ford pickup that he'd tucked under a bank of blackening azaleas to take this particular walk, which would lead him up a loop of unremarkable box houses and around a minor park of no special beauty to deposit him back here in front of Shaara's rec room window. He could say he was concerned about her loss of a guard dog. He was. But he felt more like a prowler than a security patrol—taking a step back into the shadow of a high hedge to watch the smoke curl out of Boyd Soole's pipe beyond the plate glass, and Shaara carrying a stubby glass of something-on-the-rocks, the glass held out in front of her at awkward arm's length.

Gene wished she would close the curtains. He wished (unusually) that he still smoked. He had left the theater, gone back to the trailer for a couple of beers, and planned an early night of it when he'd started seeing Shaara crossing the dark Magoor parking lot, started wondering if she'd locked her car, locked her house, wondering if she understood there had been two rapes and four break-ins in her neighborhood since last summer; until without any sort of conscious decision, he had got back in the truck and driven here just in time to see the big man unfold himself out of the little car and follow Shaara into the kitchen door. He had walked to the corner and back again. Now Kevin was leading Boyd somewhere deeper into the house and Shaara hung behind in the smoky yellow light, tucked a wisp of hair under her scarf, and rearranged, twice, a set of gewgaws on a table. She stretched her arms in front of her and locked her hands, wringing the knuckles. The agitation in her hands sent Gene out of his niche in the hedge and on up the hill.

He was interested in a lot of things—good wood, nailless construction, gardening, the Braves, Falcons, road systems, the interior tangle of a balking machine, brackish waterways and, recently, the ecological balance of the Florida Gulf Coast—but it was a few years since he'd been interested in anything against his will. It made him nervous. He was not a coward in the sense he'd grown up to understand cowardice, being both hard to startle and willing to stand his ground, but he supposed he was a cautious man. He always left the TV on when he wasn't home. At the shop he did a round of electrical plugs and (recently, again) made sure Shaara's iron was off and the dryer trap free of lint before he left. The iron was sometimes on and the lint trap was always full. It would not occur to Shaara that a loudmouth Shepherd was a safety feature in a Southern town, and this irritated him. It was none of his business and there was nothing he could do about it except alarm her. He could hardly lurk around her house night after night. Irritation sent him up the hill.

He'd been brought up to be cautious, in another Southern town about the same distance as this one from the other side of Atlanta, and what the shape of his life had mainly taught him was that caution had to be valued for its own sake, apart from whether it was any use. He checked doors and plugs for the same reason he made his corners true and caulked the joints where nobody would see them, because enclosing one space and keeping out another made a piece of order against the flung mess of the universe.

He had been ill as a child and had consequently, perhaps predictably, made himself physically strong. He had experienced early and later the deaths of those he cared about most and had consequently—less predictably—come to believe in his own mortality. What the consciousness of his mortality did for him was mainly to convince him that he'd better enjoy himself day by day; but as his enjoyments tended toward woodcraft and woods lore nobody pointed to him as a hedonist. Whereas he was likely to be twitted for his caution.

A picket fence mounted the hill at his right and he dragged a hand along the top of it as he'd done as a child, remembering the pleasant numbing thud in his palm. A mottled cat arched invitingly toward him, rubbing her back on a post, then took fright when the vibrations reached her part of the fence, and dashed into a clump of pampas grass.

His dad, for instance, had kept a shotgun and a Doberman, which he ritually loaded into the back seat of the rusty Plymouth every time he went as far as the bait shop or the bauxite mine where he worked—which made a kind of double sense because the dog and the gun were the most valuable things he owned. But when he died (Gene was nine) it was from one of the creepers, a lung infection beginning in the bauxite dust and spreading to his finger joints and phlebitis before it cut him off. His mother, a compact woman who made no show of feelings, had expressed her mourning principally in an augmented and controlled care of Gene that had nothing to do with either shotguns or cancer. When he thought of his childhood (he was past the fence now, rolling his sneakers over pine needles and cones on an unswept section of sidewalk), the first thing that came to mind was an image of his mother's form, foreshortened from his vantage point in a tree, busied at a shrub or a pepper plant. She never suggested either that he should not climb trees or that he should be careful climbing them, but when he climbed trees she commanded the territory beneath them in patent demonstration that she was not a person who would prevent a boy from climbing a tree. It was a powerful preventative; he would not have dared to face her if he fell. Her heart failed the year he left home, when she was fifty-three.

And his wife Harriet had had an infectious enthusiasm for health fads, nutrition and regular exercise. But after their only child was stillborn she had lost her enthusiasm piecemeal, some kind of creeping waste around the eyes. When they told her not to try another pregnancy it was Gene who took over health, got her into camping, bigmouth bass and the hand-tied flies that snagged them. And then when she died it was in defiance of the wrong set of precautionary measures. She slipped in her stockinged feet on the two-foot rise of back porch step and hit the base of her skull on the concrete sill. Even so it was a creeper: he stretched her out on the couch and gave her a shot of bourbon and went back to tying flies; and it was half an hour later that he noticed she was shaking and grunting, tearing at a doily under her head. He put her in the truck to take her to Emergency, and on the way she flailed at his head with her fists and screamed at him words he didn't know she knew. At the hospital they had described her condition as "combative," and raised the tubular sides of the bed, which she whacked with her forearms while she pissed yellow puddles of rage, sheet after sheet. They said "probable concussion" and made him sign a surgery release that was "just a formality" and told him to go home. He went home and drank, and was still awake at four when (he learned later) they operated, but by the time she died at six he was profoundly sleeping, and they didn't wake him. When he got there at ten it was to face the arrangements, the other forms, the Latinate explanations.

Then he went, as he told Shaara, temporarily bats. Then he did his mourning, perhaps, for all four of them, all the deaths that were too early from birth to fifty-three. He sold everything and went to work at minimum wage as water man on Interstate 10. He quit smoking, and for the first couple of fogged months on that monotonous road he supposed he was suffering withdrawal symptoms. All he did was fill and empty the truck. He lay on top of it with his foot in the tank, reading Zane Grey. When the water hit his ankle he drove to the site, stuck the hose where it was wanted, and read till it ran dry. He never looked farther than the black characters on the cheap newsprint or the threads on the water cap. He got through several hundred Westerns, following the road north, living mostly in trailers, making no enemies and no friends. But when they finished the Interstate he'd had to choose between a Mississippi transfer and a real job again. He liked Georgia. Besides, one day he found himself in Handy Dan's leafing through a *Sunset* manual on deck building, and figured he'd been bats for long enough.

At the top of the hill the neighborhood stretched out into a plateau, and Gene followed the curve to the right past older houses, mostly from the 'thirties, some bare brick and some whitewashed, some given over to the creepers. He heard shouting and the hollow rat-a-tat of a plastic machine gun ahead of him, and although it was quarter to eleven on a school night, he spotted three boys engaged in passionate warfare. Two were half concealed in the foliage, wearing khaki and camouflage out of Army Surplus, the sleeves and trousers rolled. The third, in gym shorts and a tank top, was crouched on the street side of a yellow Datsun 280Z. The streetlight, the brilliant car, and the stripes of his shirt all put the boy at a disadvantage in a guerilla skirmish. The machine gun clattered and one of the camouflaged soldiers yelled, "Gottcha!"

The smaller boy obediently dropped his pistol and died. He was good at it. He clutched his belly and staggered against the car, then hand-over-handed himself up the fender and lifted to Gene as he passed a smudged grimace of mortal pain. He wheeled away from the car and across the road into the park, lurching into a bank of azaleas—thinking, perhaps, to have a better position for the next round—emitted a groan and then a death rattle, arched his body in a last throe, and lay still. The two from the bushes sped into the park and disappeared in the pines.

Passing the next house Gene heard more shouting and expected to see another squadron, then recognized an adult resonance and a background of real crying. A woman's voice began—high, hard and hysterical—and pursued him around the loop of the park. When he was at a distance of maybe thirty yards and headed back the way he'd come, he heard a door slam, and a slight woman in Levi cutoffs and bare feet charged catty-corner across the lawn. She had giant rollers in her hair and although she was still crying she was taking the trouble to tie a wisp of filmy stuff around them, keys clenched and fumbling at the base of her neck. Gene crossed to the park to watch, with no impulse either to help or to interfere, but cautious, and nevertheless spying. Oblivious, the two soldiers passed him to the left through the trees.

The woman stopped at the expensive car and rattled the

keys against the door, stomped her bare feet on the concrete and slammed in. Into the reverberating metallic silence a boy shouted, "Go 'round the back!" and the woman turned the key too hard. The starter motor squealed and the motor gunned into a neutral rage so that the gears gnashed as they meshed. The machine gun sounded. "Gottcha!" The small boy leapt from the azalea bushes and into the road toward his pistol just as the headlights and the car came to life. Gene froze, and the boy froze in the light, arms flung to his face as if to ward off an overhead blow. The brakes squealed and the car lurched to a stop a couple of feet from him.

"Jesus Christ!" the woman screamed.

Expert at death, the boy handled his survival badly. He blinked and snuffled, edged awkwardly out of the headlights and raced ignominiously away, ankles snagging in the grass clumps. The woman sat still for a moment, breathing anger. Then she put the car more adroitly into gear and drove off. Gene, stranded in a neighborhood park with a useless excess of adrenaline, jogged the rest of the way around the park and back to the hill, where the incipient violence of gravity pulled him down toward Shaara's house.

Now, alert, even from a distance he could see the fresh tire marks under her streetlamp where Henry had been hit. He took a side turning and kept running until he got his rhythm. Well, the dog had died and the boy had not; even odds. The sidewalks ended, and he jogged in the middle of the pitted road. What the shape of his life had taught him was that ordinary life is as dangerous as war; more dangerous, because *everybody* dies as a result. And it is not after all a question of avoiding risk because you are as likely to be punished for not doing a thing as for doing it. His run took him into a neighborhood now of cheaper houses, smaller lots and frame construction, and fewer lights on inside. With the regular rhythm of the asphalt under him his thoughts contracted, steadied. The houses were darker because they were cheaper, he thought. The people who live here get up at five instead of seven, so their children go to bed at nine instead of eleven. Everybody quarrels earlier.

He ran for a quarter of an hour, turned back and walked for a ways, then jogged again. His plan was to reenter Shaara's street and just keep going, back to his truck. But he was thwarted in this because when he reached the corner he saw a taxi pulled up at her house, and Boyd and Shaara in the drive. He detoured into the next driveway to avoid the cab lights and found himself, ridiculously, in Shaara's backyard.

There is nothing for a Peeping Tom to do in this situation but sit it out. He threaded his way in the dark through gardenia bushes, sweating from the run, stealthy on crumbly ground that might have been the dog's grave or might have been fresh molehills, feeling foolish and annoyed. He sat on the damp ground, locked his arms around his knees. He heard the cab pull away and the back door swing closed, but from this angle he couldn't see in. The rec room ran the depth of the house, with smaller windows on this side, so all he had to do was wait till the lights in them disappeared, meaning Shaara had gone to bed, and then thread his way out to the street again.

But the lights didn't go off. Shaara appeared briefly at a window, her hair outrageously haloed by the backlight, and pulled (finally) the drape. There was a second window, and while he waited expecting to see her there, the back door swung again and she appeared, very suddenly, on the bright porch. For an awful second his explanations stuttered through his mind. Then she swung the lid off the garbage can and dumped inside, with an unnecessary largesse of gesture, the contents of a bronze ashtray. She stepped off the porch into the arc of lit grass and walked a few paces. Her feet, like the angry woman's, were bare now below her caftan, and she rolled each one deliberately in the grass, heel and arch, ball, toes. She dropped the ashtray and dropped to her knees, dug her fists in the grass, and came up with two rooted, dirt-scattering handfuls. She dropped these and tore out another two. She reached for the ashtray with one hand, fisted still another clump of grass and began to clean the ashtray with it, scouring in a muscular circle again and again, again.

He didn't know exactly what she was doing but he felt that her hands nevertheless spoke very clearly. They always spoke clearly though she did not know this; she worried away at words and they did nothing for her, formed no order, and she did not know this. Whereas her hands tucked back a stray lock, made a space between persons or crossed the space between them and put an end to the space, shaped cloth, enclosed, encompassed. Now he didn't know exactly what she was doing but he felt that her hands were performing a purely private act, an act of private pain. And now her ignorance of his presence obscurely frightened him, as if he were guilty in fact of criminal intent. He would like to have called out and warned her—of what he was not sure, not knowing whether the danger he sensed was to Shaara, or from Shaara to him, or in himself. After she rose and carried the ashtray back inside, and after the lights went out, he sat for a long time in the damp dark and the clay smell of her backyard.

7. *Off the Hook*

Wendy had been an embarrassment to her dorm in the early 'seventies before the middle class came back in fashion, and in many ways New York had not "taken." She was friendly with people who had gurus, analysts, rebirthings and abortions, but her conversation was distinctly tinged with tact. She had liberal views on sex, but out of the minority opinion that everyone since Freud had made too much fuss about it. "I think," she said once, "that there's more celibacy going on than people are generally willing to admit." Naiveté was much in vogue in the City at the time; its style was spacey, blown-away, and potentially committable. Wendy's was not of the style.

She had, for instance, an anachronistic confidence in anyone in uniform. She would hop into a dentist's chair with her mouth already open. She made friends with doormen and trusted cops. She would, in another era, have been perfectly certain that the cavalry would arrive in time.

On the other hand, she had high standards for such persons, and did not expect Dr. Madden of East Millstone to keep her waiting for two hours while she leafed his scabby stock of *Good Housekeepings* and *Family Circles*. She found a single copy of *Sports Illustrated* and read about scaling the Matterhorn, which she would rather have been doing than this.

Nor did she expect him to greet her first when she was already naked under a sheet offensively sprigged with blue posies. Dr. Madden, gleaming of tooth and coat, stuck out a hand to her which, in order that she take it, necessitated that she flap her right arm out from under the sheet while clasping it to her collarbone with the left. Dr. Madden said her name to the chart, removed his hand from hers, washed it, and slipped it directly into disposable plastic.

"Just relax and slide down," said Dr. Madden, while the nurse lifted Wendy's heels into the icy stirrups and pulled the sheet up to her hips. "There's nothing to be nervous about."

"I'm not nervous," Wendy said.

"Good, then just loosen up in here." He spread petroleum jelly and inserted a metal shoe tree. "You're tensing up on me."

"It's cold," Wendy explained, and briefly wished after all that she had gone to Dr. Malspies, who was chatty and fuddled and had a chivalrous awe for the bravery of little girls and women.

"Mmm," said Dr. Madden, swabbing. "How late is your period?"

"Six weeks. But I'm not very regular."

"Six weeks!"

"But I'm not regular."

"That may be," he said, fingering her belly into the shoe tree, "but I think you have a fairly regular eight-week pregnancy going here. Any discharge?"

"A little," Wendy said. "Sort of blackish. I might need a D and C."

Dr. Madden looked up at her use of the term, caught her eye for the first time. He had a cowlick and enlarged irises, like a fish. "We'll have the test results on Monday. Get dressed and stop by my office, will you?"

While she pulled on her stockings Wendy made a quick review of her reasoning. She did not want to make a decision, she only wanted the possibility of making one. She disliked Dr. Madden very much; that was an advantage. He didn't know her and she wasn't from East Millstone. She could disappear if she chose.

She started to do up the clasp of the jade pendant her parents had given her for Christmas, then changed her mind and poked it into a corner of her makeup bag. It wouldn't do to look too prosperous. She rumpled the sleeves of her knit shirt above the elbow and draped her trench coat off-center over her arm.

He would ask her why, and she would not be caught telling

him just because. She had worked it out on the train—a train always disembodied her and set the fantasies flowing with its rhythm. She would tell him nothing but the strictest truth, but she would not be caught telling him *her* boring truth: I'm not ready, I feel trapped, I don't think I was meant to be a mother. She knew that such reasons, through repetition, had lost their force by now. They came under the suspect heading of "on demand."

In his office she crossed her knees and clasped her hands on top of her bag. "Dr. Madden, I would like a D and C."

He gave her his underwater gaze and clasped his hands as well. "If you're pregnant, Mrs. Soole, it wouldn't be a D and C, it would be a termination."

"Ah, I see. I'm sorry." She dropped her eyes, as befitted a young Bostonian when confronted with a crisp coat and crisp ethics. "I see," she said again.

"You *are* married?" he asked more gently.

"Oh, yes!" Wendy looked up, earnest. "Yes, I've been married for about two years."

"Well, I don't just hand abortions out. So many women change their minds. On the other hand, if there are extenuating circumstances, it is possible. Perhaps you'd better tell me why . . ."

"Yes," Wendy said, recrossed her legs and took a labored breath. "My husband is quite a bit older than I. Almost twenty years." She hesitated. "I met him when I was doing my honors thesis on Theatrical Uses of Body Language." Dr. Madden may have suppressed a smile, so Wendy drew herself up to a dignified straightness of spine. "He's a theater director, and he was kind enough to let me do my research on the play he was directing at the time."

"I see," said Dr. Madden.

"So that's how we met. And we got married as soon as I graduated. But now . . ." She sighed. "Well, he has a son by a former marriage and has to contribute to his support. I'm afraid the theater isn't a very steady living."

"I see," Dr. Madden said again.

"I'm afraid he drinks rather more than is good for him, especially when he's working." She found a piece of lint on her knee and scratched at it for a while. "Not that that's why he doesn't work all the time!" she reassured him, and rolled the lint into a ball. Finding nowhere to put it, she returned it to her knee. "But, well, when he is working he's on the road a lot. For long periods sometimes. I'm afraid things are a bit of a mess at home. The rent isn't paid." She became confused. "I'm waiting for him to send me money, but . . ."

Dr. Madden, his hands still clasped, leaned toward her over the desk.

". . . Right now, he's down in Georgia. In a little town . . . with his former wife."

"Ah," the doctor said.

"My mother keeps trying to get me to come home, but I'm not sure. I don't like to admit to her that I haven't got the fare."

"A termination, you know, would cost about three hundred dollars."

"Yes, I know," sighed Wendy bravely. "I have friends here in East Millstone who know . . . my situation . . . that I could count on. And it's not—is it, doctor?—anything like the life-long cost of raising a child."

She had learned at home that the best lies are always based on maximum truth. College had done what it's meant to do, and codified the knowledge. Dr. Madden drew a notepad to him and offered her an abortion. She had no way of knowing that he would have done so in any case.

She hadn't told Fred and Cass Carson she was coming, because she might want to change her mind. They liked being dropped in on anyway, and always had a pot of macrobiotic something or other on the stove. There was nothing to eat in the apartment in New York, and it was already getting dark. She caught a cab.

She was exhilarated and a little frightened by her success. She had betrayed Boyd grossly. The odd thing was that he'd love the story if only she could tell it. She imagined herself sitting sideways on the couch (the apartment was spotless in this vision) with her stockinged toes tucked under Boyd's thigh, describing Dr. Madden's fishface as she said, ". . . with his former wife." In the fantasy Boyd threw back his head and howled with laughter, and—contrarily, because the impossibility of this scene had nothing to do with Boyd's absence—for the first time Wendy was stabbed with a pang of home-sickness for him. In the backseat of the cab she hugged herself, an instinctive and inadequate surrogate. Although she was preparing to defy him she missed him bitterly; no, it was because of that. She removed her hands from her forearms and folded them deliberately in her lap. Tomorrow she would have to pay her dues: make a real decision, and perhaps borrow the three hundred dollars. But for tonight she would let herself off the hook and have a "natter with Cass" on less momentous topics.

The taxi pulled up to the Carsons' in smoggy twilight. It was a ramshackle street, old brick houses with big backyards that spread in a tangle of blackberries down to a stream. Boyd and Shaara had lived in one of them—she wasn't exactly sure which—for several years. The inhabitants here were mostly pretend dropouts who worked in the City and came home to tend their beanpoles, do macramé and tinker with pickup trucks.

She paid the fare, and only when the cab had pulled away did she notice that the Carsons' place was dark. She picked the morning newspaper up off the lawn, found the mail in the box. They were gone, then, but she reasoned that they would not be gone overnight, or they would have had a neighbor take in the mail.

She sat for a while on the porch, creaking back and forth in the swing. She put on her trench coat and walked around back, stamping her feet against the oncoming chill. She tried under the mat for the key, above the doorsill, behind the oil tank. When she got really cold she decided to break in.

The Carsons would not mind this, but she checked stealthily for neighbors and dogs who might. Nobody seemed to be about. She pried a screen from a back window with her nail file, which was surprisingly easy, and poked the file between the window and the sill, which was not. The latch inside was of an old-fashioned brass kind that swiveled open, but the swivel was stronger than the file and dry with corrosion. Inspired, she dipped the nail file in her cold cream, stuck it back under the window, and rasped it around the turning point. She did this several times, intent, till she felt the grainy stuff give way and the oiled point slip into the swivel itself. Once a mole ran over her foot, but nothing else stirred. When the swivel was well greased she bent the file, shoved it under the frame, and twisted it toward the upper perimeter of the latch. Gradually it gave.

Now she found that the window was painted shut, and she had to stack bricks to stand on while she scraped it free around the edge. Where she gathered the bricks the grass was crushed and white; potato bugs surfaced frantically. She was not frightened now but she was still exhilarated, and when a dog barked a couple of yards down her heart barked back. She pounded upward with the heels of her hands on the window frame. Chips of paint snowed onto the sill, and with a sharp crack it came free. When the pulleys caught it sucked itself up.

She slung her bag inside, but before she climbed in she took the bricks—the impulse was obscure—and replaced each one accurately on its rectangle of flattened grass. Then she hauled herself over and locked the window behind her.

She was in the rec room, which they called the den, and which had every attribute of a hunting lodge except the antlers. It was dominated by a flagstone fireplace with a massive hearth. All the walls and floors were distressed pine, age-dark and glowing. The furniture was overstuffed and covered in masculine stuff, lumberjack plaids and hide. When she put on a low yellow lamp it caught at Fred's beetle collection pinned to the bare wood, and at the wall's worth of blown-up snapshots in cheap black frames. All of these, from some earlier era in the Carsons' marriage, were outdoorsy and had the attitudes of safari, though if you looked closer their content was of an amateur vacationing kind: Fred at a campfire, Cass on a dock, the two of them in a canoe. One was of Shaara in a dirndl and peasant blouse, left foot on an oak stump and her arms folded on her cocked knee. The snapshot had been in mediocre focus and the blowup gave it the grainy quality of a daguerreotype: Shaara the pioneer, in command of the wagon train, triumphant over a tree.

Still wary of neighbors who might come to investigate, Wendy felt her way through the dark house to the kitchen and made herself a snack by the refrigerator light. Sugar-cured ham and alfalfa sprouts, a pot of homemade yogurt into which she dumped Cass's blackberry jam and some extra sugar. She was agitated, had a low backache from her war with the window. At some point she'd stopped wishing they'd show up and started hoping they wouldn't.

She found the liquor stock. Most of it was quirky, as if there was something more organic about Pear Aquavit and Amandine than sour mash, but tucked in the back was a little gin and a half a bottle of brandy. She thought brandy was more calming, and that it would be a good idea to calm down, so she took that.

She balanced her meal back into the rec room and flipped on the big old black-and-white console TV. "Going far?" Little Henry Travers shivered into focus, his hand on the window of a contoured 'thirties car and his smile aimed trustfully up into the face of "Mad Dog" Earle. Bogart flexed a lip down over his lisp. "Up in the mount'ns for my health."

High Sierra was one of her familiars, from "Matinee Theaters" and "Late Late Shows" when Boyd was on the road. She slipped off her shoes, nestled into a cushion, chewed brandy into the alfalfa and prepared to be content. She would think about it tomorrow. Tonight Ida Lupino could flash her perfect eyes under the pompadour and assure Bogie that "I'm not gonna be sent back to that dime-a-dance joint if I can help it." Willie Best could dance his nigger shenanigans around the jinxed mutt Pard: "He up and die of poomonia. Big stroppin man too." She waited for a commercial before she went to pee.

The Carsons' back bath was the most genuinely rustic thing in the house. Too much damp and too many layers of old oil made it unredeemable. Thick curls of paint, brown on the outside and lime green underneath, hung from the ceiling and wall like dried leaves. Sometimes they detached themselves and drifted into the bathtub or crashed on the checkerboard tiles. Wendy sat on the john scuffing chips with her stockinged toe, a lead ache at the base of her spine. *High Sierra* ran in the background familiar as a song, a swell of pure movie music that meant the sun was breaking over the peaks, Lupino coming in with the refrain, "You kinda hope you can crash out. It kinda keeps you going."

The brandy hadn't worked, she was still jumpy, so she cleaned the paint chips out of the bath and soaked for a while in water as hot as she could take, stole some shampoo and scrubbed her hair. Trusting Travers gushed, "It's the second time you saved my life. I had thirteen cents in my pocket and a five dollar bill in my shoe." And Big Bad Bogie, soft in the center, and wanting to buy his way into the American Dream, fixed up an operation for his clubfooted niece. After the bath she didn't feel like getting into her day-old clothes, so she rummaged in Cass's closet for a robe. They were all too long except for a short happi coat thing in tie-dyed plush, which she unearthed from the bottom of a cumbered hook. The wrinkles were set, as if it hadn't been worn for years.

She belted it around her and went back to the den, picked

up her glass. Joan Leslie, clumpily leaping in thick stockings
and librarian shoes, clapped her hands. "Roy, he says it can
be fixed!"

She took the glass back to the kitchen, propped the fridge
door open for the light, and crouched at the liquor cupboard.
She fished the brandy toward her, flexing her bare toes on the
linoleum in preparation to rise. Her calf muscles caught and
hardened, taking her weight. The explosion of blood was so
painless that she felt it first as wet on her heels; her first thought
was that she had somehow spilled the brandy.

Then the backache reasserted itself, but numbly, and even
surprise was numbed. She watched the blood run down her
ankles, pool on the flecked linoleum around her toes.

Nothing further happened. She remained crouching, waiting
for a second blast, which didn't come. She wasn't sure what
she ought to do, but it seemed logical to wipe her legs and
the floor with paper towels, so she did that. She dampened
another set of towels and perfected the job. Cleaned her toes.
She found a tea towel and belted it between her legs with the
sash of the happi coat, then took the paper towels back to the
bathroom and flushed them one by one down the toilet. Bogart
was having a nightmare in the den.

She felt all right, she just wasn't sure exactly what she was
supposed to do. The dog down the street started up its barking
and the one on the set began licking Lupino's tear-stained face.
From the photograph Shaara grinned up tough over the felled
tree. Lupino was falling to pieces, she was no help, so Wendy
consulted herself for pioneer spirit. Get the wagons in a circle.

She took the phone from its table and moved onto a rugless
section of the floor. She looked up Dr. Madden's emergency
number and dictated into the answering machine her name,
the words "I seem to be bleeding," and the Carsons' phone
number. Bogart said, "I'm giving it to you straight. I got plans.
There's no room in them for you." Then he went and proposed
to Joan Leslie in a hair ribbon, who turned him down flat.
Leslie seemed to be going to the bad in her own way. "I'm
not crippled any more, Pa, and from now on I'm going to have
fun!" A few scenes on she was drinking and dancing with an
oily type. Wendy stretched her legs out in front of her and
waited for Dr. Madden to call.

By the time he did so, Bogart and Lupino were on their way
to L.A., broke, with the jinxed dog in the front seat and the

jewelry in a shoe box. Lupino had taken to wearing a hair ribbon, as if it was not at all clear who was corrupt, and who innocent. Dr. Madden, cheerful—delighted?—said, "Well, it looks like you're going to save three hundred dollars."

"Should I come and see you?"

"No need. It all sounds perfectly normal. Just deliver it into a clean jar and cover it with water. Bring it to me in the morning so I can check that it's all there."

"Is that all?"

"That's all."

"I'm not even drinking gin," Wendy said, which sounded a little demented, but Dr. Madden laughed.

"It wouldn't be a bad idea to switch over. You'll be fine. Carry on."

And she was fine. Bogart got blasted out of his hiding place in the Sierras and Lupino went hysterical with grief. But Wendy found a quart Hellman's jar in the kitchen—the label was still on—and squatted among the paint chips in the back bath drinking gin until the embryo, no bigger than a golf ball, slid itself out into the jar. She had learned in Biology that the human fetus differentiates itself amazingly early into eyes, brain, spinal cord and skin. But she could differentiate nothing, a visceral clot with frayed edges, like an anemone. She held it under the tap and ran a trickle of water into the jar until the fetus bobbed up underneath the label and, once the lid was on, she could see it no more.

She curled up on the couch with another brandy and watched a special on Three Mile Island and *The China Syndrome*, news of another defective DC-10 and an earthquake in Yugoslavia; an interview with the director of *Marathon Man*. By one o'clock she turned it off and fell instantly asleep.

In the morning she put the happi coat back under the other layers on the hook. She buried the tea towel in the hamper. She took a swipe at the bathroom ceiling so the paint chips fell into the bath. She put the mayonnaise jar in a grocery bag, called a cab, let herself out the front door, picked up the mail and the paper off the porch swing where she had left them, returned the mail to the box and the paper to the lawn. She dropped the bag by Dr. Madden's office and caught the eleven-eleven to New York.

When Boyd called Sunday, latish, he asked if she had gone down to see the Carsons.

"They had plans for the weekend, out of town," Wendy said. She hugged herself and stared at the junk mail on the floor.

"Ah, too bad. What did you do to amuse yourself?"

"Oh, I watched *High Sierra* on TV. You know. And some dumb interview."

"You saw the doctor?"

"I did, but I didn't need to. I got my period after all."

"Aw. Poor baby," he said. "Well," he said, "never mind."

8. *Starlit*

Gunilla Lind was awake at six A.M. Sunday, tangled in Farrah hair, petit point, and the smell of Lauren across the double bed in the Sheraton. Under the scent, she thought the sheets smelled slightly used. Since the Sheraton provided daily maid service this was unlikely, but the notion mixed unpleasantly with a general clamminess. The room had a synthetic decadence about it, nylon plush and flocked vinyl, the Interstate Whorehouse Franchise. Thick red drapes blocked out everything but a thin slit of moted light that fell on her toenails.

That Gunilla felt she had been raped was unremarkable, incidence of rape on Magoor campus being fourth highest in the nation. Gunilla didn't know that. But she knew that her feeling was somehow unremarkable, and that it should not be remarked on to the cast of which she was the only female member. She had not so much as spoken to the man. Nevertheless she twisted in the sheets, stung by minor memories of times she had swapped strokes, tongues, juices, for a variety of reasons unconnected with desire. She had never deliberately put herself on the casting couch, but she had been tricked and trapped many times over the past dozen years by subtler and more insidious forces; mistaken signals and misplaced tact, drink, the greed of her own uncertain ego. Now, when she had not in fact been touched (the police would have laughed), these memories erupted nastily in her mind, accompanied in some instances by real hair and jowls. The air was wet and hard to breathe.

All week she'd stayed in, studying her lines and writing her biography of the Senora, so by Saturday she'd felt slightly claustrophobic. Places were important to her. She'd spent her childhood between Sweden, which she loved, and Argentina, which she hated, while her parents' marital and financial fortunes waxed and waned. Now she was so much on the road, living in trailers on location if it was a film, or in hotels like this one if it was legit theater, that she liked to spend some time in orientation. She needed the ritual of filing her underwear in the disinfected drawers, laying out on the Formica her collection of bottles, sponges, colors, brushes, scents. She spilled dusting powder. She wound her jeweled travel clock and set the oval photo of her mother on the nightstand. She draped shawls over the chairs. Once she'd made the room hers she liked to go out wandering and, as she always explained later, "get the feel of the place." It was likely that she'd got the feel of this one.

Saturday afternoon she'd finished her biography, and she was pleased with it. She'd found a fine base of identification with the Senora, exiled on an uncivilized island, pampered and surrounded with luxury and nevertheless sick for home. Gunilla speculated (the play said nothing about this, so she was free to make it up) that the Senora had been raised, very sheltered, in a Spanish manse, and had married into exile on Haiti where she suffered equally from the provinciality of the whites and the barbarous power of those who were supposed to be her servants. She thought the Senora found Haiti brash and violent, and nevertheless numbingly dull. What she had already experienced of Hubbard had perhaps suggested these attitudes, but the feelings ran deep, and were neither new nor specific to the American South. She had felt something of the sort in Buenos Aires, Minneapolis and Malibu.

About seven she'd picked up a local paper in the lobby and gone in to dinner. The dining room was Plantation in the same stagey way that her room was Brothel—black waiters in red gabardine tails who poured water from an astonishing height and *yes-ma'amed* through the meal while they stared sullenly at her tumble of blond hair and her discreet cleavage. From a parchment menu she ordered a baconburger and Coke because it was cheap, then grossly overtipped because she sensed that the waiters were angry.

While she ate she read the local news. Busy weekend for a town of forty thousand: one fatal spelunking accident at Ofkenowee Springs, one attempted rape (foiled by a neighbor) in Alumni Housing, two convenience stores relieved at gunpoint of an undetermined amount of cash. She turned to Ann Landers on the entertainments page—and discovered, at first with a sense of gratified delight, that *The Big Heist* was playing this weekend at a cinema called The Campus Arts. Gratified because for a moment she supposed that they had somehow unearthed it in her honor. Then she realized that if that were the case, someone would have mentioned it and capitalized on her presence in the publicity. She had already been blandly miffed at Hubbard's disorganized lack of interest; in Minneapolis she'd been booked within days to meet with student groups and feminist caucuses. The one-column-inch ad in the *Hubbard Post* listed Jean-Pierre Guery and Louis Claude as the stars of the "wacky French farce," which they were, though neither of their names was as well known by now as hers.

The Big Heist was the first film she'd done that had achieved American distribution, and she hadn't seen it for what (she calculated her travels) must have been eight years. She decided she'd go to the nine o'clock showing. She'd hate it, but that was okay; it would give her a clear sense of how she'd do it differently now, how far she'd come. Remembering intense little Guy Fatras, a director of overweening and self-defeating ambition, with whom she'd briefly, mistakenly, believed she was in love, she laughed aloud. He'd been so taken with his title pun, *Bijou*—which, he debonairly explained, meant movie theater to the Americans, and would improve its distribution chances. And then when the thing was bought they changed the title because Americans thought *bijou* meant movie theater and wouldn't know it had anything to do with a jewel robbery.

After dinner she wandered for an hour or so among old brick buildings lush with creepers, getting the feel of the place. The campus was nearly deserted except for squirrels darting in the starlight, chameleons with bloated throats watchful on the foliage. The weight of the air, the wet fecundity, reminded her very much of Argentina, where she'd spent four teenage years while her father made and lost one or another of his fortunes. And that was good, although she hadn't liked Argentina, because it was a point of contact, a minor root. She half expected to see one of those extravagant tropical butterflies, their fragile stained-glass wings and their obscene furred bodies. She dragged a hand over the new leaves and followed a squirrel toward center campus.

On the steps of the administration building a gaggle of demonstrators stood disorganized. John Spenkelink and the ERA had both been killed two weeks ago eighty miles south in Tallahassee, and they were holding a wake part Baptist and part Anarchist. A minister in a bowtie quoted texts from Ephesians to condemn one or another of the deaths; a squat woman led a song. Ordinarily this was Gunilla's cup of tea, and it was possible that if she identified herself she'd be recognized as an actress or an activist or both. But she was not in the mood; if she were not invited she would not offer herself; so after a while she went off to find The Campus Arts.

It was on the most anonymous drag in Hubbard, a four-lane blinking with primary colors and smelling of gas and fries. There were three or four blocks of crumbling plaster storefronts, erstwhile dry goods and five-and-dimes, and every third one of these had been covered over with pine planks in a herringbone pattern, transforming them to health spas or head shops. The Campus Arts was thus facaded, with three chrome-framed posters of the current and coming attractions. It was not the first time Gunilla had noticed the peculiar U.S. attitude toward the word "arts," which seemed to mean foreign and/ or pornographic. She supposed this equation was not particularly obscure. Two of the promised offerings were X-rated, one of them called *Pom-pom Sex Kittens* and another *Eager Beaver*. *The Big Heist* was billed once more as "wacky" and "farce" and also "sensational" (it was none of these) and rated R. Gunilla paid for her ticket and went in.

Inside nothing had been done to camouflage the tacky age of the place, threadbare carpet and grungy drops of yellowing crepe curtain, and it was all but empty. However The Campus Arts survived, it was not with wacky French farce. While she sat waiting, a few earnest-looking student couples came in (the foreign film buffs, she recognized) and a few single men here on the wrong night. The light dimmed and the titles rolled over a lingering closeup of the window contents of a *bijouterie* that Gunilla recognized, with a sudden lurch of nostalgia, as belonging to the beachfront at Cannes. She had been so anxious in those days, so awed by authority, so willing to take any direction she was given. And for what? So that she might achieve exactly what she had achieved by the ripe old age of twenty-eight; so that she might sit in a fourth-rate movie house in a third-rate town to suffer a surge of nostalgia for Guy Fatras and (of all places) the beachfront at Cannes.

The Big Heist was one of those 'sixties comedies based on a French guess at American taste, compounded in equal parts of sex, greed and whimsy. It concerned (of course) the perfect crime executed with perfect ineptitude by a comically tall skinny thief and a comically short fat thief, one moron sidekick and the dumb bombshell girl friend of the sidekick. Gunilla was the bombshell. She had only scattered lines for most of the film, and two decent-sized scenes in one of which she did some *double-entendre* sight gags with the sticks of dynamite, and in the other of which she was supposed to seduce the night watchman while the heist was going on (only he, whimsically, turned out to be queer). When Gunilla appeared on the screen for the first time—in a dippy cootie-catcher hairdo and a sweater they'd had to buy in child size to get it tight enough—she could see herself self-consciously keeping her left profile toward the camera, and she remembered, with a tug of self-pity, that she'd had a pimple on her right jaw. At nineteen, in her first French film, it had seemed some trick of malevolent gods that she, her porcelain Scandinavian skin, should have erupted just in time for the introductory take.

She also remembered that there had been a scene a few minutes and two or three days of shooting on, where she'd been chewing gum in a full-screen closeup with her right side to the camera. She had pleaded with Guy in the rushes (even then, knowing enough not to cry, to mute her real anguish and manipulate him with a waif-eyed deference) to stop the film. He had done so, and Gunilla had gone to the screen and stood against an image of herself in which her whole height barely reached to the middle of her ear. Each of her teeth was as big as her head, and her minute pores made shadows the size of a sink drain. She had placed her splayed hand over the pimple so it appeared on her knuckles, and turned to Guy. He cut the take. But she had been more effective than she intended, with herself; and even now a closeup discomfited her. She always watched films from the last two or three rows of the house.

Now her self on the screen began with the dynamite, drew it caressingly along her neck and scratched at her ribs with it, lifting a sweatered globe of breast. Her pout was as vacuous as a pretty fish. Jean-Pierre Guery leaned down at her with a pout of his own, trying to persuade her to take part in the heist, while little Louis Claude gaped at her tits and clutched his heart. Fairly standard stuff, Gunilla thought.

She became aware of the man a few seconds before she heard him. He was behind her in the last row, two seats toward the aisle, so that in the first startled shift of her head she saw—only—his bulk and the hunch of his shoulders, the screen light reflected on the rocking forehead. She snapped eyes-front, pointlessly making the frozen face with which she always discouraged importunate admirers. The breathing was not "heavy"; on the contrary, it was as shallow and quick as the breath of a woman giving birth à la Lamaze. Gunilla's heart pounded. But the man was unaware of her; he was watching *her*, the teenage bimbo who now (Fatras knew what he was doing; Gunilla had known well enough what she was doing) tapped the stick of dynamite on the inside of her bare ankle, rubbed it against her calf, lifting the serge schoolgirl skirt a centimeter higher with each stroke till it cleared her knees to a shadow of inner thigh. Her petulant mouth said, *"M' je n'veux pas, mon chou."*

The titles recorded, "But I don't wanna, honey," and while some part of her mind registered that this translation was a cultural as well as a culinary oddity, she became aware again of the dirty damp-trapping walls, and smelled, or imagined she smelled, something sickly that might as well be a compound of cabbage and honey. Behind her the breathing turned ragged and guttural. In front of her a giant closeup caught her face in a left three-quarter pout. *"Pourquoi moi?"*

Why me?

Quick vignettes of revenge flicked through her mind. She would stand and accuse him, expose him to the scatter of audience, she would call the manager to throw him out. Oh yes? Meanwhile her enormous double on the screen would purse its vacant mouth on the end of the dynamite while she squirmed straddling a packing crate and caressed a detonator with her bare foot.

She wanted to leave but could not, feared her own breathing was audible, sat rigid with her hands clenched on the arm of her seat. In that one glance she had seen enough to know that the man was large, even huge, but it was not him she now feared but that she would be recognized. He was nothing like

so huge as the self that faced her, shielding its right profile so
as not to expose a hand-sized blemish, sucking on the dynamite
like a candy stick. Her agent was always talking about "exposure" as if it were a thing to be ardently desired. Was the
man exposing himself? What could it possibly mean, to expose
him? The camera did a slow dolly to her open mouth till it
filled almost the whole of the screen, the tip of her tongue
poised on the end of the stick for a second before the mouth
said, *"Eh bien, pourquoi pas?"*

The title grazed her underlip, "Oh well, why not?" The man
issued a sticky grunt and, now, sighed heavily. Gunilla gagged.
Then as the man shifted in his seat and she felt, not saw, because
she couldn't turn again, that he leaned toward her—oh, probably he was reaching for a handkerchief or a cigarette—she bolted,
clambering ignominiously to the aisle and out through the lobby
to the oily-smelling brightness of the street.

She stood a moment under the marquee, trying to breathe,
alert to passersby. Then she shook herself, gathered her wits
and, her bag dangling from her elbow, her arms absurdly crossed
over her cleavage and her hands tucked into her damp armpits,
she crossed the street and headed back to the Sheraton. From
the direction of the demonstration she vaguely thought she
heard a chant of "Spelunking, Spelunking," and had a vision
of diving into an underwater cave.

Now she untangled herself from the sheet and pulled aside
the heavy window drape. The air was still wet, and painfully
bright; she let it fall again. She took a third shower and rubbed
at her skin till it was red.

Gunilla was a born victim; she knew things she couldn't feel.
Her mental capacity was beyond her knack for behavior or
emotion. She belonged to a number of organizations in defense
of women, and her name had figured prominently on petitions
to do with abortions and battered wives. But her own fetal
error she had brought to term and put up for adoption. On
her own account she couldn't act except by the exercise of self-
control and by "acting," which was why she slipped so enthusiastically into personalities for whose guilts and failures she
would not have to pay. The girl bimbo, for one. She supposed
that if she had been raped it was not last night but nine years
ago in Cannes, by Guy Fatras not in bed but behind the cam-

era. What happened last night would clearly come under the legal term of "provocation."

She huddled under the shower letting the water drag her heavy hair down to her breasts; then, half watching herself, stood more erect, lifting her chin to the spray and conscious of her backbone.

That week she would hold forth several times on capital punishment and women's rights. She would mention several times that she had heard the demonstration and thought the students were chanting "Spelunking." The rest of the cast would find her, on the whole, rather a prima donna.

9. Double Take

"The Mongolians thought the world sat on a hog's back," Kevin said. "And when there was an earthquake it was because the hog shifted in its sleep."

"Huh!" laughed Boyd. "Is that so?"

"Yes, but there're a whole lot of myths that exist *to the present day*. F'rinstance, there's no such thing as a fault line."

"There isn't?" Boyd was politely amazed. Kevin sat lotus-legged on a footstool, Boyd deep in the sofa. Shaara hovered, unwilling to settle on her own chairs. She was aware of the magpie nature of her rec room, that artful clutter that Boyd always found so trying—cattails, old brass, wind chimes, curious stones and shells.

"Well, there is, but it's an effect, not a cause. It's a crack made by a former earthquake but it doesn't mean the ground is weak there or anything. The causes are way underneath the surface. The earth is like a pot of boiling stew, the heat's on the bottom where the stove is and the bubbles come up to the top."

"Huh," said Boyd. "Was that for science or social studies?"

"Science," Kevin smiled slyly. "But you just gave me an idea."

Boyd's pipe was upended in her bronze ashtray, shedding that now-foreign granular ash that was, however, familiar. The vanilla smell, the zippered pigskin pouch in which, she still knew, were a few apple peels. She mumbled an excuse, closed herself in the kitchen, and made hogback sandwiches with mayonnaise and mustard cress. She would have screamed if she could think what she would get by it.

So that was it, then. Their "reunion" consisted of a few rushed and hushed sentences at the theater and a few—it was going to become a pattern if she didn't do something about it—drinks and lunches in her house, where she felt invaded and displaced. Boyd came in a cab, which he resented, and she took him back, which she resented. She played spectator to conversations in which Boyd talked about what was going on in New York drama while Kevin said huh-no-kidding-great, and then Kevin talked about the Dungeons and Dragons Game Club while Boyd said huh-is-that-so-great. When they were both exhausted, Kevin identified a necessity in his room and Boyd turned to enlist her in the adult conversations that he found more comfortable and she, intolerable. Shaara had suggested she would take Kevin to the motel instead, but Boyd said it was so sterile and unnatural; after the pool there was nothing but TV. This bland assumption of his rights so choked her with anger that she hadn't dared to insist.

She hacked at the ham bone, tore the cress. Through their salt-and-pepper smells there was still vanilla. The smell of vanilla hurt. She did not want his ashes smudging up her bronze and yet she longed for a time when that smell simply, neutrally, identified Boyd; his presence, the presence of an illusion of permanence still intact.

She, in middle school science, would never have chosen earthquakes. She always did metabolism, dietetics, photosynthesis, things close to home. The body, she remembered, takes in protein and converts it to fat for storage; then it has to convert it back to use it for heat and energy. She trimmed the ham. Love is like that. It takes in anger and converts it to pain for storage. If it's ever to be made use of it has to be converted back.

"Kevin!" she called. "Come and make some ice tea."

He bounced through the door in a mixture of good behavior and relief. If he'd been pitting a Troglodyte against a Hobbit in the Sorcerer's dungeon, she'd have had to call six times.

"Shall I put the sugar in, or separate?"

She faced him, lowered her voice. "I'll make the tea. Kevin, you have got to tell him about Henry."

"He hasn't asked about him."

"If you don't tell him, I will, but it will be better if you tell him."

He shouldered his T-shirt and scowled at her. "He's forgotten about him. What's the point?"

"Kevin, he's forgotten but you haven't. Your Dad doesn't know you're avoiding something, and he wouldn't mind if he did. But you know, and you mind. Am I right?"

This may have been more obscure to him than Mongolian myth. He popped the refrigerator door a few times while she gathered things onto the tray. One sneaker toe trampled another. The water boiled. *It's all so painful! I can understand why it feels too unbearably awkward in a motel room, but why does that mean I've got to make the sandwiches?*

"And there's another thing," she said, with probable foolishness. "You mind that he's forgotten. Don't you?" She did not allow herself to say anything against Boyd. *It was some ways toward wicked to invite Kevin to.*

"Aw, Dad's got a lot on his mind. It's four years since he sent me Henry, after all . . ."

"Well."

"Well."

"It's up to you. I mean it: it *is* up to you."

"Okay."

Which was not entirely conclusive, and they sat over the sandwiches while Boyd, apparently released by lunch, talked entirely to her, about the conflict he could see developing between Wyman and Gunilla.

"She's so steeped in Method she asked him if he'd written his biography yet. Wyman's worked with plenty of Studio people to know exactly what she meant, but he told her he was waiting for an offer from Doubleday. God."

"Huh," said Shaara.

Boyd said, "Gunilla has less sense of humor than Malcolm X. Luckily, you don't need one to play an aristocrat or a corpse." Kevin slid from his stool to squat cowboy-style and took a mouthful of his sandwich. "Have you ever noticed how it seems to be a condition of revolution, having no sense of humor? Bolsheviks, Black Power, Libbers. I'll bet Napoleon never slit a smile." Shaara chewed determinedly. "But I wouldn't have thought the law would extend to the Stanislavski revolution. I mean, the Method turns out comedians, after all, apart from the fact that it's been the 'new regime' for half a century now."

"Say, Dad," said Kevin, and set his sandwich on the chair.

"And yet of course I'm wronging Gunilla, because you put her in a comic part and all of a sudden she brings it up from wherever it's buried, the phrasing, the timing. Have you ever seen her do a double take? Beautiful . . ."

"Is that so," said Shaara. Boyd knocked his pipe out again, and again she became aware that her environment was composed of things she shared with Boyd and things she had not. They had had a strange, inverse divorce quarrel about the division of the goods. Shaara had wanted to take nothing with her, and Boyd had never wanted any of it in the first place. Now she could have named with exact accuracy which of the cushions, throws, books, knick-knacks, had been looted from East Millstone, and which were acquisitions of herself as ex. What was obscure to her was whether Boyd had any sense of the same. Did he know he was knocking his ashes into an anniversary present from himself? Bronze: eighth.

Kevin swallowed. "By the way, Dad, y'know, Henry got run over."

"What—who?"

"Henry. The dog."

"The dog I sent you."

"Yeah."

"Oh, that's too bad. I'm sorry. Do you want another dog?"

Kevin lit up, "Could I?" And the matter bid fair to reach a sudden and satisfactory conclusion.

"I'll have something to say about that!" Shaara said, so loudly that they both started toward her. Her bracelet whacked against her tea glass and she grasped at it, caught it neatly around its sweat.

"I buried him," she announced. "Early in the morning. I dug the grave myself." They stared at her. "I had to hack the roots with an axe!" she claimed, bewildering all of them.

"I did," she emended, faltering, "a pretty good job of it."

She dropped Boyd at the theater and drove down Magnolia to where she could park in the shade. Then she followed the serpentine flagstones back, past Philosophy and Religion, skirting mossy oaks, making detours for the magnolias. The paths were from an era when students strolled. Now they were crosscut by straight lines of trampled lawn and broken azaleas. But the monkey grass was spikey with new growth, and the wisteria hung lush at every turn. Out of the day's debris something in herself stirred and sprouted, an acute and jealous pleasure at the dailiness of things, this familiar escape to her spools and braids, the one machine she really could command, the one place where she made no mistake she could not put right.

An old line of poetry rose with her spirits, "Magnificently unprepared/For the long littleness of life." The rest of the poem was awful, something about a "young Apollo dreaming on the edge of strife," but this line, which she had wept over copiously as a girl, now enriched her by its contradiction, because really life is neither long nor little, and there *is* something magnificent about how unprepared we are. Unprepared even to be caught by a lift of spirits in the tangle of old angers. She passed under a rose-encumbered arch and circled down the hill to let herself in the back door of the shop.

In a riot of Freddy Fender, Eugene Keyes was melting blocks of polystyrene with an acetylene torch. He was protected by a welder's mask but absurdly shirtless, aiming the hissing flame around the edges of a massive block so that the stuff recoiled, shriveled and transformed itself into rough rock. She leaned in the doorframe and watched him work, skinny and muscular, pleasantly absorbed. He swung the deformed mass—now it was a boulder, and once it was sprayed it would be solid granite—on top of a pile of them to his left, and took another of pristine plastic from the right. He surveyed it for a minute, stretching his plaited fingers in front of him, designing a stone. Then he took up the torch and aimed it off-center, pocked the side with a series of short blasts, swung the flame around the corners that retreated, coagulating; chipped the edges with the swiping fire.

This is what we do, Shaara thought. Somebody else takes petroleum out of rock and transforms it into plastic and taffeta. We take those and restore them to an illusion of the real. It's worth doing, probably.

It was at any rate rather wonderful to watch, the skin so taut over his bent back that every shift of the torch was reflected in a rolling shift of sinew on the wing blade. Gene set the torch aside, hoisted the block and turned. When he saw her he clowned with it, over his head Atlas-style, staggering. He was no actor, Gene. Graceful alone and at work, he became instantly awkward in company, even a company of one. Which was no doubt why he usually sat so still.

She laughed for him, though, and even so he came toward her taking off the mask saying, "You're looking thoughtful."

"Am I? I was thinking what an expenditure of energy it is, how many emotions an ordinary person goes through in the course of an ordinary day."

He nodded and waited, as if waiting for her to specify. When she didn't he said, "Coffee?"

"No thanks, I'm full of tea. I had an idea, though. Are you still game for that iguana cage?"

"Shore."

"I was thinking that if we brought the wood here to make it, you could just keep an eye on it when you have time. That way Kevin won't be hanging around the house all summer, and he and his Dad would be sort of working in the same place." She did not say: And you wouldn't be coming to the house on weekends. "I think it might be easier on them. And me."

"As long as it's not too big to get in the door."

"God, yes. I'll tell him that. And I'll make sure he understands the set is your first priority."

"He won't bother me."

"Then Boyd and Kevin can have lunch together and sort of be on neutral ground. I've got to move it out of the house somehow."

"D'you want to talk about it?" He had gone into that stillness again, in which there was no curiosity, but there was the more dangerous thing, the tear-triggering sympathy.

"No, I really don't," she said. "Thanks. What I want is not to think about it. I'd like him to go away. I'd like him just not to have come, but he has, so I want his goddam tobacco pouch off my table and I want to go set the sleeves in Gunilla's mockup and think about it as little as possible."

Which was, of course, talking about it. She sat in the costume room with the muslin pattern in her lap, gathering the puff over the slender undersleeve, so positioned that one of the mirrors in the shop across the hall showed Gene turning polystyrene into a granite wall. This meant that if he looked up he could catch her at it. But he did not.

10.   *The Method*

———————————❖———————————

"On this line, I want you to move from left to right," Boyd said.

Gunilla had made herself aggressively ugly for the duration. It was, in a way, quite dazzling that she could do so. Those points of bone—cheek, chin, jaw, tilted nose—that caught the light like diamond facets; they had become warts, witch's hooks.

No. A more mundane viciousness. She was a fantasy librarian. She wore her hair peeled back like a zucchini. The granny glasses pinched her nose. She pinched her nose, as a signal of dissatisfaction. She pulled her earlobe in deliberate awkwardness. Touted for her grace, she stood all angles on the stage. She wore Oxford cloth shirts whose shoulders hung off her shoulders and whose tails hung out. She wore clogs that made her clog.

"I don't see my intention for the move," she said.

Boyd said blandly, "Take it back from: *You mustn't expect her to answer.*"

Cumbrously Wyman heaved himself from the little table and returned stage left to where Barnard kneeled over a guitar. Every heavy step protested. Wyman had been trained, as Boyd had, to set all the movements first and only then begin to explore the meanings and intentions. Gunilla brought her Actors Studio training with her like a flag. She expected to improvise, experiment, and "let the movements grow out of the motives." Consequently, they were a week into rehearsals and Act One was not yet blocked. Wyman, theoretically on Boyd's side, had told Boyd that she needed her ass kicked, with the distinct implication that it was up to Boyd to do the kicking.

"You mustn't expect her," Boyd prompted. Orme quietly took his place against the pillar in the shadows and Barnard gave a few cacophonous strums on the guitar, smiling seraphically up at Wyman.

MOTHER SUPERIOR

You mustn't expect her to answer when you speak to her. Our poor little sister lost her voice in an unfortunate accident.

SENORA

Oh, the poor little thing! How could such an awful thing happen to such a dear sweet soul?

SISTER ANGELA

They cut it off with a knife, right down to the root.

MOTHER SUPERIOR

Sister Angela, spare us the details, or the Senora's going to go into another faint.

SENORA

Cut it off? How could that happen?

MOTHER SUPERIOR

Oh, it's a sad story, but quite a common one in the dreadful times we live in. An evil star is guiding man's destiny just now. Passions run high. Queer things happen. Old scores are settled. Sister Ines's family were very distinguished. They belonged to . . . the aristocracy.

SENORA

The poor angel. And to think that, seeing her, you would think she knows nothing of the wickedness of the world.

MOTHER SUPERIOR

When the soul is pure . . .

* * *

SISTER ANGELA
Besides, they bashed her about so much she's a half-wit.

Boyd stopped them. "Now," he said, "Gunilla, on *the poor angel*, cross right three paces away from Wyman."

"I still can't see that," Gunilla said.

"No," Boyd replied, "but do it. And we will be able to see you do it."

She rooted herself to the spot, pinched the bridge of her glasses, arched her pencil above the script. One point of this hostile stance, Boyd saw, was that they would all forget how beautiful she was, and when she appeared in costume they would be unprepared for it, thrown by it. It was a subtle and calculated upstaging, an impressive theatrical effect, but aimed at the other actors and no use to the production.

She offered him now, mute and rooted, a dilemma. He could assert his authority, and she would move to the right, which would satisfy both Wyman and the blocking schedule, but she would cross, and continue to cross, so grudgingly and unconvincingly that three weeks hence he would have to cut the move. Or he could "give in" and find a motive for her, in which case he would win his point but lose face with Wyman. Wyman stood rigid with incipient eruption.

"And Orme!" Boyd called. He sprinted onto the stage area, into the shadows where the backstage wall was beginning to take form and the one heavy pillar had already been erected. "I want to try something." His back to Wyman and Gunilla, he put a hand on Orme's shoulder and the other on the pillar. He lowered his voice so the others would have to strain. "In the second act you're going to lash Gunilla's corpse to this post, so let's establish it as your territory right from the beginning. Play with it when you're playing with her. Caress it. You might even swing on it like a bored schoolboy. Think that'll work?"

"It might," said Orme. "I'll give it a try." He would give anything a try, and most of his attempts would fruit. He knitted his brows as he stroked the pillar, thinking about it, and his face was so misconstructed that he might have been thinking about boiling children.

"It may feel awkward for a time," Boyd said. "But keep on doing it and let's see if it grows into something. For instance,

that line, *They cut it off with a knife, right down to the root.*
I don't mean you should cut at the pillar or anything grossly
visual, but . . . suppose you were leaning into the pillar, your
hands around it down here at groin height, and when you
finish *to the root,* just let your tongue hang out and touch the
pillar."

"Yu-uck!" Barnard yelled and swiped a discord on the
guitar.

"Let's . . . Gunilla," Boyd half-turned to her and beckoned
perfunctorily. "Come over here and let's try an improv for
Orme for a second. Just set the script down." He took it from
her and tossed it on the table, positioned her lightly and carelessly against the post. "You don't need to do anything but
play dead like the second act. Now, Orme, at this point you
don't know that this corpse is ever going to be in this position.
But for the moment just imagine that, in your mind's eye, it
is always here. The post *is* the Senora's body. Wyman, what's
your line to the Senora?"

"*Oh, it's a sad story,*" Wyman intoned. "*But quite a common
one in the dreadful times we live in.*"

"That's it: dreadful times." Now Boyd stepped back to take
them all into his focus, though he addressed himself to Orme.
He took out his pipe and gave the bridge of his glasses a
thoughtful rub.

"There's never been a time that couldn't be called dreadful,
of course. What's happening here is that the dreadful times
are closing in, in a way that nobody's quite aware of. The same
thing happens to children. For most of us growing up, dreadful
times are simply elsewhere. They belong to foreigners, or to
aliens of some sort with alien names: mugger, murderer, rapist,
alcoholic. And the process of growing up, or losing our innocence, is this . . . piecemeal recognition, that we live among
those things and they live in us. The boy next door is the
Boston Strangler, Ted Bundy lives upstairs. Even the first time
your dog got run over, you inched a little nearer to death.
Orme, take the rubber band out of the Senora's hair and run
your fingers through it. The first time, as a boy, you tortured
an animal, it came a little closer home to you what murder
was."

"A cricket," said Orme, fingering Gunilla's hair.

"Yes. You pulled its legs off?"

"First the wings, and then the legs." He pulled out the rubber band and dropped a lock over her eye.

"All right. Now, the Mother Superior is moving in, threatening the Senora. But you, Orme, are feeling that threat because it's inside you: you know that you're the one who is really going to strangle her, and the more the Mother Superior moves in, the more you get to feeling your fingers around the Senora's throat. The Senora is that cricket, and you're going to dismember it. Give us your lines, Wyman."

Wyman said, cold and slow, "*An evil star is guiding man's destiny just now.*" Orme followed the lock of hair down Gunilla's face with the palm of his hand. He rested it heavily on her collarbone.

"*Passions run high.*"

"Passions run high," Boyd repeated, and Orme lolled his face into Gunilla's, slack jaw against her eye. He flexed his fingers on her throat. He panted once and ran his hand the length of her limp arm.

"*Queer things happen . . .*" Wyman said, advancing, his voice rising not in volume but in reverberation.

Orme locked his hands around the post, around Gunilla's hips, and snaked against her with a low guttural sound.

"*Old scores are settled.*"

Gunilla shuddered. She broke her possum act and caught for breath.

"Right," Boyd said briskly, went back to his seat and picked up the script. "Thanks, Gunilla. The point is, Orme, not that you're going to command any attention in this scene except at your lines. But if you make murderous love to that post in your mind, some of it will stick in the audience's mind next act.

"You see," he took the whole stage in again with a gesture as they wandered back to position, "what we're trying to do here—always, onstage—is the most difficult thing in the world, to make intention concrete. It's more difficult than anatomy, for instance, because there, when you pin out the sinews and splay the nerves, you're already working with a corpse. We want to expose the nerves and keep the creature live. And here, what you mean is not in the lines; the lines are lies. What's really going on is all body language. Can we take the scene from *They cut it off with a knife?*"

Wyman stood over Barnard, his hands folded, with a saintly

smirk. Gunilla skinned her hair back into the rubber band.
Orme pondered at the pillar.

SISTER ANGELA

They cut it off with a knife, right down to the root.

MOTHER SUPERIOR

Sister Angela, spare us the details, or the Senora's going
to go into another faint.

SENORA

Cut it off? How could that happen?

MOTHER SUPERIOR

Oh, it's a sad story, but quite a common one in the
dreadful times we live in. An evil star is guiding man's
destiny just now. Passions run high. Old scores are settled. Sister Ines's family were very distinguished. They
belonged to . . . the aristocracy.

SENORA

The poor angel . . .

Wyman leaned a fraction of an inch toward Gunilla. Orme
pressed his groin into the post in a movement so obscenely
malicious that Boyd would have to forbid it a few rehearsals
hence. But Gunilla moved three paces to the right.

11. *Body Language*

———————◆———————

The rehearsal ran late, so that by the time Gunilla arrived for her fitting Gene was gone and Shaara had already called Kevin to put the chicken in the oven. She'd had time to stitch together the whole mock-up, a complete model of Gunilla's gown in unbleached muslin.

Gunilla came in haggard, spilling apologies, pulling the rubber band from her hair. She flung the hair forward, brushing it vigorously over her face with a brush made of some expensive amber laminate, clock parts trapped inside the handle.

Gunilla interested Shaara. She threw up a smokescreen of attitudes, imperious one day, fawn-shy the next, now sternly intellectual, now dumb-blonde and anxious. Under these postures the person was obscured, more unknowable than Gene Keyes in his silence or Wendy Soole in New York. Unknowable except for one clue which, in the company, only Shaara would have, and which she would protect. She went to the door and locked it loudly.

Gunilla Lind was ashamed of her body.

It was usual among actors, and had been usual long before the public saw a nude, to dress and undress, take fittings in front of each other, in the professional agreement that they paid no attention to bodies. In fact a few were voyeurs and more enjoyed the exposure; almost all conspired in the pose of nonchalance. So Shaara had been surprised at the measuring when Gunilla, who had done at least two nude scenes on film, neglected to undress until the other actors left. Then she removed her long blouse skittishly, hunching her shoulders forward as if to shadow her breasts, slipped out of the slacks concealing her thighs in stiff forearms. She had thick thighs. Her body was basically so fine, her movements so fluid, that Shaara fairly stared at the hump below the pelvic bone, the thick muscular spread almost to the knee. Then she remembered that the two love scenes had been sheet-draped at hip height, and it was Gunilla's small full breasts that took the camera's eye. She remembered that Gunilla, on screen or off, always wore voluminous skirts, belted shirts, long-peplumed suits or high-waisted flaring gowns. It was sheer luck that Shaara had chosen an Empire line for her costume, which would show a lot of shoulder and cleavage, bind her narrow rib cage and flow from there. Sheer luck because nobody seemed to know what a Spanish aristocrat would have worn in Haiti in 1804, and Shaara had more or less arbitrarily decided that the Senora would get her gowns from Paris a few years out of date.

Now it appeared that it might be more difficult than that. Gunilla was picking at the puffs, pulling at the rib-cage binding of the muslin even before Shaara had the back seam pinned. She bounced her bosom in the palms of her hands, frowning skeptically.

"Wait," said Shaara. "That won't fit until I bind you up."

"Do I have no bra?" Gunilla twisted toward the mirror, wrenching the pin from Shaara's hand.

"Uh-mmm." She took the others from her mouth. "The bra hadn't been invented. But wait till you see this trick." She reached around Gunilla's rib cage under the cloth and found the ends of the elastic she'd sewn into the binding at center front. Stretching each end just under the aureole, she pulled them up to the back neckline and secured them. Gunilla's breasts, pushed up and together by the elastic, plumped forward out of the low scooped neck, producing a cleavage that reached almost to her collarbone.

"There," said Shaara, admiring.

"But it's cut so *low*."

"Very sexy." Shaara grinned and nodded, knowing she wouldn't get away with it. She busied herself at the armhole. "I think we want to cut this half an inch higher so we're sure you can move your arm freely."

"Is there going to be something to fill in, here?" Gunilla's hand did the wafting number, her mouth the fluttering pout. "Some froufrou, a little lace?"

"Out of period," Shaara admonished. "But of course without a facing the mock-up feels less secure than it is. It'll be piped."

"I'll fall *out* of it." Her face was a mask of distress. "There could be just a little lace . . ."

"Honestly, it'll be fine. Take a long view in the mirror. You have very beautiful breasts, you know, and there's no reason not to show them off."

Gunilla fretted and looked, not into the mirror but down at her ballooning cleavage. "See," she whispered, "the stretch marks. People will know I had a baby."

Shaara, her twenty-twenty vision and true eye, peered where Gunilla's hand trembled and could just make out a few lines of translucence on the skin. A camera might have magnified them into general view (somebody had talked her in front of those cameras, though); on stage, under dark pancake, they would be as invisible as a hemstitch. Shaara, who had known what it is to suffer from breasts, found herself a little impatient at this performance. If Gunilla had wanted to hide her thighs, Shaara would have concurred and conspired.

"You know," she said tactfully, "I think you're overtired and a little upset."

"Rehearsal was terrible . . . terrible!" Gunilla agreed, and threw a hand over her eyes. "Boyd . . ." She stopped, denied herself with a flap of the hand.

"Boyd drives people very hard," Shaara said.

"Yes." Gunilla studied herself in the mirror, pressed at her cleavage while Shaara adjusted the binding. "You have been married to him," she observed.

"Elefen yers," Shaara mumbled through a mouthful of pins, and ripped open a faulty dart.

"Will you think I am prying if I ask you something? Is he . . . sadistic?"

Shaara looked up in surprise. Gunilla's eyes were averted to her sleeve and she seemed to have dropped the melodrama. She was rather pale. "Sadistic" was a long ways off the mark, but for a moment she was tempted to make a friend of Gunilla.

"What did he do to you?"

"Oh, he did nothing. It's just a feeling I have . . . I am beginning to realize how difficult it is going to be to play the corpse. If something goes wrong I can't *do* anything about it. Usually, you step in and ad lib, or cover somehow. But here, if anybody should forget his entrance, or knock over the furniture, well, I'm dead, so *anything* I did would be wrong. The only way I can defend myself—the only way I can be professional, you see—is to be completely inert." She slumped minutely, an instinctive demonstration. The impulse in Shaara was very strong, to make this the starting point of a confidence: *the only way I can defend myself is to be inert.*

But it wouldn't do. It wasn't *professional, you see.* If she allowed an alliance with Gunilla against Boyd, there was no telling what chain reaction might draw her back into the volatile intimacy of cast and director.

"Well, Boyd certainly isn't sadistic, at any rate." She pinned the dart back in place. "I think"—the cliché, which she believed, came out without conviction—"that he's really rather vulnerable." She bent to mark the hem.

"No doubt he is." Gunilla also withdrew. Regretful, Shaara stepped back to survey her work. "Look. Miss Lind, why don't I cut the silk an inch higher at the neckline? I can always cut it down again if you feel comfortable with it." She had no intention of doing this, it would spoil the line. But she wanted to offer something, a wedge in the minute fissure of sympathy between them.

"You're a darling," Gunilla gushed.

Her watch said the chicken would be dry, but the gas gauge said the tank already was, so she pulled into the Exxon. William "Bud" Rufus was busy at the self-service island with a customer wearing a Stetson, the two of them peering and poking into a wicker crab trap like a laundry basket. She took out her wallet and turned on the radio, trying to be patient.

It occurred to her she was short of somebody to talk to. That's why she regretted Gunilla's overture. Her only two female friends on the faculty had taken off as soon as term ended, and everybody else was too far away. She still enjoyed long sloppy chats with her mother in Iowa and her brothers in Phoenix and Sausalito, but wouldn't burden *them* bitching about Boyd after all this time. Same thing with Cass Carson, for whom it might be awkward now that she and Wendy were friends. Shaara slipped the credit card out of her wallet and confronted Wendy's bright face. That was it, of course: that senseless sense that she and Wendy could sit down over a drink, in front of a fire, and understand each other without rancor.

She slid the wallet to the far seat and got out to fill the tank herself. As soon as she did so, William "Bud" came loping, ready with the weather.

"Sticky one, ain't it?"

"We're due for rain, I guess."

He took off the gas tank cap with a single twist. "You're doin' it backwards, Miz Soole, filling yourself over here. If you go t'the self serve, I'll fix you up anyways."

"You'll never get rich that way, Bud."

He laughed. "Oh, I give up gettin' rich a while ago. Say, that fellow there on the way down t'the Gulf says there's a tornado watch out from Carrabelle to Pensacola. Not but what we'll just git the tail of it."

He was right. Preoccupied, she hadn't noticed how gray the early dark was, or the branches whipping. Winter was so mild here that there was no real season for dead leaves. They showered at intervals all year long, whenever the wind got high enough to spank them. They were hitting the windshield on the way home, interspersed with a few raindrops heavy as splattering bugs. They flurried in the drive as she swung into the carport, narrowly missing Gene Keyes' pickup, which was pulled up against the fence. What now?

She clucked, "Tch," for her own benefit and checked the mirror to make sure her headband was on straight. She looped her canvas bag over her arm and went in the kitchen door, calling, "Hi, love. I finally made it."

They were in the rec room, blond hair bent to black, Andy Griffith on the set and the iguana cage plans spread out on the coffee table. Gene's baseball cap occupied the exact spot vacated by Boyd's tobacco pouch.

"Hey, Gene. What's up?" She dumped her bag beside the TV set and slipped out of her shoes. Kevin bounced toward her with a sheet of architectural tracing paper crackling between his hands—Gene must have brought it from the theater.

"Look what we worked out."

"Did you turn the chicken off?"

"Gene did. Look." The cage, designed of slats crossing at the corners like a log cabin, except that they had spaces between, had been redrawn in Gene's clean draftsman's hand.

He must have been here for a couple of hours, straight from the shop. "We're going to drill the corners and put rods through with wing nuts. That way the whole thing'll collapse to get it through the door, and then when it's set up you just tighten the wing nut. Isn't that neat?"

"It's neat."

"And you c'n always collapse it for storage, or when we move, just with these four nuts."

She laughed. "What makes you think we're going to move?"

"But if we did."

Gene apologized from the couch, "It's gonna run a hundred dollars for the wood, though."

"It'll be *indestructible*," Kevin urged with the earnest inflection of a commercial.

"Hang on, just let me catch my breath. Gene, will you have a beer?"

She took the ashtray to the kitchen to scour it of pipe leavings. Kevin fell over his feet in pursuit of her while she washed her hands and twisted a pair of cans off the six-pack.

"Gene had an idea about the money, Mom. He said there's some places he needs help on the set, and if Dad would okay it, I could be his assistant and they'd pay me, and that way part of the time I'd be working on the cage and part of the time I'd be earning it. Gene would teach me to use the jigsaw, and I already know . . ."

"Hold on, hold on." She took the beer back, turned the sound down on Barney Fife's whine, and collapsed into the chair beside the couch.

"We put the screens up," Kevin said, as if this were another argument. She glanced over and saw that they had, indeed, bolted all the screens into position against what looked, now, though, more like shutter weather. The rain had begun to batter.

"That was nice of you," she said to Gene. It was nice; it also made her wary. He was very obviously damn at ease, his sneakers on the rung of the coffee table and her needlepoint cushion in the crook of his arm. He propped the beer on his T-shirt and rested the brim against his chin.

"But hold on. It's a very good idea, but it might not be that simple. I don't know that the university's *allowed* to hire a thirteen-year-old, whatever the director says. And besides that, your dad hasn't been paid yet himself."

"What?" Gene cocked his head at her. "I was."

"So was I. But that's because we're on the regular payroll so we're already in the works. The cast comes out of the Grumbacher grant, and it's hung up in the bursar's office waiting for the academic V.P.'s signature."

"So why doesn't he sign?"

"I asked Joe Dimbleton. He's on a Merit Scholar recruitment tour and won't be back till a week from Tuesday."

"You mean none of 'em have been paid? They must be pissed."

"And it doesn't make them particularly love Magoor, I don't suppose."

"Department of Redundancy Department," Gene observed.

Kevin squatted, elbows on the table and fists at his cheeks. "Does that mean we can't buy the wood?"

"Why should it mean we can't buy the wood?"

"Because we'll have to give Daddy money."

"No," said Shaara grimly, "we won't have to give Daddy money." She felt this demanded a justification, to Kevin though not to Gene. She set the baseball cap to one side and put down her beer. "I'm sure your dad can manage his finances without our help. The point is that even if he could hire you, the play'd be over by the time the papers went through."

"Does that mean we *can* buy the wood?"

Anxious, innocent, he panted up under his tumbling bangs, not even knowing he was manipulating her. Half the time none of us know, thought Shaara. "Yes, we can buy the wood." He whooped and wheeled. Gene grinned at her, and out of nowhere something stabbed her in the chest. She and Boyd had smiled over Kevin that way for eight years. In the first lonely months in Hubbard it had been the thing she missed first and most, someone to share that smile with, over Kevin's head. She rose and checked a window latch against the rain, turning her back on Gene.

She was pretty well stuck with offering him dinner, though, what with the cage and the screens and the rain. "You don't want to go home in this," she said. "Will you have supper with us?"

"Sho-ure. What can I do?"

"An' *I he'ped*!" Kevin, jubilant, turned the TV back up and flipped from "Let's Make a Deal" to Uncle Wally and back again.

Gene had baked potatoes and wrapped the chicken in foil. She mashed sour cream into the potato pulp while he made a salad, wielding the knife against the cucumbers and onions as deftly as he used a coping saw. He sliced a tomato into fancy ridges and held it up for her to admire.

"Hey," she admired, and popped open another pair of beers. Oswald Link, she remembered, had made rosettes out of radishes.

"I'm a homebody at heart."

"Oh yeah?"

"Listen." He glanced round the door frame to make sure Kevin was absorbed. "I'm sorry if I interfered. I didn't know there was a hassle with the money."

"That's okay. It's got nothing to do with it really. It's just, you know, it's not my business whether they get paid or not, but Boyd complains to me and obviously I know Dimbleton and so what do I do? All of a sudden I'm a goddamn *liaison*."

"I just thought it would be good for Kevin, to feel as if he's earning it."

"You're right, it would."

"It's also a fact I could use help on the set. I got plenty of time, but sometimes I need another body at the end of the lumber, or holding one end of the tape."

"I'm sure he'd like to do that anyway."

"What I mean is, if I hire him to work on the set, and he hires me to work on the cage, then he's earning it all the same."

She turned aghast, at his innocence or his guile, she was not sure which. "Gene, that's nuts. The logic of that is, that you'd be personally paying him for doing the theater's work."

"It's a barter."

"In which I win and the theater wins and you get zilch. You reason that way and you're going to end up screwed every time."

He chopped olives a while, crushed garlic expertly with the bowl of a spoon. "I usually get what I want," he observed, thoughtful. "It just usually isn't money."

Jesus, I'll bet you do. She stole a glance at his lean face, the high black of his lashes where he concentrated on the chopping board—and tried to imagine him with a woman. One of those miniskirted waitresses at the Sundown Diner, for instance. She picked up about three beats late that she'd just promised him he'd get screwed.

"Y'know," he continued, thoughtful as if it were part of the same thought, "the way we're brought up . . ." She observed that he leaped a thousand miles in this dependent clause. ". . . There's a lot of emphasis on the idea you can be anything you want to be. I don't think it's ever mentioned that y'might not want to. Doncha get down on yer knees every day, f'rinstance, to thank God you're not Papa Doc Duvalier?"

"Not every day," she demurred.

"Doncha thank God you're not Boyd Soole?"

"Not God, but yes." And conceded that before the summer was out—after the production, after things had settled down to humdrum—she would sleep with Gene, once. Or she would hold off till the dogwood shed, and indulge them both to a wistful scene, acknowledging that it would not do.

Kevin set the table, babbling. They ate with an eye each on the TV set, where "Sanford and Son" quibbled about a truck-load of trash. They moved back to the couch and had coffee over "The Rockford Files." Kevin and Gene competed at anticipating punchlines; Kevin won. The rain slashed and shouted now, and the back grass drowned. Gene helped her wash up, during which she could hardly tell him to go. She made popcorn for "Macmillan and Wife," opened another two beers. Gene yawned, arms over his head, so his belly button lifted out of his Levis, a ring of black hairs leaning after each other around it like a camera shutter, pale skin where the tan ended at the ridge of pelvic bone. Shaara peered into the pop-tab hole of her beer. When Dick Cavett interviewed Katharine Hepburn, Kevin decided to go to bed.

"No school tomorrow," Shaara offered brightly.

"I wanna go in with you to the theater. Will you call Dad and say we'll meet him there?"

He shook hands with Gene, kissed her, and abandoned them to Katharine Hepburn, who said, "Well, I was lucky. I had a fahscinating family. I have a happy naycha."

"Rally I do," said Gene. The rain abated a little and they shared the last of the last six-pack. Coincidentally, another channel offered Hepburn and Cary Grant in a squabblesome domestic comedy. It was after midnight and he made no move to move. Shaara, somewhere between hyped and sleepy, couldn't form the sentence to turn him out. She sat crosslegged on the floor and ate popcorn out of his cap while he commandeered the bowl. She thought this provocative of her, so she hinted, "It's letting up."

He sat while Hepburn and Grant kept falling in and out of slanging matches—and even when the national anthem stirred over the furled banner and stuttered into test pattern. "The beer's gone," she said. "How about one nightcap, I think there's a little Southern Comfort, and then I really . . ." She trailed off and wobbled to her feet, found the bottle and two juice glasses, brought them back. Gene had turned off the set in the meantime and put "Gorilla" on the stereo. She thought this was a little inept as a choice, not exactly what Cary Grant would have unearthed for seduction music, until James Taylor got around to boasting, "Hey, baby, I'm your handy man . . ."

"Lissen, Mr. Keyes," she said then, slurring a little, "I want you to understand one thing. Don't think just because you're quiet anybody ever makes the mistake of mistaking you for *shy*."

He nodded solemnly. What now? She scowled into her glass, which reminded her of the amber laminated handle of Gunilla's hairbrush.

"Boyd did something to Gunilla," Shaara said.

Gene slugged his drink and poured himself another frowningly. He had his shoes off and the couch was tousled from his sprawl. "Whad'ya mean?"

"I don't know. Gunilla is feeling threatened. He did something. I don't know what."

"How do you know?"

"I don't know. I don't know how and I don't know what but I know I know."

"Is that a know-know?"

"No, no," she said. This was supposed to be repartee but nobody was laughing. Gene kicked at the table rung a little, sullenly.

"Lemme tell *you* something. Your trouble is, you're still wrapped up in him. It's all over for him and he can't figger out what you're fussing about. But you don't move yer little finger without taking him into account."

She was suddenly sober, alert as if he'd slapped her. The blood rushed to the roots of her red hair and she swiped her headband off. "What do you fucking know? It isn't *him*." She said this, spat it, with conviction. Or was it defensiveness? If she'd really given up on Boyd, would she still be so angry with him? She wanted Gene to go now, but it was too late. "He blundered into this stupid mess. *I* could've told him he'd have to deal with a motel or else me. It isn't *him* I can't be rid of."

"What is it, then?"

"You wouldn't understand."

"Try me."

"It's Doris Day. It's Gomer Pyle. Go home."

"Shaara." He didn't move. "Try me."

"Oh, it's decency and Mr. Right and happily-ever-after and all the smarm they sold us. It's the, it's the . . . illusion of permanence."

This was her phrase, she had found it, she had studied it as if it were some stark answer to the human condition. She had never used it aloud before, and she minded using it as if she had been cheated. "You can only have it once, like chicken pox."

"Like measles," he offered, as if that amounted to comprehension.

"Like leprosy."

"Leprosy kills you."

"No, you move into a colony. The colony of the Formerly Married."

Baby James diddled over the guitar, "Hey, girls, gather round./Lissen to what I'm put-ting down . . ."

"Harriet," Gene said neutrally, "died."

Both of them attacked the bottle, and Shaara knew they wouldn't give up now until they'd killed it. She didn't care. He could give her his "understanding," which differed by not two black hairs from Oswald Link's seduction line, and he could know it'd get him screwed because he'd found the raw end of the scar that wasn't healed. He would probe it till it split again and made room for his minimal self.

"Divorce is different," she said. "You choose divorce, so you have to choose it over and over again, every day. If you know you can give up and go back, then you have to decide over and over that you won't, won't give up, won't go back, that you choose, that you decide."

"Yeah."

"Over and over. Every day."

"Yeah, that's different. With death you don't decide. What you have to learn is that you got no choice. Over and over, every day."

"With divorce you have to choose."

"And with death you got no choice."

"It's different."

"But it's not a contest, is it—who has it worse?"

"Go home, Gene."

"Okay." He sprawled without his shoes, compliant precept and stubborn example. Do as I say, not as I do. "Did you leave Boyd, or did he leave you?"

"Ask him; he'll tell you I moved out. I filed for the divorce." She rocked over the Southern Comfort, comfortless. "He'll tell you it's *semantics* if *I* tell you his *mind* moved out about three years before. About our eighth anniversary: bronze." She stared at the unpopped kernels in the bottom of Gene's baseball cap. She'd probably ruined it with a film of butter and salt, but Gene by his own admission didn't mind much of anything. He hugged the pillow in his crossed arms and made no move to go. She passed him the bottle, which he refused.

"You think I haven't got over it," she said. "But I have. That's the point: I got over it."

"I don't think so."

"It's like getting over God, I think. What do you do then? What do you put in the void? Black holes. What you believe in, is chaos."

"Out of nothing created he."

"But I was not religious. We never had God, at home. We had us. We had . . . do you know what a family is? I mean a real family? Do you know, if my brother Lou went berserk in San Francisco tomorrow and turned a machine gun on a playground, I would *grieve*. I wouldn't *get over* him, I wouldn't *give up* on him. I don't see him, you understand. I talk to him maybe twice a year and at Christmas I send him a tie he probably hates."

She leaned back against the couch, very tired. Knowing that Gene would come over now and offer her the comfort of his hand against her cheek. Wishing he would go instead, but knowing perfectly well the rules. You do not let a man stay until two A.M., get him drunk and confide in him, and then expect him to go home. The stereo had turned itself off, the popcorn and the Southern Comfort were gone.

He sat for a long time yet, though, then leaned over and slowly put on his shoes.

"You okay?"

"Sure, I'm okay."

He gave her a slow grin, picked up his cap, shook the kernels back into the bowl and let himself out the back door. She sat feeling a little bereft, a little abandoned, a little drunk. But she figured that in the morning she'd be grateful.

And she was, when she woke with a sour mouth and an axe behind the eyes. A hangover was enough to deal with, without a tacky sexual indulgence as well. Even if she might have wanted it to happen, she wouldn't have wanted it to *have* happened.

She waked Kevin and made breakfast with carefully controlled cheer, drove in to the theater and went him on into the scene shop. She closed the door behind her in the costume room and went to take Gunilla's mock-up from the dress form. Tucked into the neckline was a folded sheet of graph paper, covered with Gene's lean and limber hand.

This should be a bird feeder, because I'm better with wood than words. No 2 × 4 ever makes the mistake of mistaking me for shy.

I knew last night I could reach over and touch your face. But from my limited experience, I figure things would muck up from there.

I'm happy the way things are. Please accept my service in the matter of an iguana cage.

Gene

She read this several times, tucked it into the pocket of her skirt and sat down to take the muslin apart. All morning she was grainy-eyed and shaky with too much drink. She propped the door open a crack, though, to hear the radio in the shop, and hummed with it a little, feeling behind the seedy headache a conviction that something rather fine, rather old-fashioned and Iowa, had occurred.

12. *Let's Make a Deal*

———————❦———————

There were final notices from New York Telephone and Con Edison, and a polite reminder from MasterCharge assuring her of the probability that her check had crossed in the mail. Wendy paid the telephone.

She was spending less and less time in the apartment, which nevertheless pleased her by looking (her mother's phrase) "as if a cyclone had hit it." She left the windows open to save on air conditioning, and the city grime settled on the pillows and the floor. One day on television she saw an ad for a "Miracle Eraser" sponge and conceived the notion of sanding the floors herself. She found the same gimmick in a hardware store on upper Broadway and attacked the crumbling varnish, but after an hour she had cleared only a patchy strip about two feet long, so she gave it up. The powdered varnish rose in motes and settled with the dust. It clung to her bare feet and made sticky tracks to the kitchen.

The same day something went wrong with the iron. She had plenty of drip-dry and polyester in the closet, but she willfully dug out an old peasant blouse from high school days and belted its wrinkles into a skirt with miles of braid around the calf. She needed a haircut. Her style (feathered? layered? She couldn't remember which Mr. Lawrence called it) stuck out in funny wisps when it got too long. Mr. Lawrence charged fifty-four dollars for his genius, though, so she bound a scarf over her forehead, rakish at the ear, and thought the whole outfit had a certain style, a gypsy carelessness. It was the sort of thing Shaara Soole might wear.

Relieved of domestic employment, she became a low-budget tourist, did the zoo and the museums and the churches. She liked walking, and when her feet got sore she liked the subway too, the rich mix of sweat and popcorn and lox; and especially the spray-can graffiti, those cheerful threats. She toured the Bowery and the Statue of Liberty, checked books out of the New York Public and read them straddling the railing at Rockefeller Center. Most of them were spy novels and thrillers, but she also liked Kotzwinkle's *The Fan Man* for its celebration of junk, and wondered if you could achieve such gummy layers on the Upper West Side.

A couple of times she had dinner with friends for whom, however, her touristy discoveries were old hat. They were marginal theater and academic people, taking care of her for Boyd, and they talked mainly "endowment dynamics" and "council politics"—by which they meant how to get a grant. She didn't return their invitations because she didn't want to clean or cook. She herself was getting by on a nicely balanced diet of pumpernickel, peanut butter, cream cheese, celery and apples. She was out of liquor so she didn't drink.

But the money worried her. There was another notice from the utilities company threatening immediate cutoff. She looked around the frowsy room and imagined herself without electricity. She wasn't using much of anything in the way of appliances, and she could listen to the transistor by candlelight. She had the phone. She'd miss TV, the stereo, and cream cheese, though. She thought of calling Boyd but it was midweek and somehow or other she'd developed a strong resistance to the idea. She knew he'd send her money as soon as he had it. In the meantime he'd offer her defensive sympathy and a tirade against Magoor, neither of which was utilitarian.

The next day she considered not taking in the mail at all, but roused herself with an almost superstitious alarm at her cowardice. And this paid off, more or less. There was an overdue notice on the rent, but there was also a flyer, cheaply mimeoed with a border of doodles that looked like dollar signs on a treble clef, inviting her to a Friday night session with *Peter King the Money Guru*. It assured her, "YOUR BEST ASSET IS YOU!" and asked her how she would like to actualize her dollar dynamics and rid herself of money hassles forever. It said she was hiding her earning potential even from herself. The session cost twenty-five dollars.

She wondered how they got her name. The whole thing—though the address was in the East Sixties—seemed a bit low-rent, and she tossed it in the wastebasket. But a little later she took it out and set it on the jumble on the desk. A few hours after that, when she came back from a ramble in the Village, she had an amazing phone call, from Shaara Soole.

"Listen, Wendy, I've got no right to be calling you and you may think I'm rude or stupid. Please don't be angry at me."

She really did sound nervous, which surprised Wendy because she always thought of Shaara slashing around doing exactly what suited her without worrying what anybody thought. Shaara had a husky voice with a little twang in it, more West than Midwest or South.

"I've just been thinking about it for several days, and I finally figured I wouldn't stop thinking about it till I called."

"Sure, that's okay. What's up? Is Boyd all right?"

"Yes, he's fine, it's not that. Well, it is in a way. I mean, I know he hasn't got paid, and I thought *you* might be strapped, which Boyd wouldn't tell me. I remember what it was like trying to get a few shekels out of summer stock companies, and—you know, I thought you'd understand it would be awkward for me to offer *Boyd* a loan, but . . ."

"Sure, I can see that," Wendy said.

"Well." Shaara breathed, like relief. "The mess with the grant should be sorted out in a couple of weeks, but in the meantime I thought, if you . . . please don't think it's condescending."

"I don't think it's condescending," Wendy said. "I think it's neat." The flyer flashed up at her, "YOUR BEST ASSET IS YOU!"

"But I'm fine, honestly," she said. "The bills will wait till I get around to them, and I haven't got many expenses here on my own."

"Oh, okay, great. It's really sticking my nose in none of my business, but Boyd's pretty pissed off at the college, which I don't blame him. Could I ask you one thing?"

"Sure."

"Will you not mention to him that I called? Everything's going fine down here and I don't want to annoy him."

"I won't say a word. It's really nice of you."

"I feel better then. I'm looking forward to meeting you next month."

Are not! Am so!

"Me too," said Wendy.

But a few minutes after she hung up she found herself shaking with anger. At Shaara, for asking her to lie to Boyd? No, it wasn't that. Shaara was only being decent and the nervousness made it more so; it must have cost her some effort to call. She was mad at herself, that she had a B.A. degree in psychology from Swarthmore and a drawer full of cashmere sweaters from her lawyer father, and when Boyd got in a bind that was none of his own doing she couldn't help out by so much as a temp typist's wage. That Shaara Soole, whom she owed a hundred and fifty-six dollars for a broken leg, managed her affairs so well she could afford to worry about Wendy's. The Money Guru said she was hiding her earning potential from herself, and she guessed she was doing a pretty good job of it. What was she good at? Flower arranging and watching TV, just like her mother.

There was forty-two dollars left in the account. Friday night she put on the peasant blouse, tied the scarf around her hair, and walked across the park at Seventy-second against the traffic. You were not supposed to do this, but she was not going to spend a full fare when it was less than a mile. There were plenty of headlights and she kept her hand in her shoulder bag, around a spray can of Houbigant Chantilly that her mother had tucked in the last package, and which she figured would sting anybody's eyes. Nothing happened, though.

Peter and Mrs. Guru and their three noisome children lived in an enormous apartment off Third Avenue, with high ceilings and tall French windows looking onto minibalconies. A fifteen-hundred-a-month sort of apartment, though the walls had the usual painted-over cracks and the curtains and couch covers were made out of cheap Indian throws.

There were about twenty people scattered around the room, mostly pretty young girls who settled right down on the floor with their elbows on the goatskin rugs (Wendy took a chair); but also a few young men, a plump one with albino hair he couldn't keep out of his eyes, a weedy one that picked his acne. There was a grandmotherly woman with a jiggly bosom. At the far end of the couch sat a suave man of about forty-five in a blue-gray pilot's uniform, who lightly twirled his cap where it hung on his knee. He had a silver moustache and matching sideburns down to the turn of his bronze jaw, and wide-set dark eyes. He looked generally like he wasn't hurting for subway fare.

Peter King straddled a straight-back chair in front of the fireplace, greeted them free and easy, "How's your head?" and folded his arms limp over the back while a bouncy blond daughter passed out stapled handouts with the money-music doodle across the top. The Guru was wearing a sweater with dollar signs knitted into it in gold Lurex thread. He had auburn hair and a Jesus beard, though he was older than Jesus got to be. He stretched his arms and legs out in front of him to yawn, the most relaxed man in the world, a smiler.

Wendy accepted a pencil stub and looked at the handout. On the top page was a single imperative:

$ELL YOUR $ELF!

The rest of the pages were blank. She looked at the exclamation, which reminded her of something, a little pamphlet her dad kept in the glassfront bookcase in Boston. It was very old and dog-eared and by somebody named Elmer Rice. It was called *Don't Sell the Steak, Sell the Sizzle*. Wendy began to be discouraged.

The Guru clapped his hands happily and entered on a rambling account of how he had got rich. He was a struggling student at CCNY, he said, with a wife and a baby and one on the way, and he realized he was "spending more time chasing debts than chicks." The girls on the floor and the albino giggled. Well, he did this odd job and that part-time job, and this happened and that happened, and the point, when he got around to it, was that he woke up one day to ask himself why he was spending so much unproductive energy doing stuff he didn't like to do and still not paying the bills.

"So I asked myself, what do I like to do? And I replied: I dig money and math, I like interpersonal relations, and I sorta like to be the center of attention. So how can I make a fortune out of that?"

He put his chin on his hands and smiled around, letting them get the point maybe for a minute before he said, "Now tonight, you're going to cough up about five hundred dollars between you, just for me sitting here interacting with you a couple of hours. Isn't that beautiful?"

"Wow," said one of the pretty girls. Mrs. Guru in a loose brown bun came around with a Coke bottle and a coffee pot, and the bouncy daughter followed with oatmeal cookies on a bar tray. They surely did seem to be a happy lot.

"The secret of success," pontificated the Guru, slouching comfortably, "is the one they've been hiding from you. The secret is: mix business and pleasure! OK, everyone, now take a sheet of paper and number it from one to five. Then list five things you *really* like to do."

Wendy duly numbered her paper and searched her preferences. Beside number one she wrote without hesitation, "Traveling." Then she thought that was strange because apart from a week in Mexico City with her folks (a graduation present) she hadn't done any traveling to speak of. And she hadn't enjoyed that trip much—her mother measuring pills into the water all day and her dad judging everything Mexican as either shoddy, illegal, or in bad taste. Apart from that she'd only been back and forth to Boston, and to a few of Boyd's provincial openings. What she really meant was that she liked shuttles, buses, planes, trains, being in movement and in flight, seeing strange buildings and confronting people who had whole sets of different assumptions under their life-styles. Beside number two she put, "Being on my own." She scratched out "on my own" and substituted "free," but this had a maritally disloyal ring to it, so she crossed that out and wrote "alone."

Then she ran through the things she was good at: flower arranging, shopping, decorating, giving parties. She rejected all of them as not being what she *really* liked to do (she hadn't done a smidgen of any of them since Boyd was gone); and quickly penciled "Reading" and "Watching TV." This was a grim revelation of what a thin person she was; she grimly let it stand. What it didn't suggest was what reading and TV meant to her. It wasn't as if she watched game shows and cartoons. It was Bogart in *High Sierra* . . . she thought about last weekend, breaking into the Carsons' house and leaving without a trace. "Having adventures," she wrote beside number five, and then looked at her dumb list. "Traveling, being alone, reading, watching TV, having adventures." She looked up and saw that she was the last to finish. The Guru was gently waiting for her.

"Now," he said, "let's see where we are." He stood and stretched, smiling around at them. "Check over your list. Is there anybody who doesn't make money with a single one of the things he likes to do?"

He was looking right at her. Maybe he was a real Guru after all, and had some psychic means of knowing what a flop she was. She grimaced boldly back at him and put up her hand.

"Mmm." He clucked, and pursed his mouth, and sighed. "How'd your life get to be such a mess?" He grinned to take the sting out of that, like part of a bedside manner. The girl on the floor said, "Wow," commiseratingly.

"I don't know," said Wendy.

"Well, read us what you like to do."

She was angry at being the center of attention in such a stupid scene, so she stood up to read defiantly, "Traveling, being alone, reading, watching TV, having adventures."

"Again," said the Guru. She read it again. He scratched at his beard, then repeated her list, twice, ruminatingly.

"Would you . . . what's your name?"

"Wendy."

"Wendy. Would you cross over to the sideboard and pick up the coffee pot? Take it over and offer a cup to Captain Tesoro over there."

Wendy crossed and took the pot, walked back to the handsome airline pilot. He lifted his cup and grinned, encouraging. She pursed a grim little smile back and shook her head. She returned the pot and went back to her seat.

"Good. Will you say a few sentences for us?"

Wendy said, "I'd be happy to, but I really don't have anything to say. What would you like me to talk about?" The Guru applauded this with one clap, and a few people laughed as if she'd said something clever, so she continued, "I feel a little on the spot so everything's gone out of my head, and not a single topic of conversation comes to mind. I like your curtains."

She didn't much like the curtains, but several people clapped as if she had passed some sort of test. "Isn't Wendy beautiful?" the Guru asked. The audience murmured agreement. The pilot said, "Very."

"Far out," said Wow.

"How tall are you?" asked the Guru.

"Five four."

"Well." He spread his arms to full crucifixion length and shook his head, lovingly. "You're *easy*. Anybody here can tell you. Tell me, anybody. Here is Wendy, beautiful and five foot four. She moves gracefully and she has a cultivated voice and a charming manner. The things she likes best in the world are travel and adventure, and things she can do alone, like reading and watching TV. What should she do, to make a start, at earning her fortune?"

Light dawned in little patches round the room. The albino raised his hand, the grandmother leaned and gestured in the direction of the airline pilot.

Wow said, "She should be an airline hostess!"

Her neighbor on the floor said, "Wow."

Wendy sat down stupefied and the Guru turned to solve somebody else's life. She glanced, eyes blazing, in the direction of the pilot, who shrugged, hands up to shoulder height. She was supposed to pay twenty-five dollars for advice she'd been getting from dumb classmates half her life for free. Move out of flower arranging and into serving soggy sandwiches to drunk businessmen—no thanks! She had a notion that the cup of coffee on Captain Tesoro's knee was the last one she was ever going to hand over in her life.

The Money Guru was telling a ballerina to check out disco dancing. Wendy hiked up her shoulder strap, smoothed her skirt, stood and walked out. Nobody stopped her.

She went toward Third Avenue, clutching the spray can, furious, undecided whether to take the crosstown bus. At the light somebody touched her on the elbow, and she turned, whipping the can out, finger on the button. It was the pilot.

"I'm sorry if I startled you. I was wondering if I could offer you a drink." Cap on, he had the glossy good looks of the *nouvelle vague*, wicked of moustache but kind of eye. His dark skin glittered rosy in the traffic light.

"I'm married," Wendy warned, returning the can to her bag.

"Congratulations."

He was probably laughing at her, but his eyes were very benign and she found that she instinctively trusted him. She had, in fact, been trusting him for the last hour in that company of geeks and gurus—probably out of something Bostonian and disgusting, like an instinct for good breeding. Also, he was in uniform.

"I just thought it would be a good idea to establish it," she said.

"Very wise. I think I'd like to offer you a job, but in any case I'd like to offer you a drink, to talk about it."

"What sort of job?"

He seemed to hesitate and then, from a quick intake of breath, to take a risk. "Adventurous."

"Like airline hostessing?"

They both laughed, which meant she had accepted the drink, though she hadn't meant to.

"My apartment's just around the corner, but I assume you'd rather go to a public bar."

"Yes please," said Wendy primly.

He swiveled her downtown with another touch on the elbow, took off his cap again and swung it, a tall man with an easy jogger's stride. Wendy stretched her legs to keep up.

"You're pretty handy with that Mace."

"Oh, it isn't Mace." She showed him the pink perfume can with its gold scroll. "But if you thought it was, it's just as good as, isn't it? I walked across the park, and I just thought of it."

"You walked across the park? At night?"

"Mmm-mm."

"You're a tough lady."

Wendy perked up at this. She couldn't remember anyone's suggesting it before. When a wino staggered at them from the curb she gave him a haughty stare and didn't miss a step. The captain ushered her into a bar with a front wall of leaded bottle-bottoms and clusters of overstuffed chairs around clawfooted tables. A European sort of place, tasteful. She began to have a good time.

"What would you like?"

He gave their orders to the waitress, Grappa for him and a Black Russian for her, smoothed a paper napkin out on the table with long brown fingers. He put one peanut in his mouth and leaned back, chewing it, smiling at her, appraising.

"Sandro Tesoro," he introduced himself, and formally offered his hand.

"Gwendolyn Soole," said Wendy.

"I gather you didn't feel especially enlightened by our Guru, Gwendolyn."

"*I'm* clutching at straws, I guess, but I couldn't figure out what you were doing there."

"Oh, Peter and I have known each other for years. It's true, all about being a struggling student and so forth. He's found himself a wonderful gimmick, and every once in a while he hits on a real plan for somebody—mostly he makes them into regional money gurus. It was good for my ego, too. Unlike you, I earn money doing what I like."

"What do you like to do, then?"

"Travel, live on my own, eat and drink well, watch TV." He was teasing but he probably also meant it.

"That's four."

"The other I don't get paid for."

Wendy blushed. She did not take sex very seriously, and had not since the first prod of a cock in a backseat. But Sandro Tesoro was out of her league for urbanity. She dropped her eyes. "Maybe I should be a pilot."

He leaned forward and started folding the napkin back up, into a paper hat—no, airplane. "Anyway, that's not quite an honest answer to your question. What I was really doing there was looking for you."

Wendy found this nonsense thrilling, like something Bogart might have said if he had an Italian accent. She gave him a sassy moue to make sure he understood she did not believe it.

"Me meaning who?"

He chose his words. "A refined and captivating woman who is not easily flustered when she's put on the spot."

"Ah." She considered this too. She tried it on—just window shopping. Tough, refined, and captivating. She felt her chin lift to the left. "Are you going to put me on the spot?"

"I hope not." When he laughed the skin around his eyes crushed into crow's-feet; somebody who had spent his life squinting into the tops of clouds. "But if you don't mind I would like to more or less interview you, before I explain the opening."

"I haven't applied."

"I know," he apologized.

"Well, all right. Interview."

"Do you have a valid passport?"

"Yes."

"Are you free to spend four days in Europe next week?"

Wendy's stomach hopped. "I could be."

"Your husband would not object?"

"My husband's out of town," she said rashly.

"He travels, in his line of work?"

"He's a theater director."

"Oh, *very* good. Are you an actress?"

"Me!" Her laugh attracted attention from a couple of men at a table farther down, so she leaned in and lowered her voice. "I have a degree in psychology, but sometimes I think the two professions are not . . . altogether unrelated."

"How do you mean?"

"I like to watch people and, um, fit in. Well, get them to respond. I'm not an actress, but sometimes I think I'm a chameleon." She offered this saucily, but he took it with such solemnity that she was reminded she was sitting in a bar with a stranger who seemed to be offering her a trip to Europe. "Look, Captain Tesoro . . ."

"Sandro."

"Captain Tesoro. This job you have in mind. Is it legal?"

He sighed, rather theatrically, and rather theatrically looked her straight in the eye. "No, very strictly speaking, it isn't legal, but it *is* moral. Is that a distinction you make?"

"Ye-es," she said tentatively, "in certain instances. Are you a real captain?"

He signaled the waitress for another drink and pulled out a packet of plastic I.D. cards and a Pan Am contract, spreading them eagerly out, pointing to seals and stamps and signatures of authenticity. "That's why I wore the uniform, to convince you."

"Whoever I turned out to be."

"If you should turn out to be."

"Tell me about the job."

"I'm originally Italian; naturalized. I have the papers to prove that too, if you . . ."

"No, no, I could've guessed that." Wendy laughed again, liking his style, these little eruptions of earnestness in the worldly mien.

"My family has owned vineyards in Chianti country for several generations, just outside of Florence. One of the nice things about my job is that I do the New York–Rome run, and every three months or so I have a layover long enough to see my family."

"That's nice," said Wendy, meaning that it would be nice to like going home. She was overdue for a call to her mother and would have to make it in the next few days. She'd say the floors weren't sanded yet, which was true enough.

"There were only two of us, my brother and me, which is a sort of a disaster in an Italian family, though not as bad as having *girls*. And then I emigrated in my teens—I got sick of picking grapes and wanted adventure, I wanted to fly from the first time I saw a plane. At first the family was wretched, but then I became an American pilot and everybody was *proud* of me."

He made an expansive gesture, welcoming the prodigal, and Wendy could see it like a film: the vintner in his peaked cap in the arbor and the cousins standing around with their hoes while plump mama ran down the gravel path to greet the uniform.

"It's a flourishing vineyard and exportable Chianti—you've probably drunk it. My father died, oh, seven-eight years ago, and my brother took over the business. My mother died last year."

Wendy was not sure whether sympathy was indicated, but he seemed to be presenting forthright fact, so she held herself to a nod.

"My brother and I came to a very simple agreement. He has the house and the farm; he's earned them. It's right they should belong to him." This struck her as very Italian—that familial piety that sifted right through to the Mafia. "Besides, there are no girls. So we agreed I should get Mama's jewelry, which is worth nearly as much as the house, some of it handed down four generations. In fact there's not much of it, a dozen pieces only, but Mama, and her mama, and her mama, had some very strict ideas about quality."

"My mother is the same," Wendy sympathized, wanting to raise herself a notch or two in the middle class. Her mother liked "quality" jewelry, but her velvet-lined boxes of it wouldn't have bought a house.

"So there is the problem. The jewelry is mine, I paid the death taxes on it, I'm free to sell it. I can get about three times as much for it in New York as I can in Italy, I'm an American citizen, and all the same I can't bring it home without paying about fifteen thousand dollars' import duty."

"Ah," Wendy said.

"I'm caught in a Catch-22 of the law."

"That's smuggling, though," she said, a jump ahead of him.

"If I bring it in without declaring it, chances are nobody questions me. But if they should, what am I, an unattached male, doing carrying around diamond necklaces and emerald bracelets? I not only lose the jewelry, I also lose my job which I like very much and I'm good at. And probably I get jailed."

"Wouldn't I get jailed?"

"How can you? It's yours. You travel with it, you wear it. It's been in your family for generations. None of it's new and most of it isn't even Italian, it's Dutch and French. My mama's mama had very fancy tastes."

"Ah," Wendy said again. She wasn't at all convinced it was as safe as he said, which excited her very much. She was on her third Black Russian after a couple of weeks of abstinence, and the low glow of the bar had begun to shimmer like a smoke-and-Kodachrome chimera. They were talking in low voices like lovers.

"How much are you offering for this . . . job?"

"All expenses and three thousand dollars, a thousand before we leave and the rest when you give me back the jewelry. I'll give you cash for the ticket. It's more expensive, but if I don't make the reservation there's no way of connecting me to you. That's why you had to be a stranger. I'll just happen to be the pilot of your plane."

She scarcely heard the details, after the three thousand dollars. That was half of what Boyd was making for the whole Georgia production, and his expenses came out of that. She flashed onto herself at New York customs, that droopy hat and the diamonds wrapped in a scarf at the bottom of her carry-on.

"Why should you trust me?"

"Shouldn't I?"

"How do you know I wouldn't try to walk off with them?"

"Well, for one thing, the first thing you asked me about the job was: is it legal?"

"So I did."

"Besides, I trust my instincts." The captain gestured at her dirndl. "You'd probably need some new clothes."

"Oh, that's all right," Wendy assured him loftily. "I was slumming tonight. I have some much more . . . cultivated clothes than this. I'd probably need new luggage, though, something rather Gucci."

"All right."

"No, something American but expensive, leather-trimmed tweed from Saks. I'd need a haircut. Would that come under the heading of an expense?"

"Why not?"

"And a hat."

"A hat?"

"Yes," said Wendy firmly, "a hat. A woman who still wears a hat and stockings on an airplane, is a woman who would carry a dozen pieces of jewelry on a four-day trip."

"That's it," he said, admiring.

"I should pack a couple of evening dresses, and I should go to the theater and the opera, just stick the programs in my suitcase, on top of my clothes."

"Wonderful. You can come to Florence, why not? And bring back reproductions from the Uffizi. And you should shop, not enough to take you over the customs allowance, but enough to declare. A couple of good leather things."

"Suede boots," said Wendy. "With gold heel trim."

They sat back mutually pleased with each other. Then Tesoro's expression took on a romantic cast and he leaned forward and covered her hand with his. "Does that mean you can do it?"

"Certainly I *can* do it."

"And you will?"

"Let me sleep on it."

"Oh, yes." He sighed sentimentally and kissed the tips of her fingers. "I'd so like to sleep on it with you."

Wendy's stomach hopped again and her vision skidded but—tough and refined, not a woman to be easily flustered when put on the spot—she let her hand rest lightly in his, and arched her eyebrow. "You'll just happen to be the pilot of my plane," she reminded him with an urbane grin.

"That's true," he conceded. His earnest eyes sought hers, his head ducking slightly as if this were an effort. "But then one *can* mix business and pleasure." He rubbed his lower lip across her fingertips, which had the effect of letting her know, midstomach, that she was rather tipsy.

"It isn't a condition of my getting the job," she told him, not a question, and realized she had accepted the job, though she hadn't meant to. Realized that this third offer was also something she could do if she chose, that she had the power to say yes or no. The idea of adultery had never crossed her mind before. It crossed now, with a sickly thrill, as something more dangerous than smuggling. It was something her mother would *never* . . . neither would Wendy, of course. Still . . .

"Certainly not!" He kissed her fingers again, wafted them across his lower lip, touched the index finger with the merest tip of his tongue.

"Ah," Wendy said.

14. *The Late-Night Double-Feature Picture Show*

Motel life suited Boyd. Its emptiness honed his concentration. He liked the plastic monotony of the café menu, grilled burgers and shrimp with hush puppies; he liked the paucity of his belongings among the glossy fake paneling, the discount Aztec bedspread on which, every time he came back from a breakfast of ham and grits, he could bounce a quarter.

He wasn't lonely, or else what loneliness he felt had a melancholy density he could enjoy. Wyman and Barnard had taken a shabby sublet on Lake Takullah, and Gunilla stayed at the Sheraton in town, but Orme lived across the pool at the Campus Side, and they did an occasional drink or flick together, deferential to each other's privacy. Once Boyd picked up a woman in the motel bar, an efficiency consultant doing pit repairs for the Magoor administration. It was okay; she was warm and forty and soft-breasted, which was odd after Wendy's limber flatness. But later—probably it was the breasts—he had a confused dream in which Shaara was screaming at him, naked, as she had never screamed.

Most evenings he prepared the next day's rehearsal and then settled into Jack Daniels and TV. He had whatever the opposite of claustrophobia would be—claustromania?—with the drapes closed and the television set as his one window onto the world. It told him that the airlines and regulations people were still squabbling over the DC-10's, that a quake had jolted Lake Isabella in the High Sierras, that Carter's popularity had dipped to thirty percent whereas eighty-eight percent thought Theodore Bundy had clubbed those two Chi Omegas to death down in Tallahassee. Usually at one A.M. he could pick up a golden oldie of the ghoul world, some of it stuff he hadn't seen since Hollywood, *Brides of Fu Manchu* and assorted Draculas and, a disinterred treasure, Roger Corman's *Not of This Earth*. Late shows were a luxury; at home he didn't feel free to sleep in the next morning, even when he wasn't working. And his mind being now a single receptacle for the production, he could usually suck in something to make use of the next day. For instance, it bore in on him that the best monsters, Wolf Man, King Kong, Frankenstein's, Creature from the Black Lagoon, were the unwilling ones, the tender-hearted wreakers. He fed this into Wyman, and could see a rich paradox beginning to emerge in the character of the Mother Superior, seconds of real saintliness in back of the cigar and the treasure mauling. It was still not a happy cast, and every day he had to deal with some recalcitrance in either Wyman or Gunilla, but he dealt with it, he was in control, and the moments when his stomach caught with fear got fewer and shorter.

Nor did he miss Wendy, at least not in the sense of wishing she were here. What was better than missing her was the warmth he felt when she crossed his mind. After he talked to her on Sundays he always had an anchoring sense of normality up there: the refrigerator had cut off and leaked rotten water all over the floor, she'd had a haircut and bought a classy new weekender for the trip to Hubbard. He supposed that meant MasterCharge hadn't dumped them. Wendy had taken a pert and endearing attitude toward the late check. "I don't suppose the landlord'll turn me out on the sidewalk before the academic veep gets back to Magoor."

He loved her for this sentence specifically. The worst period in his life—far worse than the aftermath of divorce—was the two years following his folks' crash on the L.A. freeway and the selling of the Hollywood house. He'd been in college at the time and had money to spare for the first, only, time in his life. He'd used it up around Europe, where it seemed he was filling in a debarkation card or a hotel register every twenty minutes. Every time he had to fill in "Permanent Address," he panicked. He never had the guts to write "None." He'd sweat, and wait, and then put down the old Hollywood house number in a sick sensation of void and fraud. He'd see the house uprooted, hovering a few inches off the ground, peopled with literally faceless strangers, celluloid shapes under rubber hair.

Now, Wendy told him, she was walking a lot and reading a lot. He could see her in a pool of lamplight, lean bare legs tucked up, the apartment almost as quarter-bouncing neat as the motel, but in her crisp good taste. He liked being where he was and he liked her being there. She was his permanent address.

And in fact the only thing he didn't feel good about was Kevin. He blamed himself; he hadn't thought it through. Shaara was right all those years ago, he planned ahead for work down to the least pause or prop, but he thought family matters should take care of themselves. He was also right about Shaara (rub a couple of guilts together and they'll burst into blame)—she'd mouth over any emotional nuance like a cud. When she was short of yardage for a costume, she used to say she was "chewing ravelings." He thought she chewed ravelings at home too, always a yard short on affection, feedback, togetherness, response, whatever.

Whatever, he was feeling it with Kevin. They couldn't talk. Probably it wasn't natural for parents and thirteen-year-olds to talk anyway, but in New York there was a routine for him to fit into, and nobody noticed. He'd thought—or not thought—that in Kevin's context it would be easier still. He hadn't reckoned on Shaara's stiffness, which made every sentence an effort. He hadn't thought about being stuck in the motel without a car, and nothing to offer his son beyond a swim and a grilled burger. Now, even when the check finally came through, if he rented a car Shaara would take it as her triumph, and what would they do with it, besides drive to a farther pool and a farther diner?

Orme Sullivan had rented a little Volvo, and did his bachelor thing, exploring the area, soaking up local color in the form of sinkholes and stately homes. But Boyd didn't want to intrude a thirteen-year-old on that, and besides Kevin had seen it all. In the meantime Shaara had managed to job Kevin into the scene shop, where he spent his days in a radio racket with the redneck carpenter. Shaara probably thought this was a brilliant ploy—no, give her credit, she probably thought it was easier—but the theater was exactly where Boyd was most distracted and could least afford distraction. Also, Barnard had taken to hanging around the shop when he wasn't on call, half helping and half camping, adorning himself with pine shavings and bits of metal debris. Boyd didn't know what Kevin might understand about queers and hoped it wasn't much. He didn't want him picking up either ideas or mannerisms. Half the time when he arrived to fetch Kevin for lunch he felt the fun and games stutter to a halt. Then Kevin would drop his hammer and follow him, monosyllabic and polite. Boyd felt an empty longing for his son, and could not get through.

At least they had movies in common—they saw *Alien* and *Moonraker* together and disagreed enthusiastically about both—so when Orme stopped by to suggest a drive-in, Boyd took him up on it.

"There's a low-budget thing called *The House on Dead End Street,*" Orme said, propped on the TV, sinister and mild. The usual disasters played under his elbow on the late news: student accused of setting his grandmother on fire, rebels attacking Somoza. A cockroach crawled across the bureau, and Orme leaned over to trap it gently under an ashtray. "I've worked with one of the kids in it. He's a real punk but it should be good for laughs. I think we should take in a local drive-in, don't you? No tour of the rural South complete, et cetera?"

"Would you mind if I brought Kevin?"

"Fantastic. We'll do popcorn and jujubes."

That was Monday. Rehearsal was due to knock off at eight on Wednesday, so Boyd and Kevin made a date for the late drive-in, Kevin to stay over at the motel. Shaara was not so enthusiastic.

"Is it some sort of horror thing? He said *Alien* made him sick to his stomach."

Exasperated, Boyd charged, "You took him to *Exorcist.*"

"And regretted it."

"Bullshit. He told me it was great. You're the one it freaked."

"Well."

None of this was what he meant, and he was too tired from his struggles with Wyman and Gunilla to go into it, how her protectiveness was actually possessiveness, a way of putting a wedge between father and son. Her reasonable tone enraged him; he muffled the rage.

John Wayne died Tuesday night and rehearsal Wednesday was oddly awkward on account of it. Wyman had been visibly weeping; he had great Irish bags under bloodshot eyes, and this embarrassed everybody else. Gunilla naturally considered Wayne a rotten actor and no sort of human being at all, a couple of steps above Nixon for right-wing hypocrisy. In rehearsal she played the innocent Senora with the wrong kind of hauteur, and Wyman lost all his saintly undertones. From time to time Boyd could see him doing a bowlegged swagger under the muslin rehearsal skirt.

Afterwards he and Kevin went with Orme for pit barbecue at a place enchantingly called "Mother Joe's." The Wayne talk continued, Kevin sloppy with the sauce, spraying his T-shirt as he declared, " 'My country right or wrong.' I think that's a great saying. Great."

This ought to have been less embarrassing coming from a thirteen-year-old than from a sentimental Irishman, but Boyd felt responsible for his son.

"You don't mean where Vietnam was concerned."

"Sure. Well, I mean, maybe we shouldn't've gone in there, but once we did, we should've gone *all out* to win."

Boyd sighed and tried to catch Orme's eye, but Orme was delicately mopping hickory blood from his five o'clock shadow.

"Where do you get these ideas?" Boyd smiled, with an indulgence as phony to his own ears as Kevin's cliché. What he meant was: Where *do* you get these ideas? Not from Shaara, he was sure, and yet it was Shaara who had brought him down here to live in cracker country, go to school with Klansmen's sons. Surprised by his own bitterness (because really he and Shaara had an amicable relationship, didn't they?) he chuckled and filled his mouth with hush puppy.

"I'm a conservative," Kevin announced.

"O-yeh? Capital punishment? Keep women in their place?" Upset, angry, he was still grinning, his mouth still full.

"I read somewhere," Orme remarked, "that conservatism is based on fear and radicalism on anger. That's an interesting notion, don't you think?"

"John Wayne wasn't afraid of anything," Kevin said.

"Oh, I think he was," said Orme. Boyd shifted uneasily in his chair, seeing how naturally and without condescension Orme spoke to his son. "He was just better at facing it than most of us. You know . . ." Orme turned to include Boyd, eyes musing under the murderous brow, "it occurred to me in rehearsal today, watching Wyman: there are fewer hypocrites among conservatives. Conservatism comes out of self-interest so there's no *need* to be insincere. The liberal stance is based on brotherhood and the other fellow, a harder thing to feel; the self-interest involved is likely to be a high opinion of your own virtue, so hypocrisy's a constant danger. Conservatives only get phony when they pretend they're *not* operating on self-interest. You know, 'the dignity of this great office,' or the Mother Superior's 'we must save the poor child' stuff."

"Mmm," said Boyd. And wondered if he could use this. Kevin, obscurely knowing that he'd been defended, bobbed his blond bangs admiringly at Orme. Boyd's unease shifted into higher gear.

The drive-in was a stubbled field on the highway south. Ordinary lightbulbs surrounded the marquee, and a few of these were out. Orme slowed to inspect them and pointed out gleefully that they'd been shot at, probably with a BB gun. The ancient cashier peered sleepily in at Kevin when Orme said, "Two adults one child," and for a second Boyd thought they'd be turned away. But the old man mumbled, "Kids are free," and relieved Orme of a mere four dollars. There were only a dozen cars on the undulating dirt, most of them humpbacked old Dodges and a couple of pickups. Orme cut the lights and coasted to the front row, then had to back up again when the first two speakers they tried were broken.

"Isn't this a kick?"

They bought stale popcorn from a waitress in a red check minidress and a blond beehive. "It's a time warp!" Orme whispered jubilantly, and entered into a solemn discussion of chocolate raisins with her. Kevin caught his mood and skipped pebbles from one trough to another back to the car, then got in front with Orme because "*You* c'n see over my head." The patched screen was showing local ads in the tinny Technicolor of the fifties—for real estate, dog racing, the Sundown Seafood Diner and Gum's Ranch and Garden Center. When the feature came on it was in so much the same brash contrast of oranges and blues that Boyd didn't recognize it. A beefy kid, all pores and leather, sidled across the screen, hams bouncing. He flicked a sneer like a cheap switchblade.

"That's him, the punk," Orme said.

Kevin said, "He looks like Meatloaf."

"Like who?"

"Meatloaf. Y'know, from *The Rocky Horror Picture Show*."

"You've seen *The Rocky Horror Picture Show*?" Boyd asked,

while the punk on the screen did a pelvis-swing and the credits started rolling over: *The Last House on Dead End Street.*

"Sure, six times."

"He's a conservative," Boyd observed to Orme. "Just a sweet conservative from Transexual Transylvania-a-a."

"It's a tacky blow-up," Orme said. "They must've done it in Super 8. This is going to be the worst!"

The punk continued to walk, presumably down Dead End Street, toward what looked less like a house than an abandoned school. Abruptly the scene switched to a "subliminal" flash-forward of the same punk in shirtsleeves lifting a double hand-ful of dripping guts. For a second, center screen was occupied by visceral clots of slime oozing through thick fingers. The shot stayed long enough for them to register, in the background, the dismembered body of a blonde on bloody sheets. "Sheece," Kevin let out through his teeth, and Boyd understood by the familiar wringing of his diaphragm, as if someone had squeezed it in a fist, that this was a mistake. Somehow for the next hour and a half they were going to work up to, and through, that dismemberment and that disemboweling, and he would not be able to take Kevin away because it was Orme's car and Orme would be having a good time.

"The way they do that," he put in quickly, leaning over the seat to edge his face next to Kevin's, "is just get a butcher to save them cow intestines. It's practically free, and very effec-tive." Kevin nodded and said nothing.

Such plot as there was unfolded: the punk was going to trap and torture everyone who'd had a part in sending him to prison, and make a film of the process to sell on the hardcore market. It was unrelievedly boring except when relieved by flashes of the sickening. It was a movie about unredeemably trashy peo-ple, but without any redeeming contrast because it was made by unredeemably trashy people. Kevin started covertly hiding his eyes against his shoulder, but since he hadn't the skill to foresee when the flash-forwards would come, the buzz saw through the flesh and the dangling body parts, he hid at the wrong time. He became very still. Orme enjoyed himself, mocking, and Boyd joined in because it seemed that the best option open was to make light of it. Had Kevin not been there he might have enjoyed it too; had Orme not been there he'd have made a moralistic speech about artistic distance, and taken him away. Stuck, he joked, placed a reassuring hand over the seat to stroke Kevin's shoulder, playfully covered Kevin's eyes when he guessed more knowledgeably that the blood was going to run.

"This is not a horror movie," he explained academically. "It's just a horrible movie. The horror genre requires something supernatural, so you have a sense that people are pitting themselves against the unknown. And then you keep the horror offscreen as much as possible, so it's our own imaginations we're struggling with." Meaning, he supposed, that what they were watching was not "horror" because it was altogether too possible. Kevin tried a wan smile, tried to laugh at Orme's quips, once or twice he braved a comparison of gore—"D'you see that fish tank thing in *Silent Partner?*"

But it was different, different from all the TV blood, different from the spitting metallic Alien, as far as possible from Wayne's right-minded violence; because Boyd could sense, and Kevin could sense, that if people made such a movie as *The Last House on Dead End Street*, about making a movie about people who would make such a movie, then there were such people.

It dragged through half an hour, an hour, a chase through corridors to a locked exit door, an hour and ten minutes, the victims strung up by their wrists to the water pipes, an hour and a quarter, a Black and Decker drill through an eyeball. "The obligatory drill through the eyeball," Orme said, but grew a little disenchanted himself. Twice he turned to ask them if they'd had enough, if they wanted to go.

But neither Kevin, huddled toward the door, nor Boyd, his stomach cramped with leaning over, could admit this. "I've seen worse," Kevin claimed, and Boyd, "Might as well sit it out." The best Boyd could manage was, for the last five minutes, a mock parental tone: "I think I'm censoring this. You put your head down and I'll let you know when you're allowed to look." Kevin was obedient. The punk hacked through the blonde's legs, finally, and returned to the original stance of sacrificial triumph. The lights came up and the Dodges started sputtering to life. Orme pulled into line with them on the dirt exit ramp and headed back to town.

"I counted the boom in the shot seven times," he said, and, "Amateurs shouldn't be allowed to play with studio sound." But in fact he was a sensitive man, knew the outing was a disaster and would have been grateful had Boyd released him earlier. Now he suggested a midnight swim, and at this their spirits all buoyed extravagantly. Orme turned on the radio and they sang along, "The devil went down to Georgia . . ." At the motel pool they horsed and splashed; Kevin flung himself bellyflop after bellyflop into the purifying chlorine.

After which he slept at once on the far side of the vast bed. Boyd mixed himself a stiff Daniels and turned the TV on low. A late news recap informed him that a homesick ex-defector had hijacked a Delta jumbo back to Cuba, and that the Theodore Bundy trial was being taken to Miami. "Theater Bundy," Boyd said under his breath. "The last house on Dunwoody Street." He turned it off and slipped into bed, listening to Kevin's steady breathing, holding himself rigid on the edge of the mattress because he would like to have crawled toward that pubescent warmth, to have wrapped himself around his son and cried.

When he woke it was from a new form of the old dream, not the naked dream but the pleading dream, his other standard. He was in a huge Goodwill van with his parents, on the way to dispose of the Hollywood house effects. His father sat professorial and remote in the black recliner, and his mother bent over a sock on a darning spindle. Boyd was cross-legged on the floor of the van with an extravagant book in his hands. It had a padded leather cover decorated in gold scrollwork, a flap from back to front with a medieval gilt clasp. He had never seen such a book outside the hands of Vincent Price, but he knew what it contained, and he was pleading with his father not to give it to Goodwill.

"They *sell* these things," he whined as the truck shuddered down Ocean Drive in the direction of the big box dump. "Don't you understand, somebody will *buy* it and *read* it." His father adjusted his glasses and made notes; his mother darned. When he tried to stand, the book imploringly held out, the truck swerved and tipped with a squeal of brakes.

It must have been one of those instantaneous dreams, because the squeal was Kevin. He'd thrown the covers off both of them with the violence of his sitting up, and had his hands hard one over the other over his mouth, through which double barrier he issued short squeaks, one after the other. Boyd flicked on the light and flung himself across the bed to take Kevin in his arms.

"It's okay, 'tsokay, 'tsokay," he repeated. "You had a dream. 'Tsokay." But his heart was contradictorily hammering, himself only half awake, half back in the Goodwill truck. " 'Tsokay," while the squeaks subsided into choppy breathing and Kevin let himself begin to cry.

Boyd knew what was in the book and could even see the handwriting, small and sharply slanted leftwards, though in fact he had seen it not in a book but in one of the stack of green spiral stenographer's pads, neatly bound together with rubber bands. Each had a water-green cover with the word *Rexall*, and a long-nailed hand holding a quill.

"You just had a dream," he said, and Kevin nodded, hiccuping. "It was Henry!"

"Henry?"

The script had a tendency to slant down as well as left, like the drag at the corner of his father's mouth. He had, he now realized, always associated the two. The script spelled out: "It won't be a plan or even a conscious decision. Just one day I'll have a choice of turning the wheel or not, and I won't choose until a second past the necessary moment."

"It was Henry, he came back up, he came down the backyard with those guts hanging out, he was after me!"

Boyd realized he was talking about the dog. "It was just a dream," he said again. "Never mind, never mind."

They had found no explanation, at L.A. traffic control. The car did not appear to have been going fast for freeway traffic. It was in the outside—slow—lane. Witnesses agreed that no one had cut in front of him, and that the car had simply continued straight where the road curved, crashed the barrier and somersaulted onto the lower level of the clover leaf. They had asked Boyd, once, whether there was any reason to suppose his father might have taken his own life; and Boyd had scoffed, sincerely angry. But that was before he'd begun to clean out the desk, in preparation for the selling of the house. He still had the notebooks up in New York, locked away from Wendy in a strongbox at the back of the closet. He did not remember if he'd given any of the junk to Goodwill.

"I want to go home!" Kevin blubbered, and home came into Boyd's mind: the Spanish tiles, the stucco arch over the porch, the big blue ceramic pot where his mother trained some kind of dinky purple flower. He rocked Kevin back and forth, stroking his head, comforting and taking comfort in the hot face at his chest. Then the heat spread into a wave of pure anger, that "home," to his son, meant Shaara.

"Come on, it's the middle of the night," he scoffed lightly. "We can't go wake her up, we'd scare her to death."

Kevin nodded against his chest and repeated—apologizing now, "He was all bloody, and he was after me."

"You know," Boyd said when he was fully awake and they had both calmed, "a very famous poet wrote a poem about just that, having a dream about his dead dog. I'll get a copy of it for you, shall I?"

Kevin nodded again, released Boyd, and moved back to take possession of himself.

"It's probably a very common thing to happen, having a dream about a pet you loved." He regretted the warmth gone from his chest. "Let's see about getting you another dog, shall we?"

But Kevin was already up, moving toward the bathroom, holding himself erect, hitching the elastic of his underpants like a holster belt.

"We'll have to see what Mom says." Friendly but remote.

"Everybody has nightmares," Boyd said again. "It's nothing. They're not real."

15. Buried Treasure

A professional misunderstanding arose, about the Senora's jewels. Since Gunilla brought them onstage in a casket, and they were only incidentally worn—once when the Mother Superior furtively tried them on, once when Sister Angela gobbed them on the corpse—Shaara had assumed they'd be taken care of by props. Props, in the person of Dora Fisher, assumed otherwise.

"Joolry is definitely costyoom," Dora said. "If somebody brought a dress on in a box, and then later put it on, you'd never expect *prawps* to make it." Dora was a chipper and officious virgin, an M.A. candidate in Theatrical History. She had the soul of a schoolmarm in the body of a koala bear, an inordinate desire to be with it (she frequently claimed to be "grossed out" when in fact she had probably "felt repugnance"), and a passion for professionalism. Like many amateurs, she equated professionalism with her own dignity.

However, "I'll be re-spawnsible for the *caskit*," she assured Shaara brightly. "Unless you'd like to take it up with Boyd."

"No, that's okay," said Shaara. "I'll hit the garage sales this weekend. I've got time."

Satisfied, Dora jounced up the stairs to preset for the afternoon's rehearsal. As soon as she was gone, Gene appeared in the doorway.

"Joolry," he said, "is definitely *prawps*."

"Nyah," Shaara shrugged.

"Unless you want to take it up with Boweed."

"I'm not worried about confronting Boyd, I just don't mind finding the junk. I'll enjoy it, in fact."

"But if you spend the weekend at the garage sales, you'll miss the unveiling of the Great American Iguana Cage."

"Not necessarily. Depends how many people's grandmothers died this week. I might get it all out of one attic haul. And anyway, I've got better taste in trash than Dora."

"What Ah've got," Gene said, "is a better *ahdea*." He always thickened his accent for emphasis; something about the backbone of the South, no doubt. "How's your bud-git?"

"Brilliant. I got all the fabrics at K-Mart and T.G.&Y. Why?"

"How pressed are you?"

"Not."

"Well, let's knock off and go do the junk shops around Tifton."

This *was* a better idea. The junk shops around Tifton had yielded most of her own bangles, in fact, and searching the jetsam for bargains was one of her favorite pastimes. Also, Gene was holding his naked torso taut in the doorframe, as if holding his breath. Something skipped in her own midriff, so it was hard to find an adequate objection.

"We'll pick up some sausage and wine and do a picnic."

She found one. "But Kevin stayed over at the motel with Boyd, and when they get here we'll be gone."

"We'll leave him a note. All's he's got to do is put another coat of polyurethane on the cage."

"I don't know."

"Shaara, it cain't *do* any *harm*."

She did not entirely agree with this—that is, her head did but her midriff didn't. However, she folded up the habit she was working on.

"Can we be back by five?"

"No sweat."

They left the note and took Gene's pickup. He donned a new baseball cap, which probably meant she'd spoiled the other one. She hadn't been in a truck since Iowa, and being so high off the road was exhilarating. They stopped by the Exxon to fill up, and Shaara watched Gene and William "Bud" in deep converse, old boys over the radiator. Being at the station put her in mind of Wendy Soole. She no longer had to take out the photo to see it, that clean Peter Pan innocence against a backdrop of Atlantic Ocean neverland. This in turn put her in mind of her agitation over Boyd. She did want to go look for the jewelry, but if she hadn't, she would have done it anyway, because she'd lied about that; she wouldn't confront him. Couldn't. She felt obligated to a show of cheerful competence, and everything she did in his presence was crisp with strain. She rummaged now in her bag for a wintergreen, something to do, and was about to drop the scrap of wrapper on the floor when she realized that the truck, although it was a '72 Ford giving in to rust along the panels, was as scrubbed inside as the cheekbones of Wendy Soole. She shoved the paper back in her bag.

William "Bud" came back to her window, a forward drag at his shoulders that looked out of place on his usually resilient frame. "Miz Soole, I was just telling Mr. Keyes here that I wanted to warn my reg'lar customers, I'll be closing down weekends from now on."

"Oh, I'm sorry. Are supplies short?"

"Yes, ma'am, it's caught up to me." He had a greasy version of Gene's hat (popcorn would not have harmed it), which he took off and twisted, literally cap in hand. Shaara winced. "You get in by six on Fridays, I'll be sure to fix you up."

"I will, thanks, Bud. Never mind; it's got to get better soon."

"Yes'm," he said doubtfully.

They pulled out on the road to Tifton. This was precisely the sort of thing that got to her, injured birds and common courtesy. The dumb tears rose and she scrambled for another wintergreen, flipped on the radio. "I doan know . . . if I should . . ."

Gene flipped it off. "What's up?"

"Nothing. Don't say anything."

So he said nothing. It was Flag Day, a holiday disused except perhaps in rural Iowa and Georgia. The farther out of town they got, the more frequently the banners furled, some on real flagpoles rigged up to porch posts, some draped like awnings over wooden window frames. Most of them were stained or ragged, and they spotted only two with fifty stars. When Shaara had swiveled her sentimentality around to a proper liberal rage, she explained, "Oil profits up eighty percent and it's Bud Rufus getting screwed. Probably the only ones that'll go broke are him and the other four honest people in the industry."

"Prob'ly he won't."

"No, probably he won't. Probably he'll just have to go without the Sunday roast and a new used car. But it's shit anyway."

"Yeah . . . if he's as decent as you think."

"Don't tell me about decent. I grew up on it. I went in for

a water pump once and he fixed it with a gasket. Last week he told me to go to the self-serve island 'cause he'd serve me anyway."

"Maybe he knows the value of PR."

"Shut up."

So he shut up. But when they stopped at a Majik Market for Almaden, peaches and Slim Jims; when they got back in the truck; when he stuck the bag at her feet, started up and slipped into gear; he held the clutch to the floor and put his arms around her, stroking her astonished hair. Then he released both her and the clutch and drove to Tifton.

Where the pickings were fat. There were two barn-sized junk shops and a half a dozen converted houses, some of which called themselves things like Antique Boutique and Carriage Wheel, but all of which were permanent rummage sales. They found trays' worth of Coro and Trifari out of the 'fifties, gilded fleur-de-lis pins with pearls of impossible size, tiered earrings long enough to slash a shoulder. Shaara figured she could afford to squander fifty dollars without breaking her budget, and most of the pieces were priced at a quarter or fifty cents. When the shopkeepers realized she was bent on buying this dated stuff, they unearthed boxes of it. The owner of the Carriage Wheel, who was herself wearing Coro earbobs under a gray marcel wave, went from drawer to drawer of the used furniture, both arthritic and spry, saying, "Wait now, wait now, I think I put another . . ." Regretfully, Shaara turned down a whole menagerie of rhinestone-studded animals.

"They're not the right period," she explained, but the old lady assured her with the firmness of a connoisseur, "Oh, that's 'fifties, I'm sure. Was it something earlier you wanted?"

"Rather earlier."

"So few people appreciate . . ." the woman said, after which Shaara hadn't the heart to tell her she was buying props, so she took a Jiminy Cricket with bulbous eyes and a glittering coat. The woman unlocked a case and withdrew a rope of minute sky-blue glass beads, each of them no bigger than a pinhead, hand-strung and twisted to a length of nearly a yard, with tassels of the same beads at each end.

"This is the nineteen-twenties, but I'm afraid it's fifteen dollars; it's a very special piece." Shaara took that too, for herself, and asked for a separate receipt.

"Do you have a tiara?"

But no, she hadn't, and they needed a tiara, so they went on. They stopped to eat their lunch in a miniature park, barely bigger than the shade of its one iron oak, and Gene kicked through a pile of leaves at the curb.

"I always like to check the free trash too," he said.

"Do you? Are you a trash picker?"

"The best. I am the Rocky-feller of trash picking."

Exhilarated by their success, both of them had a little more energy than they knew what to do with. "Once I got a genuwine U.S. Navy pea jacket out of the middle of the road. I said to myself, 'That looks like a dead pea jacket in the middle of the road.' And it was. It must've crossed in the rush hour."

She choked on her wine and coughed. "No, pea jackets are nocturnals."

"Put your hands over your head."

She put her hands over her head, a Slim Jim in one fist. The coughs subsided. "I got a leather hat out of a Dempsey Dumpster once. I had to drown a month-old black kitten, well, that's a long story, but the vet was on the other side of town and there was a tornado watch, and I wasn't going to leave Kevin home alone while I went out in a tornado, and the kitten had terminal diarrhea anyway, so I put it in a pillowcase and drowned it in the bathtub, and then I didn't want to put it in my own garbage can, so I walked up the road to the apartments. The wind was howling like bejesus and I thought, 'God doesn't want me drowning kittens.' Only when I opened up the dumpster there was this perfectly beautiful split cowhide hat sitting on top of the potato peels. So I decided he did."

"Thass a in-spiring story," Gene said, knocked back on the grass by the inspiration of it.

"Sure. My mother taught me that."

"What, kitten drowning?"

"No, well, that too. But I mean, the value of trash. 'Something out of nothing' was her favorite phrase. She made patchwork quilts when it was out of style to make patchwork quilts, and tacky little pots of calico flowers, so she wouldn't waste the scraps."

"I thought you came from a inte*llect*ual family."

"Oh, no, I got intellectual all by myself."

"One of them libbers."

"One of them."

They still needed a tiara. There was a big-barn junk shop yet to do, so they stuffed their treasure into the glove compartment—one of the truck doors wouldn't lock—parked on the highway and crossed the asphalt. This place was the bottom of the heap and sold mostly rejects from the Salvation Army—unfixable appliances and half a pair of anything. They minced sideways through the aisles to avoid the dirt, uncovering nothing but destuffed animals, volumes H through M of defunct encyclopedias, holey-soled shoes and lids without a pot to go under them.

"I suppose this is an unlikely place for a tiara," Shaara said.

Nevertheless she found one. From a jumble of nefarious headgear she turned up a wedding veil on a wire frame, the cheap tulle crushed and yellowed, the crown of daisies bedraggled, but the wire still strong. She put it on over her headband to test the spring of it.

"Look, this will do."

"Oh, it's juss *you.*"

"No, but if I strip it down to the frame and paint it with epoxy, I can roll it in glitter and sew on some of those rhinestone thingamabobs. It only has to stay on Gunilla's head for five minutes ten performances."

"Okay."

She started back through the aisles to the cashier, but halfway Gene called to her, "Look here a minute."

He'd sideswiped a window drape and knocked it off an old Zenith console radio, the speaker slots cut in the unmistakeable curves of the early 'forties. It stood waist-high, gutted, the tuning dial smashed and the brocade over the speaker shredded.

"When I was a kid," Gene said at the same moment Shaara said, "*We* used to have . . ." They both stopped and laughed.

"Fibber McGee," Gene swore. He scratched at the cracked varnish, which flaked easily even under his stub of a nail. "That's teak on top and mahogany on the front panel."

"Super."

"You could strip it in about ten minutes. Couple of coats of polyurethane and it'd be better than new."

"Except there's no radio."

"That's a problem."

"What could you do with it? Besides set a fishbowl on it or turn it into a planter. Like those cutesy butter churns in *House Beautiful.*"

"An iguana cage?"

"No thanks, already had one."

They made their way forward to the cash register, where the paunchy good ol' scalper insisted on a dollar and a half for the wedding veil.

"What're you asking for that Zenith console back there?" Gene asked.

"Forty-five."

"*Dollars?*"

"Yessir. They don't make 'em like that no more."

"But it's a radio without a radio."

"Suit yourself."

"How 'bout fifteen?"

"Forty'd be my lowest, and I'd be gee-ivin' it away."

Gene gave him a look, which he ignored, and steered Shaara by the elbow back out into the sun.

"You ask me what I know about decent," she said, "that ain't it."

"Varmint. All the same, it's too good for him, oughtta be rescued from his foul clutches."

"Not for forty dollars."

"All the same."

All the same, it sparked their talk the whole way back to Hubbard: "Amos 'n Andy," "Ozzie and Harriet," "One Man's Family," Benny, Hope, "Grand Central Station," and "Our Gal Sunday."

"Can this girl from a mining town in the West . . . ?" Gene wondered.

"I was taking something called *adagio*, which is sort of tumbling, because my mother thought it would make me *graceful*, worse luck. We'd have Ernie Pyle with supper and afterwards I practiced headstands and chest rolls to the radio while my brothers carried on. They'd say, '*I* can do that,' and then sit on the couch imitating my grunts. They liked to catch me in a backbend when Fibber McGee was about to open his closet, and then tickle me when all his stuff came crashing out of it."

"What I used to do is, when I got sick, I stayed on the couch while my mother cleaned, so I could listen with her. Then I'd get hooked on Stella Dallas and think I couldn't go back to school not knowing what was going to happen, only I couldn't admit that *no ways*, so I'd sneak greasy stuff I wasn't supposed to eat till I got sick again."

They pulled into the Magoor theater lot about four-thirty and unloaded the glove compartment, took the stuff in still giggling over Fibber's closet, and went to find Kevin in the scene shop.

He was there, the cage was polyurethaned, but he seemed a little clinging and subdued, which was not like him. Usually he didn't notice whether she was around or not. Naturally Shaara was stung with guilt.

"How was the drive-in?"

"It was the pits."

"Not scary?"

"Dad said it's not a horror flick at all, just garbage."

"Speaking of garbage . . ." She showed him the jewelry, which except for Jiminy Cricket was not of particular interest, until Barnard came in and began adorning himself, camping the Mother Superior's lines. "*A thousand years of riches, of blissful nights and carefree days . . .*" while he bangled his arms to the elbow, and so forth. Then Kevin cheered, perked up, and strutted in the wedding veil. She took him home by way of Wuv's and let him get a double fries *and* a shake. She played an hour of Dungeons and Dragons with him, though the labyrinthine complexity of the rules exasperated her; played it nevertheless for her own sake; prevention of guilt. By ten o'clock he was tired, and displayed normality by downing a tuna fish sandwich, three brownies and two glasses of milk before he went to bed.

After she'd bathed and slipped into a zippered caftan, she took out the rope of blue beads, knotted it around her hair Alice style, Indian style, tiara style; struck poses at herself in the mirror, then hung it around her neck and looped it loosely at the breast. It was a find, no doubt of it. But she and her double seemed thin company to appreciate it. She missed Henry.

She sat on the couch with a new book on the masks of the *commedia dell'arte*, making notes for her fall seminar in Costuming Comedy. September seemed a long way off, though, and the project of minimal urgency. After a while she gave it up, gave in, and reached for the *TV Guide*. She had a choice of "Barnaby Jones," "Sports Highlights," or Jimmy Stewart in *It's a Wonderful Life.* Jimmy Stewart every time.

She didn't remember seeing *It's a Wonderful Life*, but she recognized it in such a way as to suggest that she'd seen it as a child, and never since. The *TV Guide* said '46, but movies never made it to Burlington the year of their release. She might have been five or even six. She recognized the bridge from which Jimmy was going to jump into the swirling black waters, remembered Henry Travers as the bumbling Angel Clarence who came to save him, found familiar the notion that an angel gets his wings every time a bell rings, though she thought perhaps she had thought it was his halo. She did not remember the plot, the series of flashbacks showing how Jimmy had been trapped into small-town domesticity by his own benevolence, or the fantasies where Angel Clarence showed him how life would have been for the town had he not lived. She remembered Lionel Barrymore as the oily exploiter, but did not remember Jimmy Stewart shouting at his kids and throwing a newel post. She didn't remember the drunk scene in the bar but she did remember the scene of salvation, the whole town crowding into the living room, showering coins and bills in a heap on the parlor table.

Soap opera at its purest, the fugleman of melodrama. By the time the bells rang for Clarence's wings she was blubbering into her bosom, wailing for the time she believed life ran along this plan, villains foiled and virtue exalted, guardian angels and the redeeming love of ordinary people. She chewed on the bead tassel and howled.

At this point Kevin appeared, hovered across the coffee table in his underpants. "Are you okay?"

"Sure," she sobbed, laughing. "I was just watching some soppy movie and let it get to me." But she bawled on, couldn't stop, was undone precisely by his solicitous frown. "Oh, well, and I guess I'm lonesome sometimes."

He came around to sit, gave her shoulder an awkward flat-handed pat. "For Daddy?"

"No, not for Daddy."

He accepted this, apparently, and reached to pat the farther shoulder. "I was lonesome today when you weren't there. Well, I was lonesome last night; I had a nightmare and wanted to come home, but I was afraid it would hurt Dad's feelings."

She was done crying now. "That was brave of you."

"I wanted to be brave."

"If you have a nightmare tonight, wake me."

"Dreams aren't real."

"Of course they are. What else would they be? Remember when you used to be afraid of vampires? I thought we cleared that up. Vampires aren't real, but the fear of vampires is as real as the nose on your face. We closed the windows to keep out the fear, not the vampires."

"Right; I remember."

"If you have a dream tonight, wake me; we'll chase it out."

"Okay. I won't."

"But if you do."

He went back to bed and she gave him time to sleep, letting the late news offer its antidote to *It's a Wonderful Life*. Here were the friends and families of '79: Mr. Randall Dallas Mayo shot by his drunk buddy Willie F. Vause, with rifle fire that "tore through his body from one shoulder to the other." In Greenville a Martin Morgan—who had been "nervous" ever since, eleven years ago, he'd accidentally put a torch to the gas tank of his car—blasted his wife eleven times with a twenty-two, then blew her face off and killed himself, orphaning three. The brother Curtis Morgan, interviewed, said, "He did tell us he needed some kind of help. He just wanted to talk to some-body."

She cracked the door of Kevin's room to make sure that he was sleeping, then went to lock up in back. At the kitchen door she was startled by a swing of headlights in the drive. She clutched the knob and checked the lock. The headlights died. She killed the kitchen bulb and peeked through the curtain, heart like a jackhammer. At the back of his pickup, Eugene Keyes struggled the Zenith backwards off the truck bed. He hugged it, staggering, toward her door. She turned on the light and opened up.

"You're crazy."

She made way for him to lug it, reeling like a drunk, into the rec room, where he set it in the middle of the floor.

"It's fantastic'ly heavy. That's no veneer, it's hardwood to the core."

"You're out of your mind."

"See, what I got to thinking, if I sliced the front panel off and hinged it back on with a magnetic catch, it'd make an ideal cupboard for storing fabric."

"Did you go all the way back to Tifton?"

"That scalper."

"And paid forty dollars for it?"

"Well, he was closing when I called, and there wasn't no way he was going to keep open for any less."

"It's robbery."

"They don't make them like that no more."

They faced each other over the radio. There was a period of dead air.

"Are you," Shaara asked cautiously, "trying to buy me for forty dollars' worth of Fibber McGee?"

"No, ma'am."

"Sold," she said.

He took off his cap and twisted it like Bud Rufus. "No, I'm not asking to spend the night."

She turned and crossed three paces. "Why not?"

He turned the cap. "I figured to bring you the radio."

She wasn't having that. She sighed elaborately and folded her arms fishwife.

"Because," he said, "if I bite I'll run with the line. All's you'd have to do is hang in there till I exhausted myself and then reel me in. Gut and filet me, fry me."

"That's not especially flattering."

"I'm sorry. All I mean is I might be over my head."

"You can swim."

He set the cap on the radio and took a breath. "I mean, I might fall in love with you."

"I know what you mean," she said. "But then you're already in love with me."

"That's a problem," he agreed.

She crossed into the open bedroom, to the far side of the bed, unknotted the rope of blue beads and let it slither into her palm. She ran her zipper down and shed her caftan. Gene followed as far as the dresser and pulled his T-shirt over his head.

"Put your clothes in the closet," she said. "Kevin might have a nightmare, and if he wakes you've got to be prepared to hide in there. It's a house rule. Your dignity notwithstanding."

"Okay."

They slipped in under the comforter on opposite sides of the bed and lay for a second separate before he reached across to follow her hairline with an index finger, lay it lightly on her collarbone.

She hadn't given it much thought, but without thinking she had supposed he might make trucker-love, quick and bruising. He made love in no more hurry than he made a solid join. He probed the curl of her ear, tasted her nostrils, pressed a tongue at the inside corner of her eye before he even reached against the length of her. For a while she lay still, afraid to provoke him beyond this caution. But when the while was up, she stroked him too, the wing blade she had watched across the shop, the whorl of hairs around his navel.

"Harriet," he said, touching her, "had small breasts." And for some reason this observation, neutrally made, was a gift of enormous intimacy. A phrase of Yeats's flowed into her mind: "A loosening in the thighs . . ." And she parted her thighs, but somewhere else, somewhere in the open space inside, something more delicate than a dogwood bloomed.

16. Private Parts

Sandro Tesoro was a spectacular lover. He could probably have taken the world title for sexual longevity, if there were women enough to attest to the miracle, which no doubt there were. They made love in New York, Rome, Florence, and Rome again. He liked to lean over her propped on his hands, lids lowered but in fact slit to watch her writhe. She writhed accordingly. He liked to make her come and then, still in her and over her at one hard arm's length, reach for a cigarette, smoke it while she recovered whimperingly, and begin again.

You had to admire him. She admired him afterwards, alone in the shower, making herself come again with the soapy cloth. Once he explained to her that he had had total control over his cock since the age of fourteen. He could raise or lower it at will. (Like the flag?) Wendy heard him say this, and nodded, and admired; wondering incredulously if he could believe it made him more valuable. She fantasized about it. If she should tell him that it immeasureably chilled her, if she should explain to him that it was the most insulting thing she'd ever heard, would he believe her? Would he be crushed? If she told him: oh, I can lubricate at will—would he get the point?

She also fantasized being raped, by someone of greater penal proportions than Boyd but by someone who desired her in the extravagant desire of Boyd. She fantasized being raped by Boyd, and understood that a fantasy of rape was not masochistic, it was a fantasy of power. In the fantasy Boyd was driven beyond control by her desirability. He was mindless, obsessed. She was his obsession. She felt driven and warm, frightened and comforted.

She also understood clearly for the first time that Boyd was not a father figure to her. Sandro Tesoro, who was also old enough to be her father but *also* old enough to be a matinee idol, the Mastroianni of the Skies, bestowed an orgasm on her as a father might bestow money. Boyd, on the other hand, lost himself; Boyd making love was a lost man, needy, lovable.

Once when they showered together Sandro confided to her that, of course, women stink. He said this affectionately; it was a confidence. Wendy's flesh rose in goose bumps between the sprays.

"You're cold," he said solicitously.

Wendy said, "Ah."

Apart from his prowess, she liked him a lot. He was an enthusiastic shopper, a buoyant tourist, a gourmet, and so skilled a wine connoisseur that he knew more than he felt compelled to say about it. They ate wonderfully, then walked it off. He chose her hat—though in fact the one he chose precisely matched her image of it, a desert tan felt, moderate of crown but *slightly* extravagant of brim, so that it dipped Bacall-like over her left eye. He paid a hundred and fifteen dollars for it without blinking, and two hundred for a suitcase at Saks, leather-edged and understated in the same tan.

When she got home that first Saturday afternoon she found that the utilities had indeed been cut, and the fridge was soggy-rotten. She cleaned it up and propped it open, but although by Monday she had a thousand dollars in a new account, she disdained to pay the bill. Let them keep their juice; she'd listen to the radio by candlelight.

By the time they got to Rome Wednesday they were as familiar with each other as a married couple—or rather, except for bed, familiar as brother and sister. He took her to the Trevi Fountain and they tossed a dozen Susan B. Anthony silver dollars in. He paid for two hotels but they slept in one. The next morning he was off to Florence—they agreed they should gather evidence of separate itineraries—and she had two days of Rome on her own.

She liked this even better.

She did the standard things, the Forum, Coliseum, Pantheon, Vatican and St. Peter's Basilica; liked them all, liked the hot smell of centuries rising off the stones, was suitably imaginative about togas, scrolls, and ancient plots. Better than that she liked the wild cats stalking the Coliseum, better than that the tourists themselves, some straining after ecstasy in the Sistine Chapel, some sidestepping dog shit in the streets and clearly wishing they were back home in Tokyo or Liverpool or Chattanooga.

Best of all she enjoyed herself. She had in the extreme the disembodied sense that travel always gave her, that as long as she was on the move she was beating time, need never grow up, or be fixed, or give in to age. She could shop for personalities as easily as boots, strike an attitude without a past and have it taken for her own: hauteur, waiflike timidity or hip offhandedness—just looking, thanks. She changed her clothes a lot (it was hot, and otherwise what was the point of bringing them?) and found that her observations altered with them. The first morning, for instance, she put on designer jeans and a tie-dyed tunic, the long chiffon scarf bound theatrically around her hair, and near the Coliseum she saw a German smother his baby in a *trattoria*.

No, he didn't smother the baby, and maybe he wasn't even German—too lean, maybe, suck-cheeked lean with a hooknose hollow at the bridge, a little scrub grass of blond beard.

He was very unhappy. He sat in front of an empty *cappuccino* cup and a glass of milk, and his single purpose, a kind of inert drive, was to let the baby sleep. The baby was certainly Teutonic-fat, his face pocked with mosquito bites, his chin rolls damp. The father had his hand over the baby's eyes, shielding them so that the baby would sleep. But it was a hand like a cricket bat, like a side of pork. She had seen spatulate fingers before—Boyd had them—but the supposed *tedesco*'s fingers were not spatulate, not flat, but fat on a body otherwise entirely lean, each one a puffed knockwurst of a finger, wet and heavy, so that, Wendy thought, if they were on *my* face, I would smother before I slept.

The baby waked, cried, fretted, stuck his fist in the milk and laughed. Wendy reached across and offered a foil-wrapped mint, which the father took gingerly between his enormous thumb and index finger and passed to the baby. She grinned at him, girlish, and he smiled unhappily back.

Whereas in the afternoon it threatened rain, so she put on her Bogart trench coat and Bacall hat, very high heels, and let the scarf trail elegantly. She walked to Ferragamo on the Via Condotti and asked with Bostonian grace to try on the gold-trimmed doeskin boots in the center window. She assumed that if she assumed the clerk spoke English, it would indicate she was used to superior service. And this was apparently the case. The small man, bald, and dapper in 'thirties lapels, brought her not only the doeskin boots in three different widths, but four other pair as well, and half a dozen "coordinated" handbags.

"Madame has a vairy high arch," he would observe, and she, "Do you think the narrower heel will be in this year?" and he, "Of course the doeskin should fit more snugly as it will geeve more than the suede," and she, "Which tone do you think is the more adaptable?" At the end of forty-five minutes she bought the pair she'd tried on first, and which she'd picked out the night before, but having convinced him that he'd convinced her to do so, so that they were perfectly charmed with each other and performed a pantomime of good-byes like old Polo or Yacht Club friends.

In the evening she put on a drape-necked black Quiana gown and went to see *La Traviata* performed in the ruins of Terme de Caracalla. She carried a lace shawl and a black satin clutch bag, and (though it was the nether end of twilight when she arrived) wore large tinted glasses. She threaded down the stone steps with an arrogant sway; a teenage girl with a Brooklyn accent whispered, "Look. That must be somebody."

She collected theater and museum tickets, postcards of the more elegant interiors, paid twenty-five dollars for a leather address book in a chic shop so she could put it on her customs declaration. Friday afternoon she took the train to Florence and added the playbill of Pirandello's *Henry IV* to her batch. This one was in a little experimental theater off the Piazza del Duomo, so she went as a student: the jeans and a T-shirt and the trench coat hanging carelessly open. Boyd had produced this play last year on Cape Cod, so it was a double pleasure to her—that she could follow the action, and that it was not nearly so good as his. Afterwards she walked the narrow unlit streets back to the hotel, alert to doorways and alleys, her hand on the button of the Chantilly. But nothing happened.

Sandro met her at the hotel, approved her evidence of wealth and culture, made love to her, and asked if she would like to meet his family next day.

But she had had a taste of making her own way in a foreign country, and wanted to perfect her palate. "It's wiser not, you know," she regretted, raising an eyebrow.

"I suppose."

So she did the Uffizi, the Duomo, and the Ponte Vecchio, bought more postcards, a whole Genoa salami, a wallet for Boyd and a medieval dagger for Kevin, then on impulse an absurdly expensive *commedia* mask, thirty-five dollars though it was only papier-mâché. But it was handsomely formed, the hooknosed hauteur of the Venetian merchant, glazed in bronze and marbled in metallic blues. By four she was back on the train for Rome, by nine at dinner with Sandro, who had the jewelry in a plastic bookstore bag. At her hotel he spread it on the bed and she got out her old velvet jewelry box, which she had brought along for the purpose.

It was rather disappointing stuff, excessively valuable no doubt, but clunky and ostentatious, not a piece in the lot she would have chosen for herself. There was a filigree collar with a pendant amethyst the size of a duck's egg, a bracelet shaped like a polyglass tire with diamonds stuck in the treads. Oh, well, Sandro's forebears probably had more body than she on which to support such weights. She chose a smaller emerald bracelet to wear on the plane, and, the only thing she liked at all, a pendant watch with seed pearls both on and around the face, hung on a gold chain with a pearl clasp.

"Does it work?"

"So far as I know. Try it. Why?"

"If it works, it makes more sense that I should be wearing it."

He admired her methodical intrigue.

She stuck a pair of diamond earrings in her makeup kit, put the rest in the jewel box and stuck this at the bottom of her shoulder bag.

"There's not a chance they'll check it," Sandro said. "But if by any fluke they should, be astonished but *very* polite. Don't get defensive whatever you do. Give them the Boston address and say you'll get any sort of proof they want, that of *course* it's yours but you know they're just doing their job."

"I know what to do."

He returned to his hotel at four A.M., and at six she bathed, doused herself in duty-free Femme, donned her eggshell linen traveling dress, her trench coat, hat and scarf. The watch didn't work after all, but she wore it anyway. On the plane she was perfectly charming, though a tiny bit demanding, with the hostesses, who shelved her hat for her, brought her *Vogues* and dry martinis and several cups of coffee. "It must be such interesting work," she murmured to one of them, who smiled dryly. She watched the first-class film, *Silent Partner*, so well into her role that she was neither too amused by Eliott Gould nor too upset by the beheading of his girl friend. Altogether the passions involved in it seem a little excessive to be occasioned by a mere forty-eight thousand Canadian dollars.

She filled out her customs declaration and neatly stacked her receipts. Although the boots had cost a hundred and fifty, she was still sixty dollars short of the three hundred dollar allowance, and this worried her; it seemed out of character. She remembered that she'd paid twenty dollars for the salami, so although she had no receipt for it, she added that. Then she rang for the hostess again and bought another bottle of perfume, a fifth of Courvoisier, and a carton of Dunhills. What she'd do with the cigarettes she didn't know—Sandro smoked Gitanes—but this brought her declaration up to $294.56. Excellent.

They were through Passport Control and into the New York customs shed by noon Eastern Standard time, though it was now six P.M. for her, and she'd had only two hours' sleep. There were three flights ahead of theirs for clearance. The travelers stood in ragged lines, kicking their luggage before them, fed up and burdened, babies and children wailing at the wait while the adults went in for more sophisticated bitching. The air conditioning was set at 78 as per the Carter rule for government buildings; the actual temperature was near 90. The fluorescent light bounced off the walls like handballs. Here and there a temper exploded in the words "red tape," "bureaucracy" and "snafu." Optimists answered with reminders of the DC-10, and that at least they were safe on the ground. She saw Sandro pass with the rest of the crew through the Nothing-to-Declare line. Somebody said there'd been a full-scale hurricane in Jamaica last night, leaving thirty-two dead and hundreds of millions of dollars' worth of damage, and that this had probably messed up the landing schedules. Somebody else pointed out that the schedules couldn't be messed up by planes that *didn't* arrive. Wendy was next. Her shoulders ached from the long sit and the weight of her bag. She tried to roll them with finesse.

"I swear, man, I think everything sucks," whined a voice behind her. She glanced discreetly back. Two teenagers—two *children*—in Air Force blues were shifting their duffle bags from one hand to the other.

"My dad got cancer, my girl died."

"What happened?"

"My girl died."

"What happened?"

"Three weeks before I shipped out she borrowed a car and got creamed. Elvis Presley died, Bing Crosby died. My dad smoked one too many cigarettes and he died. John Wayne died, and now I'm stuck in this fucking airport."

Wendy felt the giggles rise. The couple ahead of her swung their X-chalked bags off the counter and the customs man said, "Nee-ext."

She choked the giggles down under what felt distinctly like a smirk, lifted her suitcase onto the counter and handed her declaration form across, lowering her head to shadow her face. She cleared her throat.

The customs official had puffy eyes like steamed clams, as if he hadn't slept last night either. He stood with the chalk raised above his shoulder, ready to swoop it down on the bag, while he squinted down her list, moving his fat face back and forth, rather than his eyes. Wendy tried to compose her mouth and tilted her head back to the Boston angle.

"Whussis," he said. He seemed bored. (Boredom, she had learned in sophomore Psych, is always submerged anger.) The clams closed and slit open again; he shoved the list across, jabbing at it toward the bottom.

"Whussis?"

The shoulder bag swung phenomenally heavy as she leaned across to see what he meant.

"Oh, that? A salami. A Genoa salami, you know. It's the best sort anywhere in the world, except possibly the Ardennes."

He sighed. Bored. "You'll have to open up."

She had to set the shoulder bag on the counter and dig in it to find the key, which was in her makeup kit with the diamond earrings. She found it, did up the clasp of the kit, zipped the handbag, undid the lock on the suitcase and unzipped that. She was careful not to hurry, although the man stood with his thumbs hooked in his belt while she accomplished all this, kneading the chalk against a palm impatiently.

He lifted the lid back, and she was reassured to see that the case contained no surprises, no stacks of newly minted bills, no machine-gun parts; just her black Quiana dress on top, the boots arranged around the corners, a stack of postcards and playbills balanced by the brown wrapping of the foot-long salami. He lifted it out.

"*A'm* sorry, ma'am," (he wasn't), "the Yew-Ess Customs regyalations forbid the importation of enny meat or dairy producks. I'll have to confiscate this."

Wendy was aghast. "But it's salami."

"Yes, ma'am, a meat produck." He unwrapped it and held it up by the string as if in proof.

"Well, it's meat but it's, you know, *cured.*" Her "cured" was a little shrill. A taller official down the counter looked up and came over to them.

"What's the trouble?"

"A salami," Wendy appealed to him. "Salami was invented to make meat keep. I mean, it kills the germs, so you don't have to keep it in the fridge—you know, for hot countries."

"Yes'm." The taller official, though more polite, stood ready to support his colleague. "But you can't bring in meat products. It's a case of animal diseases."

"I know, but that's the *point*. It's cured just so it can't have any hoof-and-mouth or anything. Look; it's got a government seal!"

"I'm only doon my job, ma'am," said clam eyes. They faced each other loggerheads, Wendy and the Abbott-and-Costello team across the counter. The child hero in the Air Force blues said, "Man, that sucks. You can't take her salami." Wendy was dumbfounded at the notion that they might let her slip something like a hundred thousand dollars' worth of hot rocks into the country and confiscate her lunch meat. The incompetence!

"But you c'n buy Italian salami at any deli in Man*hat*tan."

"But it's da law."

"The law's *crazy*," Wendy wailed.

"I can't help that, ma'am. It's my dooty to confiscate this meat produck."

The Air Force said, "It sucks," but Wendy gave it up. She

didn't have a prayer of getting away with it. She zipped her suitcase and the official X'ed it with the chalk. She fumbled with her shoulder strap and heaved the suitcase off the counter.

But she had high stadards for men in uniform. At the gate she turned back and tossed her brim bitterly. "Enjoy your lunch!" she called.

Just beyond the barrier, Sandro Tesoro was leaning against a pillar reading a Sunday *Times*. It shook in his hands like high winds off Jamaica.

17. *Father's Day*

Sunday the seventeenth, dawn came rosy-fingered over the Campus Side Bar and Grill. It was going to be a scorcher. Having sat looking into the dark, he closed the drapes on sunrise. He breakfasted as soon as the grill opened, and dawdled over the Sunday papers, but all the oil-crunch, hurricane and summit news was stale because he'd seen it on TV the night before. The only thing to hold his interest was a psychological profile of Theodore Bundy, whose "command of legal language" and "ingratiating manner," coupled with the viciousness of the thirty-six murders of which he was still legally innocent, offered a direct parallel to the Mother Superior, her biblical phrasing and deceptive empathy. He tore the article out to save for Wyman, wandered back to his room and took his shoes off. It wasn't yet eight o'clock. He usually didn't call Wendy till late afternoon; Kevin probably wouldn't be up for hours. He tried TV but there was nothing on except Baptist brimstone and gospel crooners—till he flipped over to the university PBS station and found them oddly doing a Sunday morning rerun of the Cavett interviews with Hepburn. He'd already seen them, but he watched.

"The whole warld is petrified," she said cheerfully, nodding to her Parkinson's disease. "Anni-bahdy who's intelligent is afred to do anni-thing."

Kevin had had some project with his iguana cage Saturday, and Boyd had spent most of the afternoon in the college library looking for the Richard Wilbur poem about the dog. It was yeoman's work because he didn't remember the name of it or which volume he'd seen it in, and Magoor's scanty Wilbur collection was scattered among the Dewey decimals on the third floor, the humanities collection on the second, and the undergraduate stacks in the annex. The catalogue listed seven of the possible dozen books in one or another of these places, but when he got there most of them were either out, stolen or otherwise AWOL. After an hour he was disgusted but after two he was compulsive, the way he sometimes got about achieving the right timing or gesture onstage. He pestered the delicious belle at the front desk (he should send Gunilla over to see what librarians really look like these days) until she turned up a pile of modern anthologies for him to leaf through. He took them into a carrel and pored over the indexes for another hour before he decided the poem he remembered might answer to the name of "The Pardon."

> My dog lay dead five days without a grave
> In the thick of summer, hid in a clump of pine
> And a jungle of grass and honeysuckle vine . . .

Purse-mouth triumphant, the way he sometimes was when he finally got the timing right, he copied the poem out on his directing pad, his boxy script splaying across the page from one edge to the other.

> I who had loved him while he kept alive
>
> Went only close enough to where he was
> To sniff the heavy honeysuckle-smell
> Twined with another odor heavier still
> And hear the flies' intolerable buzz.

He spoke the lines as he wrote, practised the controlled drone inherent in them, applauded Wilbur for that impeccable restraint, like an actor whose emotion is nine-tenths contained, the tension between passion and craft.

> Well, I was ten and very much afraid.
> In my kind world the dead were out of range . . .

* * *

He was back at the motel before he realized that the poem
would no more serve its purpose than *The Last House on Dead
End Street*. It was no poem for a child. There was pardon and
redemption in it, yes, but intellectually achieved, whereas all
the force of the images went into the maggoty corpse, the
dream where the dog came:

> In the carnal sun, clothed in a hymn of flies,
> And death was breeding in his lively eyes.

He hoped Kevin would not remember he had mentioned
it. He tore the page off his pad and crumpled it into the wastebasket. But this was no use, to him. He'd always been a quick
study; by the end of a run he could recite any play he'd directed
from first to last. He always jumped the prompter by two beats.

Now he had the poem by heart, or it had him by the balls,
or something. It droned through his head over dinner and
louder than TV, stuck itself between the lines of Flannery
O'Connor's letters when he tried to read.

> I started in to cry and call his name,
>
> Asking forgiveness of the tongueless head.
> . . . I dreamt the past was never past redeeming:
> But whether this was false or honest dreaming
> I beg death's pardon now. And mourn the dead.

He didn't dream because he didn't sleep. Or rather, he slept
but in such wary sleep that he must have waked every time
his mind warned him that he might dream. He gave it up about
five and sat in the dark looking over the still pool, seeing the
strongbox at the back of the closet, the Rexall notebooks in it,
the cramped pages after pages recording, exploring, inter-
preting, scratching away at his father's nightmares. He had a
powerful desire to call Wendy, wake her, make her go look in
the closet and make sure the strongbox was still there; and the
asininity of this desire alarmed him more than anything. She
would think he was crazy. He thought so too.

Now at nine A.M. he mixed a drink—he didn't mix it, but
poured it straight over a scoop of ice—and tried to defuse his
mood by reciting the poem in Hepburn's lilt:

* * *

"Ah *draint* the *pahst* was *nevah pahst* redaiming:
Baht *whethah this* was *false* ah *awnist draim*ing . . ."

Luckily, though, he wasn't drunk by nine-thirty, when he
had an amazing phone call, from Shaara.

"Good morning. Happy Father's Day."

"Oh?"

"Yes. Didn't you know it was Father's Day?"

"No." He composed himself toward her hearty voice. "I only
read the bad news."

"Well, it is, and Kevin and I have an idea. I don't need the
car today, so why don't I fix you two a picnic and drive over
to pick you up. You can drop me back here and take a look at
the new iguana cage, which he's dying for you to see, and then
you can take off for the lake . . ."

She chattered on, chirpy and chummy, offering olives and
beer, full of goodwill. Or full of shit? She sounded real enough,
the way he remembered her holiday enthusiasm in the good
times. Wonders, said Sister Angela among others, never cease.
I dreamt the past was never past redeeming.

"How soon should I be ready?"

"Whenever. Now, if you like."

And she was there in fifteen minutes, flushed and shining
in cutoffs and one of her everlasting Madras shirts, spilling
high spirits all over the dashboard.

"I thought Father's Day you ought to be able to get off
together."

"I was thinking of renting a car once the check comes through,"
he offered, edging to meet her at conciliation.

"Those stinking checks. Is everybody in the cast all right? I
mean, I know they're livid, but are they all right?"

"We're all living off American Express, all except Wyman
and Barnard, and I guess their landlady's used to late rent.
It's rotten for morale, though."

"I'll bet."

"I think we should charge interest."

"I think you should."

Kevin had a load of blankets, baskets, balls and rafts heaped
on the front porch, and fairly leaped with enthusiasm as he
led Boyd back to his room. One whole end of it, wall to wall,
was taken up by the new cage, split-level slats with a climbing

frame made of thick Tarzan vines. These led to a mezzanine where the dirty cast provided an extra perch. Kevin had got his mother's magpie genes, all right. Bette Davis liked the cast. She straddled it, tucking her scaly toes around the edge, the soft spines along her back waving gently like tentacles. The dewlap quivered on her Godzilla face, the membrane over her eyes slid up and down. On the whole, Boyd thought a *dog* a good pet for a boy. But he admired.

"How'd you get it in here?"

"That's the great part. You just undo these wing nuts and the whole thing collapses flat so you can move it anywhere."

"Not that we're going to move," Shaara said.

"That was Gene's idea. You know, the carpenter?"

"I know. The redneck with the accent sired by Atlanta out of C.B. radio."

This fell palpably flat. Kevin laughed uncertainly and Shaara performed a quick moue. Boyd said, "He's a great carpenter, you can learn a lot from him," but Shaara had turned on her heel and gone out, to the kitchen apparently; he heard her banging around. They followed.

"Well, you'd better get going if you're going to catch a real sunburn." Her brightness had an edge now. He wondered briefly if there could be something up between Shaara and the carpenter, then dismissed it. Shaara always had intellectual taste in men, and was more likely just defensive about living down here in the sticks. She'd wanted so bad to get out of Iowa and into the big time that it was probably rough on her to have ended up in Hubbard, Georgia. Whereas he would have dumped New York in a minute for someplace you could afford to leave your door unlocked and walk safe down an unlit road.

He still loved her, her rusty hair and her loose way of standing. (She stood stiff now.) He still loved every woman he'd ever loved, and couldn't understand the kind of mind that wanted to cut things off completely. He'd no desire to live with her anymore, god knows, or even to bed her, but he'd have liked to tell her at least that he thought she and the South were fine. New York and Boston were rotting; cultural dry rot, cerebral termites. Stick close to Atlanta and the big time will come to you, he wanted to tell her. But she was standing stiff and shooing them.

"Stay as long as you like."

They loaded the car and took off. Boyd hadn't handled a stick shift in years, and made the car lurch until he got the hang of it, while Kevin jeered.

"Where do you want to go?" Boyd asked.

"Let's go out to Lake Takullah. Maybe Barnard's there and we can use their dock."

This would not have been his choice. He'd have liked the day alone with Kevin, and a day off from Wyman's furor toward the bursar, Barnard's dollybird routines. However, half the point of Father's Day is being a model father, isn't it?

And it worked out well, because Wyman and Barnard weren't home. The public side of the lake was chock a block with families and college kids, but they felt free to use the private dock in front of the crumbling clapboard house, from which they could launch the floats, paddle across to the public sunning raft and back again.

They spent, on the whole, a pleasant day. Oh, not that he ever entirely shook off either the strongbox or the poet's dog, but he kept them at bay. Kevin seemed scarcely to surface long enough for a breath in the whole six hours. Boyd lay on the dock till the sweat ran off his chest, then slipped into the cypress-stained water and swam figure eights through the cypress knees. *To sniff the heavy honeysuckle-smell.* He drank beer and nibbled at Shaara's fig cake—made, she had boasted before her mood soured, from the tree in their own backyard. Kevin accepted half a salami sandwich over the edge of the dock, treaded water to eat it, and then took off for the pontoon platform again, maybe a hundred yards away. He did it underwater on just two breaths.

Boyd dozed a little, didn't dream, though when he waked with the gently lapping water stretching away across his line of vision, his father's handwriting danced on the lit crests.

. . . it was the same scene,
But now it glowed a fierce and mortal green.

Professor James Soole, Anthropology, was forty in 1955 when the notebooks began. Boyd had been sixteen. He was forty-four in 1959 when they stopped. Boyd had been twenty. Boyd was forty now. For four years almost daily James Soole had recorded his nocturnal terrors and his diurnal sense that his life was a vacuum, his youthful dreams blasted, his ambitions past retrieving. What the ambitions had been or why he should feel this he never said. There was scarcely a reference to the life he led either at home or in class, no confessionals, no guilty secrets, no remarkable failures. Nor was there any reference to taking his life outside of the one passage, "It won't be a plan or even a conscious decision . . ."

Instead, bloodlessly, he noted the contents of the dreams. "Corridor w/ two Orc-like creatures. I growing hair from palms of hands. Class bell signal for them to advance. G. Jensen appears, I warn her back, realize she is with them. Know hands are useless because of hair." Then a Freudian analysis of this dream. Then a Jungian. Then a comparison of the two interpretations. Then a critique and rejection of Freud's wish-fulfillment rule. Then a comparison with former dreams. The Orc one would be referred back to later, so that the whole project knitted in on itself and added up to an intricate pattern, something out of nothing, a mythic system with no reference point, pointless, leading nowhere but to a cloverleaf on the L.A. freeway. *I started in to cry and call his name.*

In the whole stack of notepads Boyd was mentioned only twice, when he'd appeared in relatively minor roles in his father's nightmares.

He lifted himself on an elbow and checked idly across the water for Kevin, but couldn't immediately spot him. On the sunning deck there were only three college kids, a youth with his hand on his hip, cock-foremost for two girls in bikinis who gestured from the wrist as if being teased. All the heads he saw in the water were either dark or too small or too long-haired. His stomach started its slow twist of fear, but he stilled it. Probably Kevin had gone on to the public beach. He reached for his glasses and put them on, scanning the brown surface.

It took him with a jolt that the youth on the raft *was* Kevin. The lanky figure shook the water from his hair, flipped it back off his forehead with an arrogant hand, then flicked one of the girls backhanded on the thigh while she squealed and jumped out of the way. Kevin tossed them a wave and dived, a clean Olympic jackknife, then breaststroked slowly toward Boyd, showing a lot of shoulder muscle.

But halfway to the dock he disappeared again, and when he came up he was bobbing and crowing, "Lemme have a piece of that cake. I'm starved."

Boyd watched this transformation three or four times. On the raft Kevin hung his weight on one hip and flicked at the boards with a foot, cool. At the dock he flopped or squatted, bounced ass-first into the water and shot out again, a kid. It was as if his voice was cracking through his whole frame. Bemused, Boyd followed him out to the deck to see which was the presiding genius in this conflict, himself or the girls. But Kevin was too clever for him. As long as Boyd was on the raft, he lay back sunning, legs straight out before him and hands under his neck, a position of no particular time of life. Boyd sat up and grinned at him, loving him, amused. "How soon do you want to go?" And saw that, the way Kevin lay, the sucked hollow of his diaphragm threw into relief a long bulge under his tight orange trunks. His son had a hard-on. Last summer that penis had been a pencil stub. There were curly bronze hairs in the armpits, too. Boyd wanted to reach over and hug him, which, under the circumstances, was not appropriate. What was appropriate was to go back to the dock and leave him to the giggling girls, which he did, stroking slowly against the water and against his will. He pulled out and ate another sandwich, had another beer. Elated and abandoned, he lay wanting Wendy until he was hard himself, the poem lapping irrelevantly through his mind with the rhythm of the water against the dock:

I who had loved him while he kept alive

Went only close enough to where he was
To sniff the heavy honeysuckle-smell
Twined with another odor heavier still . . .

When Kevin surfaced for the last time, he had a phone number written across his thigh in ballpoint pen. Boyd pretended not to notice. He drove back, skillful with the clutch by now, to Shaara's house. Her mood seemed to be in good repair again, and she asked him in for a drink. But he was tired and stinging-taut with sunburn, and wanted to call Wendy, so he turned her down.

At the motel he realized this was a mistake. Wendy was out, and while he sat letting the phone ring ten times, fifteen times against his ear, the weight of last night settled in on him again. He sat with his pipe looking out over the mirrored pool. The emptiness of the room, which he liked, was peopled now only with the images that intruded on it, television and dreams, poem and strongbox and the news. He had the drink, called again, had another, called again. After the third try he found himself in the motel closet, pushing back the clothes to check the corner, as if he would find the strongbox there. This startled him. By the time Wendy answered he was clutching the receiver, halos of moisture around each fingertip.

"Where were you? I've been trying to get you since five o'clock."

"Oh, *I'm* sorry. I was out shopping."

"On Sunday?"

There was a short pause.

"Well, I took it into my head that I wanted some Genoa salami, I've been out and around for hours. You ought to be able to pick up a Genoa salami, even on a Sunday. But I've come home without any."

Boyd laughed and tears stung around his sunburned lids. Genoa salami. Wendy Soole. Salami and normality and a permanent address. "You're a kook. What else have you been up to?"

"Not very much. Sightseeing and shopping mostly. I got a pair of terrific Italian boots, doeskin with a little gold bar around the heel. I'm gorgeous."

"I'll bet. Listen, baby, you'd better cool it with the Master-Charge, though. I'm putting everything on American Express, and that fucking check probably won't be through for another week."

There was a longer pause, so that at first he thought she resented the admonishment. Then he caught on. "Your mother's been sending you money, hasn't she?"

Wendy sighed. "She *likes* to, Boyd."

"I don't care. Let her buy you a whole closetful of boots. Only don't ask her for the rent."

"Boyd! That's the last thing I'd do!"

"Are you okay?"

"I'm great, I'm fine. What are you up to?"

"Oh, Kevin and I have been out in a cypress swamp getting a roaring sunburn all afternoon. Shaara lent me the car, special dispensation for Father's Day."

"Is it Father's Day?!" she wailed. "Oh, Boyd, I didn't even notice, I was running around so much."

"I don't know why you should notice. I'm not *your* father."

"I *know* that." She gave a throaty chuckle, seductive, and a sucking sound. "As a matter of fact, I've been thinking specifically about that, how you're not my father. God, if I had you in bed right now I could show you how well I know who you are."

The hard-on leaped to life. The sunburn flamed along his thighs. It was *not* like Wendy Soole to talk sweet-and-dirty in earshot of Ma Bell.

"Hey," he said. "Don't do that to me, baby. I miss you enough as it is. It's too long down here. Jesus, I wish I had the cash to fly you down right now."

The pause was longer still, so that he said, "Wendy?" and she said, "Yeah, I'm here."

"Do *not* ask your mother."

"I won't. I wouldn't. But I wish I could come down."

And he should have left it at that. If he were a perfectly sane man who loved his son and missed his wife, he'd have told her how he thought of her on the dock while Kevin horsed with the nubile girls; he'd have said something sweet and dirty, and hung up for another week.

He said, "Would you do me a favor? There're some papers I need, in the strongbox at the back of the bedroom closet. Could you send it down?"

"The whole box? Couldn't I find what you need in it?"

"No, I've got the key here, and if you wait to get it, it'll be too late. UPS should take it. Is that a bore? Have you got money enough to send it?"

"Sure, I've got enough, but it seems like I could break it open."

"Just send the box. All right?"

"All right."

But the mood was gone. She'd closed up on him the way Shaara had this morning. He didn't blame her. He said goodbye, hung up, mixed himself another drink and turned on the evening news.

18. *Energy Crisis*

For Gunilla the days were long and hard to fill. Rehearsals ran six hours on weekdays and three on Saturday; she was needed for only about half of them, and for half of those she had nothing to do but lie limp and let Orme and Wyman carry her around. She was good at being a corpse and she worked at it, but it was purely technical work, controlling her breathing so as to make it invisible, resisting any impulse to help them by using a muscle, supporting herself at the post on a turned foot so that it looked as if the ropes took all her weight. Sometimes, propped there, consciously relaxing till the blood tingled in the tips of her fingers, she wanted to scream out with the boredom of it, the exhausting effort of doing nothing.

And after rehearsal there wasn't much more to do, in Hubbard, Georgia. She'd worked in a lot of provincial rep before, but it was the first time she'd been the only woman in the cast, and she missed the camaraderie. She'd thought at first that she might like the costume designer, but Shaara Soole had snubbed her and, wrapped up in her son and her home life, disappeared straight after fittings. Finally the locals took note of her presence, and Gunilla was asked to do a couple of local talks, one for a NOW group at so low a level of consciousness-raising that she had to stoop and tug; another for the Lady Lions, who struck her as the gutsier and brighter bunch, though their blued bouffants and pant suits discouraged her from pursuing any friendships there. She had lunch with the cast sometimes, and dinner once at Wyman and Barnard's house, but Wyman always dominated, and she despised Wyman.

She truly despised him, as perhaps it's natural for a Swede to despise an Irishman. He was loud and sloppy and did too much of everything, drinking, eating, reciting, confessing, boasting. Even at lunch he'd get fulsome drunk and rant Shakespeare at them as if this was supposed to make him *educated*. He told endless anecdotes of stage disasters and his supposed powers of ESP; interpreted their horoscopes for them and reminisced about all the celebrities he'd worked with—all of whom seemed to be "intelligent" and "warm" in direct proportion to their fame. Gunilla had worked with Olivier, Dreyfuss, Ullman and Newman, but she wasn't going to parade them for Wyman Path. He even boasted of his conquests with "gorgeous" women, though from the arrangement of the beds in the cottage and the way they fussed at each other in the kitchen, it was obvious that Wyman and Barnard were having an affair. Gunilla was a gay rights champion and had once neatly baited Anita Bryant on a talk show. Nevertheless, the idea of all that slouching mound of jowl and belly in bed with lovely Barnard made her stomach turn.

All of which she could have forgiven Wyman Path—or at least she could have dismissed him—if he had not been perfectly brilliant in his role. He did everything wrong and it turned out right. He did everything backwards—technique, device and contrivance before feeling—but when he got around to feeling it was there. He broke up, fluffed, dried, coached the others behind Boyd's back, distracted them onstage and exasperated them in the wings; but when a scene was worked out you could have tested a cardiograph against the way he made a heart race or stop. He was terrifying and saintly, towering when he raged, piteous when he wept.

The more she realized how good he was, the more she realized how little scope the part of the Senora offered her. She was duped in the first act and dead in the second. She had the paradox of innocence and hauteur to play, and that was it. She compensated in the only way she knew, the only way any good professional knows, by treating her inadequate role as if it were Medea, by taking it deadly seriously, perfecting it, exploring it for nuance, polishing the pace. The more expansive Wyman was, the more severe she became. The men wore muslin rehearsal skirts to get used to the feel of them, but Gunilla knew what a skirt felt like, and she dressed in shirts and trousers, her hair in a bun, in case anyone should mistake her for a silly starlet. She had convinced Boyd that the corpse would be much more horrible if she played it with her eyes open, and he'd agreed to let her try it. She was determined that by opening night she could do the whole twenty minutes without one visible blink.

It was grim work and, above all, there was not enough of it. Sometimes when they were rehearsing a scene in which she didn't appear, she'd find herself cut adrift at one o'clock in the afternoon, in either steaming heat or a thundershower, with the choice of a paperback or a third-rate department store. By the second week both of them had palled. She avoided going to films.

Luckily, her body took a lot of time. Often she spent the afternoon on it, working up a Yoga sweat on the carpet of her room on the top floor (which was called the eighteenth but was actually the seventeenth because the Sheraton Towers had no thirteenth). Then she soaked in Badedas for as long as two hours while she sanded her heels with a pumice stone, shoved back her cuticles with an oil-tipped stick, tweezed the blond hairs one by one from her upper thigh. She was a connoisseur of makeup offstage as well as on, and like a connoisseur of wine, knew which labels excelled in which areas, and when the *ordinaire* was better than the vintage. So she preferred Germaine Monteil on her lids but Revlon on her lashes, Erno Laszlo as foundation, Clinique for powder, Princess Marcella Borghese on her lips and Lauren behind her ears, but Cover Girl on her nails. She creamed herself with Pacquins to high gloss.

Then, too subtly and expensively bedizened to stay in, she took to spending her evenings in the student bars.

She stuck to lighted streets, drank very little, skirted the campus and kept as far as possible from The Campus Arts; though these precautions were prompted less by the memory of the incident in the movie theater than by innate discipline. Discipline she had, and when the seedy theater, its sickly smell or the man's breathing crossed her mind, she staunchly relegated them to their proper perspective: occupational hazard.

Summer term was in session from the second week of rehearsal, and her favorite place, a noisy beer hall in a converted railway station, was always full of earnest philosophers and pool-playing jocks, fresh-faced girls who were nevertheless too modest for jealousy. They ogled, but they included her. They asked her opinion of everything from the SALT agreement to "Mork and Mindy," and deferred to her without sycophancy. Though she wouldn't tell film star stories for Wyman, she let them draw her into show-and-tell: "What's Dreyfuss *really* like?"

Afterwards she'd let one or another of the youths walk her back to the hotel—they explained very solemnly about the rape statistics, and that there was a network of protection for women at night. Sometimes at the lobby door, with a wistful quickness she knew perfectly well to be effective, she would kiss her escort good night. She was never tempted to take one up. It was the company she wanted, perhaps the flattery, not sex. She admired the jogging fitness of them. Their anxious deference salved a sore ego. She may have been causing a few minor breakages of heart, but a little time would relegate *that* to a proper perspective, and in the meantime she could think of no less pernicious way of killing time.

By the fourth week of rehearsal Boyd had worked them through the whole play twice, once for movement and once for spine and shape. Now they were back in the first act taking everything apart again. She was grateful for the longer hours and for lines to say. All the same she felt frustrated and abandoned by Boyd, who gave her too little direction and seemed to squander his considerable talent on the men. Maybe he just couldn't handle women. Or maybe Wyman intimidated him; if so, she despised Wyman all the more.

Boyd was good. She'd played a hunch on that, a gut feeling, and on the surface she'd been proven right. Part of the proof was that he'd managed to assemble such a superior foursome for this provincial project. It was a play that couldn't afford one flaw in the cast. If it was "uneven" it would be a disaster. Boyd had picked without a flaw. Wyman was brilliant. Orme had a narrower range but that was right for the balance of the parts, an efficient and intelligent projection of menace. She of course was a *coup* for him. And Barnard he had caught at the passionate beginning of what could be a quick rise; they were all going to hear from Barnard Jones.

All the same, if he'd been a *really* good director, he'd have made them a happy cast as well as a fine one. Usually—always, in her experience—actors who admired each other's work got past any personality clashes to enjoy each other offstage as well, and the camaraderie fed back into the play so that they supported and fed and covered for each other. Here only Barnard, the novice among them, was trying for a coherent company. Orme remained a loner, Wyman was surly and bombastic, Gunilla felt cheated, and Boyd didn't seem to be able to do anything about it.

The casket scene was a case in point. It was *her* scene. The nuns asked nervously to have a look at the jewels with which they were all supposed to finance their escape, and the Senora, like Our Lady of the Gullible, bestowed a gift on each. Over the Mother Superior and Sister Angela's four little ejaculations (*"Marvelous!" "God, how they sparkle!" "They're like stars . . . like suns . . ." "A fortune!"*) Boyd spent half an hour. He talked about church art, ritual and the symbolism of relics, put Orme and Wyman in touch with a passion deeper than greed, coaxed out a rich, tense texture in which treasure and mysticism merged. He reminded them of the revolution outside; of how even here and now, surrounded by the collapse of society, by mayhem and madness, we look for salvation to the material objects we hardly know how to protect.

Her speech followed. She trailed her fingertips over the surface of the junk jewelry and looked forward to exploring the Senora's emotions in the same way.

Every one of those jewels is full of memories for me. . . . They stick to my skin, heavy with pictures of the past. Some of them are family heirlooms, others presents from my husband. Other pieces I bought for myself, out of vanity, boredom, the pleasure of spending money.

She raised her eyes to the ecstatic faces of the nuns.

Wait a minute!

She drew the chest to her and paused, fingers tentative and stroking over a plastic cameo and a green glass ring.

Let me see . . . yes, here they are. Take this, Reverend Mother, as a present. This cameo belonged to my husband's mother.

* * *

Gunilla intimately understood the Senora in this scene, and all she needed from Boyd was some help in externalizing what she understood. She knew what it was like to be a permanent exile, so thoroughly uprooted that even home was a foreign place. She understood how, to such exiles, portable objects become the only root, wandering and stretched and thin, but still connecting fibers and tubers to the self that elsewhere was. Why else did she carry the oval photo of a mother dead, the Saint Christopher medal given her by Aunt Eva but never worn since her middle teens, even the real sea sponges bought in Cannes and St. Tropez that were never used because the synthetics gave a finer patina with the pancake? Her skin was too delicate for greasepaint; nevertheless she carried all over the world a half-dozen sticks of it given her by Carl Lundh on the occasion of her professional debut. Nothing she owned was as precious as the Senora's jewels; her father had been both stingy and moralistic about such things, and she herself despised ostentation. But the principle was the same. She understood that to give something from a former life was to part with a piece of self, and that when the Senora bestowed her jewels on the sisters, she was performing an act of faith more intimate than religion. She even understood the danger of receiving, and that sometimes to accept a gift was a greater risk of commitment than to give one, a nearer terror than locking bodies. She knew all this; she knew it was what she had to play, and she waited for Boyd to draw it out of her and let it reverberate in the simple lines.

Boyd only murmured, "Good," and let them carry on into the nuns' acceptance speeches. So thrown was she by this lack of attention to a crucial moment, that she missed her next cue and they had to back up through Orme and Wyman's lines again. Wyman clucked annoyance, under his breath but loud enough for everyone to hear. Gunilla gritted down her fury and turned to Barnard with a seraphic generosity born of pure self-discipline.

As for you, little sister, I should like you to wear this cross always around your neck. A cousin of mine wore it for her first communion, and the day she died. She was a sweet, kind girl. Nobody deserves it more than you.

* * *

She looped the aluminum cross around his neck and kissed him on the cheek. Barnard's face crumpled. She raised her eyes to Wyman.

What is it, mother? What's the matter with her?

Wyman lifted his hands in benediction.

Take no notice. It's just being given a present. She isn't used to it. The simple-minded can't understand when happiness knocks at their door. That's why they cry.

"All right." Boyd jumped into the playing area and sat on a trunk. "Let's take a look at that. Gunilla, from: *As for you, little sister.*"

The pent energy escaped her pores and Gunilla fingered her hair back, gratefully ready to work. Boyd left his seat in the house only when he intended a real session. She repeated, savoring it:

As for you, little sister, I should like you to wear this cross always around your neck.

Once she had given Guy Fatras a little cross, a useless half a pair of earrings of which she had lost the other half somewhere in Argentina, but precious because they had been the first pair of earrings she was allowed to own. He had stuck it through his buttonhole at the opening of *Bijou*, but later he had lost it, without fuss, without regret. He hadn't understood, as Sister Ines understood, that we give mineral and stone because the treasure of the self is too well hidden to be mined.

"Yeah, stop," said Boyd. "Now, this is a crucial moment because this is the moment that makes for the shift in loyalties. Up to now, Ines, you've been entirely under the Mother Superior's influence, but it's this scene that's going to make you try to prevent the murder. And eventually cost you your life. What we have to be able to see is that, at this exact instant, you fall in love with the Senora. What's the line, Gunilla?"

"A cousin of mine wore it for her first communion and the

day she died," Gunilla supplied, not acting. She smoothed her shirttail and waited very patiently for Boyd to get back to her.

"Now watch the Senora's face when she says that. Since you're deaf you don't have any idea what she's saying; you have to drink it all in through the eyes. And then although she's the one who's speaking, you have to *take* the audience's attention. So don't let your face collapse too quick. First we want to see the radiance build up inside. Radiance, hell, *radiation*, so when you cry it's like Three Mile Island going up, exploding and falling from inside, burning through the China Syndrome." His powerful hands grasped the air, demonstrated explosion and collapse and meltdown. "Take it from . . . no, wait." He left the trunk and paced, clawing his words out of the space in front of him while they perched and sat, now, intent and relaxed. Gunilla tried to relax.

"See, here's the point. Here's what you play. Up to now you're doing all right as a deafmute, you're used to it, it's no big deal. You understand everything you've got to understand, and you haven't got anything in particular to express. You bring them what they want and plunk at that guitar and all you need is an occasional pat on the head. But now she's offering you the cross, saying something you want to hear. For the first time in your life you know what *mute* means. Barnard. Have you ever loved someone, wanted to hold them, kiss them, comfort them, confess to them . . . and you were absolutely tongue-tied? Mute, in fact?"

"Oh, my dear," Barnard rhapsodized, but Boyd wouldn't let him fool around.

"What would you have said? If you hadn't been blocked and stoppered? Go over to Gunilla and tell her you love her. No cock-sucking talk, I mean *love*. Think of her as your sister. Think of her as your son. What do you want to say?"

Stung by the admonishment, Barnard came to her with his face flushed but composed. They all knew he had neither a sister nor a son. He pressed his hands to his cheekbones, concentrating into the light behind her head, his thick lashes quivering over round bronze eyes. She leaned and focused her attention on his mouth, to help him. He was silent a long moment, his lips barely moving with effort.

"I do love you," he said, and again just, "I *do* love you." And then, with a breath from the throat, "Oh, my God, don't you see, the last thing on earth I want to do is hurt you. It isn't your fault, it's the way I am . . . oh, Christ, you'll never understand, it's . . . Mom, it's *because* you taught me how to love . . ."

His eyes caught light and the tears surfaced, overflowed a second before his muscles crashed.

There was a stillness. "The simple-minded," Wyman said with a gentle resonance that had nothing to do with the Mother Superior, "can't understand when happiness knocks at their door. That's why they cry."

Gunilla, also moved, felt her elbows flex with the impulse to put her arms around him. She looked at his cherubic face and saw for a second the swaddled face of the baby boy she had put up for adoption.

"All *right*," said Boyd, and Barnard snapped back into a self-pleased pose and flicked the tears away. "Now remember you're saying that to her. And, that's good, Gunilla. You remember it too."

Which was the only direction he gave her the whole afternoon. She did not resent Barnard's taking the attention away from her. Boyd was right about the moment and its meaning. But she wondered very bitterly, clamping down on her raging energy, where Boyd came up with these effective goddam analogies, a man who had obviously never once found himself at a loss for words in his whole goddam life.

19. Summit Meetings

Shaara Soole, B.A. cum laude from the University of Iowa, M.F.A. in Design from the Yale School of Drama where she had been assistant fellow to Frank Bevan; winner of the Peabody, Head and RCA awards in costume; was in love with a cracker carpenter.

She sat at the president's conference table along with the other members of the Arts and Sciences Budget Steering Committee, checking out contemporary academic fashion. Harvey Nims was in forest-green polyester houndstooth with a newmown shade of button-down and an olive-and-rust rep tie. Michael Ogburn had a three-piece pale blue seersucker with a fob across the front. Ellen Chiesa sported a natty black ribbed vest over a strawberry nylon turtleneck. Larry McElhaney, that romantic, had shed his blazer onto the chair back and showed his hairy wrists below the sleeves of lemon-on-canary batiste. It was ninety-four degrees outside. What's the *matter* with these guys?

The problem was, that they'd got a bequest of seventeen thousand dollars for new stringed instruments, but the strings were preattached. Their money had to be spent before September first on such violins, cellos and/or violas as the Music Department deemed necessary, but on such items alone. None of it could be spent on a humidifier, and if they stored the instruments in the Music Building through the winter in that blast of old-fashioned furnace air, the sounding boards would warp and crack by the time Budget Steering got in a request for next year. If they shifted enough OPS funds to buy the humidifier, then History wouldn't get its computer link-up to the registrar, which was already ordered.

Shaara put Eugene Keyes into forest-green polyester houndstooth, in her mind's eye. She put him in lemon-on-canary batiste. She put him in a black vest and a strawberry turtleneck. She giggled and said, "Excuse me."

Ellen Chiesa warned, "If you try to take that computer away from them at this point, you'll have Oswald Link to deal with!"

Shaara supposed that some of them—Larry, anyway, and probably Mike Ogburn—wore Levis and T-shirts at home, grilling steaks out on the sun deck. She tried linking her arm in Gene's and pulling him through the Ogburns' vestibule out back to the brick patio with the potted wandering Jews. But this didn't work very well. She was bumping into him and snagging her caftan on the corner of the Queen Anne whatnot with all the Hummel figurines inside. Gene was whistling under his breath at the crystal-drop chandelier and the two wallpapers, gilt fleur-de-lis on the west and south, parchment stripes north and east. It was a matter worth some noetic speculation that Michael Ogburn could spend the afternoon in the Rough Draft Club doing a subtle exegesis of the beauties of a poem by Keats, and then go home to that vestibule.

Harvey Nims suggested that they move the funds out of travel expenses and "let the superstars pay their own way to MLA," but Ms. Chiesa protested vigorously, and Joe Dimbleton explained that travel was on the wrong line and not convertible to equipment.

Who else was there on the Ogburns' patio? Sergio Chiesa in a snaky narrow-lapeled sort of thing, and very likely the academic V.P. and his Scottish wife with her pince-nez voice. "I'd like you to meet Eugene Keyes." "Sunch a pleh-jah." "Howdy." Nope. She checked her watch. She had a dinner date.

"Joe," she leaned over and whispered, "did the V.P. get back?"

"This morning."

"Did you get to him about the Grumbacher release?"

"Not yet. He's been in conference all day."

In fact she was not the only one distracted. Late June in

academia is a sluggish time, and they were all having a little trouble steering the budget this afternoon. At one point Larry leaned over to ask her if she'd heard about the trucker being killed by sniper fire in Tuscumbia, Alabama. Nearly everyone had digressed to deplore either the skyjack from Kennedy to Shannon, Governor Graham's signing of two more death warrants in Florida, or the Sandinista shooting of the ABC reporter in Managua. Dimbleton, who usually ran a tight meeting, seemed a little fatalistic about this one, and was cleaning his nails with a letter opener.

"Why not let Una Pendleton take them home and keep them in her attic?" Shaara suggested. "She's got a humidifier."

"Security would never buy it," Harvey said. "Not seventeen thousand dollars' worth."

"Well, then, why not leave the heating *off* in the Music Building this winter? We could do without the humidifier and we'd probably get a commendation from Carter for energy conservation."

She was half-serious, they half-laughed; and in the end they left it unresolved. Joe was steered into taking it up with the academic V.P. as soon as he could get in to see him.

"But Grumbacher first," Shaara pleaded.

It was already five-thirty and she needed a bath, a hair wash, an ironed shirt, and to feed Kevin. She nipped down to the parking lot and drove home fast, reminding herself to get gas before six tomorrow. She threw a can of tuna and mushroom soup together and put the noodles on to boil.

"But if you get them to pick you up later," Kevin was saying into the hall phone, "we can go over to Wuv's afterwards and get a double suicide." Being a cum laude and an M.F.A., Shaara knew that a double suicide was a thirty-two-ounce mix of Coke, Sprite, Mr. Pibb and Orange Crush.

Kevin Soole and his mother both had dates tonight, and on the whole Kevin was handling his with more finesse. He was on his back on the shag already showered and dressed in jeans and a white shirt with a barbershop collar, the sleeves rolled just so below the elbow. His sneaker wandered over the wall. He had done something to himself this week. Something like deciding to be a teenager and transforming himself into one. He'd mowed a lawn and gone to have his hair styled—as opposed to cut—without even asking her to pay. Then he mowed three more and bought himself a Supermax II hair dryer with which he stood in front of the mirror for an hour at a time training the front locks back off his face. Moreover, his date was an older woman: fifteen. She even had a learner's permit, which Kevin clearly found a little daunting. He'd agreed that Shaara could drop him at the Skate Inn, "but on the corner and I'll walk in. You can see it isn't the thing to have your *mother* drive you." She could see it wasn't the thing.

It wasn't the thing to be so skittish, either, but Shaara had it all: the early-waking can't-eat shower-humming heart-skipping gold-hatted high-bouncing works. She hadn't slept alone for a week and she liked it better than she liked to think. As a matter of fact, she probably liked it better than she liked to *think*, which is not something a Yalie wants to face up to on a Thursday afternoon. They kept agreeing to take an evening off, cool it, see you at the shop tomorrow; but every night some time before midnight the pickup would materialize in the drive, and by the time it did she'd've been half nauseous with the conviction that it wouldn't. So far Kevin hadn't waked, and Gene was up and out before the birds were singing, after which she was singingly awake herself, making elaborate breakfasts of biscuits, ham, grits and omelettes which she didn't touch but which Kevin downed, uncomplaining, in their entirety. By nine they were at the shop, but never ahead of Gene, who'd be bellowing Conway Twitty over the buzz saw.

"You are *not* moving in," she told him Tuesday. "I am *not* clearing out a drawer for you. Do *not* bring your socks and underwear." He nodded firmly, understanding, agreeing. But now when she went to bathe she had to hide the Winn Dixie bag in the closet—two changes of J.C. Penney jockey shorts, a toothbrush, and a can of Rapid Shave.

She'd confronted him with the Winn Dixie bag and he absolutely agreed; couldn't agree more. That's why he was cooking dinner for her; she'd have to leave at ten-thirty to pick up Kevin, and they'd both get a good night's sleep. The only trouble was that Shaara was having a hard time getting tired.

Kevin noticed her fresh top and the blue glass beads as they drove to the Skate Inn. "You going out?"

"Yes, Gene's cooking dinner for me at the trailer."

"You dating him?"

"Yeah. Okay?"

"Okay."

"Thing is, I don't mean you should lie or anything, but I'd

just as soon you didn't volunteer any information to your dad about my social life."

The new Kevin could finesse this too. "I'd just as soon you didn't volunteer anything about mine."

"It's a deal."

She dropped him at the corner, carried on, then doubled back and drove idly past the parking lot to watch him saunter across, hands in his pockets, and offer a casual window-wipe of a wave to a raving beauty in raven hair and *breasts*. She thought maybe it was time to check up what he knew about contraception. She understood perfectly well that puberty was a period of grief, disaster and parental anguish, but she swore to God, so far it was mainly funny. Heading out of town she turned on the radio. "Picture-rearranger earthquakes, as one resident described them, have subsided after three days in northern Imperial County. Reaching as high as four point two on the Richter scale . . ." She switched bathetically over to the Country 'n' Western station.

She'd been to the trailer before, on Sunday while Boyd took Kevin swimming. It was a rented double-wide on a piney lot with a creek too dinky for anything but wetting your toes. Gene's cuffs were rolled as if he'd been wetting his, and he waved the grill tongs at her with a whoop. She felt about two years younger than Kevin herself. She clambered out catching her shirttail and stubbing the sole of her thong sandal under her foot so she had to draw it back and press it flat again. Usually when they met there were a couple of minutes and about three feet of distance between them, and Shaara was never sure if this was awkward or anticipatory, some kind of savoring control. Then they fell at each other.

"I gotcha Delmonicos and chicken-fried okra; I know how to treat a lady. And Chianti wine."

"You're wasting it. You know I won't be able to eat."

"And I've got something else I wanna show you. C'mere."

He led her to the trailer, turned with a hand on the knob and put the other up flat-palmed, firm.

"Now, if you don't want this, thass cool. Just say the word."

"What is it?"

"Okay, but I mean it, hear?"

"All right, all right."

He opened the door and a pint-sized hound pup tumbled out and rolled down the steps.

"Oh, Jesus."

White, black-spotted, with one black ear that cocked on a faulty muscle, it did puppy things; pranced on her sandal, licked her big toe, tugged at Gene's rolled cuff and ran a circle yapping while Shaara sat down on the steps. The pup peed on the doormat and she picked it up.

"Oh, Christ."

"Now, I mean it, he came from the pound, he was free. If you don't want him it's no big shit."

"It isn't that." She let the pup slaver over her blanched cheeks. "What's his name, then?"

"Temp'rarily it's Fibber McGee, unless Kevin wants to pick another. It's a good calling name. He's deerhound and terrier, just a mutt, but he was the pick of the pound. Look, Shaara." He put a hand between her cheek and the dog's. "If you'd rather not, I'll just keep him. You don't need to look so blasted. If I have a dog maybe it'll keep me home sometimes at night, huh? I don't care. Really."

"You will care, though," she grumbled into the wet nose, which recoiled. "That's the thing. You're going to be pissed off at me for the first time, and I don't know how I'll handle it."

"What d'you mean?"

"It's not that I don't want it. I do want it. It's that, you know, Boyd gave him Henry, and when Henry died Boyd wanted to get him another and I wouldn't let him. I made a scene of it. If I accept one from you . . ."

"Oh." Gene considered. Recoiled, maybe? What did he think the rest of the unfinished sentence was? If I accept one from you I have to admit you to Boyd? There's no loving way to turn down a gift. Gene said, "No, I can see that. I prob'ly should have thought. No, I can understand that. And it wouldn't be any good if you got him from the pound yourself?"

"It'd be the same thing, it'd be some kind of contest over Kevin, one-upping Boyd."

"Yeah. Well. I can see that, Shaara, I'm not some rhinoceros hide. I really don't mind, you know."

And whether he did or didn't, he spent the evening making sure she knew he didn't. It was Shaara who minded. She sat mawkish watching Fibber McGee flounder around the trailer, chew on the rugs and shit under the couch. She was unhappy enough to eat; the food was terrific and the place, apart from Fibber's leavings, immaculate. They talked about other things.

"I think it's very macho of you to be such a good housekeeper," she tried. "It means you didn't lose your independence, being waited on by a woman."

"Oh, I always did the cooking and cleaning. It puts my mind in order."

"You did? What did your wife do all day?"

"She was an accountant for Tel. and Tel."

Shaara blanched again, stung with her own sexist snobbery. And within five minutes they were into what felt distinctly like a first quarrel. She made an amusing anecdote of Kevin and his older woman, but when Gene had got done being amused he started insisting that Kevin should be "told."

"Told what? I told him tonight that I was going out with you." She was guiltily aware of having asked Kevin not to tell Boyd. "I'm not going to tell him you live in my bedroom between midnight and six A.M."

"If you don't tell him, I will. God, Shaara, he's thirteen."

"Tell him what, though?"

"How about I'll tell him I love you. That'll make it clear enough to prevent a shock, won't it? I'll ask his permission to court you. How about that?"

"I don't know."

Actually, she did. Not Lying To Children was her parental touchstone, the one thing she never had to consult Spock for. But Kevin's knowing was like a Winn Dixie bag in the closet. How was she going to extricate herself from this affair when she came to her senses?

They made love with the jinxed mutt pulling at the sheet corners, and that was sweet and fine. She stole a snapshot of Gene standing on the Interstate, and stuck it behind the photo of Wendy Soole behind her Exxon card. But when she picked Kevin up and went home, she knew the truck would not appear tonight, and it didn't. She slept alone for the first time in a week, and she liked it less than she liked to think.

20. *Nothing Doing*

❧ ━━━━━━━━━━━━━━━━━━━━━━━━━━━━━━━━━━━━ ❧

"No, the floors aren't sanded yet." This was true enough.

"They're taking a terribly long time," said Pauline Greton.

"I'll say. You can't imagine what a mess I've got here." This was also true; her mother would probably not have the requisite imagination. Without air conditioning, the apartment had taken on a permanent film of humid grit. Smells of must and mildew long buried in the sofa stuffing released themselves into the air. She'd been dropping her dirty laundry in the hall and hadn't washed a dress or a dish or a tabletop in four weeks now.

"Well, when do you think you'll be able to get away?"

Wendy hesitated. "Ummm." She wanted badly to fly down to see Boyd, but she couldn't because he didn't know she had the money. She didn't want to go to Boston, but she could because the Gretons didn't know she hadn't. "I'll try to have everything in order by the first; that's the week before I go down to Georgia. All right?"

Mrs. Greton said it was all right in such a tone as to indicate that it was not precisely wonderful.

"We'll have the Fourth of July together," Wendy promised.

She took down a Watteau print and hung the *commedia dell'arte* mask, but the place was so littered she couldn't tell if it looked good or not. She leaned the picture against the baseboard among the grit and fluff. She'd paid the rent and the MasterCharge minimum and still had two thousand dollars left, but she hadn't paid the utilities. It satisfied some sour impulse in her to be without electricity in an energy crisis. The carton of Dunhills sat useless on the TV set. She had no idea what she was going to do with *them*. The only person she'd ever known who smoked Dunhills was Bettaline Leric at Swarthmore, who used to crack up the dorm by parading naked except for a fur coat, flashing her pendulous tits. Betts also sometimes put clothespins on her sweater at the nipple so the squeamish ones (Wendy) would go, "Ooough!"

She flipped on the TV before she remembered there was no juice (it didn't matter; it would be "The Munsters" reruns and "Tic Tac Dough" at this hour; who needs it?), then tugged at the cellophane end of the Dunhill carton and shed the crumpled wrapper on the floor. She pried at the box and undid a pack, let the smaller cellophane skin float toward the other, took out a cigarette and waved it at arm's length in the air the way Betts had always done. She rummaged in the kitchen drawers for a match but couldn't find one—even the drawers had got jumbled since Boyd left; some hidden entropy at work—then remembered that there would be matches in the bedroom under Grandmother Greton's brass sconce that hung on the wall.

She found the match and took shallow puffs until the tobacco caught, then shed all her clothes onto the rug and posed in front of the mirror like Betts, wafting airy emphasis. "Dahling," she said without conviction. The wax ran down the side of the candle, frozen in the position of its last lighting, the night before Boyd left. It occurred to her as it had occurred to her before, how shocked Grandmother Greton would be if she knew what lascivious use her brass sconce had come to; but this had always delighted her, and now it stung her with some sickly sense she couldn't identify. She took a deep drag on the cigarette and was surprised by the way it caught a sharp pain under her lungs, sent her vision askew as if she were going to faint. Her reflection was breastless, fleshless. She was pale as something that lived underground. There was an angry insect bite high on her right thigh, and as soon as she saw it, it began to itch. As soon as she scratched it the telephone rang. She started as if caught and stubbed the cigarette out in her pin dish, hoping it would be Boyd, hoping it would not be her mother calling back to say she had a ticket for the fireworks or the symphony, hoping it would not be Sandro. But it was Sandro.

"Lovely," Sandro greeted her, while Wendy sat naked in the litter of four weeks' mail and scratched at her thigh. "I've missed you terribly." His trace of accent had a calculated unction about it; a line. He had always had a line but she had never found it distasteful before.

"Hello," she said, and the one word came out petulant, inadequate. Sandro didn't seem to mind. He invited her back to Rome—they could do anything they liked now that the jewelry was safely here, he said—but it was a short run, there tomorrow night and back on Sunday, and he allowed as how it was a long ways to go for a Strega and a fettucini. This put her in mind of Bettaline Leric's favorite story, how Emlyn Williams had flown to Italy to try to talk Richard Burton out of marrying Elizabeth Taylor, and had called back to his wife in the States, "I have just spent fifteen hundred dollars for a plate of cold spaghetti."

"I don't think I can," Wendy said, but this was not enough. Sandro waited for the excuse that she would invent in order not to tell him that their affair was over, so that he could pretend to believe it in order not to have his pride scathed. "I have a previous commitment," Wendy said.

"Previous commitment!" She could see the eyebrow raised above the glittering eyes he used to such effect. He raised the eyebrow every time he teased her, which was often. "Twitted" was the word he used; not a word she cared for.

"Yes, I have to . . . I'm having . . . the floors sanded," Wendy told him, and despaired.

But he was not rancorous, and the truth was probably that ten days and five thousand miles was a standard sexual run, for him. "Well, look, the plane doesn't leave till ten. Let's have an early dinner at least, and I'll drop you home on my way to the airport."

She couldn't say no to that, she owed him that much, though how she had got to owe him anything Wendy was not certain. There's a point at the beginning where you have the power to say yes or no, but if you don't pay attention, you lose that right.

"Yes, fine," she said. "Lovely."

She went and put her clammy clothes back on, looked at

the dregs of food in the kitchen cupboard—peanut butter and sardines, marmalade and artichokes vinaigrette—drank a glass of tepid water and sat in the gathering dusk. She knew that she ought to make herself do something but she could not think what. What was it she used to like to do when she had liked to do anything? Traveling, reading, watching TV, having adventures, being alone. She had no TV. She had just turned down the adventure of a trip to Rome. She hadn't the energy to concentrate on a book. She was alone, all right.

She went back to the bedroom and lit the candle, lay on the bed and longed for Boyd, watching the flame sputter till she fell asleep in her clothes.

Friday she woke at dawn with her thigh itching, and had been scratching at it over a cup of hot-tap instant and a cold Danish for half an hour before she bothered to take a look. When she looked, it was not an insect bite as she'd supposed, but a convex flaking white disk about the size of a Cheerio, surrounded by a rim of angry red. A ringworm, she recognized immediately. She'd had them as a child. She sat looking at it, high on the inside top of her right thigh so that if she bent her leg too far she would risk spreading it to her belly, and though a ringworm is not a terminal disorder, Wendy found herself profoundly discouraged and faintly disgusted. As if it smelled, which it didn't. It was so tacky somehow to have to suppose she picked it up in Italy, which was exactly what either or both of her parents would have predicted from Latin countries and alien sheets. *I have just spent fifteen hundred dollars for a minor fungus.*

She lay in the bath and soaped her thigh—thank God hot water came with the apartment and not from Con Ed—imagining the little diseased flakes floating toward the drain. When Supaclene had come to do an estimate on her mother's carpet up in Boston, they said her "soil content" was composed of animal hair, silt, lint and body ash. Pauline Greton had asked what was body ash, and they said particles of dead sloughed skin. "Can you imagine!?" Pauline had cried to Wendy over the phone. It was as if she'd been served a warning from County Health. "It must be the dog," Pauline had said.

Now when Wendy let the water out the drain was sluggish, and she had to bend a safety pin and fish out a clog of hair filmed with old particles of Ajax and, presumably, body ash. She decided she would not go out with Sandro, but by midafternoon when she had not managed to call and say so, she felt stir-crazy and a little desperate, and that she had better get hold of herself. When you feel most apathetic is when you most need to rouse yourself, she remembered from Psych, and she roused herself as far as the corner drugstore, where she bought a tube of Tinactin antifungal cream, came home again and spread it on her thigh. She would have forced herself to go out walking, sightseeing, but the temperature was in the upper eighties and she knew it was important not to sweat, so she sat indoors and sweated. The itch turned to a burn as the medicine began to work, and she sat constricted, moving gingerly in her bikini pants and a tank top, feeling a little sluttish, a little sick.

She wanted her utilities back now, but she didn't get them. She dialed the number, but a slimy Bronx voice told her to hold and never came back. She held for half an hour. Then she must either dress to meet Sandro or call him, so she called and said she was sick. She didn't tell him she had a ringworm, which seemed undignified; she told him she had a fever and nausea. He was extravagantly solicitous, admonished her to get plenty of rest and fluids, to take care of herself; he assured her so many times that he would call her as soon as he got back that she knew he would not. And this was what she wanted; all the same, when she hung up she felt a little panic of abandonment that he was on his way to Rome without her. She sat with her hand still on the receiver, not daring to call Boyd, not daring to call Cass Carson. When the notion of calling Shaara Soole came into her head she decided she'd gone a little mental and went back to bed.

It had seemed fair enough to break her date with Sandro; being sick was one way of rescinding an obligation. But now, having done so, she found herself obligated to be sick. She did have a fever. She had diarrhea although she had eaten almost nothing for four days. She lay with the chalky taste of Kaopectate in her mouth and the burn of Tinactin on her thigh, thinking uneasily of Boyd. It wasn't guilt, exactly. Wendy wasn't given to guilt, and besides, though she and Boyd never discussed fidelity she sort of assumed—well, he was away so much. But that last call from Georgia had something wrong with it, and what was wrong seemed to be mainly at her end. The stuff about the salami, and her mother sending money. One comfortable thing about Boyd's dark imagination was that you could trust him not to be shocked or judgmental, which, considering the atmosphere she grew up in, was like entering some freer neverland. But there was something wrong with that phone call all the same.

While she'd slept last night the candle had burned itself down to the socket and dripped tallow on the dressing table. Her mind, idly racing, planned to clean it up before Boyd got home, replace the candle, burn the new one down just as far as the old one had been burned. But she had never brought Sandro here. If she felt no guilt why should she replace a candle innocently lit? She fretted, slept, waked in the dark with a hazy headache, slept again.

Saturday the ringworm had turned angrier, the red rim bubbled with tiny pustules. Now it both itched and burned. That was all right, it meant the medicine was doing its job. But it also meant she stayed in once more, filling the tub and then deciding she'd better shower instead, sitting indolent in her underpants, almost stupefied.

About noon, staring at the blank TV, she caught sight of the Dunhills, of which there were still one hundred and ninety-nine, and she thought again of Betts Leric, thought nostalgically of her, because it was Betts who had pointed out, "There's nothing new about *body language*. If actors and audiences hadn't understood *body language* from the beginning of time, there'd be no such *thing* as thea-tah." And so was responsible for her senior honors thesis, and so responsible for her meeting Boyd. Betts had dropped out to go study at the Actors Studio in New York, but according to the grapevine she never got in. Wendy didn't know what had become of her. Sluggishly she tugged out the Manhattan Directory and flipped to the L's: Lepley, Lepper, Leppert, Leran, Leric. There she was: Leric Bettaline 235 W. 11th . . . 471–8059.

Technology makes Merlins of us all. What else did they mean, those old tellers, by "conjuring out of the past"? She looked at the peculiar configurations of little numbers, like a spell: 235,11,471,8059. Why not? What else did she have to do?

The purring was replaced with a metallic scratching, then a voice distantly recognizable that said, "*This* is Bettaline; look, I cahn't get to the phewn right now but I shall be destroyed to miss your call . . ." Betts must've got into some acting school, because she'd put on more than four years' worth of stagey

accent. Wendy was about to hang up when the scratching cut
off with a click, and the same voice said, "Shit. Hellew?" against
a background clamor of something punk, Clash or the Sex
Pistols.

"Hello, Betts? This is Wendy Soole."

"Hoo?"

"Wendy Greton, remember?"

"Hoo? Hoo?" Betts hooted. "Theh's a shitlewd of noise
heh—weh heving a film potty."

"Ah," said Wendy. "It's all right, this is just Gwendolyn
Greton Soole. We went to Swarthmore together."

"Oh, *Swathmah*." Betts seemed to remember Swarthmore.
"How on uth did you feigned me?"

"You're listed." A sigh of elaborate amazement, as if Wendy
had done something a good ways witchier than hanging clothespins on her nipples. Wendy figured out hat Betts was stoned.
"Actually," she said, "I thought of you because I have a spare
carton of Dunhills and I don't know what to do with them."

"Yaw magnificent. We must have launch."

Betts must have moved because the music blasted louder
and a man's voice cackled heavy laughter near the phone.
Wendy had a sudden flash of panic at the image of meeting
Betts in Yellowfingers or Tavern on the Green, being hailed
over the heads of lunching matrons by those cooing decibels
and an armload of bangles. How come, if Betts didn't even
remember her, she had got herself back in the position of lying
to say no? "Sure," Wendy said. "Call me," and hung up, staring
at the ragged mail.

A surge of restlessness cut through her inertia and she stumbled to the hall to rummage among the clothes and pick out
something, the rumpled linen traveling dress. She would accomplish one thing today. She would get rid of those damn
Dunhills. She pulled the dress on, took the cigarette carton
and her keys, and when the elevator didn't come at once she
lurched down eight flights of stairs, the rough texture of the
linen chafing at each stride. The doorman was in his cubicle;
she headed past him eyes down and made for the litter bin
outside. But when she got there she hesitated, some debilitating
impulse of thrift holding her with her hand poised on the rim.
She was aware of the burn of the ringworm, the ooze of the
cream, the linen catching. Finally she turned and set the carton
open on the sidewalk, the broken pack leaning against it.

This seemed to have exhausted her, and when she got back into the apartment she dropped the dress where she was and pulled a chair to the window. For perhaps three hours she sat, hunched so her bra straps were hidden by the sill, watching the cigarettes on the sidewalk, waiting to see who would benefit from her jetsam. No one did. People passed by, around, stepped over the carton, occasionally gave it a furtive glance but hurried on. A brown boy no more than seven or eight circled it once, peered in all directions from its corners as if looking for the string, too streetwise to be fooled. A couple smart in designer jeans and straw hats doubled back from the corner, walked past it, held a furtive conversation at the lamp-post but finally crossed the street. Once when the shadows had started to lengthen an old man picked a butt out of the gutter but gave the most cursory glance, suspicious to the point of disdain, at forty dollars' worth of imported nicotine. Wendy put her chin on her fist and thought about how little trust there is left in the world. She sat so long that the box, its little shadow inching toward the building, began to seem unreal to her, as if it were painted on the sidewalk, and she remembered an Escher print that used to hang from a plastic dowel on Bettaline Leric's wall in the dorm, the one with the rolling papers and the cactus plant, the reptiles crawling out of the artist's pad getting real and then turning into drawings when they crawled back in again. She went to pee, to spread a new layer of medicine on her thigh, and when she came back the cigarettes were gone.

Sunday the red ring had paled and she felt physically well again, but this made it all the more alarming that her lethargy had not abated. She picked the dirty travel dress up off the living room floor and started to put it in the hall, then changed her mind and shoved it into the garbage bag in the kitchen with the banana peels and the Danish wrappers. She pushed the broom a few times over the kitchen floor but sweeping made her cry so she left the broom propped against the sink and sat huddled in her terry robe until Boyd called.

"Believe it or not, I've sent you money."

"That's good."

"Did you send the strongbox?"

"Yes."

"Thanks. What have you been up to, lovely?"

"Not a thing. Not a damn thing worth doing." And that was true too.

21. *Breaking and Entering*

---❖---

The strongbox finally arrived on Monday, so after rehearsal he went down to borrow a hammer and chisel. It wasn't true that he had the key, which was in the paper clip tray in his desk in New York. He would not have wanted Wendy to see those notebooks; they bespoke a dark nature utterly out of her range. Shaara and the carpenter were already gone by the time he went down, but the shop doors were open into the hall, and he didn't suppose anyone would mind his taking the tools. Probably he could get them back before they were missed.

At the Campus Side he poked the chisel into the slit between body and lid and hammered a few sharp strokes against the bolt. It was surprisingly easy. He let fall the castrated lock and took out the Rexall spiral pads.

From which he learned nothing. They contained the secrets, but no surprises. The cramped hand he could almost have forged from memory, the green of the pads themselves he could have matched on a color wheel. He did not remember all the dreams, but he recognized them as he read, and the endless exegeses, done to death, so it seemed that no possible further insight could have been supplied even if someone had been mad enough to wish to. He became dull, and even bored.

But not drunk, though he downed glass after unmeasured glass of bourbon on the rocks. A little before midnight he put the notebooks back in the strongbox and the strongbox at the back of the closet, and propped himself on the bed to watch *Rosemary's Baby*.

His mind wandered, sneaked away from him, though it was one of his favorite films. He remembered reading somewhere—in that Fowler book on Nabokov?—that every author has only one story to tell, and it appeared that the same was true of screenwriter-directors. Polanski had "wardrobe" for an *idé fixe*, all the way back to that early short where the two men carted a cupboard across a sandcastle-covered beach. Probably Polanski had been locked in a wardrobe for punishment as a child. Here was *Rosemary's Baby*, the same film precisely as *The Tenant*: moving into an empty apartment where someone has died; finding menace in the old wardrobe, a mystery behind it, so it has got to be moved; the nearly normal interference of the neighbors. And this produces a hysteria that everyone takes to be insanity; it turns out that even those outside the building are in on it, when the protagonist turns on them for help.

Little Mia Farrow, so like Wendy in her bones and hair, so unlike Wendy in her hesitant fragility, sat at the kitchen table as if chained there. What can be more ordinary than the menace underneath a cup of milky pink dessert? Terror attaches itself to the solicitations of the neighbors, to the screech of tires, dark rooms and musty smells, the simple squeaking of a rusty hinge. The occult is invented as an explanation of our pain and terror, as gods are invented as an explanation of our hope and awe. Really we do not know why we are wounded, terrified.

Mia moved around the apartment, impregnated by and with the devil, afraid of the place and afraid to go out; but Boyd was unmoved by it this time. His thought took another direction, intellectual and detached: so many modern dramatists have centered on the room. Pinter where the room is safety and the danger is the opening door. Albee where the room is a trap. Ibsen's Hedda smothered by the drawing room, his Nora constricted in the doll's house until she slams the door. Beckett's *Endgame* where the room is a deranged mind—or is it? Polanski's various new tenants, whose innocence is destroyed by something present in the place, the walls.

And isn't this a natural obsession for a dramatist, where the "fourth wall" is removed and the enclosure is exposed?

The bourbon that hadn't made him drunk had ended by making him sleepy, and he shut off the TV before the film was finished. He wasn't really watching it anyway. He went to bed.

This one was the exposure dream again, a more profound uncovering. The fourth wall of the motel room had been removed. The audience was sitting, swaying, on a tarpaulin stretched over the pool. A floodlight struck him from behind their heads, washing out the colors of his room and flickering on the moted air, so that he could barely make out the TV set, where he was also on the screen. He watched a mirror image of himself—the film was overexposed as well—watching himself on the set and fiddling with its dials to turn it off. It would not turn off. The closet had turned into Polanski's wardrobe, wooden, carved, elaborate and massive. The door swung open on its hinges to reveal the mutilated strongbox. Boyd knew what his part called for, what he was compelled to do. He had to take the notebooks out, sit at the dresser and pour a drink. He had to read his father's dreams aloud from first to last, acting them out where called for, all the way up to the L.A. freeway. He chose not to do it. He moved toward the wardrobe determined that he would not do it. But his body wouldn't work for him. His sinews seemed independently, contrarily convinced that the show must go on.

The bourbon that hadn't made him drunk had given him a hangover. And when he got to rehearsal it was clear that Wyman was not going to be in a helpful mood. He buttonholed Boyd in the hall.

"D'ye *know* what that bitch is doing with her spare time?"

"Gunilla, I presume?"

"Barnard and myself dropped into town last night for a bit of drink, that student bar they made out of the old railway station. Well, there she sits, dolled up like a Dublin tart with her titties harnessed half up to her nose, and she's laughing and waving her pretty little arms about for a bunch of snot-nosed kids. Who are naturally making goo-goo eyes and hanging on her every word."

"Well. It's her spare time, Wyman."

"No doubt it is. But doesn't it strike you, she comes in here looking as much like a grandmother as she can manage, and never gives a howd'ye'do to her fellow actors, or cracks a half a smile. And then she fluffs out her gorgeous hair and goes down to perform for the local teens?"

Wyman's brogue thickened right back to J.M. Synge when he was angry. Boyd shrugged and put on what he hoped was a commiserating look, but he really couldn't go into it. Maybe Wyman would come around in rehearsal; they were running the second act and working on the final scene. Wyman would get all the attention and Gunilla would have very little to do.

But Gunilla was late, and Barnard had apparently gone down to the shop again. The stage manager was chalking the floor and Boyd couldn't find a spare hand, so he asked the prop girl, Dora, to go tell Sister Ines they were starting. Dora assured him she would do as she was asked, with such a twittery-martyred implication that this was *not* her *job*, that Boyd said, "Never mind. I'll do it myself."

He descended, remembered he'd left the hammer and chisel in his briefcase, decided not to go back. Maybe he'd tell Dora they were prawps, and send her down. The radio was blasting away and Kevin and Barnard were holding up the massive doorjamb, Barnard camping peek-a-boo around it while the carpenter tried to fix a bolt and Kevin doubled up in laughter.

"Barnard! On stage!"

Beyond the other doorway, Shaara looked up over the wimple in her lap. "Good morning."

He went in. "Shaara, can you please explain to me what is happening about the money? I'm going into the fifth week here now, and all I've had is the check that I was supposed to get the day I arrived. I've sent it all up to Wendy so she won't get evicted, and I'm *still* living on American Express. What is going on?"

"I know," she said. "You see, the regular paychecks are issued every two weeks, and the bursar doesn't have a release for an irregular payment, so he assumed that the second check should be made out two weeks after the first one."

"Well how in God's name does he get a release?"

"It'll have to be issued by the V.P., but he's down in the Florida Keys this week. Taking what Joe Dimbleton describes as a well-earned vacation."

"Jesus fucking Christ."

"I know, Boyd. You've got every right to be furious, I'd be just as mad myself. But there's nothing *I* can do about it. It's not my job."

He turned on his heel and stormed back upstairs, scattering the stagehands off the set. Gunilla had arrived, as astringently outfitted as usual.

"Places for the opening of Act Two!" Boyd barked. "I want a run-through up to the place we stopped yesterday, after the death of Ines. As of now, every run-through is to be treated as a performance. I won't stop you, and if you crack up or dry you have to get out of it yourselves. I'll give notes this afternoon and we'll go back over what doesn't work. Is that clear to everybody? Good. Places. Music. Curtain."

It was too early in a seven-week schedule to do this. But sometimes anger works. They sailed right through it. Wyman, who could not remember half his lines yesterday, reeled them off. Barnard projected a helpless terror that put him in mind of Mia Farrow. Orme, who had to tread a careful line not to overplay the sinister, trod it, sure-footed and vicious. And Gunilla was truly dead. If he had not watched her technique these four weeks, he'd have had them stop and make sure she was all right.

As he watched, a different kind of agitation welled up in him. That other terror, the one you can't sort out from hope or love. They had two weeks yet to work before they went into dress rehearsals, and if he kept them fresh the production might be really good. No, but *really* good. The breakthrough production. The one he was always after, crafted and funny and passionate. Burt Reynolds would be there for opening night. Reynolds—who had already used Orme in his "Mean Machine" in *The Longest Yard*—would watch Boyd's work. If it was as good as it could be and Reynolds recognized how good it was, who knows what could happen? Orme would be sure to introduce them; they would go out for a drink together. Reynolds was said to be open and easy; Boyd could talk about his career. . . .

He didn't stop them when they got to Ines's death, and, obeying his injunction, they carried on to the end. He could see with great clarity what had to be done with the final scene. When they finished he walked onstage casually, not betraying his excitement in his step. "Now, I lied to you. I didn't take any notes because I wanted to have a look. Has it occurred to any of you, the possibility that we might have a *show*?"

Barnard beamed, and even Gunilla gave him a half a smile.

Only, unfortunately, Wyman's spirits had not been lifted by his own performance as much as Boyd's had. After lunch he went grudgingly back to work, not acting badly but not concentrating either. Half the lines he had known this morning were either forgotten or reworded.

> When I've sold my share, I think I'll buy myself a castle and put . . .

"What is it?"
"And put spikes on all the . . ."
"Yeah."

> I think I'll buy myself a palace and put spikes on all the walls to keep everybody out. I've seen people enough to last me a lifetime.

Wyman broke character and turned. "How can I do this with my back to half the audience?"

Boyd had put Orme and Wyman back to back on a trunk for this low-key scene, the calm before the final storm. Wyman was playing it too big, with gestures, trying to make himself visible around Orme's body to the other side of the house.

"They don't need to see you, Wyman. They know what you look like by now."

"I can't abide this bloody round." Boyd had given up trying to tell him it was an arena stage and not a round. "I can't be acting with the back of my bloody neck!"

"Wyman," Boyd soothed. "Of course you can. You're acting with the back of your neck all the time. You act with your armpits and the underside of your toes. It's getting across, I promise."

"It makes me bloody nervous, being looked at on all sides at once."

"Well then, use that, Wyman. Go ahead and think of the audience as threatening. They're the revolution and you're surrounded. You picked this basement because you thought it was the one safe place to be, and now it's trapped you. You're about to be exposed. Look, Wyman, stop thinking of this as a play about Haiti a hundred years ago. It's New York 1979. It's Georgia now. You know there's danger on the streets, coming at you out of every person and machine; and you're cautious, you protect yourself, you're nobody's fool. But then you get to the place you really think you can relax. Your motel . . . your cottage on the lake. Your dressing room. And all of a sudden danger comes at you from the place you least expect. It's hiding in your closet. It's at the window. Backstage."

"Damn right," said Wyman, but still meaning it as anger, not productive work. Gunilla tossed her head in hauteur. Boyd thought it would be a good idea to get rid of her, so he excused her gently, "It's a waste of your time, when we're just picking their lines to pieces."

But Gunilla declined, and continued to stand tied to the post by the ribs, dropping into the character of the corpse every time one of the actors said a line. She used her industry as a punishment, like the prop girl. She was by far the most difficult of the four to direct, partly because she worked so hard herself that she left him little to do. She had written reams of the Senora's autobiography and was always coming in already having worked out the idea he was going to give her. Then she took his few suggestions so doubtfully, with a scrupulous obedience, that he'd learned early on, the best way to direct her was not to direct her at all. When he wanted a feeling from her he worked on somebody else, and let it emerge as reaction.

Today with Wyman in a snit her very presence was an accusation. He took them back over the trunk scene after the smothering of Ines—Barnard, now he was dead, had been perfectly happy to take off down to the shop—and tried to convey the menaced calm he wanted. "Let's try for the moment . . . that the play is already over. These lines come *after* the curtain. You know the way you feel after a performance, spent? All you want to do is sit slumped over a whiskey?"

"Not me," said Wyman. "I like a roaring party after the show."

But Orme would work for him. The gesture he flapped toward Gunilla was almost as limp and graceless as the corpse itself.

That one broke up when she fell. Anyway, I don't think it was a good idea digging her up. People always want to know what's been going on. And they always end up finding out. We'll have to bury her again.

* * *

"That's it," said Boyd. "It's just something that occurred to you. It hardly has anything to do with you. And your mind's wandering, back over the past." Orme lit a cigar and backhanded it over his shoulder to Wyman without looking. Boyd laughed aloud. "Good! Keep it."

I knew a sailor once who used to say: You've got to smoke a lot to put a curtain of smoke around the world. He always smelt of gunpowder, baccy and rum. A real man, he was, a hell of a fellow on land or sea.

Boyd worked them gradually forward, concentrating on Orme since Wyman was not in a cooperative frame of mind. But it was frustrating, knowing so well what he wanted, unable to get it. And when the Mother Superior got to her confession, which was absolutely crucial to his concept of the play, he couldn't let it slide, not even till tomorrow. The stage manager dutifully hammered on a bench with a rubber mallet, to represent the revolution at the door.

I've a confession to make. That hammering on the door? . . . I, I made it up. So you'd leave me alone. I could never tell with you, you're so unpredictable.

No, it wouldn't do. Wyman believed what he was saying. There had to be a whole mesh of motives under it, self-deception and fear, manipulation, hope.

"Wyman, was your father a drunk?" Boyd asked, and stepped onto the stage. Wyman jerked a look at him, not clear yet whether he was going to be offended. His eyes glinted a second's anger, then he changed his mind and let a smile spread out into his jelly jowls.

"I do believe he was one of the three or four drunkenest men in Dublin."

"How do you feel about that?"

"Oh, proud as a peacock in the mating season. What's that got to do with the Mother Superior?"

"How did you feel about it as a child?"

Wyman hesitated, suspicious, smiling. "I'd've given 'im a trophy if I'd had the price of it."

"Did he beat your mother?"

The anger was rising again under Wyman's chosen pose. He stiffened and the smile took on a rigid edge. "Just a cuff or so about the ears of a Saturday night. Nothing you'd be wanting to make a fuss about to the authorities."

"Did he beat you?"

Wyman gave it up and glared. His fists flexed. "I don't remember."

"Right." Boyd sat on a stool and let the tension string out. Not because he needed to think but because he needed the transition. His own father appeared to his mind's eye, the cold mouth, and then the down-drag of the handwriting in the notebooks. Gunilla, lashed in the position of the corpse, was alert, and Wyman registered her alertness with the back of his neck.

"The point about this speech of the Mother Superior's," Boyd said finally, "is that she's trying to make light of something that really holds a lot of pain and terror. She wants to make it so by saying it, but underneath, she knows. She can't protect herself with the words. Do you see what I mean?"

Wyman saw. He took up his position again, ruminating. Then he did a comic double take and asked, "Was *your* father a drunk, then?"

Boyd grinned to the jowls and gestured airily. "Oh, no. My father was a Professor Milquetoast. He had other problems."

They didn't quite get the scene right, but they got a ways in the right direction. They knocked off around five-thirty, and Boyd waited till they'd left, then took the hammer and chisel out of his briefcase. He thought the carpenter would be gone and he could return them the same way he got them, but from the stairs he could hear that the radio was still playing. Shaara wasn't in the costume room. He pushed on the shop door, prepared to confess his unauthorized borrowing.

But the overhead lights were off and there was only one little pool of it, over in the corner under a hatted bulb. The carpenter, Gene, was sitting on a stool with his arm lightly around Kevin's shoulders. Kevin sat on an upended crate looking up, his face lit. The hound was doing a His Master's Voice number at the two of them. Boyd couldn't hear a word over the music, but he could see that the conference was intense. They seemed to finish and got up. Kevin put out his hand and the carpenter took it in both his own. Then Kevin started to walk away, turned back and flung his arms, with a chilling, childish innocence, around the other's neck. The carpenter hugged him in the swinging light.

The sweat sprang to his brow. He should have shoved the door, discovered and confronted them. He knew this, chose it. But his body would not obey. He dropped the hammer and chisel and escaped back up the stairs.

22. *Body Snatching*

There now. Another example of her penchant for the soapifying and smarmifying of the trivial. How a woman who dealt so sturdily with the real-life stuff of mothering, divorcing, and breadwinning could choose to cause herself to suffer so heartily over a cock-eared flop-assed polka-dot half-breed from the Hubbard pound was . . . beyond her. Nothing altered with Gene, who began bringing Fibber McGee to the shop, where he took to following on the heels of Kevin, who enjoyed this a lot. Gene did not mind, Kevin did not covet, and Boyd did not notice.

Gene also began bringing Fibber McGee into her bedroom at night, where he gradually got house-trained, and where he settled down under the bed till he was waked with the birds. He slept very soundly and so did Kevin. Anyway there were dogs enough in the neighborhood that Kevin wouldn't have noticed an extra bark or howl unless he was right at Shaara's door.

And as regards the actual telling of Kevin, she had made too much of that too. Gene said, "He gave me a hug, well, he gave me a handshake and then a hug. Has he said anything to you?"

"Yes. He said you make better chili con carne than I do. I think it was an official sanction."

She was normalizing now, beginning to function in normal patterns of sleep again, of metabolism probably, of bowels and ovaries demonstrably; though there was no use pretending she brought any willpower to bear on it. Did that make sense? Did the *though* belong in that thought? She was aware that she was not always perfectly aware of how words and thoughts related to each other, though a more acute observer might have observed that if she had wit enough to be aware of this much, she did better than most. She did not observe this.

The relationships of which she was perfectly aware were of armpit to armhole, pleat depth to hip shape, thread count to drape. Her eye had a logic that her math did not. If she measured it came out wrong. If she meditated the armpit, then the sleeve would fit, so her eye was better than her math, better than her logic. And better than her heart, maybe, which still functioned irregularly. She was taken with fits of tachycardia when she felt under no stress. And her heart chose wrong. Over and over, it chose wrong. It had chosen wrong, clearly and overtly, now. Nothing but grief would come of it, this unlikely liaison, this unacceptable union, this stunted flowering.

In the meantime they were both working remarkably well. Shaara had finished all six of the nuns' habits, hung the three most perfect for the first act, stuffed the others in a damp drawer in the kitchenette so wrinkles would set before she got round to breaking them down for the second act. Now—saving best for last—she was putting the finishing touches on the first of Gunilla's two yellow gowns. She had time to do them with identical care, and expected to have trouble deciding which was for the breakdown.

Gene was making a door more or less on the same principle as the iguana cage, which would shatter much more effectively than the one the designer had called for. He was supposed to band crate wood with two-by-fours top and bottom so it would give when hammered on from backstage. Instead he was setting timbers into a frame and bolting them with wing nuts. When the nuts were loosed from behind, the rough wood actually fell askew against itself as if it were just about to crash.

The frame was heavy and he needed both Kevin's and Barnard's help. Now and again they even enlisted Dora Fisher, whose work brought her often into the shop. Dora disliked Barnard because he was a queer, and Barnard disliked Dora because she was a bore. He baited her by parodying her own fanatic fussiness with the props. "Dora, I'm just *worried* that this censer is going to reflect the light. Could you possibly give it a coat of matte varnish?" Or, "Darling, the rope is too pale, it just doesn't *read Haiti*. Couldn't you get us something more in the hemp or jute line?" Dora never knew she was being mocked. Dislike him as she might, she would accede religiously to such demands. She confided to others that he behaved as if he were the *stawr*.

When none of these people were about, Gene and Shaara would naturally dip into each other's shops for an illicit snuggle, multiplied by the mirrors—the odd couple of identical height but mismatched structures, she big-boned and -breasted, he V- torsoed and narrow-framed, as if they had been constructed to different scales.

"Listen, we've got to pay more attention to locking up at night. I found a hammer and chisel on the floor in the hall. Anybody could get in the third floor and just come on down and he'p themselves."

"I'll try, but I was raised in Burlington, Iowa, you know. It goes against my nature."

"Go against your nature, then."

"Okay. Speaking of which, will you please not sweep up the shop for a week? I'll be ready to do the breakdowns about next Friday, and I want a lot of gunk in there."

"Awright. You have a late fitting today?"

"Gunilla, yes."

"Why don't I take Kevin home and make some split pea soup? Did you ever notice how split pea soup smells like warm dog shit?"

"A lot of good things to eat smell like warm dog shit."

The logic of this exchange was such that it required a complicated kiss, which the mirrors gossiped around the room.

But ten minutes after he had taken Kevin off in the truck, she missed him. Missed him! The shop was too big and the silence had a faint suggestion of an echo on it. She wished with irrelevant anger that Boyd would leave town. She tried to imagine waking up one morning and finding herself suddenly indifferent to Eugene Keyes, but—normalizing though she might be—she could not picture it.

While she waited for Gunilla she put the gown on the dress form and admired it critically. She had found a gray tricot, shot with dull silver, that just matched the embroidered flowers. She had gathered the yellow satin into extravagant, almost Renaissance, puffs from which the slender silver undersleeve protruded, cut to fit like second skin halfway down Gunilla's hand. She had bound the rib seam with the same silver, used it to pipe the deep scoop of the neck, made ropes of it to lace the back, which was triple-boned on either side. She had given the skirt a slight train and faced the hem in the tricot, so that it moved with soft authority and sometimes revealed a flash of silver underlay. Shaara knew it was the best costume she'd ever built, and knew that Gunilla knew she'd not get a better in New York or Hollywood. But Gunilla still complained about the neckline.

Today when she arrived—she always began a fitting with a vigorous brushing of her hair—she pulled a newspaper clipping out with her hairbrush and waved it theatrically across. "Have you seen this?"

Shaara had, and had heartily hoped Gunilla hadn't. At Wimbledon, Linda Siegel, across the net from Billie Jean King, had lost a strap and dropped a breast out as she slammed the ball. Actually, the picture in the prudish *Hubbard Post* didn't show the breast exposed at all, but it tittered through the details, "Staid old Wimbledon blushed," etc., and quoted the unfortunate tennis star as saying, "I thought it might be dangerous because I couldn't wear a bra."

"Yes," said Shaara, "but did you notice Billie Jean King's advice? 'If you're well-endowed, show it.'" Gunilla was not mollified. As usual, she picked at the piping while Shaara bound her breasts and pulled the laces, kneeing her in the back. "She just had little spaghetti straps. You've got a whole construction of sleeves and stays." Gunilla eyed her shoulders doubtfully. Shaara was annoyed at this niggardly appreciation, and jerked a little harder than necessary.

But when Gunilla finally looked up and got the full effect in silver and sunlight satin, she said, "Oh." The décolleté scooped slightly outward from the shoulder line, curved just over the aureole of her offered breasts; her slender ribs were tightly bound, and the long clean fall of the skirt gave her height, dignity. She arched her neck, taking on the Senora's character, and preened for a view of the back. "It *is* lovely." Isn't it peculiar for an actress to have so little imagination? Did she think she was going onstage in muslin?

"I want one more adjustment of the left dart," Shaara fussed, unwilling to betray her triumph. Too bad Gunilla couldn't have yielded a little earlier. They might have been friends.

Shaara had a sense that someone was hovering outside the door, and Gunilla, leaving, passed Boyd on the threshold. He came in and stood about, admiring the dress in a throat-clearing sort of way. Shaara wondered if he was going to bring up the money again.

"How's it going with Gunilla?" he asked.

"Okay. Frankly, I think her costume may be the best one I've ever made. *Frankly*, I think it may be the best she's ever worn—at least, what I've seen in films. On the other hand, she isn't easy to deal with in a fitting."

"I can believe that. I feel for you." He hesitated, hemmed. "I don't know that I've ever got around to telling you in so many words, Shaara, that I think you're a fine artist."

The word embarrassed her, as it would not have embarrassed her back at Yale. She turned the bodice over and basted the new position of the dart. "Oh, well. Costuming isn't an art."

"How do you mean?"

"I mean it's a craft, like carpentry. It's not creative. The playwright gives you essentially what it has to be, and you just fill in with the material."

"I never heard such addlepated crap."

"No, I mean it. You don't make something out of nothing."

"You make *character*, out of cloth."

"Oh, well."

"I can't believe you're saying that. You! What do you think creation is? God created out of the void, maybe, but creation as we know it. . . . Matter can't be made or destroyed, didn't they teach you that in school?"

"Sure, but that's not . . ."

"Everything in the world is made by selection and arrangement. A play, an onion, a fetus—they begin with a conjunction of unlikes. And then other things—cells, ideas—accumulate around the join. An onion or a fetus or a costume design. Selection and arrangement, Shaara. That's what creation *is*."

"That's what craft is, like a carpenter." She looped the thread through itself and bit it off.

"Don't you know the difference between art and craft?"

"Apparently not. Why don't you tell me?" She did not know what he was doing in here, lecturing her about onions and fetuses. He was stalling about something. He had put on a professorial demeanor not his own, which he only adopted when he was covering something else.

"The difference is, that a craft can't be done too perfectly. In a table, you want exact symmetry, and the finest sanding, and the most perfect polish. But in art there has to be a balance of exuberance and craft. Too much discipline can destroy the life. There has to be craft, but there always also has to be a certain risk."

She flung the gown over the form and kneed it in the small of the back in earnest this time. She despised his eloquence. "Well, you didn't come in here to theorize. What's on your mind?"

"Yes." Now he did clear his throat, and sat rather awkwardly. He filled his pipe. "I guess you realize that Barnard Jones hangs around the shop a lot, with Kevin and the, Gene. I think Kevin has grown very fond of Barnard."

"So have I."

"Yes, well, I think we ought to take into account the fact that Kevin has grown up largely without a father. I'm not blaming you, it's common enough and it's the way things worked out, but, he might be more susceptible, especially just now, going into puberty and all."

"What are you saying?"

"Well . . . I have reason to believe that Gene, the carpenter, is queer too."

"You have *what*?"

"I know it seems incredible on the surface of it, but I have more experience than you have in . . ."

"You have *what*?"

"I wouldn't encourage Kevin's spending too much time with him. Believe me, in that prison in New Jersey I saw great brutes you'd never believe it of. In the theater we get mainly mincing types like Barnard. But I could tell you tales . . ."

She had the scissors around the handle, daggerwise. For a scary second she thought she would sink them in his diaphragm. Then she caught sight of his reflection and wheeled her rage off course to that, threw the heavy steel blades straight into his silvered face. A true eye makes for an unerring aim. The mirror shattered and flung shards as far as the table. Boyd rose amazed.

"Lemme tell you a tale, Boyd Soole. You can lecture me

any time of day, about art and craft. You can cast me an *intellectual perception* and I'll swallow it right down to the bobber. But you tell me about how *people* work and you can shove it up your intellectual ass. Lemme tell you something about people that you might be able to make use of. Pro-fessionally. You know, real people, the kind that have children and divorces and eat and fuck and die? They aren't so altogether different from the characters in plays. As a matter of fact, the people who write plays?—well, *on* the whole, they take a look at the way people act and react and mo-tivate themselves before they sit down to write. And there's a fuckin' goddam rumor that now and again a director even does the same, and tries to understand a few—flesh and blood, mind—actual stinking human beings before he tells his actors who they are. And I think you're bloody brilliant on the stage, but if you want to get into my life or Kevin's or Barnard's or Gene-the-blinking-carpenter's you better start doing your homework because you're about forty years behind!"

"I don't know what you're talking about."

"Good. It's a pleasure to be over your head. But you needn't think I like this, dredging this up, digging up the past."

"The past? Dredging what?"

"Your goddam density. The reason our bloody marriage died. I want to leave it dead, I want to be rid of you forever. This stuff is grave-robbing to me, body-snatching, necromancy. Is that clear enough? I'd like to scatter the ashes of our marriage over the middle of the Atlantic Ocean!"

"Shaara . . .?"

"Just get out of here, will you?"

He left her and she continued to fume. She stalked the length of the shop, grabbed the broom and dustpan from the laundry room and wielded them carelessly to gather the glass. Gene Keyes queer—oh, what a wonderful perception! Everywhere she turned Boyd mocked and hampered her, he and his goddam presence and his air of authority. She wasn't sorry she'd broken the mirror and if he was there she'd gladly have broken another one. God knows she'd already put in her seven years' bad luck.

Boyd went back upstairs to gather his things into his brief-case. He was not reassured about Kevin, and he had no idea what had set her off, but he thought her fire rather fine. She flashed and flashed. He would like to have had a videotape of it. She reminded him of the Shaara in the dream, except she wasn't naked. He wished he could get just that incandescence of eruption out of Sister Angela in the second act, where she grabbed the jewels back from the Mother Superior and loaded them on the corpse. He'd have to remember it, in the run-through tomorrow.

23. *Bad Trip*

❧ ━━━━━━━━━━━━━━━━━━━━━━━━━━━━━━━━━ ❧

Wendy caught the shuttle to Boston on the morning of Monday the second, having lost the courage of her prevarications. People were already flinging themselves around the country in celebration of the nation's Independence, and LaGuardia was packed. She was wearing jeans, which would get the visit off to a bad start with her mother, but she couldn't seem to care.

The ringworm was healing nicely, but her spirits had not begun to heal. She'd moped around the apartment all week, had sat in the silence in the dark. She'd shifted things from one part of the living room to another, but the grime defied tidying and sapped her energy. She had four thousand dollars again, two from Boyd and two left of her own. All she spent was for burgers and cheese sandwiches twice a day at the grill on Broadway. Her splendid Saks suitcase was full of dirty underwear and unironed shirts, like a college kid taking the laundry home to Mom.

She got in the boarding line just ahead of a dark-haired girl as young and small as herself, so immensely pregnant that Wendy wondered if the airlines didn't have *rules*. The way her luck was running, the woman would go into labor on the plane. Or maybe it was because she had such little bones that she looked farther gone than she was. Wendy would have looked like that toward the end, if she had gone through with it, or if it had gone through with her.

She turned forward and stared at the hulking back on an

overgrown kid in a work shirt, with a transistor clamped to his ear, a Panasonic with a briefcase handle, big as a hardback book.

"Don't bring me day-own," the radio said. Wendy knew the airlines had rules about *that*; he'd have to turn it off. The way he held it, leaning his sloppy platinum hair into it, reminded her of Peter Plendl, the great big number 59 from the Wellesley High football team.

The line turned the corner and she got a glimpse of his face. It was! "Peter Plendl!"

He turned around and looked at her, not registering right away. She'd probably changed a lot; she used to wear ponytails and pageboys back then. But he'd just got a little softer. He had that same jutting underlip, so swollen-looking that you always thought he'd been punched in the mouth last night. His pale hair was getting thin in the front already, and his eyes were puffier than before.

There was something wrong with his eyes. They seemed to be skittering around her face, not as if they were alert but as if they couldn't catch onto anything. "Wendy Greton, from Wellesley High," she said, and he mumbled, "Yeah, yeah, right, hi," and turned his back to her. He propped his head up with the transistor and held his shoulders strangely askew.

It was very peculiar seeing him, and especially seeing him in bad shape. He'd always been shy and secret, but a sweetheart, really, the only one on the football team who was also on the yearbook staff, so he always did the sports. It struck Wendy she'd been moving backwards ever since she wasn't pregnant after all. First she was not a mother and then she acted as if she wasn't married and then she talked to Bettaline Leric from college and now here was Peter Plendl from Wellesley Senior High. And she was headed home to be coddled and instructed on her table manners. She wished the damn plane would crash.

Sure enough, when he got to the door, they told him to turn off the radio, and he took off with it across the tarmac in his seven-league lope. She remembered it on the field, though he wasn't the one who made the touchdowns. That was Burton Seel, usually, so gorgeous that half the cheerleaders, Wendy included, bounced themselves directly at him. Wendy paid her fare and walked toward the plane, undecided, remembering other things. Like how when they put the football photos on the bulletin board, all the girls stood around gaping at Burton Seel, but she and Mara Laine said, "Look at that great big number fifty-nine!"—out of loyalty because they were on the annual too. Once Peter pointed out to her that they had something in common, because she was the only *cheerleader* who was also on *The Welleslian*. But he didn't have a crush on her or anything; he didn't go out with girls.

She looked for him on the plane, and he was sitting next to the window with the aisle seat free, so she said, "Is it okay if I sit here?" He nodded, his head down over the radio in his lap. She sat down and did up her belt, smiling pleasantly at the gray-haired executive type across the aisle.

"I'd've wished you didn't do that," Peter said, to the radio.

"Do you want me to sit someplace else, Peter? That's okay if you do. I know what it's like to want to be alone."

After a while he said, "No, I mean I'd've wished you didn't get on."

"Shall I move?" She was already unbuckling the belt.

"No, no, no." He took a ragged breath that made his bulk shudder, so she stayed where she was. She saw now that he was afraid of planes.

"Hey, it's okay, Peter," she said softly. He glanced aside at her, pathetic, a huge man that could butt his white head full-tilt into another hard-skulled bruiser. It's amazing the safe things people are afraid of, airplanes and cockroaches and dreams and garden snakes, and then they'll run right into real danger without batting an eye.

The plane taxied and took off and Peter Plendl hung onto the radio till his knuckles whitened. She thought it would help if she could get him talking but she didn't quite know how to start. He had the radio face down and she read off the back of it in raised plastic letters: CAUTION—TO PREVENT SHOCK DO NOT REMOVE COVER. NO USER SERVICEABLE PARTS INSIDE. A piece of the handle was broken off so it was only attached at one end. It might have been one he'd had back at Wellesley; it was old enough.

She didn't think he was up to answering questions so she dived right in. "I'm on my way back to spend the Fourth with my folks, and I am *not* looking forward to it. It seems like the minute I walk in the door I turn thirteen again, and my mother is telling me to wipe my shoes. You know what I mean?"

He turned his sad, disfocused eye on her and she figured

she was on the right track. The NO SMOKING sign went off and the executive across the aisle lit a cigarette—her eye was taken by the flame and then startled by the way he maneuvered the light from his left hand to his right, which was withered into a rigid crook. She hadn't realized they were in the smoking section. She waited for the hostess to give them the emergency spiel.

"I'm married now, to a theater director named Boyd Soole. We live in New York on the West Side, but he's away right now, directing a play. What have you been doing all these, what, six years?"

His mouth worked before he answered and she leaned to him, helping. "I got in a, I got a muthufug depression, man."

"Ah." She could see this was no lie. He sat with his hands, limp now, around the radio; a vibrating inertia and a slightly sour smell. Whole sections of textbook appeared unbidden in Wendy's mind: *Involutional Melancholia. . . . The person realizes that life's ambitions and dreams will probably never be wholly fulfilled. . . . Women are more particularly the victims of this affliction, perhaps because a sense of uselessness and isolation comes to them with special abruptness. . . .*

"I am sorry."

It occured to her for the first time that she had been depressed the past two weeks. Involutionally melancholic, not able to sweep the floor. Wendy had never been depressed that she knew of. She'd been sad, disappointed, frustrated, irritable and often angry, but she'd never been unable to dial the phone, so she didn't recognize a depression when she got one. *Women are more particularly the victims . . .* but wasn't that supposed to be in middle age, when the kids left home?

"I know what you mean." He rejected this with a jerk of his head. His swollen underlip twitched. "Like you can't get up off the floor."

"Yeah," he conceded.

The stewardesses were coming along with the drinks cart and Peter eyed their clankings nervously.

"I've been living in filth since my husband's been gone. It's not because he's gone. I don't know. It seems as if . . ."

"They keep away," Peter said in a louder voice, higher pitched than he'd used up to now.

"What, Peter?"

"Tell them keep away."

"The hostesses? They're just bringing the drinks cart. Do you want a Coke or something?"

"Get away fug'n out of it!" Peter yelled and rose up, holding the radio above his head, but his seat buckle was fastened so he stood in a strained half-crouch. One hostess wheeled around with a can of club soda in her hand and sprayed some of it over the gray-haired executive across the aisle, who looked alarmed and strained against his own seat belt.

"I gotta bomb in here!" Peter shouted. "I blow this muthufug airplane outta sight!"

People in earshot turned stricken, you could see the I-knew-sooner-or-later-it-would-happen-to-me looks on their faces, and the people beyond, aware of the bodies shifting, turned as well, like dominoes to the front of the plane. The far hostess ran, *ran* forward to the cockpit, and the other one, abandoned, stumbled after the drinks cart, shoving it into the coatrack and swinging around to hide in the kitchenette. My God, the incompetence! Aren't these people supposed to be trained for emergencies?

Of course, Wendy was the only one who knew Peter didn't have a bomb. She had heard the radio playing. If it was a working radio it couldn't be a bomb. But she could not say this, because she also knew that if he was hysterical, contradicting him would make him more so. And although he couldn't blow them up he could inflict a lot of damage because the hysterical have extreme, sometimes superhuman strength. She was aware of the straining strap against which he tried to stand, could hear the metal of the buckle grind like teeth.

"It's all right, Peter. They're gone," she said.

He still stood, shaking the radio over his head as if he were shaking someone's shoulders. The muscles filled out in his soft upper arms, biceps conjured out of the past. He was really sick. Sicker than anyone she'd ever taken peanut brittle and paperbacks to in the psych ward, sick and dangerous. Wendy had a painful sense of waste. "Hey Peter." And she had a powerful sense of his power. She knew something about that, firsthand, from long before she knew anything about depression: the strength of weakness, the binding potency of disease, the looming of the small. Her mother, when she had a migraine, commanded half of Boston. She thought of this, and on the heels of it came the most outrageously irrational impulse she had ever experienced: that she would rather like to write a *term* paper on it: "Weak Strength: A Study in Manipulation."

Peter gradually subsided and hunched back beside her. People were still giving them furtive looks, and somebody was crying softly. She slid her eyes to her watch. The flight had only twenty minutes to go. The stewardess in the cockpit would have had them radio ahead, and if she just kept him calm that long he wouldn't hit anybody or scare them worse than they were already scared.

"I can see you're upset," she said, out of the textbook. "Can you tell me what happened?"

"Outkick'n' my coverage," he blurted, which she didn't understand, but she got the gist of it, that he'd got out of his depth somehow.

"Where was that? New York?"

"No, fug'n' Coast. Screwed up bad, mu-fucks, I'm'a blow this plane up, I'm'a blow it!"

"Yeah." She didn't think she ought to touch him, but she leaned far over, so that her head was really in his space, confidentially. "It's not such a bad idea maybe. They fucked me over too. I was thinking standing in that line that I wished the plane would crash. I was."

Peter said nothing so she guessed this was okay. "Do you want to tell me about it?" He said nothing. "Can I tell you?"

He nodded barely perceptibly, swiped his hand across the radio and turned it over, thumb on the tuning dial. "I had a, I had a miscarriage, and I had to do it all alone and put it in a jar; and then I got involved with an airplane pilot that wanted me to smuggle some stuff for him and I thought I could handle it . . ."

"Ah-sheece." Peter shook his head, his shoulders shook again and his face crumpled sympathetic pain. His great lip wobbled. "Those mufug'n' mufucks."

The cockpit door opened and the hostess came out followed by one of the pilots, she round-eyed and he grim. They started down the aisle. Peter raised the radio again and shouted, "Keep 'm away!"

Wendy turned to the man across the aisle and gripped his wrist. She was embarrassed to realize that she was holding the withered arm. His cultivated, weathered face had calmed now, though his cigarette was pinched flat where he held it in the other hand.

"Go *tell them*," Wendy said, "just to stay right up front. Peter and I are having a little talk, and everything is *fine*. You tell them to keep out of it like he says. *Convince* them, hear?"

The man nodded, smashed out the cigarette, undid his seat belt and rose cautiously. He walked, back flexed like a back with a pistol aimed at it, to the stewardess and pilot, who had frozen at the kitchenette. All three of them went into the cockpit.

"See," Wendy said, "they think you're trying to hijack the plane."

"I'n wanna hijack anything, 'm just gonna blow it up."

"I know, but they don't have any idea where your head is, see. They think anybody with a bomb wants to go somewhere else."

"I do wanna go s'm'ere else," he mumbled darkly.

"Where do you want to go?"

"Out of it. Out. Out."

"Yeah. I know what you mean."

This put her in mind of Mr. Bruno Grant back at Wellesley High, one afternoon when he woke up half the class and freaked out the other half with a fanatical spiel, over their heads, about prepositions. She said, "Or sometimes I want to go back. Where it was simple. Do you, ever?"

His head jerked obliquely, neither nod nor shake. "You know what I got to thinking, because I ran into you? Do you remember when Mara and I used to stand in front of the bulletin board with the other girls and say, 'Look at that great big number fifty-nine!'?" She realized she was abnormally awake —it was the first time since Italy that she had felt awake— realized it because she could hear the prepositions as they went by: *to thinking, into you, in front, of the board, with the girls, at fifty-nine.* She had never admitted that she almost knew what Mr. Grant was talking about, but even back then she really did, and she understood it clearly now. *Through the air, on the floor, out of debt, inside your head, back to Boston, down to Boyd, in bed, with him, at home.* "All thought originates in a preposition," Bruno Grant had told them, intense and passionate for the first time in his lethargic life. "Spatial relationships are the primary function of the mind."

"I remember," Peter said, so sadly, and enunciating so, that she dared to put a hand on his arm.

"Do you remember Bruno Grant?"

He smiled a little. "That boring muthufug."

Wendy skipped the part about the prepositions. "How Bud McBride glued up his roll book?"

"Yeah."

The gray-haired man appeared at the cockpit door and waited there, as if asking permission to proceed. Wendy held her palm up to keep him where he was. The plane tilted minutely downward, not the usual frank direction of descent, but one degree at a time, as if caution were in the metal itself.

And now she was so awake that it suddenly occurred to her that she could not really see this, the downward angle of the plane. Outside in the milky cloud bank there was no point of reference; no land could be seen, no cumulus, no horizontal. If she thought she saw the nose of the plane pointed earthward it was that she felt it in the drag of gravity on her flesh, the strain of her torso muscles to stay upright in the seat, the shift of balance in her inner ear. She wanted powerfully to talk to Boyd. She could taste the sound of his voice as surely as she could see the plane descending.

"Did you see that very pregnant woman behind me in the line?" He shook his head. "Very pregnant; I think she must be just about to have the baby. I guess it's a crime to bring children into this shitty world, isn't it?" This was an awful risk, it was either too subtle or too bald. *Into this shitty world*. If he wasn't functioning he'd think it was just chatter, and if he was he might know he was being manipulated in the crudest way.

But she was lucky, and he was somewhere in the messed-up space between. *In, up, between*. Wendy had always had a lot of luck. He said, "Ah-sheece," and started crying and handed the radio to her.

"Don' set it on WBCN."

"No, no, I won't."

He cried into his mammoth hands. Rather like the hands of that German in the café in Rome. He'd been depressed too; almost smothered his baby to let it sleep. Wendy beckoned with the tips of her fingers to the gray-haired man still standing in the aisle, and he walked slowly toward her and bent politely for his instructions.

"Tell the captain that when we land, everybody is to stay put until Peter and I get off the plane. I'll take this with me"—indicating the transistor.

He nodded and withdrew. Wendy reached across and touched Peter's arm. "You know, they'll have radioed ahead for a doctor for you. I think you ought to talk to him." He looked up despairingly and she pressed his biceps more insistently. "See, you'll have to see him anyway, but if *you* choose to see him, they'll know you're okay, really, just a bit depressed."

They came down through the clouds and in sight of Boston. *Down, through, in, of.* She thought they would never land. The No Smoking sign came on, and the intercom. "This is your captain speaking. When we arrive at Logan Airport everyone is to remain seated, with seat belts fastened, until I give you the signal to deplane. This is for your safety and is an absolute order. I repeat . . ."

They touched down shuddering and the door seemed to open the second they came to a stop. Everyone sat mouse-still and quiet. Wendy got up and tucked the radio under her arm, underneath her shoulder bag. She gave the other hand to Peter, who got up and followed her off the plane.

She had known there would be doctors and police. What she wasn't prepared for were the hovering goons in the rubber suits. They stood behind the tires as if that were some kind of hiding place, great metal space masks on their heads like a cheap-shot movie. One of them came to her holding out his thick-gloved hands.

"It's just a radio," she said, and he took it away.

They even had somebody standing by with a straightjacket, but when the two suited doctors had talked a few soothing sentences to Peter they just led him away.

"Good luck, Peter!" she called. She didn't even know what had happened to him on the Coast, who *they* were and what *they* did. *To him.* She was very tired again.

Then the police were around her, the passengers were coming off the plane from behind and the reporters from the front.

"I told you she wasn't with him," the gray-haired executive said to the pilot.

"Please don't put my name in the papers," Wendy said. "My mother would never get over it."

They said they would not put her name in the paper, though they made her tell what happened several times, and took it down. The police said they might need her for a witness. When things settled down a bit, the man with the bad hand came to her and thanked her.

"Alan Tobin," he introduced himself. "I want to say, you are really somebody."

"Ah." She shrugged, embarrassed.

"I mean it. Are you a counselor?"

"A counselor? No, well, I have a B.A. in psychology, but really I just knew Peter back in high school."

"I want to say . . ." He took out his wallet and, using the crooked fingers with remarkable efficiency, handed her a calling card. "If you're going on for a higher degree and you're ever looking for a job, I hope you'll let me know."

The police dismissed them. Wendy dragged on toward the terminal and her parents, who would be both alarmed at the danger and irritated at the wait. She looked at the card. It said *Exxon* in red-white-and-blue, and underneath: *Alan Tobin, Personnel Division, Career Counseling,* and a Manhattan address. So. He was a counselor himself. In careers; a sort of Money Guru at the top. *In, of, at.*

She went *toward.* The reporters hung *around.* The goon in the rubber mask came *across.* He spoke *to.* The policeman stopped her *at.* He said again they were indebted to her *for.* . . .

It was a bomb.

24. *The Pardon*

Kevin having his face telexed and printed on a T-shirt in Underground Atlanta. Kevin buying a natty peaked tweed cap in Peachtree Center. Kevin ice-skating in the middle of the Omni in the middle of the summer in the middle of the hot Deep South.

Boyd sat on the sideline benches reserved for parents and other cowards, glancing back and forth from his newspaper to his speeding son. Kevin had made the transition from roller skates to ice in about fifteen minutes and four falls, and now he was taking the corners foot-over-foot with a bounce and lift at the knee, limber, graceful. Grace was the point of the sport; nevertheless it made Boyd uneasy.

He had given the cast and crew four days off for the holiday—unheard of this late in a rehearsal run, but he had his reasons. They were too ready, too primed, and the main danger now was their getting stale. They were ready for costumes, but the costumes wouldn't be ready for them until Monday. And if they went into partial dress they would have been ready for an audience before there was one. He wished he'd scheduled an earlier opening, but he'd wanted it to be a weekend (God knows how many people could be got out to the theater on a weeknight in Hubbard, Georgia), and he hadn't even wanted to suggest an opening on Friday the thirteenth.

And he'd been taken over again by his own sort of fright and phobia. It happened at the end of any season, any rehearsal period. He began to feel sapped and dry. He became aware of his own rhetoric, and so could not believe in it, and so could not pull it off. We prize self-knowledge but health is at odds with it; you become aware of the working of the viscera only when it is diseased. When you know your heart pumps it is in disorder. Boyd knew too much about the way he worked.

So now in the penultimate week he'd given them Tuesday to Friday. They'd do run-throughs this weekend and have five full nights of dress to build back their pace.

Orme was taking the holiday in Miami. He'd had a call from his agent to say that Ian Hopkins had fractured his hip, three weeks before he was due to start rehearsing *Man of La Mancha* down at the Reynolds dinner theater in Jupiter Beach. Orme had been asked to fill in for him, in the role of Sancho Panza. It meant both that Orme could play a sympathetic character for once, and that he'd have work from the closing of *The Nuns* right up to his next TV filming; and Orme was anxious to fly down and clinch the deal. Boyd's first reaction had been stinging envy, but by the time he and Kevin had dropped Orme at Atlanta Airport yesterday—in exchange for which they got to use the car—Boyd had decided that this was a stroke of luck, another link with Burt Reynolds; and was nearly as anxious as Orme to have it happen. "You can pull that tenor out of mothballs!" Boyd had encouraged him.

Now he and Kevin would take in the fireworks tonight at Atlanta Stadium and drive back to Hubbard late. He'd thought Shaara might make trouble, but she was so damn capricious she thought it was a wonderful plan. "He has a key," she said.

Boyd would really have liked to keep Kevin in Atlanta for the whole four days. But he couldn't afford it. The trouble with living on plastic is that you can get a filet mignon but not a Whataburger.

They got a filet mignon. They got the T-shirt and the cap. They got a plush double on the sixty-third floor of the Peachtree Plaza, its curved outer wall solid glass so that the carpet ended in space over a sixty-three-story drop. *The fourth wall has been removed*, Boyd thought when he first saw it, but he put that out of mind in Kevin's enthusiasm. Neither of them was afraid of heights.

Now the other fear took precedence as he watched Kevin gliding, twirling, in the middle of the ice in the middle of the

Deep South summer. When he read his paper, the news was even more bizarre. The Bundy trial had started, with live television coverage of proceedings on the admissibility of contested evidence. This meant that the sequestered jury were the only people in the country not allowed to see such objects, witnesses and background info as the judge deemed inadmissible. The country was making up its mind on the very stuff that was being held back from the twelve good men and true. In Lake Elsinore, California, a woman and her twelve-year-old daughter had walked half-naked around the woods for two weeks thinking they were fleeing a murderer because they'd overheard somebody talking about shooting a raccoon. Whereas on the New York–Boston shuttle another woman, unidentified, had talked a psychotic out of blowing up the plane with what she thought was a transistor radio. Jesus, the Boston shuttle. Wendy could have been on that plane as easy as not. There's danger everywhere you turn.

Kevin turned adroitly and stopped himself by crashing into the railing. "Is it time for dinner yet? I'm starved."

"It looks like hungry work. Let's go."

He'd picked the restaurant carefully tonight, had asked around. Because all of life, like the syndicated horoscope that Wyman kept bringing in, is a self-fulfilling prophecy. What's on your mind is always in your path and at your fingertips. They'd driven down Peachtree Street last night searching for a place they liked the look of, and it wasn't until they had their menus and their water glasses, admiring the etched screens and the antique brass, that Boyd realized there wasn't a woman in the place, and that he'd brought Kevin to a gay restaurant. He had meant to initiate a serious conversation with him. All he could think of was that *they* thought *he'd* brought in a kid young enough to be his son.

Again at lunch he'd meant to try, in the delicatessen, and Kevin had appeared to give him an opening with some off-the-cuff comment about his "faggy math teacher."

Boyd said, "Do you know what that means?"

"What?"

"*Faggy.*"

"Oh, sure, it's just an expression. All the kids use it."

"What I mean is, for example, do all the kids use *nigger*?"

"Nah, you say *black* now. Only grits say *nigger*."

"Well, but there's a big difference."

"Sure, I guess."

"Do you know what the difference is?"

"Sure, blacks like to be called blacks and they don't like to be called niggers."

"That's a big difference."

"I never say *nigger*, dad, if that's what you're getting at. Mom's a fanatic about it."

"So am I."

"Okay, sure."

"But what about *fag*, then?"

"*Nerd, dork*, it's just an expression."

"There's no such thing as just an expression, is what I'm getting at. *Expression* is the way people live with each other. How do the homosexuals feel about being called fags?" He had the feeling he was not getting at what he meant to be getting at.

"I don't know any *gays*."

"Yes, you do."

"I do? Who?"

"Barnard, for instance."

"Oh, yeah, but I mean at school."

"Well, how would Barnard feel about being called *faggy*?"

"He's not faggy, he's funny. Hey, Dad, listen, don't *worry* about it. I wouldn't call Barnard a fag. I'm not a dork."

Tonight at the Coach and Six they tried veal scallopini and bouillabaisse, and Boyd tried again.

"Y'know, the way things have worked out, you've spent a lot of time growing up without a man around. I guess your mother and I owe you an apology for that—that we couldn't work it out."

"That's okay, Dad. I got used to it. I'm not saying it wasn't rough at first. But half the kids I know, their parents are divorced. It's no big deal."

"I realize that, but one of the things it means is that I haven't been in on some important parts of your growing up. You and I have never talked about sex, for instance."

"Oh, they do all that stuff in school."

"I know they do, but there are always things it's hard to bring up in school. I know when I was your age, there were things I got really confused about because I didn't have anybody I could ask. Well, I did—but my only source of information was a bully on my block. He knew even less than I did, it turned out, and he gave me some pretty bass-ackward ideas."

Kevin laughed. "I know the kind."

"I just wanted you to know you can ask me anything you want."

"Okay, sure."

That appeared to end it. "I mean anything. Whatever—kinky, whatever."

"I 'preciate it, Dad."

"Well? Is there anything?"

"I want to ask? Hmm." Kevin pondered. Boyd couldn't tell if he was nervous or just trying to oblige. "There's one thing. What's *cunny lingwis?*"

A mushroom, a sprig of tarragon and a silver of milk-fed veal; Boyd swallowed and explained in words of one syllable and, where possible, fewer than four letters, which conjunction of human parts was designated by the term *cunnilingus.*

"Yeah, I thought so," Kevin nodded. "Sorta half a sixty-nine."

The fireworks were fireworks. Boyd was restless and a bit wry about the tangled ironies of This Great Nation of Ours. Kevin clapped and cheered with a little strain—as if, perhaps, it was the last Fourth that he would clap and cheer. It was nearly midnight by the time they shouldered their way to the parking lot, and nearly one before they got on the road.

There were a few miles of expressway, then they turned onto a two-lane state road southeast, an hour and a half to Hubbard. Boyd offered Kevin a milkshake, but they were both still stuffed with *haute cuisine*. Kevin was sleepy and Boyd knew his chance was gone; he'd be pushing it to try again. Kevin drummed on his knee to the radio, and after a while he propped his head against his windbreaker and slid off into sleep. They passed few cars at this hour, but when they did Boyd glanced at him in the headlights, tendrils of shadow swinging across his cheek from his unkempt hair. Boyd's stomach felt heavy, as if he'd overeaten fatherhood.

When they got out into pine country the mists began. Ankle-high white wisps crossed the road and stirred at their approach—some perfectly explicable conjunction of heat, damp, earth and nightfall, which Boyd didn't understand. Downhill the ground mist thickened so it was impossible to decide which lights to use. Boyd flicked to the low beam and could see only ten feet of road, went back to bright and was confronted with a wall of smoke, out of which someone else's headlights suddenly loomed.

He didn't keep a car in New York—too many hassles, and too expensive—and it was years since he'd driven in open country at night. He tried to remember when the last time must have been, but all he could remember were the first times, in California fogs more general, less capricious, than these crossing Caspars. When he was discovering beer and petting (no pot and damn little sex back then), he used to save his money for gas and take his date as far as Balboa, Riverside, even La Jolla, hoping his father wouldn't notice the speedometer. And when he got home, beer-foggy and blue-balled, impermissibly late, James Soole would be sitting in his study in the black recliner, accusingly at work. He never said a word; the cold look and the hand out for the keys were all Boyd ever got.

I started in to cry and call his name . . .

There his father was again. Wherever there was night or mist or trouble or a car; that remote man in his remoteness, his night and mist and trouble, and his car. The fog had cloaked a curve of the white line, which appeared suddenly on his right. Boyd caught the wheel with a little surge of adrenaline and glanced to make sure that Kevin hadn't waked. All it takes is to decide to turn the wheel a second past the necessary moment. He slowed to forty and shook himself wider awake, straining forward. To keep awake, and for the confrontation of it, he recited the Wilbur poem, aloud but low, over and over.

Well, I was ten and very much afraid.
In my kind world the dead were out of range . . .

At three o'clock they hit the trailer parks and fast-foods that indicated the edge of Hubbard, and Boyd put the radio on again and gently jiggled Kevin's arm. Kevin stretched and yawned and further tousled his hair. "We here already?"

"That's easy for you to say. I've been staring into the fog for two hours. Listen, Kevin, it's three in the morning. Is it a better idea if we just go to the motel?"

"Nah, Mom expects me back. She'd be worried in the morning."

"Okay."

He pulled onto the wooded street and crept quietly into the drive. A high lamp on a power pole shimmered over the tops of the trees. He got out and opened the trunk for Kevin's duffle bag and packages.

"Hey, Dad?" Kevin stood with his hand on the door, head cocked. "Dad? Some'n's wrong," he whispered.

"What do you mean?" Boyd whispered back.

"I don't know. Something funny. It's a feeling. It . . . *smells* wrong."

Boyd sniffed and listened. He could smell nothing but that moldy freshness of Georgia dirt, hear nothing that couldn't be accounted for by several million leaves. Then maybe there was a larger scurrying from somewhere behind the house.

"Just a cat or dog?"

"Or a possum. That's not it, though. Let's go check."

Boyd found a camping lantern in the carport and they headed stealthily into the backyard. Shaara had left the porch light on, but beyond its perimeter there was the same milky blackness he'd been driving through, with the faintest shudder of shadow on it from the power-pole lamp. The beam of the flashlight picked out molehills and fallen leaves, a gardenia bush in bud that would be in bloom at sunup, monkey grass, azalea bushes in need of a clipping.

"Swing it over here."

Where the grass thinned at the foot of a poisoning palm, there were fresh scatterings of rusty earth, which got thicker as they followed them in the narrow beam, to where they turned into a mound, and then a hole.

"Oh, Jesus, Dad."

The dog's corpse, half in the grave and half flung out, was only bone and matted fur by now, and bits of rotted blanket adhering to it in patches. The juice was gone. There were no guts or maggots, nothing overtly horrible, no stench. Boyd's stomach turned not on his own account but because he could have wished . . . he could have wished there might be God enough in the stinking universe to spare one boy the sight of one pet dismembered in its death. Kevin gagged and turned into Boyd's shoulder, and Boyd put a steadying arm around him, playing the beam over the grave. Part of the hide had disintegrated like a ragged-out glove, and the bone shone white at the joints, shoulder, spine and skull. Both femurs had been tossed out, and part of the spine and several ribs. The face lay sharp as a scissors blade, the empty sockets padded round with bits of lid. He held Kevin hard. "Possums, I guess."

"Or dogs."

"We should bury it again."

Kevin nodded and took a breath.

"Are you okay, Son?"

"I'm okay."

Kevin showed him where the tools were kept, and Boyd sent him in to look for kerosene or charcoal lighter.

"If we burn him, we'll wake up Mom."

"We're not going to burn him. The smell will keep whatever dug him up from doing it again."

"Oh. Okay."

Boyd went back and propped the flashlight so it shone into the grave. He spread his trench coat on the lawn and shoveled the front quarters up onto it, then hastily reached around in the dark to gather the other bones. He wanted the corpse assembled before Kevin got back to him. The bones were smooth and damp and gave off a musty smell. *Asking forgiveness of his tongueless head.* God, he was glad he'd never showed that poem to Kevin. He stepped down into the pit and put his weight on the shovel head. Tightly wrapped, the bundle was small enough now that he only had to make a deeper trench in the middle. Kevin came back with a gallon jug of Clorox and a can of lighter fluid.

"Will this do?"

"We'll use them both. The grass won't recover for a good while here. I hope it doesn't kill the palm."

"Nothing will kill that old palm."

"Do you want to dig?"

He got out and Kevin got in. They were both sweating and streaked by the time Boyd was satisfied.

"Dad, that's your coat."

"I want a new coat." He started to put the bundle in the cleft, then out of some minimal sense of ceremony turned and offered it to Kevin, who took it, hugged it to his stomach, stepped into the shallower end of the grave and pressed it into the trench.

"Bye, Henry," Kevin said . . . *to cry and call his name.*

Boyd poured the Clorox while Kevin poured the charcoal lighter. The two smells, chemical and violent, overpowered scents of sod and greenery until they filled the grave. But by the time they tamped it and strewed armfuls of leaves, night, nature, grass had taken over the air again. They sat panting for a minute. Boyd put his dirty arm around Kevin's damp back.

"Are you all right?" Kevin nodded. "I'm sorry you had to go through all that."

"No, it's okay. It's probably good. I sorta hadn't, you know, said good-bye to him or something."

I beg death's pardon now. Boyd looked out over his head into the white darkness, the breathing trees. "Son, I want to tell you something I've never told anyone. Not even your mother, not Wendy. I guess it's always troubled me."

"Yeah, Dad?"

"My father . . . your grandfather Soole that you never knew . . . you know, the accident they had, nobody knows but me, that it wasn't an accident. I found notebooks after their death, my dad's notebooks, that made it pretty clear he was going to take his own life."

"Really?" Kevin looked up and strained to see him.

"I can't be sure, but he was a troubled man—alone, remote. I think you have a right to know, because he was your grandfather, and . . ." He couldn't think what was meant to come after the conjunction. His voice wavered a little, and now it was Kevin who put an arm around him. Kevin still strained into Boyd's face, and there occurred suddenly, in his own, one of those understandings beyond the edge of understanding: a miracle, out of the mouths of babes, release.

"*You're* not your father!"

Boyd felt the air balloon into his mouth and throat, turn to helium in his lungs.

"I mean, *I'm* not *you* . . ." Kevin offered in explanation of his explanation.

Boyd looked away from that blinding insight, into the mist over the recovered grave, the smell of immaculate decay. . . .

And the pages appeared as usual, their endless exegeses, to which no possible further perception could have been supplied even if someone had been mad enough to wish to. . . .

Except the leftward and downward drag of the cramped script, which, as any fool could plainly see, was utterly other than his own sprawling hand. *I dreamt the past was never past redeeming.*

"Dad, listen, now we're doing this, there's something I haven't told you too. I mean, I don't know if you want to know, but I made it with a girl."

"A girl?"

"Well, of course a *girl*, but I mean I really did. It's okay, I mean, she's on the pill, she's *fifteen.* . . ."

Visibly to his son's astonishment, Boyd lay back in the grass and laughed, tears streaking through the dirt and the sweat in his effort not to wake Shaara.

"That's great. No, I mean it, Son; that's great."

Just before daylight he drove to the cottage on Lake Takullah and parked beside the dock. Wyman and Barnard were off doing northern Florida in the break. He tied the notebooks together with a roll of twine, found a jagged rock and knotted it securely with a slack of about a foot between stone and pads. He went to the end of the dock and, putting all his bulk and heft into the end of his arm, cast the whole caboodle into the cypress swamp.

25. *The Perils of Pauline*

The Greton family sat at the lunch table. There were Mr. Greton and Mrs. Greton and little Wendy. On the table were lots of good things to eat, cheese and bread and grapes and apples.

"My, my," said Wendy. "This is good cheese."

Mr. Greton said, "Your mother is a good cook."

Tar, the dog, came into the room. "Hello, Tar," said Wendy. "Do you want some of this good cheese?"

"Arf, arf," said Tar. Tar was big and black and very old. Tar sat on the floor beside the table.

Mrs. Greton said, "Don't give any cheese to Tar. Don't feed her at the table."

Mr. Greton said, "That dog is old. We must have her put to sleep."

Mrs. Greton said, "Now, now, George, don't talk that way. Don't talk that way at table."

"No, no," said Wendy. "You must not put Tar to sleep. She is my dog and I love her."

Mr. Greton said, "She is too old. Her breath stinks and she cannot hold her water."

Mrs. Greton said, "Don't talk that way at the lunch table."

Mr. Greton said, "I will talk any way I damn please."

"Arf, arf," said Tar.

* * *

For the first day and a half they treated her as if she had
the flu, but after they had determined that she was hale and
a trifle irritable, the Gretons were reassured that Wendy was
none the worse for the ordeal of being on that plane. Mrs.
Greton, whose own mother had believed that no lady got her
name in the papers, but was herself less orthodox on this point,
was nevertheless relieved to see that Wendy was not mentioned. "Peter Plendl!" she said. "Wasn't his father that Belgian
dentist?"

"Orthodontist," Wendy said. "Viennese."

Wendy took up her customary position as the receptacle of
smiling insults between George and Pauline. Each spoke to
her, in the third person, of the other. Wendy wondered what
happened when she wasn't there. "Your father is so crotchety!"
Mrs. Greton would trill, laughing to deny that she was saying
this. "I think we'd just better keep out of his way for a few
hours!" To which her father would reply, "Just like a woman.
Your mother takes everything *personally*." His manner was a
long-suffering lift of the eyebrow, meant to be humorous.

Both were lean and handsome people, her father of middle
height but her mother diminutive. Mrs. Greton's dignity was
in her carriage, and in an upswept hairdo that bespoke the
war years but still suited her. Of the two, her father was aging
with more grace. He still had a certain swagger born of Cor-
poration Law, of civil suits over larger amounts of money than
he himself had ever seen, of executive lunches with men In
Office, of mahogany and boardroom leather. Mrs. Greton was
still houseproud, still dusted the Queen Anne tables with her
fingertips as she passed them, still plumped the mauve-and-
aqua quilted cushions at the least sign of a dent—everything
in the Tudor house was either spindly or overstuffed—but
Wendy thought that her mother's conversation wandered more
than before, more than her sixty years called for. Her hand,
Wendy thought, wandered, to hide her creping neck. Sometimes she had a tic just below her left eye, and the hand would
rest there, unconvincingly by accident.

"Tell me about your floors. Did they do a good job?"

"I can't say I'm altogether satisfied."

"No, isn't it the truth. I tell you. Do you remember when
we had the chiffonier refinished? No, that would have been
when you were away at school. Your father!—he's always wanted

to rush in and have things done any old how, it was the same with the new handles upstairs. And how is Boyd?"

"He's fine, he thinks the production may be really good."

"But I worry, Wendy. It's such a hard life you've taken on, his being away so much. I know when your father is away, well I always think I'll get some peace and then I don't know what to do with myself."

"I really don't mind it, Mama. I always find plenty to do."

It occurred to Wendy that she would enjoy being a tourist in Boston. If it weren't home, if she were not locked here in the mauve-and-aqua quilting, constrained to set a coaster under every glass, to make sure that her knife and fork were crossed upside down on her not-quite-empty plate, that her blouses hung symmetrically on their hangers; she would tour. She would walk Beacon Street up and down and peek into the plush foyers of the old publishing houses, she would do Newbury Street and Harvard Square, go out to Concord and Lexington and be suitably imaginative about Paul Revere. As it was, she had trouble getting off for a few hours with old friends. Pauline Greton let her go with elaborate protestations of pleasure that made it clear she felt rejected. "Well, of *course* you'd want to see Cheryl Webster—what is her name now? Have a good time and don't worry about us. What time do you plan on being back?"

Her name was Walker now, Cheryl Webster Walker, and she had three children under three in a slum walk-up with clotheslines on pulleys like a Victorian novel. Magwitch in a ditch. They had no real talk because Cheryl's conversation wandered, of necessity, more than Mrs. Greton's; with injunctions of "don't" and "danger" and diaper changes and uncoverings of the breast. Her breasts wept and sagged and she spoke almost entirely of money, its scarcity. Wendy said she understood and that her utilities had been cut off. Unlike Peter Plendl, Cheryl clearly did not believe her. "But your husband's in the theater," she said, as if the glamour of this would pay the bills. Cheryl's husband was in blenders, sales division. It was a relief to get back to the clipped and dusted Wellesley neighborhood.

On the Fourth of July Pauline Greton did an American centerpiece, deep red roses and blue iris nestled in white baby's breath. She had a major talent for floral arrangement, and always seemed to know how to pick buds at that precise moment before full bloom, when they would unfold indoors and last as long as possible. Even Jimmy the gardener—who was nearly as black as Tar and had teeth nearly as bad; from time to time Mr. Greton would suggest getting rid of him as well —even Jimmy, who was a jealous and possessive professional, would admit, "Your mama knows flowers. She *knows* them flowers."

The bouquet burst extravagant on the dining table. Mr. Greton, pale-faced in a gray suit, and Mrs. Greton, gray-haired in a pink dress, bent over their pink sherbet and macaroons. The roses rioted in the center of the table, the iris thrust their stiff heads left and right, the baby's breath showered like fireworks. Wendy felt her own pallor and despaired.

"Now, tomorrow," said Pauline, who had already said this several times, "I want to take you in to the sales. Filene's is closing out their summer stock and I do think you need some decent things."

"Your mother thinks money grows under cabbages," said Mr. Greton humorously.

"Don't make any plans for tomorrow, all right, Wendy? Just this once, and after that you can go off as you like."

"No, I won't, Mama, that's fine. But I don't want you spending a lot of money on me."

"Don't listen to your father, he just likes being wheedled. All men like being wheedled. It makes them feel powerful!"

"I haven't had any power around here since the day you were born," Mr. Greton said humorously, "and the two of you ganged up on me."

"I have plenty of clothes, really," Wendy said, "It's just that with the mess in the apartment I couldn't get to them."

"We'll spend the whole day, mind," said Mrs. Greton.

"She'll spend half of Chase Manhattan," Mr. Greton said.

"Do you remember that navy-blue velvet with the embroidered duck? My, you felt grown-up to have a *dark* dress! I'll bet Boyd likes to be wheedled, now, doesn't he?"

"I don't know, I don't wheedle him," Wendy said.

Mr. Greton said, "Well, then it's beyond me what you learned from your mother!" Humorously.

This sort of thing went on. Wendy would escape to her old room, sit in the wicker rocker among the chintz forget-me-nots, hold a book in her hand but not read it, nervously judge when she must go down again. If she misjudged she would be brightly called. "Wendy, darling, I need your advice about this opal brooch. Do you have a minute?"

She had too many of them. Up in her room, redolent of proms and diaries, down in the dining room with her parents dwarfed by the flowers, out in the garden taking old Tar for a piddle. *In treating involutional melancholia, the physician stresses the importance of a nourishing diet, adequate sleep, a healthful and pleasant environment, proper exercise, and absorbing avocations.* She walked Tar around the rose arbor and along the hedges.

"Remember we're going shopping tomorrow!" her mother called from the veranda.

In the evening they watched the fireworks on TV. Mrs. Greton said, "Ooh!"—it was after all a twenty-one-inch color set—and Mr. Greton said, "Thank God you're past the age that your mother'll make me haul you down there in those crowds." They had a snack of finger sandwiches, smoked ham and cress. Mrs. Greton said, "Well, we'd better get a good night's sleep. We have a full day tomorrow."

But in the morning, when her father had gone to the office, Wendy thought Pauline Greton seemed less bright. She only half-cleared the table, lost her keys and her glasses, perched on the edge of a chair with her hand against her cheek, as if to think. With her head bent to her hand, she lost something of her splendid carriage. The upsweep of her silver hair seemed to Wendy oddly brave.

"Why don't you drive, dear?"

Wendy had not driven in Boston traffic for several years, and would rather not have. But she took the recovered keys and backed the Continental down the drive, paid attention to signs and signals, and found her way well enough.

"Filene's first?"

"Well, no, now, if you don't mind, we ought to stop off at Dr. Todd's. You remember him. He did your tonsils and I don't know what-all."

She remembered Dr. Todd. He was the occasion of many a smiling harangue between her mother and father, because he was too expensive for the Gretons. He was general practitioner to genuine Yankees and D.A.R.'s. He had elegant offices just behind Beacon Street, and a tendency to refer everything but the common cold to specialists. It was when she became president of the Wellesley Garden Club, the closest she ever got to Old Boston society, that Mrs. Greton had taken her migraines to Dr. Todd.

"Of course I remember him. What for?"

"Oh, he just has some test results he wanted to discuss with me. You know how he is. I thought perhaps you wouldn't mind coming along with your poor old mother. It shouldn't take too long, and then we'll get right on the sales."

"What sort of tests?"

But her poor old mother professed total ignorance on this point. "Some something up at the Neurological Institute. You know he's always making you spend your money on tests. But don't tell your father I said so!" she trilled.

Wendy sat in the spacious white-and-gold waiting room with a magazine on her lap. It was the same *Sports Illustrated* she'd read a month ago in Dr. Madden's office in East Millstone, with the article about scaling the Matterhorn. Which she would rather have been doing than this. She was so used to her mother's bravery over imagined slights and sicknesses that she couldn't sort it out from the real thing. Which was it now? Gilt mirrors gave her face back, tired and round-eyed. Her haircut had softened around the ears and in another three weeks it would be too long again. *A healthful and pleasant environment, proper exercise, and absorbing avocations.* Her shoulders ached from too much sitting the past four days.

The door opened and a nurse beckoned her, ushered her into Dr. Todd's office, where her mother sat upright in a leather chair brass-studded and outrageously oversized, to advertise its comfort. Across a football field of desk, gray-templed Dr. Todd put out his hand and welcomed her in the mellifluous voice that had earned him a hundred thousand a year as general practitioner to the D.A.R.

"Nice to see you again, Wendy. Your mother's a little bit doubtful about my asking you in here, but I think I've convinced her. Isn't that right, Mrs. Greton?"

"I don't know." Her mother smiled a false and timid smile. Wendy sat down in the chair next to her.

"What is it?"

"Well, I've had your mother go for a series of neurological tests, because she was experiencing a little discomfort. And as I suspected, she's experiencing . . ." Dr. Todd paused ever so slightly, with an incline of his handsome head, and Wendy remembered that his patients never "suffered" anything, they always "experienced" it. She herself had experienced tonsillitis, vaginitis, a broken leg, and cramps. ". . . A *very* mild and *very* early form of *paralysis agitans*."

"In plain English?"

"Parkinson's disease. But, as I say, we've caught it in good time, and she's otherwise in excellent health, so there's every reason to believe she can handle it beautifully."

He went on, and Wendy asked questions. Pauline Greton asked none, sat effortfully upright, smiling vaguely as if she had happened into this conference by mistake. Wendy could see now that the hand she lifted to the tic did not wander, it trembled and tapped. Dr. Todd was in a wonderfully positive mood. It *was* a wonder, fully worth a hundred thousand dollars a year, how soothingly he could convey the information that there was no cure, that Parkinson's disease was the result of degenerative changes in the brain, that the patient shows slowly increasing bodily rigidity, associated with tremors of the head and limbs, that the patient's arm no longer swings when he walks and walking may become difficult, that the voice tends to lose its natural inflections and becomes monotonous. That intervals of as long as a year may occur between phases of development from one limb to another.

"It's never fatal," Dr. Todd said, having dealt the symptoms out so skillfully, letting them adjust, that by now this seemed a cause for a holiday, "and we can control the rigidity with levodopa and anticholinergic drugs. Baths and massages help too, and there's been a technique developed at the University of Chicago, to deaden a portion of the basal ganglia, which has shown marvelous results in letting that portion of the brain function more normally."

He said, in effect, but in other words, that it would be a good many years before they had to stick needles into Pauline Greton's brain. Wendy and her mother thanked him and Mrs. Greton wrote a check in the outer office. They went outside and got back in the car.

"*Now* Filene's," said Pauline Greton.

"Oh, Mama." Wendy dropped the keys in her lap to signal that she would not move until they had this out, or had taken it in. She looked at the pleasant Georgian street, its pillars and window boxes and scrubbed steps. "Oh, Mama. Does Daddy know?"

"My goodness, your father? Wendy, don't you dream of telling your father."

"Mama, he's got to know. If you don't tell him, I will."

"I would never, never," she held up a forefinger and it shook like an advanced form of the disease, "*never* forgive you if you told your father."

Wendy didn't like to point out in so many words that her father would be able to *see* it. "He'll have to know eventually," she said.

"Oh, eventually. After I've had time to get used to it and learn how to deal with it. These modern drugs are miraculous, you know."

"But Mama, Daddy would want to know. It's not the kind of thing you keep to yourself. He'd be terribly *hurt* if you didn't share it with him."

Pauline Greton laughed a short bark, something like the bitterness of the old command. "Really, Wendy, I wonder what they taught you about psychology. Don't you know that men can't handle disease? Doctors, hospital smells, weakness—they simply can't handle that at *all*. It wounds their pride, you see. Your father never gets ill . . . well, he does, but he *won't*. He goes to the office with the Asian flu. And when I'm ill, why . . ." the fine tracery of her skin changed angles as her face fought itself. She had lovely bones and lovely skin. George Greton, when he was not in his crotchety mood, was fond of saying that she got prettier every year. ". . . why, Wendy, you know about the dog, you can see it yourself. You can *see* the way he feels about *Tar*."

Wendy picked up the keys and kneaded them in her palm. She could not reply to this. "Mama, you must think very little of him if you think he wouldn't want to know."

"I think the world of your father!" Mrs. Greton said sharply. "And I'll think very little of you if you don't let me handle this in my own way!"

They tried things on. They put them on their feet and around their necks and over their heads and behind their ears. They bought some. Mrs. Greton wrote the checks and got out the charge-a-plates and Wendy let her. They dawdled a long time in a special Italian section where Wendy saw, at twice the price, the dagger she had bought for Kevin in Florence; and where she bought, at twice the price, one of the paramilitary jumpsuits she had seen in Rome, all epaulettes and brass and khaki. They got home after six with a delicatessen rotisserie chicken and tomato aspic.

"Well, am I broke?" Mr. Greton greeted them.

"We're demolished!" Pauline Greton claimed, and dropped into a chair with her bundles. "The crowds are dreadful! But I think we got some decent things. Wendy, put on that army uniform and model it for your father." She leaned to George and placed the left hand firmly on the padded chair arm. She confided, "It's very smart, the latest thing from Italy, but Wendy has some doubts about what Boyd's going to say. He's, you know, rather antimilitary."

After supper, surprisingly (it was Thursday), Boyd called from Georgia. Wendy took the call in the stairwell, out of earshot but in sight of her parents, who were deep in mauve-and-aqua quilting before the TV. Boyd professed anxiety, but in fact he seemed in high spirits, almost jubilant.

"I read about the bomb scare on the shuttle, and I thought, my God, you could have been *on* that plane."

"I was."

"Wendy! Did you realize what was going on?"

"More or less."

"You must have been terrified."

"Not really. I knew Peter Plendl back in high school."

"The hijacker?"

"It wasn't a hijack."

"The psychotic, I mean."

"That's what they said. I don't think so. I think he's an involutional melancholic."

"Didn't that freak you out? Knowing him?"

"No well, really it made it easier. I knew he was a sweetheart underneath."

"Wendy, you are something else!"

She wanted to say: something else than what? She said, "How's it going down there?"

"Too well. So well I gave them a few days off. Kevin and I have been doing Atlanta, and . . . we had a real adventure over his dog. I'll have to tell you all about it when I see you. It's a kick having a kid, I tell you. We should try it sometime. Wendy? Are you there?"

"I'm here," she said.

"What have you been up to in Boston?"

"Not a whole lot. Mom and I spent the afternoon at the sales. I'm pretty much worn out."

In the living room she could see that her father was making some deprecatory remarks about "The Waltons," could see it from the corporate courtroom tilt of his head. Her mother sat with her left hand at her left cheek, unconvincingly by accident. "Boyd!" she said.

"Yeah, love."

"I need to tell you . . ." She fingered the corkscrew of aqua telephone wire and stared into the busy pattern of aqua primula on the stairwell wallpaper, tugged at the cord to diminish the distance between them. ". . . that I got an Italian outfit, sort of military. I'm not sure that you'll like it." Across the hall her mother tapped the cheek and replied to her father, some bright lie. And now her father made a humorous remark, the eyebrow lifted as he had lifted it last night at dinner: *it's beyond me what you learned from your mother!*

"Also, Boyd . . ." She tugged at the wire. The clear necessity of telling Boyd the truth—a truth, any truth—appeared before her in the mathematically spaced holes of the telephone receiver that would carry such a truth as far as Georgia. "Also . . ." The thing she had learned from her mother, how to lie to a loved man, flowered in the primula on the wall. "Also, I, uh, bought a dagger for Kevin." And for the first time in six weeks, perhaps for the first time in her life, Wendy was aware of mortal danger.

26. *Breakdown*

The first requisite of a good breakdown is a glue gun with a diluted mixture of latex-based mucilage. If the spittle is too thick it will read embroidery under the lights even when decorated with dirt. Dribble, glob and smear the mixture in the desired area and drag immediately through silt, sand and sawdust. When working on heavy fabrics (e.g., a gabardine nun's habit), it will be efficacious to place the garment on an ironing board and to "press" it with an orbital or belt sander at hem, cuffs, elbows and other points of natural wear. Dregs of paint may be used, dark on light and light on dark; avoid primary colors. An acetylene torch will make more convincing holes than a knife or scissors. Many designers otherwise knowledgeable stumble through life without realizing that the most valuable assistant in the matter of rips and tears is a hound dog in the chewing stage. A slice of bologna or a thin solution of sugar water applied in the desired spot will cause the hound to produce irregular and frayed apertures of an eminently realistic appearance.

Shaara washed the shop windows with Gunilla's satin gown and cleaned the grease off the jigsaw with it. The fabric was not absorbent enough to do a good job on either windows or jigsaw, but they did a good job on it. Gene played tug-of-war with Fibber McGee over the wimples. Shaara took a screwdriver and ripped several of the silver and lavender day lilies to shreds. Gene did action paintings on the habits with a compound of shellac, 3-in-One oil and ashes. Shaara set fire to one of the sleeves and put it out with cranberry juice. She took a rasp to train and bodice.

Gunilla's gown was the easier because it started out so light and bright. Satisfied, Shaara threw it on the floor and wiped her bare feet on it. But the habits didn't yield so well; the cloth was too dark and strong. As every actor knows to his chagrin, a costume can be stiff and stinking and still look bandbox under the lights.

"What we need is to get some kind of allover patina of dirt. I don't like to paint it, I'm afraid the strokes will show."

Fibber, sensitive to the general atmosphere, was tunneling aggressively through the garments on the floor. Every now and again he stopped to challenge a wimple with karate noises. He was lengthening every day in face and haunch, and he was a bit of a breakdown himself in glue and grease. Classes were back in session on the third floor, in Theater History and Improvisation, but the company was still on break, and Gene and Shaara had the theater and shops to themselves. Kevin and Boyd were touring sinkholes in Orme's car.

"I've got a can of beige flat wash here. Why don't we just dip our hands in it and wipe 'em on the habits?"

"Okay, let's try it."

Gene levered the can open and Shaara picked up Sister Ines's costume. They stuck their hands in the paint, shook them half dry, and began wringing them through the fabric, she from the shoulder and he from the hem. There were seven yards in the skirt and it was a long job, not as exhilarating as a belt sander or an acetylene torch.

"Howzat?"

Shaara put it on a hanger and hung it from the doorframe, stepped back and trained a work light on it. "Not bad. It's a little blotchier than I'd like. That's okay for Ines, though. She's been scrabbling around in the grave. But I wish we could get it sort of more general on the others. Maybe I better try a brush."

"Or how 'bout this? If I paint a big square on the floor, we can put the habits on and roll around in it."

"That's it! I'll sweep the dirt into it." She took the shop broom and worked from the corners inward, to where Gene painted a king-sized square of rubbery beige. Metal filings, sawdust, shavings, ashes, fluff and general gunge settled over and into it.

"Lock the door, Gene. I don't fancy the academic V.P. walking in on this." She bound her hair in a shop rag, kerchief-style, and tucked it in. She stripped to her bra and panties and Gene to his J.C. Penney shorts. Her bosom would not go into Orme's habit at all, so Gene put it on and zipped it as far as it would zip, loose at the waist and straining at the shoulders. Shaara crawled into Wyman's voluminous shape; the whole thing hung long and large.

"Let me cover your hair too." She made him a mammy-kerchief out of half a towel and jeered at the result. She bent over and tested the paint with her fingers—it had to be tacky, not wet, or it would be too obvious.

"All right."

They lay down on either side of the square and rolled toward each other through the paint and dirt. "Wiggle around." Fibber, excited by the smell but unwilling to wet his feet, yapped at them and tried to catch the fabric as it passed.

"Oh, say," said Shaara when they met. "I do just fancy you as a nun."

"You are a superior goddam mother. But your costumes fit something awful."

They rubbed each other's sleeves in the muck. They rubbed each other. Gene lifted her habit and stuffed it into his waistband to reach her thigh.

"What are you doing?"

"I'm girding up your loins."

"Stop that, now."

"The door's locked."

"But the windows."

"It's lighter outside than in."

"Someone will come."

"Fibber's a good guard dog."

"We'll be excommunicated."

But they sinned. Very slowly, their skirts tangled around their waists and the sleeves crushed up as far as they would go. Fibber got bored with them and wandered off somewhere. Shaara's kerchief slipped and she murmured amorously, "Paint in my hair," and took a deep breath of latex flat wash, which made her high, the chemistry between them.

The breakdowns were spectacularly good. And they were not walked in on; it was fully an hour later, both of them dressed and more or less washed up at the laundry sink, when Joe Dimbleton dropped by.

"Oh, Shaara. I was looking for the cast. I thought they'd want to know that the academic V.P. was in this morning and signed the Q-80 form. I've got their checks right here."

"Oh, thanks, Joe, terrific. I'll be seeing Boyd later tonight and I'll play Santa Claus if you like."

"Yes, well, I suppose that would be . . ." He cast an eye askance at the mess on the floor and the mutilated costumes, but he handed her the envelopes. "How is it going? Aren't they, uh, rehearsing?"

"They're taking a break because Boyd thinks they're too ready. They'll be back tomorrow for run-throughs."

"Ah, yes. We're certainly looking forward to it . . ." He took, she thought, note of the dog and the paint in her hair, and took his leave.

"Jesus, Gene, that was chancy."

"Yeah, but the Lord looks after his own."

She tucked the checks in her bag. She shooed Fibber off Gunilla's gown. "Oh, Christ almighty."

"What?"

"Look what he's done. I told you we'd be punished."

"What?"

"He's chewed through her piping."

"Can't you fix it?"

"Yes. I can zigzag some tape underneath, it'll be okay. But Gunilla's paranoid about the neckline. She'll pull some kind of number."

She took all the breakdowns into the costume room and hung them with plenty of space between, to finish drying. Gene had locked the shop and stood in the doorway, her handbag dangling from his curled fingers. Shaara set her palms on the shoulders of the dress form and surveyed their work with satisfaction. "We make a super team," she said, and when he did not reply she turned and cocked her head at him. He still had a streak of beige aslant his forehead where the kerchief had ended, paint in the cracks of his neck and hands. A spot of it jumped on his Adam's apple when he swallowed.

"What is it?"

He hesitated, frowned. "I think we should get married."

A sick sensation. She gripped the dress form, could feel the hole where she had stabbed it with the scissors.

"Don't do that."

"Awright, I won't."

"You've done it."

"Awright, I've done it. It's there for you if you wanna take it out and look at it sometimes. I won't mention it again."

"Like you won't move in your underwear."

"I swear to God, Shaara, I'm not gonna wake up one morning and change my mind, and if I do I'll tell you so, so if I don't, you can consider it's been said. I'll take my underwear home too, if that's what you want."

"No."

But in the parking lot she stood outside the pickup, mawkish, and kneaded the strap of her handbag. "Don't come home with me tonight, okay? I think I ought to be alone awhile and get my head straight. I don't mean I want to be, I think I ought to."

"Okay, yeah, sure."

"I'll call you later."

"And if you don't I'll call you. And I'll see you back here in the morning with your head straight and everything just the same as before."

"I'm sorry, Gene."

"You got no call to be."

It was only midafternoon and she had nothing in particular to do. Boyd and Kevin seemed to be having a high time together these days, and would probably be home late. She didn't even need to get dinner.

She wanted to call her mother but she had talked to her mother only yesterday—who had picked up on Shaara's high spirits and accused her of being in love, had taken a girlish delight in it. She wanted to call Cass Carson. And tell her what? That she was not going to marry the cracker Boyd thought was a queer?

In the end she decided that the best way to straighten a head is to clear it out first, and she went to a movie. At four on a Friday in the second week of its run in Hubbard, Georgia, she had *In-Laws* entirely to herself. She ate popcorn and dug the paint out of her fingernails while Peter Falk and Alan Arkin broke their asses to amuse her. "Zany" and "madcap," as the ads had promised, the milquetoast dentist and the spacey agent raced around robbing Mint trucks, hopping the Wong Airlines to Honduras, dodging bombs and firing squads. Shaara, finding all this funny, sat glum. It all turned out all right, of course, with a successful million-dollar heist and a wedding full of farting balloons. A dog padded after a retreating car. Shaara dropped her popcorn box on the floor and went home.

It was only early evening and she had nothing in particular to do. She picked through the house looking neither out the window where the jays and nuthatches squabbled over the teak feeder, nor at the Zenith which was refurbished and full of cloth, nor at the Winn Dixie bag in the closet. She tried to recapture the dull self-sufficient sense of evenings here alone before there was any prospect of the pickup in the drive, but this met with no success. She decided to dust Kevin's room.

It puts my mind in order, Gene had said. She hadn't dusted in here since the day Henry died, and there was plenty to do. The iguana cage had several hundred feet of slat. Bette Davis was not in a talkative mood and watched her slit-eyed, grumpy. Shaara went over the shelves, polished the pile of plastic vomit and a length of prewar barbed wire that Kevin had told her was a "collector's item." She thought over her "youthful ambitions" in Iowa and at Yale. *There's a lot of emphasis on the idea you can be anything you want to be*, Gene had said. *I don't think it's ever mentioned that you might not want to.* She had thought she wanted to, though. She had imagined herself a city dweller, *costumier* to the theatrical elite. By the time she found out that the center of her life was really at home, Boyd had found out that his wasn't, and the center wouldn't hold. Now she was a teacher at a two-bit college and had one son and one lizard for a family. *Don't you thank God you're not Boyd Soole?*

"I am the same thing as a state baton-twirling champion, for the Arts," she said to Bette Davis.

"What I do would take the blue ribbon in the Four-H hemstitching competition." This to the tank treads and the squirrel skull.

"I have come a long way, from Burlington, Iowa, to Hubbard, Georgia. A world traveler." She cuddled the dustrag under her cheek.

"There's no such thing as a *second* chance at *permanence*."

She tried to imagine waking up one morning to find herself indifferent to Gene, and could not. She tried to imagine going back to things the way they were, being content to be alone, and could not. She tried to imagine telling Boyd that she was providing as stepfather to his only son a Maintenance III about whose sexual proclivities he was in error. And could not. But Gene had suggested it, the cat was out of the bag, the jig was up. Gene was somebody who could take a lot of rejection, but nobody can take a lot of that kind. And so things, as Gene had predicted once, would muck up from here.

Kevin's bookbag spewed its contents over the floor where he'd dumped it a month ago when school let out. She started sorting wadded bits of paper into the basket, setting aside a selection of tests with A's on them, and reports in Kevin's round schoolboy hand. She ran across the one on earthquakes, on the top of which the teacher had shrilled, "C – Your ideas are good, but your spelling!" Shaara read it through, thinking that Mrs. Stripling, Science, was a sour peabrain. The world is full of copyreaders. You need exuberance as much as craft. After he'd dutifully dealt with the encyclopedia stuff, Kevin recounted the myths and metaphors of the swallowing earth. He reported that cows and pigs wouldn't go into their pens when a temblor was pending, that frogs jumped out of their ponds, and that these phenomena were a more accurate prediction than the Richter scale. He ended with an apocalyptic account of a major quake:

> First there is a little tremore. Nothing happens except a few plats slide off the shelfs. Then their is a little crack in the earth. It may close up again. But it doesnt this time. Peple and houses fall into it and die. The lanscape is permently changed.

Shaara set the report aside and stared into space. The particular space she stared into was inhabited by the Kodachrome teeth of Wendy Soole triumphant over a bigmouth bass. Kevin's smirk made a dozen dimples in the muscles round his mouth. The bass had no expression at all. *If I take the bait I'll run with the line*, Gene had said. *Gut me and filet me*. Nothing in nature is as accusingly round as the lidless eye of a fish out of its element.

The frogs jump out of the ponds. First there is a little tremor. The mouth, the vagina, the heart, loosen and begin to open. They can recoil and seal themselves again. But they don't this time. The damage is irreversible and complete. The landscape is *permently* changed.

27. Crashing Out

The Saturday run-through was pretty well a disaster. Wyman had lost half his lines and even Orme seemed distracted, maybe by visions of himself as Sancho Panza. Gunilla had disapproved of the four-day break, and in her usual martyred way, she'd stayed in town the whole time, so she was restless instead of rested. But Boyd wasn't worried. It was natural to have gone off their stride, and it would naturally scare them into doing better tomorrow. He whispered his notes into a minicassette and delivered them afterwards soothingly, or with a shrugging assumption that they all knew it was awful.

And Sunday was better, almost good. For one thing, Shaara produced the checks, which she admitted she'd had since Friday and forgotten! Remembering he'd told Wendy that Shaara was a little flaky, Boyd wrote *her* a check for Kevin's broken leg. She seemed to have forgotten that too. But the company's spirits were significantly raised by money.

Monday the costumes threw them a little—natural again. The habits were heavier than the men had anticipated and they sometimes misjudged the swing of them into the furniture. On the other hand, Gunilla looked so spectacular in the yellow gown, her hair swept up in front and tumbling at the back, that the crew gaped and even Wyman was driven to a whistle. This clearly did Gunilla good. There was an awkward moment in the second act when the Mother Superior shoved the tiara on her head and a speck of glitter got in Gunilla's eye. It spoiled

her stare and she ended shutting her lids, which failure of
discipline upset her. But Shaara said she would dip it in polyurethane so it couldn't happen again, and Gunilla seemed satisfied. Tuesday, in second dress, they were on target again.

And by Wednesday, up through three-quarters of the second
act, they had got everything back—pace, paradoxes, tension,
laughs. From the moment Sister Angela, saintly-satanic, bit
off the end of his cigar and whined, "I don't like it when things
look too easy," you knew disaster was on its way, and likely
to come from whatever corner seemed least likely. The costumes helped by now, the skirts loosened their movements
and Wyman learned to use the chinstrap of his wimple so that
his jowls hung over it, sometimes comically, sometimes ugly.

The trouble came in the last fifteen minutes, when the Senora's corpse had already been bedecked with earrings, necklaces, bracelets and tortoise-shell comb, and Sister Ines was
staggering to hold her upright. Orme had the back hem of his
skirt pulled through his legs and tucked into the front waistband so the breakdown habit looked like some kind of pirate
pants. Gunilla's flesh was powdered a rotting greenish-gray
and her staring eyes circled with shadow. Sister Angela snatched
at the Mother Superior's ragged skirt.

> When you're used to fighting like a rat in a trap, nobody's
> got the right to shovel pity over you! I didn't talk to her,
> but I shut her mouth for good and all.

Orme faced the corpse and flicked at the dead hand dangling
from the burned and bloodied sleeve.

> Now look at you, in all your laces and silks! Look at you
> now, you lump of rotten meat!

He turned back to the Mother Superior and pulled the knife
from his waistband.

> Come on, make yourself useful. Cut me a bit of this
> rope.

All that was all right. Wyman reached into the coil of hemp
on the floor and faked slicing two lengths of it, laying the knife
on the trunk where the audience would be aware of it until

Ines took it up for her attack. He handed the rope to Sister Angela, who flung one piece around the Senora's thighs and tied them to the post, cursing at Ines. But while Barnard propped her shoulder and Orme looped the second rope around her ribs, something went wrong.

And we're getting used to the smell. We're made that way. Put a man in hell and after a couple of weeks he'll get used to it.

The rope had caught too high on Gunilla's bodice, and when Orme jerked it into the knot, it dragged down on her piping and one breast popped out, startlingly pale and perfect below the line of gray makeup.

There was a second's panicked silence. Then Orme started to carry on with his line, but Gunilla broke character, shoveled the breast back in and yelled, "I *told* her that would happen!" She stood still bound to the post, face flaming under the makeup, her circled eyes alive again, furious.

"All right. Cut." Boyd peered into the house where the crew was scattered. "Shaara?"

"Yes, I'm here."

"Come on down, will you?"

"I've been saying it since the first time I tried on the mockup. It's too low!"

Wyman, who had held the pose of the Mother Superior up to now, gave it up and swished over to the pillar.

"I think it's a spectacular effect. Maybe we should keep it."

Gunilla twisted and strained against the ropes. "Undo these things!"

"All you'd have to do is carry the makeup a bit further down," said Wyman, maliciously reasonable. Orme let the ropes fall and Gunilla turned on Wyman, hands at the claw.

"Shut your drunken mouth!"

"Well, you've shown your pretty tits on the cinema screen to more folk than we're likely to have in here, Miss Lind. I trust if we have a little accident in performance you're not going to break and spoil it for the rest of us."

"You! You're afraid to expose the back of your fat neck!"

"All right, now," said Boyd. "Let's see what we can do to make sure it won't happen again."

"I do think we should keep it in," Wyman said sweetly.

Gunilla, her fury unspent, turned it on Shaara, who had come to the edge of the stage, understandably rigid and redfaced.

"How many times did I tell you?"

"It's only because the rope caught," Shaara said defensively.

"Yes, well, the *rope* is in the *play*, isn't it?"

"Gunilla. Calm down, please. Nobody is going to let that happen to you in performance." Boyd could see how Shaara smarted under the attack, and smiled at her as warmly as he could. "Let's see if there's anything we can do to the cut of the neck. Shaara?"

"Look here," Gunilla fumed. "It's been cut right through the piping."

"That's part of the breakdown," Shaara said. "If you feel it, Miss Lind, you'll see it's reinforced behind. That's not a problem."

"The *problem* is that it's *cut* wrong!"

"All right," Boyd said again, but Gunilla had gone too far and now Shaara was stiffening.

"I'll never be at ease with it," Gunilla insisted.

"Actors are not meant to be comfortable," Shaara replied, arch. Boyd had heard her say this before, in less crucial contexts, and recognized a quote from Frank Bevan.

"Could you," he suggested, "perhaps fill in an inch or two, with lace, or some of the silver?"

"That's what I told her from the beginning!"

"It'd be a pity," Wyman put in piteously, and Shaara was standing on her dignity by now.

"The line would be completely ruined."

"And it's so pretty in the first act," Barnard said.

"And it's true to period," Shaara said.

"Well, but maybe we have to sacrifice that to security."

Shaara faced him. He thought there was a little of that flashing anger he had provoked somehow that day in the costume room. "Costuming," she enunciated deliberately, "is an art. There is always a little risk involved."

Ah, good for her. She took the point. And in fact she was right; the costume would lose half its effect if they covered Gunilla's breasts for the sake of her misplaced modesty.

"Well, let's try something else. Gunilla, apart from the rope catching, you feel secure in it, do you?"

"I suppose," she said, subsiding, grudging. "But the rope can always catch."

"Then we have to change the rope. Let me think a minute." The two women still stood coldly facing each other. Boyd hoped that Wyman was not inventing some saintly barb to set them off again. He circled the post and thought.

"Somebody get the carpenter up here. Dora!"

"Oops, sorry," Barnard said, clutching his knees Charleston-style for guilt. "I sent her out for jasmine incense. The sandalwood hurts my nose."

Typical. Officious Ms. Fisher was never where she was wanted; but Boyd curbed his irritation. "I'll go," said Shaara. He thought it a good idea to release her.

"All right. Tell him to bring a hammer and nails, and see if he's got a cleat—you know, the kind with a double hook that they use on a ship?"

"I know. I think he's got some."

"Now Orme, Wyman, suppose we reblock it this way. Wyman, just cut one length of rope instead of two. We'll have the other one hanging from the post through the whole play. That'll look good, in fact, it doesn't need explaining. It's like the knife. The audience is aware of it, and then they have the satisfaction of seeing it used."

"I could play with it in the first act," Orme suggested.

"Sure, we'll look for a place to work that in. Then, you take the rope Wyman cuts you and tie up her thighs as usual. But the other one is already hanging here at neck height, and you tie it around her neck instead of her ribs."

"Around my *neck*?" Gunilla protested.

"Wait now. You don't really put any weight on it anyway, right?"

"No."

"Well, I've got an idea. Look here." The carpenter was there with the cleat and nails. Shaara hung back out of the light. Boyd showed Gene where to attach the cleat at the rear of the post and nail the rope to the side of it through a heavy knot. "Now, Gunilla, take your position. Stage management? Mark the position of her feet. Barnard, make sure her feet hit the mark when you prop her."

"Right."

"Now, Gunilla, I'll pull it around your neck just as far as it feels comfortable, and mark the rope, okay?" He wrapped the rope around—it effectively crushed her dirtied hair. "Is that not hurting?"

"It can be tighter than *that*." Good, she was getting back the other arrogance, the stage spunk. He inched it over one hook of the cleat till it barely pressed into her flesh. "That okay?"

"Yes."

"Sure?"

"It's fine."

"Okay." He pinched the rope between his fingers just where it touched the hook, loosed it and tied a knot at that point. Then he wrapped it around her neck again, put a finger over the hook and gently pulled it through till the knot caught. "Orme, see this. As long as you run the rope between your finger and the hook, you can actually jerk it—we'll do it slowly at first. It'll look like a vicious yank, but in fact it'll stop just where it's comfortable for her."

"Yeah, okay, let me try it."

Half a dozen times Orme wrapped, set a finger over the hook, cautiously pulled the rope until the knot caught, and secured it in a figure eight around the cleat.

"That work okay?"

"Fine."

"Gunilla?"

"Let's try it faster and I'll make my head bob when he jerks it."

"Great, okay."

They ran it a dozen times. They went back to Barnard's dragging her to the post and ran that half a dozen. Then they went halfway back into the second act and finished the dress rehearsal.

Like so many theater disasters, it turned out to be a serendipity. Gunilla, distracted from her prudery with a new effect to play, managed to keep the rest of her body wholly limp while her head seemed to whip with the rope and then loll against it. It gave Orme a new depth and emphasis to his line, ". . . *Put a man in hell* . . ." (yank! whip, loll—then, wrapping the figure eight) ". . . *and after a couple of weeks he'll get used to it* . . ." The crew gasped and applauded.

Boyd felt good about it, both the result and the way he'd handled it, without a single catch of apprehension. He was feeling pretty warm toward the world these days, and he was also proud of Shaara. There was a time she'd have been intimidated into giving up the cut of a costume that mattered to her, to mollify a starlet or a director. Funny to think that in a backwater college in Georgia her attitude was becoming more professional.

Even the news that night was laced with triumph. It was true that Arthur Fiedler had died, and that the Bundy trial was piling insanity upon insanity, the *defense* now claiming that pictures of the victims' wounds were too horrible to be used in evidence. But also, Skylab had crashed down in the Indian Ocean without killing a mortal soul. And off the Florida Keys a bunch that called themselves the Treasure Salvors had come up with a fortune in gold chains, bars and quoits from the Spanish galleon *Nuestra Señora de Atocha*.

28. *American Express*

❦ ━━━━━━━━━━━━━━━━━━━━━━━━━━━━━━━━━━━━━━━ ❦

Back in New York, the first thing she did was to get her electricity turned on. Then she called the sanders. The only company she could find that would do the floors in four days wanted six hundred dollars for it; she agreed. The rent, the telephone and MasterCharge were due again. She paid them. When she got down to two hundred dollars in her own account she started using the joint one.

While the sanders refinished the bedroom she slept on the couch, cleaned the desk drawers, washed the curtains, shampooed the rugs. She took down the *commedia* mask and put back the Watteau print. While they were in the living room she lived in the bedroom and kitchen and used the fire escape. She scoured and tidied and stocked the fridge with real food again: steak, eggs, orange juice, butter, peas. She took the iron to the repair shop, and when they said it wasn't worth fixing she bought a new one, threw out half her clothes and pressed the rest. She took down her grandmother's brass candlestick and flushed the old tallow out with boiling water, then polished it to a high shine. She fitted it with a fresh candle, which she left whole against Boyd's return.

On Wednesday, as if she were being mysteriously rewarded, another thousand dollars came from Boyd. She called CUNY and inquired whether it was too late to register for fall graduate courses in psychology. It was not. On Thursday morning she sent for her transcripts, went down and enrolled in a seminar in Neuropsychological Disorders and another in Current Research Topics: Career Problems. After tuition they were left with $1,600 to live on until Boyd got another show, plus whatever was left of his last check after he paid American Express.

On Thursday afternoon, when the sanders left and the apartment was in order, she called Cass Carson in East Millstone.

"Wendy! It's such a long time since we've heard from you."

"I kept meaning to see you ever since Boyd was away, and then I didn't. Now all of a sudden it's time to go down for his opening."

"We should have called you. Do you want to come out this weekend?"

"No, it's Boyd's opening Saturday. I'm going down to Georgia tomorrow."

"Lord, is it already? Summer's half gone."

"Yeah."

"How have you been?"

"Restless. You know what I did this morning? Went down and registered at CUNY. I think when Boyd's away so much it's not good for me to have nothing to do."

"I think that's terrific."

"Do you?"

"Well, sure. You're not the type to sit around the house and do nothing."

"Maybe not."

"It's a good thing not to wait like I did, till all you can go back and learn is macramé. What does Boyd think?"

"I haven't told him yet. What do you think he'll think?"

"Oh, Boyd . . . he'll like it. I mean, he always liked Shaara's having a career. You'll be meeting her—Shaara."

"Yes."

"Are you nervous about it?"

"I don't know. No, I'm not. I'm looking forward to it, really." Are not! Am so!

"And are you going to do that, have a career?"

"I was thinking about job counseling. It would be sort of appropriate to the trade. I mean, the schizos always go into abnormal psychology and the depressives counsel widows and divorcees. If I don't know what to do with myself I probably ought to tell other people what to do. I'll be a Money Guru." Cass laughed. "Anyway I'll take the classes. It'll keep me off the streets. What's up with you guys?"

"Not much. Well, I guess we've had a sort of bad summer too, so far. Nervous. 'Bout a month and a half ago Fred and I went out to Montauk Point for a sail, and we got hung up on a sandbar in falling tide and didn't get back till the next day. And when we got home somebody'd broken into the house."

"Oh? How did you know?"

"That's a funny question."

"Is it?"

"I mean, how do you usually know when your house has been broken into?"

"Oh. Stuff stolen?" Wendy guessed.

"No, that's the point, that's what makes me nervous about it. We didn't even realize it until Sunday afternoon when Fred went out back and found the window screen propped against the house."

"Ah."

"And then he could see that the paint had been scraped away around the window. But we still figured he didn't get in until—get this, Wendy—I went to do the laundry and I found one of my own tea towels buried in the hamper, all covered with blood. Human blood. We called the police and they analyzed it and then they were crawling all over the place. They found traces of it on the kitchen floor and in the bathroom and between the floorboards in the den. But that was it, no evidence of violence, nothing out of place—it'd all been sort of cold-bloodedly *cleaned up*. Millions of fingerprints but nobody to match them to except Fred's and mine. And we don't have any idea whose blood it is—or was."

No, Wendy thought. No, I don't really, either.

"We kept thinking we'd find something missing, but the most he might have taken is a drink or two. Otherwise he didn't get away with a thing."

"No, I guess not," Wendy said.

"For a week they had a patrol car doing the neighborhood, but there's nobody missing and no clue of a crime, let alone a solution. It shakes you up, you know?"

"God, I'm sorry you had to go through that, Cass. I really am."

"I mean, you go into the city thinking you're taking your life in your hands and when you come home . . . it's all on your doorstep. Spooky. Do you remember that old joke about the guy that decided to opt out of the war, and took a vacation in the Philippines? You're probably too young. But anyway it's changed my feeling about the house. I never even realized how safe I felt in my own rec room, and now I don't."

"God, I'm sorry," Wendy said.

"There's no way of knowing, but can you imagine what *might* have happened if we hadn't just accidentally been away that night?"

Wendy could imagine. "God, I'm sorry," she said, perhaps a little oddly, again.

After the call she took out one of the green stenographer's pads that she had bought to take notes in class, opened it and penciled on the inside of the front cover:

Goals:
Tell Cass miscar.

She thought a moment, then wrote underneath:

and CUNY

and put a check beside it. One of the tricks of rehabilitation is to reward yourself for what you do accomplish. Then she wrote:

Tell B.:
Miscar
Smuggle
Plendl
Mama
CUNY

She did not think it necessary to put Sandro Tesoro on the list, except as her employer in the smuggling. One of the tricks of rehabilitation is not to expect your own perfection. She made herself a steak sandwich and poured a glass of orange juice, surveyed the room, its order. Then, like every compulsive list maker, having set herself a few minor tasks, she had to add a monumental. Under the column of things to tell Boyd, she wrote:

The Truth

* * *

She took the notebook to the bedroom with her, unzipped the Saks suitcase, stuck it in the pocket on the lid, and turned to the closet to choose her wardrobe for Hubbard, Georgia.

29   *It's a Wonderful Life*

Lurking again. Gene parked the truck on the corner, under the azaleas, which had been clipped and now sprouted next April at every node. He skulked past her house and up toward the park, unready but determined; caged, contained. He was going to take a risk; he was going to tell her about herself, who she was and what she wanted. She was not a woman who would appreciate the information.

They had agreed not to meet tonight. Tomorrow was final dress, was Wendy Soole's arrival, was likely to be full of short-circuiting tempers. Shaara wanted to rest up for it. Kevin had done the evening at the Skate Inn and Shaara left the theater around ten-thirty to pick him up. The agreement was that Gene would lock the shops and go back to his trailer. He did so. The agreement was that they would both get a good night's sleep. He did not. He had a beer, scratched and cuddled Fibber, had another and went into a nighttime daydream on which, when he roused himself, he focused with some care. He prowled the trailer. He checked the clock. For something like half an hour, what he had been doing was designing the refurbished and reconstituted house in which Shaara lived. The plan was excellent. He would extend the living room wall beyond the L it made where it met the bedroom, install a second bathroom in that space with a sunken tub and a one-way plate-glass view into the pines, continue the wall to make a double studio, woodwork and sewing shop, with an outside entrance as well as one from the bedroom. He would slice the left window of the rec room into a sliding door and enlarge the back porch into a deck, cedar two-by-sixes in a herringbone pattern with a brick barbecue at the upstage edge. Then dig a carp pool beyond it—it would drain naturally enough under the deck when it wanted draining—and above that a freeform terrarium so Bette Davis could have the sun in sunny weather. The gutters needed replacing on the north side of the house. The elbow joint of the toilet was corroded between tank and bowl; the kitchen cabinets wanted stripping and refinishing. Jesus, didn't she know she needed him?

But what? Was he going to argue marriage on the grounds that he could improve the value of her house? He dragged his palm along the picket fence and headed into the park. He had left Fibber, indignant, at the trailer, and now saw no form of fauna, neither cat nor quarreler nor callow soldier past midnight on a summer's night. His impulse was to jog but it was curbed by a rarer eddy of vanity, that he didn't want to show up sweaty at her door.

No, he was going to spoil her good night's sleep to tell her who she was; and she, one of them libbers, would not like it. He was going to tell her that he could make her happy and she'd have to take his word for it. Because the thing was, Shaara was wrong about herself, she thought she was a snob. She was in a half-glamorous profession and she thought she wanted the glamour of it but she didn't. She wanted the cloth. He'd let himself get promoted to foreman if she cared about that, but she didn't. She didn't care if he read the classics, she cared about the way he caulked a joint. She cared about Kevin and love and food and sex and making things with her hands just like every natural homebody since people starting living under roofs; and she cared about him, Gene, and he was going to tell her so.

But he had, of course, promised not to bring it up again, and ever since he brought it up the first time she had been, everywhere but bed, skittish and withdrawn. (In bed she was, he thought, a little desperate.) Forcing an answer meant he risked a no. He leaned his head against an oak, bashed it lightly a couple of times on the gritty bark, wiped his forehead, and started back.

When you hit forty you start to realize there are some things you're never going to have. You wanted a kid of your own and it isn't going to happen. It's no big deal, lots of people don't have kids, but damn it, it's your life. You wanted something steady and simple like getting through life with one person, and something happens, death or divorce, and your life takes off on some other tangent. But that's no reason not to take what you can get. Desire gets keener, as a matter of fact. He wanted Shaara and Kevin in a way that he'd never wanted Harriet or the stillborn baby because in those days he'd had no taste of knowing there were some things you would never have.

He'd tell her so? Gene was not much on tactics. He'd never tried to talk anybody into anything in his life. Maybe he should just go in the back door and make *her* come out with all of it, just go in and say: Okay, you tell me. Why not?

Maybe he should just go home. But when he neared her house, trotting with the pull of gravity, remembering that other detour into her backyard, he figured he was as ready as he'd ever be, and he made himself keep pace to the lit back door.

Which opened almost immediately. Things never turn out the way you planned even if you weren't sure what the plan was.

"Where have you *been*? I've been calling you for nearly an hour."

She was still dressed, even still shod—unusual for Shaara. Her hair was escaping her headband, wisping around her cheeks, which were of a blanched pallor that showed up freckles he had never noticed. And her voice was urgent, distraught enough that for a second Gene thought she was accusing him of being with another woman.

"I been taking a walk. What's the matter?"

"He wasn't there." She rounded back into the rec room, her hands busy, touching a lock of hair, each other, fingers meeting and parting. "I was a little late; they were just locking up and there were only two kids still waiting for their parents. Neither of them knew when he left. I made the manager open up again to check the john and then I went over to Wuv's—they go for junk food sometimes—but they were closing too, and of course they didn't know if he'd been there or not, just another skater kid."

"Hang on," he said, and held her hands to still them. But at that she gave a shrugging laugh, kissed him, said, "Hello," sat, and, now, slipped off her shoes.

"I'm sorry—I'm not really worried. I'm really not. He's just a punk thirteen-year-old and he's sitting at some friend's house sneaking a beer and eating fried rinds and he's got some terrific reason for why he forgot to call." She laughed again, a competent-mom laugh, but her fingers scratched an ankle, bounced at her thigh; sign language of stress in counterpoint.

"Has he done it before?"

"Oh, sure, shit. We have a running battle about his not making it home for dinner. But this is a little different, Gene, because he knew I was picking him up. I waited around until twenty past eleven, but what was the point? Everybody else was gone by then. So I came home and called a few of his friends. Bobby and Otis weren't skating tonight and David Charleton didn't remember him leaving. I asked if Kevin had taken a spill or anything, and David said, oh, sure, he thought he hit his head but it was no biggie, he was up skating again right afterwards. I said, great, maybe he's wandering around with concussion. Look, I'm really not worried. If anything like that had happened the manager would've been all over me—when he broke his leg they took him straight to the hospital, they're so paranoid about getting sued."

"Right," said Gene, and noticed how oddly he slipped into a deeper register than natural, macho coloring, the protective male. What was maybe odder was that while she was talking he'd been aware of the left rec room window, and some piece of his mind was measuring the beam it would need to shore the wall between the joists for the sliding door. Some part of his mind was antsy to get past this minor sidetrack to the real order of the evening. But the word *concussion* concussed him. He felt a numbness at the back of his head like seeping anesthetic, or more like booze because he also became instantly careful of his motor control. He saw things one at a time. He saw he'd wasted screwing up his nerve; it wasn't going to be tonight. He saw Harriet quiet on the couch and then the way, half an hour later, she began to thrash and mumble.

"Can you think of anybody else he might be with?"

"Those are the only ones I've got phone numbers for. But of course I don't know everybody he knows, or anybody's father's first name to look up."

Then, casual, "Did you check the hospital?"

She smirked guiltily. "Yeah. Nothing."

Yet. "The police?"

"Oh, c'mon, Gene, if every thirteen-year-old who stayed out late was turned into a missing person . . ."

"Did you call Boyd?"

"Hey!" She jerked up startled. "I called *you*." This had more of an edge to it than he could quite understand. The color had come back into her face all of a sudden; she had a face like a mood ring, Shaara. It was one of the things he loved. She might *tell* a lie, but her face and hands came from a long line of cherry trees.

She said, "He's not with Boyd. Boyd won't have left the theater till after midnight."

"I don't mean that, but it's one o'clock, maybe you should let him know."

"I can't have Boyd over here!"

"Why not?"

"Oh, geez, Gene, let's not go into that. Boyd doesn't *know*—about us."

He thought this pretty irrational and now it was his tone that had the edge. "So?" But she shrugged it off. He fixed her a brandy and himself a cup of old cold coffee. His mind hopped from detail to detail as if it would not settle on the matter at hand. He saw the rec room window and himself hoisting the beam, saw Shaara's lean forearms fidgeting and Harriet's thrashing at the raised bedrails.

"Y'know," he said against these images, "he's getting to that age he'll start pulling at the reins a bit."

"I know that. That's why I'm not really worried."

Which is the way it is. You're not really worried but the form not worrying takes is that you aren't doing anything else either. They drank their drinks. Shaara rehearsed all the times that Kevin had failed to get home on time, and the hilarious hypocrisy of his excuses. When she ran out of those she went over the times she had panicked on his account for what turned out to be no real reason: colic, fevers, a playmate with lice, the broken leg.

"Not very many of them kill themselves," he agreed, and offered a few memories of his mother's stoic terrors, but in fact felt underqualified because he had himself never had a child over-whom-to-worry-over-nothing, and because apart from the rec room window and the thwarted intention of telling Shaara who she was, all that was really in his mind was another thing he was not going to mention: what he knew about the stages of concussion.

She was wearing a print wrap skirt from the hem of which she picked minute balls of lint; her strong hands fiddled impotent at the buttons of her camisole. By one forty-five the strain of not worrying was shaking him up as well. He stood her up for a hug but it fell short of reassurance.

"Look, here's what I think we oughta do. You stay here for the phone and I'll go drive around the area just in case. And mebbe drop by the hospital. If I find anything I'll call you, otherwise I'll be back in less than an hour. If he's not here by then we better get the police in on it."

"Okay," she agreed sighing.

"And Shaara—I really do think you oughta give Boyd a call."

She toyed now at the buttons of his shirt, head down over her hands and the electric hair tickling his nose.

"You don't understand about Boyd."

"He won't blame you."

She looked up, fixed him with an ironic grimace. "You'd be surprised who Boyd can blame for what."

He started to protest—he wasn't crazy about Boyd but thought him pretty straight among the theater and academic types—but decided better of it, slugged back the awful coffee and headed for his truck. She hadn't even noticed it was not in the drive.

He drove out 319, wishing he'd brought Fibber along and wondering if he should carry on past the Skate Inn to pick him up, idly speculating if Fibber would be hound enough to follow a scent if Gene had known how to put him on it. Also noticing how his mind still idled, grasping this thought and that as a way of not worrying. He passed the outskirts Whataburger, a couple of grubby bars, a Texaco with a few winos hanging out around the pumps; took a right on the red at the empty intersection of 319 and Peach, scanned the grassy ditches on either side. He swung through the parking lot of a minor mall—dry cleaning, bowling, Standard Oil and Shop 'n' Save—out again around Stuckey's and the now deserted Wuv's. He circled the Skate Inn and then turned a wider rectangle of streets in the low-rent residential district behind it. It was pretty pointless. He had not expected to see anything and the only reason for doing this was to be doing something.

He turned back toward Peach, toward 319, back to town. He had to pass within a block of Shaara's house in order to hit the western artery and Hubbard Memorial, but he didn't stop because he didn't want to mention the hospital again, or that he was headed there. The image of Harriet had narrowed like a cameo to the whack of forearm on tubular chrome.

He swung into the back entrance of the concrete block cube and parked illegally at the entrance ramp to Emergency. He braced himself against the antiseptic stench, but except for a whiff of creosote at the swinging door onto a corridor, the place mainly smelled of the popcorn machine in the far corner of the waiting room. There was nothing particularly alarming—a black woman with a fussing baby, a skinny pale man in his twenties looking more hung over than terminal. Gene approached the reception desk and sat just in time to see the girl behind it whisk away a paperback with a cover like pink boudoir wallpaper.

"May I help you?"

She was exceptionally pretty with the prettiness that is inseparable from stupidity; a tumble of towhead curls insincerely tucked into the crisp cap, vacuous eyes with a rim of unconvincing jet, a smile to show the cheekbones.

"Yes, my . . ." he hesitated, did not think it was worth going into any complication with this person, ". . . son should've been home a long time ago and his mother and I are worried about him. I just wanted to check he hasn't had an accident and been brought in here."

"Oh. His name, please?"

"Kevin Soole, but you wouldn't necessarily know his name. I mean, have there been any unidentified teenagers . . ."

"We had a hit-and-run about an hour ago, but I don't know who it was, I was on break."

The forearm hit the chrome. "Could you check for me?"

"Oh, I'm not supposed to do that," she said, but with a cornpone insistence that made it perfectly clear she would do anything for which the credit would accrue to her, and all Gene had to do was sound enough like her paperback book, and make a down payment of gratitude.

Discouraged, he paid. "Please, it's *real* important. Just lemme know if it's a blond boy, thirteen, about five six. You'll really set my mind at ease."

This was not enough. "I'm sorry . . . regulations . . ."

"It's my *only son*."

When she lowered her lashes, mumbled something of saccharine sympathy, and minced back through the swinging doors, the stupidity of it rose in him as rage, and subsided with a dullness in his chest.

A strange old-fashioned phrase came into his head: my heart is heavy. And though he must have heard that phrase from a hundred sources over the course of a lifetime he knew exactly where he had heard it in such a way that it came to him now. He was about ten, his dad had been dead for about a year. He came into the house at twilight, dinnertime, and found a pot of okra burning on the stove. The kitchen was full of smoke and the smell of scorch blotted out any smell there might have been of food. He knocked it off the burner with his baseball glove and turned off the gas. He didn't know what else to do and went to look for his mother, was shocked to find her in the dining room right next door, where the smoke was already curling and the smell was fulsome. She stood at the window staring out at the ragged plot of dusk-dim lawn, holding the closed photo album against her chest in folded arms. She didn't hear him even though he called her twice, and when he touched her she jumped. She hadn't been crying. Her eyes were a scary distance away—though she brought them back immediately, gave him a perfunctory hug, and went to the kitchen with an embarrassed briskness. She picked the pot up in an oven glove, turned to him, and to his repeated, "You okay, Mom?" she finally gave a measured answer. "Oh, yes. It's just my heart is heavy." He remembered now that she had taken another faraway look at the pot and, with an unnecessary largesse of gesture (and largesse, since there had not been much money for such things as replacing pots), dropped it from the height of her hand into the garbage bin. It occurred to him now, although there had never been a moment of evidence of it save this, that his mother had been, over the death of his father, temporarily bats. It occurred to him that the gesture with the pot was the same gesture he had seen in Shaara's backyard when she dumped the ashtray. It occurred to him now that loss is hard to lose, and the thing we are deprived of we are also required to dump or drop over and over again. He did not want Shaara to have to endure the loss of Kevin.

He did not want himself to endure the loss of Shaara. He was a man of few and therefore irreplaceable affections. His heart was heavy.

But it was not going to be that either, or at least not here and now. The dumb towhead lilted through the swinging doors, flashed him a smile that took all the credit, and cried triumphantly, "It's a woman!" He stared at her, at that phony complicity in his relief which was somebody else's tragedy, and he snarled, "Thanks a lot," and bolted. Maybe he handled his survival badly. He jumped into the truck and drove in anger back to Shaara's.

The house was more brightly lit than when he left. She met him in the door again, calling out before his motor died, "It's all right!" She swung out to meet him, barefoot on the concrete. "He's coming home in a squad car, the little shit. The police picked him up hitchhiking out on 319. What the hell he was up to I don't know, but I'm going to burn his ears!"

He squeezed an arm around her, followed her in, and was glad to let her chatter. "A highway cop called about twenty minutes ago and said he spotted him in front of a bar—he hasn't been drinking, apparently, that was just accidental—but the cop thought it was a dangerous place for a kid that young to be, so he stopped. And Kevin has some cockamamie story about how he got stranded and was trying to get home, so the cop asked me if he should bring him or send him home in a taxi, and I said if he didn't mind I'd like him to do it because I'd like Kevin *scared*, which he thought was a good idea too."

"Me too."

"So, listen, when he gets here I am going to be an absolute draconian dragon, and you back me up, okay?"

"You got it."

She giggled, but when the highway patrol car pulled in the drive, she put her shoes on and drew herself up to a fair imitation of a dowager, went out and formally thanked the cop, who took off his cap and smoothed his cowlick—he was probably still getting I.D.'d in the bars himself. Kevin hunched out, his skates hung over his hands by the laces, with a scowl that meant he was scared, all right. But not particularly concussed.

"'M sorry, Mom," he mumbled. "I'll go right to bed."

"No, you will not. You will go sit down in the rec room and wait for me there."

Kevin did as he was told. The stripling cop said politely, "He seems a good kid . . ." but Shaara still in her despot role interrupted, "Yes he is. That's why I don't want him getting mugged or buggered out there," and the cop murmured, "Yes, ma'am," and took his leave looking glad to be out of it. Gene grinned at her but she glared back. "Back me up."

"Shore."

Back inside she said, "*Now*," and chose the only hardbacked chair, folding her hands on her knee. "I'm going to hear your story, but first I want you to understand, apart from what you put me and Gene through, just what risks you ran."

Kevin moped at the floor and played his hand on the top of one of the skates, rolling it back and forth on the carpet as if testing the efficiency of the bearings.

"I know it's very amusing to you when I play anxious mother, but the fact is that grownups are cautious because they've been hurt, and they have learned the hard way that actions have consequences. Look at me."

He looked, if he could see through his hair, approximately at her left ear.

"A thirteen-year-old, hanging around that section of highway 319 at one or two o'clock in the morning, can get mugged, or raped, or murdered, by people who are drunk, or drugged, or crazy, or just vicious. Am I right, Gene?"

"That's where the winos and the pushers hang out," he backed her up.

"I am not particularly worried about your morality but I am rather attached to your bones and I would just as soon you kept as many of them intact as possible. Do you understand?"

"Yes'm." Sullen, he apparently took this as permission to drop his eyes again, and concentrated on the pattern of the skate wheels in the carpet.

"I mean it, Kevin. People *die*, from just such carelessness and thoughtlessness, which is why there are hospitals and police and why Gene and I have been checking the hospital and would have called the police if they hadn't called us first."

"I'm *sorry*, Mom."

"Now just exactly what happened?"

Kevin lifted his hair to get at the sweat underneath and

glanced at several spaces between Gene and Shaara—a rung, a corner of the coffee table, nothing higher than a knee. Shaara cleared her throat with a sound that was almost a harrumph; Gene loved it, this sensible and necessary charade, and for the first time in an hour remembered why he had come over here tonight.

"Well, me and some of the guys went over to another guy's house that lives a mile or two from the Skate Inn, and David's sister was supposed to come pick us up . . ."

"I spoke to David. He knew nothing about it."

Kevin's eyes skittered and darted and then zeroed in directly on Shaara's. Gene recognized the pattern of a decision to stone-wall. "Not David Charleton, another David, I don't know his last name."

"David said you fell down."

"Huh?"

"David said you fell down and hit your head."

"Y'always fall *down*. Everybody falls down."

"All right. Go on."

"Well anyway this guy's sister didn't show, so we walked back to the Skate Inn but everybody was gone."

"I waited till eleven-thirty."

"Yeah . . . I guess we must've just missed you. So anyway we walked *back* to the other guy's house to use the phone, but by that time the lights were all out and we didn't want to wake 'em up, so . . ."

"There's a phone outside the Skate Inn, Kevin."

"Yeah but we didn't have a dime!" An exasperated cluck, a sullen glance; the rechanneled energy of panic. "So we went to 319 to look for a phone but every place was closed except the bars and I mean"—an inspiration—"I had the sense not to go in there!"

"What happened to the other boy?"

"Oh, him? Uh, he got a ride . . . he was going the other way."

Shaara had apparently decided not to push him any further; a wise move. "All right," she said. "Now here are the rules. In future, when you go to the Skate Inn, you will not leave the grounds."

"Mo-*awm*!"

"You will carry a dime with you every time you leave the house, and you will not spend it except when you need a phone.

If you're ever without it, you'll dial the operator and tell her it's an emergency. If you can't get me, you'll get a taxi, and I will leave a twenty dollar bill under the silverware tray in the kitchen drawer which is to be used for that purpose and that purpose only. Understood?"

Impressed with this rapid-fire organization, Gene saw that her adrenaline was pumping as fast as the little liar's. The next exchange did not impress him. Kevin dragged up the laces of his skate shoes and said sulkily, "Yes'm. Can I go to bed?"

"Yes. Wait. Kevin, I won't tell your father about this, but if it ever happens again, you can be sure I will."

Kevin was already halfway across the room. He turned back so that his skates swung around and hit him with bruising strength on the back of the thigh. "Oh, Jesus, *Dad* wouldn't give a damn!" he said, and stalked out.

Shaara sat in a baffled stare. Gene was a little stunned himself, but not at Kevin.

"What do you suppose he meant by that?"

"Shaara . . ."

She dis-matroned herself head and toe, slipped off her shoes and wiped her headband back to comb her fingers through her hair. "God, do you think he thinks his father doesn't care about him? Is he old enough to begin realizing how cut off Boyd is?"

"Shaara, he was with a girl."

"What?"

"All that stuff was smokescreen. I thought you picked up on it. He was at some girl's house, and knew what he was getting into, and decided to pay the price."

"Oh."

"What he meant was, his dad wouldn't't've made him lie about it." Shaara stopped scratching her hair and cocked her head, taking a look at this possibility. "When you volunteer to lie to his dad you just underwrite the con."

But now she flared. "Oh, lie to Boyd. I didn't volunteer to lie to Boyd."

"You did, y'know."

"God, you always want to make it simple with Boyd, and you don't understand the least thing about the way he works. He's got so many twists and hangups . . ."

"You're the one with the Boyd hangup!"

"Am I? So you're always saying. Well, maybe I just have the bad luck to know how backwards he gets everything, like for instance that he doesn't want you hanging around Kevin because he's come to the brilliant conclusion that you're queer!"

Now it was his turn to be stung. He got up. "Well, it's been a long night. Mebbe we better catch some sleep with the rest of it."

"Gene, *I* don't think you're queer!"

He grinned, but without feeling it. "Naw, well, all the same I don't guess I'd better offer you any proof tonight. I'll see you tomorrow, okay?"

"Okay . . ."

She dragged a foot seeing him out. They kissed stiffly at the door.

"Gene, I wish I hadn't . . . it isn't . . . hey, how come you came over here anyway?"

"Psychic, I guess," he said, and then leftover anger eddied up out of his heavy heart. "I came to tell you that if you don't want to get married, I think I should be moving on."

And without letting her answer hopped in the truck and headed back to 319.

30. *Curtain Line*

———————————————◆———————————————

Thursday was excellent but slightly technical, as if they were holding themselves back for an audience. Boyd told them so, and they agreed—the first time there'd been a company consensus.

"*I* think," said Barnard, that scatterer of universal sunshine, "that we're all scared it might be good. Like, you know, a bleedin' smash."

"Yeah, I do know," Boyd admitted. "I have the same worry myself"—though it was a worry on which he slept dreamlessly while Gene and Shaara were waiting up for Kevin.

And Friday, the day of final dress, there was a kind of electric apprehension that filtered right down through the crew and caused the prompt girl to purchase a new three-ring notebook and lick two hundred and seventy-nine reinforcement holes for the pages of her dog-eared script. Dora Fisher set the props at ten A.M. and then set them again at noon, after which she was caught whistling in a dressing room, and was required by the others to perform elaborate penances and ritual warnings-off of evil.

At the box office business was brisk, and it looked as if opening night would be a sellout. Even the ticket girls and the student ushers, in for briefing, caught the smell of controlled urgency, and combed their hair a lot. The *Hubbard Post* reviewer (actually the Woman's Page editor) would be there tonight, along with a few other carefully selected invitees: Joe

Dimbleton, such Theater Department staff as was on summer duty, the chairman of the local Little Theater, and the PR man from Magoor Administration.

Boyd had advised the cast to stay home Friday, to play and rest. But Barnard sailed in and out of box office and backstage, offering encouragement and junk food: moon pies, onion rings and four different flavors of poisonous pop under plastic caps, into the orifices of which he stuck straws, tasting each one before handing it around—"Strawberry tutti bonbon, I believe. Rocky Road pecan cola."

Orme at the Campus Side and Wyman at the lake first swam and then rested, as admonished. Gunilla at the Sheraton bathed. She had nothing better to distract her from the play; putting it out of mind was the one sort of discipline she could not command. She ran her lines while she pumiced her heels: *Sister Angela! Her name matches her intentions* . . . and while she massaged a layer of Erno Laszlo deep into her pores, to protect them from the heavy makeup of the second act: *Oh, Reverend Mother, when I think what might have happened to me if it hadn't been for your advice. You know as well as I do—or even better—that a woman on her own is easy prey, especially when there's a danger around.* It amused her grimly that she had such lines to say to Wyman Path, whom she considered no less a hypocrite than the Mother Superior. Typecast. While her hair dried she went back over her notes from the earliest rehearsals, right back to first reading, where Boyd had said: *The wrong dream comes true. It's just a story, and then it isn't.* They had caught that rhythm in the play now, and it was a rhythm of the real. Life does imitate art; you make things up and then they happen. Men dream of going to the moon, and some century or other they'll blast off. You play the part of seductress and sooner or later you'll be assaulted. She had heard the myth of the dangerous South and had not found it to be so; yet after seven weeks as a corpse in Georgia she had learned to be a more guarded person.

Shaara, having twisted in and out of sleep through the hot dawn, left Kevin a note and came into the shop midmorning, pressed everything for the first act and wrung fresh wrinkles into everything for Act Two. Her eyes stung, and the steam from the iron seemed to condense under her lids. Her head ached, and her back; and whenever she stopped ironing to stretch against the lumbar pain her hands shook so that to still them she had to go back to work. When the costumes were done she began sorting scrap from the bins, rolling each separate fabric into a tight spiral and securing it with a pin: habit gabardine, wimple linen, satin, silver. But there was no urgency in this, and no stillness. She caught sight of herself in the mirrors and advanced to take a closer look: eyes red, face pale, jaw tight, and on her brow the minute crow's tracks of the tension underneath. She had a disheartening image of what she would look like in ten years.

She escaped to the scene shop, or maybe it was less escape than test. The debris of the set was still stacked in the far corners of the room. The bed of beige paint would be on the floor for years to come. One of Gene's T-shirts was slung over a vise. He and Kevin were supposed to come in this afternoon for a final tidying, and to oil the machines. She would go back and pick Kevin up, but she didn't know whether Gene would come in or not. She felt the huge emptiness of the shop in her diaphragm. She sat on a stool and leaned her elbows on the jigsaw bed, leaned her headache in her hands. When the pressure of the opening was off, he would ask again. And then she would not only have to reject him, but would have to falsify her reasons, though he would not be fooled. He had said he would be moving on; that meant he would quit his job, and somebody else would share her hotplate. She hoped he would not go back to minimum-wage road work. Fall semester loomed drearily, the long littleness of the academic year. She lowered her hands around the saw and laid her head against the cool steel, let the tears fall on the oily base. So that Barnard, entering with the gift of a McChicken burger, found her in apparent profound embrace with a Black and Decker, and sensing his intrusion, stealthily backstepped toward the stairs.

Boyd stayed away from the theater all day, waiting for the hour of Wendy's plane, grabbing at anything that would occupy his mind. He wanted to wipe the play right out so he could see it fresh tonight. He finished Flannery O'Connor's letters and tucked away in the back of his mind, in case he should ever need it, what toughness was, in the face of debilitation and disease. He watched *Grand Hotel* on a midday Garbo festival, enjoyed seeing Wallace Beery bludgeon John Barrymore with a blunt instrument over a pearl necklace, and reflected again that Garbo's face held up but her acting didn't. He read the news, which was full of resurrections. The DC-10's were back in the air, Nixon was parading himself with the Shah in Mexico. Carter was preparing some sort of shock tactics for a comeback in the polls. In Brazil and India two newborns had been christened Skylab after the drowned debris. In Shanghai, eleven had been killed in the biggest earthquake of the year, registering six on the Richter scale and forty aftershocks, but the real news seemed to be that the Chinese were owning up to it and publishing details. Boyd took a swim and tried to take a nap, took a drink but not another; it was better to be jumpy than not to be alert.

At two, by prearrangement, he took Orme's Volvo to the stark little airport and watched Wendy's Cessna-411 bounce and buck down out of an apparently placid sky. His stomach left him. But she, chic in a brimmed hat, clipped across the tarmac brisk as a breeze, and twice as welcome. They clung to each other for a moment, broke and smiled, deferring the real hello. Boyd saw a certain sexy brittleness in her movements he had never noticed before. It didn't strike him precisely as a change, so probably it had always been there.

Wendy, once her bag was stowed and she had taken in the shock of heat, settled into the passenger seat and put a hand on the vinyl dash. She registered the Deep South pines and the water mirages undulating off the asphalt, while Boyd asked her about the trip, the refrigerator; admired her hat. She responded to all this but she didn't let go of the dashboard or her resolve.

He said, "What is it?"

She took a breath. "We are not domestically incompatible," she observed.

He wondered whether he had heard her correctly.

"We are not sexually at odds," she said.

"Of course not."

"But we have got to find different modes. Of behavior. I will take the responsibility for this."

He didn't know what she was talking about. He was somewhat distracted by a final dress. He said, "You had a bad time in Boston, didn't you?"

"Yes."

He pulled up at a red light beside the tacky Campus Arts Theater. "I thought I heard that in your voice when I talked to you up there. Your folks get you down?"

In, to, up, down. "Worse than that. Mama's got Parkinson's disease."

"Oh, love." He went to put an arm around her, but the light changed and he had to shift into first.

"It's in the early stages and the doctor's encouraging and all that. What upsets me most is that she won't tell Daddy, and she made it—you know the way she works—she made it impossible for me to tell him either. And that scared me a lot, because . . ." Her heart was pounding a little, and she visualized the list on the cover of her notebook, stiffened her spine. ". . . Because I've done the same thing to you."

"What do you mean?"

"I lied to you about getting my period."

"You *are* pregnant?"

"No. I had a miscarriage."

"Wendy? God. Why didn't you tell me?"

"I didn't tell you"—she gripped the dash until there were little halos of moisture around her fingertips; she wanted to get it right—"because I was glad."

There was a period of dead air. She glanced sideways and said, "Boyd?" and he shifted gears. "Yeah. I'm here."

"I might have had an abortion anyway. It just let me off the hook. Boyd, I'm not ready to have a baby. You don't have to tell me how sappy that sounds, but I don't care, it's just the truth."

"It doesn't sound sappy."

"I'm not ready to have a baby, I'm not even ready to have a job, I'm not ready for anything. Except, I think it's possible I might be ready to be your wife."

"You're a knockout of a wife."

"Boyd! Don't talk to me as if I'm cute. My mother is sixty years old and she has Parkinson's disease and she's still cute. When they stick the needles into her brain the nurses will think she's cute."

"All right," he said, his voice chastened, and was silent for a second. He pulled into his space at the Campus Side and cut the motor. "Nobody is their parents, Wendy, but sometimes it takes a long time to learn it. I have stuff to tell you about that too."

"We'll talk."

"Yes."

Inside, while he swung her suitcase onto the bed, she doffed her hat and loosed it like a skipping-stone in the direction of the bureau top, kicked off her shoes, and came at him with a fierceness that raised his skull as well as his sex. She actually tore a button off his shirt with her perfect nails, and when they both laughed Boyd shoved the suitcase on the floor, drew her to him hard, and whispered, "*Cute* is not exactly it."

Around two Shaara went home, fed Kevin, and brought him back to the theater. Her driving was erratic and she made no effort to conceal it. It had the distinct advantage of keeping Kevin mum, and once they got there he went to the shop and stayed religiously out of her way. She returned to ministrations of the most contained and minuscule busyness. She stored the trim, sorted the snaps and hooks by size, separated the silk pins from the bead-heads. Stage management and the lighting crew were milling about by now. Every step on the stair, every shove of the back door that was not Gene's step or shove, sent her viscera into a tight turn and pounded half a dozen drumbeats at the base of her skull. At four, with the student dresser, she delivered the costumes two by two to the dressing rooms, in one of which Dora Fisher pontificated about making a checklist of every item. Each time she returned to the costume room she listened for evidence of Gene's arrival, and after the fourth trip she heard the radio in the shop. Kevin might have turned it on, of course. He had developed a taste for Country 'n' Western music over these weeks that meant she would have to be hearing it for months or years after Gene was gone. She wished *The Nuns* had been one of those shows with a chorus or a gaggle of extras, where everything is a panic of unreadiness up to curtain. As it was she could think of nothing better to do than make a pot of coffee that was the last thing her nerves called out for.

The water sloshed in the pot and the coffee grounds of the last scoop spilled over and scattered on the counter top. She turned in irritation for a rag, and Gene was there. He put his arms around her, pressed her face into his neck and stroked her hair. She would have liked to cry now but she could not cry. She said, "I'm sorry," but the crews were milling, and there was not time, and this was not the time, to specify what she was sorry for. She said, "Just let me get through the opening," and he said, "Sure, Shaara, sure," and stroked her hair; but Barnard was sailing by and she could not stand this, so she released herself, leaving Gene to finish putting the coffee on to perk; and as she lurched over the threshold of the costume room she was greeted by a mirror-peopled panorama of forty-odd Boyd and Wendy Sooles perched against her cutting table holding hands.

"Oh," she said.

The current and former wives of Boyd Soole met in different frames of mind. Sated and scented, Wendy reached out with an expansive sweep, wanting all to be right with the world. Shaara performed what felt to her like the skip and flap of a cartoon ostrich, and wiped the sweat of her palm down the thigh of what she now realized, by contrast with Wendy's latest—*Vogue* paramilitary chic—was a wrinkled wraparound she had been wearing three days straight. She touched the tips of Wendy's fingers and immediately withdrew her own. There followed a series of inanities in rapid and overlapping aposiopesis.

"Shaara, this is . . ."

"I'm so glad to . . ."

"I've been looking . . ."

"How was your . . ."

"Boyd's been telling . . ."

"I'm afraid I'm a little . . ."

Shaara wheeled away, and to hide her confusion began extracting from the drawers the laces, piping, trims and pins she had just stowed there, while Wendy duly took this for extreme professional pressure, and felt that her arrival had been ill-timed.

"Well, I'll leave you two to get acquainted," Boyd said, "and go check on things backstage." It is probable that his two wives concurred in a moment's harsh assessment of his tact. "Wendy, you know how to get up to the theater when you want to?" He left, and Wendy said, "I know you're busy. I don't want to be in the way."

"No, no, not at all. I've been so looking forward to meeting you."

Have not!

"Can I do anything?"

"No, no, thanks very much. The costumes are all delivered. Really I've got more time on my hands than I know what to do with." But she laughed insincerely and continued opening and closing drawers, and Wendy could tell that this was mere *politesse*. Wendy shifted her weight off the table, shifted from one foot to the other. Shaara shifted a bolt of fabric from a shelf to another shelf.

"There'll be coffee in a minute, would you like a cup?"

"Oh, no, thanks, don't trouble yourself."

"It's no trouble."

"Thanks all the same." It occurred to both of them that this could go on forever. "How's Kevin doing?"

"Oh, fine, fine, fine. He's just across the hall in the scene shop if you want to say hello."

They both latched on to this as a blessing of release, and Wendy promised, "We'll get together later."

"Yes, after the show, yes, yes," Shaara stuttered like a shooing-out.

Then Kevin rebuffed her too. When Wendy uncertainly entered the shop, he stopped his sweeping just long enough to give her a peck on the cheek, carried on with his broom with his back to her, and glanced over his shoulder almost furtively. "How's your trip?"

"Fine."

He made no move to introduce her to the men across the shop, so she said as she had to Shaara, "See you later," and went out.

Abandoned, she mounted the stairs among a purposeful bustle of people with a right to be here. She passed in the hall a woman of breathtaking loveliness, whom she thought she recognized as Gunilla Lind, but even she was garbed in sturdy slacks and a work shirt, and was palpably in a hurry. All that good mood spoiled, Wendy felt absurdly costumed and in the way. She decided to sit in the theater until Boyd came for her.

By now the crew was haggard with anticipation, and had sent out for pizza. Dora Fisher, who had gone twice in the course of the afternoon to check the props, ticking them off one by one on her list with a red pencil, went back again to have another look. She wanted to be the last person on the set before curtain so she was certain nothing could go wrong that could be laid at her door. She counted the objects on the backstage table, meticulously confirming that they were in the same position as usual, all but measuring the distance between them. She did the same with the props on the set.

This is how it came about that Wendy and Dora encountered each other—Wendy seated on the aisle on a lower tier, Dora padding among the set pieces with her notebook and her pencil. Wendy watched her, admiring her meticulousness and envying her function. For someone unfortunately endowed with features round and blurred, the girl clearly had a confident nature and a sharp sense of purpose. Wendy had been sitting uncomfortably reminded of her inertia in New York, still smarting from Shaara's officiousness, and the sight of the girl was cheering. When she came to the edge of the stage space to verify the objects on a trunk, Wendy stood up.

"Hello."

"Arrgh!" Dora hopped and flapped a hand to her breast.

"I'm sorry! I didn't mean to startle you. I'm Wendy Soole. Boyd's wife."

"Oh, Miziz Soole! Dora Fisher. It's just wunnderful you could make it down." Honored to be so accosted, Dora stuck her pencil through the spirals of her notebook and gave Wendy's hand a hearty shake. "I've been looking forward to meeting you!"

This was more like it. "Boyd's a fantastic director," Dora gushed. "I mean, we are so fawrtunate to get him at Magoor."

"I'm glad you think so."

"Oh, I do, I really do. Did you get a chance to meet the cast, Miz Soole?"

"I just got here really."

"*Well*. They are very professional. But I tell you the truth, I think Boyd has had his *hands full*. Gunilla Lind? She's a pro but she's real high-strung and timpramental. And that Barnard Jones is just as demanding as a stawr. I didn't say: I'm prawps."

Wendy laughed. "I've been admiring how careful you are. You seem pretty professional yourself."

Dora blushed and tucked in her chin and mumbled a disavowal, while Wendy for her part felt a little better, that at least someone had acknowledged her.

"Is there anything I can do to help?"

"Oh, really, that's kind of you, but really I have to take care of things myself. I'm respawnsible."

"Of course. Don't let me hold you up."

Wendy went back to her seat and continued to admire the girl's dogged precision. Dora was so overcome by the compliment—from the wife of the director!—so devoted to perfection, and so aware she was being watched, that she did several things wrong. She straightened a cover on the stage-left trunk that stage management had deliberately set awry. She swept out a pile of wood shavings that Shaara had dumped by the upstage door. She found a knot in the rope on the pillar and, impatient with the stubbiness of her nails, she took it out.

31. *Final Dress*

Boyd assembled them in Gunilla's dressing room, which, having been converted out of the gym shower stalls, was the largest space they had offstage, the nearest thing to a Green Room. Gunilla did not mind this (Boyd had checked). She hostessed from her chair at the dressing table—perhaps she queened it a little—flanked by potted begonias and backlit by the traditional rectangle of mirror and bare bulbs.

"Well, here we are," said Boyd, with the same deliberately casual voice he'd used at first reading. "Anyone for final dress?" But now he was not in awe of them; all the terror was bound up with expectation. "I have no notes for you on the play. I think you've got a fair idea of what you're doing. I *would* like to say a word about superstition."

They laughed, and Barnard offered, "Fur-iday the thurteenth!"

"Well, that too. If you should happen to be awful tonight, I *might* try to chalk it up to Friday the thirteenth. But what I have in mind are the superstitions peculiar to the trade. I have a lot of respect for them. I do not whistle in the dressing room—I understand the prop girl did, and they made her go through the whole purification. I do not mention *that* play anywhere within four miles of a theater, and I won't wish you anything but *break a leg*. The theater is ritual, and every ritual has its peccadilloes.

"But there's one superstition I don't allow in my company,

and that's that a bad final dress makes for a good opening. That one was made up by a loser and a fuck-off in the eleventh hour. What you do tonight is a performance. If it's bad, you gave a bad performance; if it's good, you get a rave. As a matter of fact, that's probably the case, because although the Atlanta critics won't be in till tomorrow night, the local press is here, and it's the local press that gets to our audience. We don't know what our audience is going to make of this play—I don't guess any of us has worked *quite* such a boondock as this, unless it's Wyman in Galway rep—but as far as I'm concerned, from now on this is Lincoln Center and the dozen people out there tonight are the cream of Broadway critics."

"Hear, hear," said Barnard, Wyman, Orme, Gunilla—the second time he had brought them to consensus.

"Places, then. Break a leg."

He picked up his cassette and watched them up the back stairway, then ascended the other one to the front of the house. The scattering of audience was in place, the invitees and those crew members whose work didn't call for them backstage. He found Wendy sitting with Dora Fisher on the fourth row aisle, and beckoned her up with him to a better vantage point in the penultimate row, slightly off-center in the U, far enough back that his whispered notes wouldn't distract anyone else.

"Sorry I had to leave you, baby. Have you been bored?"

"Lonely. It's okay, I get you later."

He settled. "Places!" he called again. "Lights and music!"

The theater blacked out and the cacophonous tune began, one they'd taken from a prison blues and distorted with drums and a flat piccolo. When the lights faded up again the Mother Superior was seated at a laden table, delicately mopping her chin. She motioned to Sister Ines to pour more wine, and Sister Angela stalked in from stage right, leering under brows and wimple. Boyd was so used, by now, to the notion of male nuns, that the titter from the guests in the front row took him by surprise.

You think everything will go all right?

Everything . . . fine.

You don't think there'll be any hitches?

No trouble at all.

You may think so, but I don't like it when things look too easy.

Across the U from Boyd, Gene mounted, Kevin following. He slipped into the back row beside Shaara, slid his hand down next to hers between the seats, and their fingers slotted back to back. Shaara sighed, permitting herself a hiatus in her angst, and began to watch the play. The lights caught surreal at the set, a squalid glitter. The truth was, she was better pleased with the costumes than she expected. They were more than adequate. Orme's habit in particular she'd cut to emphasize his emaciated height, the waist just a little lower than was natural and the sleeves a shade too long. When he shoved the cuffs back with a macho carelessness, she recognized Joe Dimbleton's guffaw.

The more I think about it, the more I reckon it isn't the Lord lousing things up, it's you.

The truth was that Joe Dimbleton, the critic and the Little Theater chairman were uneasy at their proximity to the stage. They were used to the barriers of proscenium and pit, and—as the nuns unfolded their plans, the Mother Superior chanted her *kyrie eleisons* and Sister Angela, like a latter-day Lady Macbeth, goaded her on—the guests had a tendency to hold their knees aside and protect their laps. Boyd noted this and whispered into the cassette, "Be prepared for front-row fidget. Tense, not bored." And by the time Gunilla entered, Garbo-boned in the overhead spot, the porcelain skin of her lifted breasts both fragile and erotic, the audience was caught, had forgotten their knees and been subsumed into the fantasy.

Oh, without human sympathy, Mother, the world would be an impossible place. But you deserve more than sympathy for all the kindness you spread around.

They weren't holding back tonight. As the Mother Superior spun her horror tales, as the Senora commiserated with them on the squalor of their lives, Boyd reflected that perhaps the hostility in the cast was finally another serendipity. The Mother Superior's beneficence toward the Senora had a flicker of contempt beneath it that was more than first-rate acting. The Senora's condescension had a more than illusory edge. And Barnard, novice nun to his toes, fluttered anxiously as if he might smooth out the tension between them with his bird-light gestures, his beatific smile. Of the four, only Orme had none of his role in his real character, and had to invent maliciousness entire.

On stage, Orme leaned against the pillar and fingered the nail head by which the rope was attached. He watched Sister Ines bringing food and smelling salts for the Senora, sliding his hand down the rope in preparation for his line.

How could such an awful thing happen to such a dear sweet soul?

They cut it off with a knife, right down at the root.

Orme let his tongue hang out and slapped the rope against his skirt. But Boyd was vaguely aware that the look of it was wrong, too limp for the effect they had yesterday.

"Angel: *down at the root*—slap rope harder," he dictated into the cassette. It was only the fourth note he'd taken, and the rest of the first act needed no more than half a dozen others. Barnard was a beat late strumming his awful guitar, and missed the laugh. Gunilla describing her dreams (*I wanted to run away but I couldn't move . . .*) overplayed just a shade in the jitters of final dress. Wyman did the same thing accepting the cameo, though Barnard's collapse into tears was breathtaking. Wyman, gloating over the jewels (*A thousand years of riches . . .*) and loading them on over his neck and arms, struck an effeminate note that Boyd hadn't noticed before, and that shouldn't be there. Orme, having killed the Senora offstage, reentered not out of breath enough, and having forgotten to shove his wimple back off his head.

Apart from that, it was all Boyd could have wished for. In the intermission he went from dressing room to dressing room, saying, "You've got it. Just keep it." Gunilla, seated in the ragged gown and stretching her eyes for the makeup man, couldn't answer, but flashed him a look of triumph. He passed Shaara and Kevin in the hall, and felt free to compliment her, "Costuming is an *art*."

"It looks okay, doesn't it? The production's *good*, Boyd."

"What do you think of it?" he asked his son.

"*Creepy*," Kevin very satisfactorily replied.

Wendy had stayed self-effacingly in the auditorium while he made his rounds, but when he went back to join her she trapped his arm in both her arms and hugged his elbow to her diaphragm. "I married you," she declared, "for your imagination." And proceeded to deliver exactly such perceptions as he hoped to find, otherwise phrased, in the Atlanta reviews. "It's the little stuff that's scary," she said, and, "I don't know exactly what I mean, but everything in it's full of sex."

He'd told them to keep it, and they did. If anything, in the second act they were freer and larger, beginning to feel the reactions of their audience. Sister Angela got a full laugh when she tucked her skirt up into baggy trousers, then silenced them sharply when she turned on the Mother Superior:

I suppose you're going to leave me to do all the dirty
work as usual?

A score of people is too few to get the real play between audience and actors, but there was enough of it to gauge what tomorrow could be like. You could feel a faint shudder when Orme caught Barnard scratching at the grave, and his malevolent face lit:

Why don't we dig her up?

And again when the corpse came on, hanging potato-sack in Orme's hug, then thrown back to reveal the gray face and the staring eyes.

She weighs more now than when she was alive. And
she stinks like a cesspool.

Orme propped her in a niche in the wall and enlisted Barnard to hold her steady. Every time Sister Ines shifted weight the body slumped as if to fall, and the audience wavered between laughter and alarm. The Mother Superior started sneaking drinks from a hidden flask as Sister Angela, berating the corpse, wrung rings on its fingers and snapped earrings in its ears, twisted the matted hair up and shoved the tortoise-shell comb in place. The Mother Superior fell to her knees and into an insane confessional prayer, while Sister Angela rouged the corpse.

When you're used to fighting like a rat in a trap, nobody's got the right to shovel pity over you!

Barnard dragged the corpse to the post, bangled arms dangling, and put his weight against it to maneuver it into place. Orme followed, flicked at the dead hand, stormed back to Wyman.

Come on, make yourself useful. Cut me a bit of this rope.

Unconsciously, still chanting her litany, the Mother Superior complied, and Orme tied Gunilla at the thighs.

And we're getting used to the smell. We're made that way. Put a man in hell . . .

Orme saw that the knot was gone. Froze. Judged. Jerked on the rope and felt it stop with a softer sensation than before. Secured it in a figure eight around the cleat. He had a line to say, and carried on.

Gunilla felt the rope too tight. She felt the panic in her esophagus. But she was not going to break, not for them, and certainly not in final dress. She had lived most of her life one day at a time, and often in performance one minute at a time, coping, getting through on pride and discipline. Now she got through one second and the next, saying, I won't break now, I won't call out yet, I can take this second, and this one, and this one. In the last second of her violent silence before she lost consciousness and dropped her weight against the asphyxiating line, she thought: *I'll show them. I won't break for Wyman Path.*

Shaara, sitting in the back row of the darkened house, marveled at her technique; how her eyes bulged and her sockets purpled in the counterfeit of death.

Boyd saw it too, and marveled but was not surprised. He had known ever since she skinned her hair back and put on clogs, that she was holding back something to stupefy them all. Wyman would give everything from the beginning like popcorn and balloons at a Grand Opening; but Gunilla would save it back to dazzle them at last.

Wyman saw it when he went to crown the corpse: the angle of her head was wrong. The tiara slipped forward twice and wouldn't take a grip. He ended by shoving it over the tortoise-shell comb, but it spoiled his timing, so he turned with special fury into Ines's attack. The two scuffled, knocked the corpse askew at the hips, and fell with unusual impetus onto the bench where the Mother Superior took up a cushion and bore down on it over Ines's face till her arms stopped flailing and fell limp.

"Fight best ever," Boyd dictated into the cassette, flicked it off and then flicked it on again to complain, "But Barnard, you're breathing."

Orme and Wyman sat panting on the trunk, as spent and still now as Boyd had wanted, and when Orme back-handed the cigar over his shoulder the audience laughed aloud in the break of nervous tension. Wyman daydreamed into space:

When I've sold my share, I think I'll buy myself a castle and put spikes on all the walls to keep everybody out. I've seen enough people to last me a lifetime. Pass the bottle.

The voodoo drums had stepped up both pace and volume, and the tension rose again. The drumbeats became inter-spersed with muffled blows at the backstage door.

I've a confession to make. That hammering at the door? I made it up.

The blows got louder now and the panic took them, while the front-row audience strained forward into their space. Sister Angela retrieved her knife and tested the blade, the Mother Superior bound up her skirts, they started tunneling wildly in opposite directions.

Lord, don't let anything happen to me! Don't hold any-thing against me!

The lights dimmed, gathering toward the corpse's staring face. The hammer blows got louder still and the massive door began to slide and fall.

* * *

Angela! You're making a mistake! That isn't the right way.
Follow me! . . . the light's over here. Just a little further . . .

The lights contrarily went out. The guests and the crew
clapped, cheered—a thin promise of tomorrow night's response. Wendy gripped his arm. "God, Boyd!"

"Bravo!" Shaara called. "Brava!"

"Yes!" Boyd said. "Curtain calls and then notes. Gunilla?
Bring her down. Orme, get the rope. Gunilla?"

32. *Opening Night*

So the Grumbacher-funded Magoor Summer Arts Theater did not open. It wasn't immediately clear whether they would have to refund the grant. The academic vice president, who might have been able to deliver an opinion on this point, was at the Mid-Atlantic Coalition of Senior Administrators, and could not be reached.

What was curious was that, of all the people, Gunilla included, responsible for her death, it was Orme who blamed himself. He had pulled on the innocent rope. He fell apart. In the first couple of hours' confusion of ambulance and police, nobody had noticed how Orme was shaking and sweating in a corner of the set. Then Boyd picked up on it, talked to him and decided it had better not be fooled around with. Orme kept repeating himself and getting mixed up in his words, "I knew it was not, I thought it was the knot, not, the knot was not." Boyd sent Wendy back alone to the Campus Side, put Orme in the Volvo and followed Gunilla's body to the hospital, where Orme was treated for shock and kept most of the night under observation. He wouldn't let go of Boyd, lifted up off the bed and reached after him, the murderous brows clenched and the lantern jaw quivering. The doctors said Boyd could stay, and so he stayed. By dawn Orme, sedated, was calmer and seemed to have withdrawn into himself. The hospital counselor decided that the best thing to do was to release him into Boyd's care, and Boyd took him back to the motel.

They managed to ward off the Swedish consul and the black senator. Burt Reynolds was already en route from California, and he arrived at the appointed time. Wyman went to the airport to pick him up. Wyman thought him "intelligent" and "warm," but this time everybody agreed, including Gene Keyes, who took him out in the pickup for a pit barbecue breakfast, where Reynolds asked about the construction of the Interstate. Back at Boyd's motel Wendy fetched pots of coffee from the Bar and Grill while Wyman, Barnard, Orme, Boyd and Burt huddled around the telephone to New York, Stockholm and Jupiter Beach. Reynolds turned out to be a help because he knew how to get in touch with everybody fast on a Saturday morning, Gunilla's agent and Orme's and the producer of *Man of La Mancha* that Orme was due to start rehearsing in ten days.

Stage management and the crew rallied brilliantly, stuck to the theater all night and all day coping with the press, sending out notices over local radio, and refunding tickets. Except for Dora Fisher, who had a stomachache and disappeared, they handled it like professionals. Kevin and Shaara collapsed about two in the morning and went home to get two nights' sleep, but by late morning Shaara was back again, first at the theater and then at Campus Side. Gene offered to take Kevin to the movies for the afternoon, and Kevin concurred that he'd like to take another look at *Alien.*

"We'd just be in the way here, Mom," he said sagely.

By two o'clock the hospital and the police were done with Gunilla. There seemed to be no necessity for an autopsy. There was no immediate family, no relatives at all except for a second cousin in Stockholm, no "survivors" to report for the AP man who'd got wind of it and set up at the Campus Side. They put a call through to the second cousin, who supposed they'd better bury her where she was. Boyd insisted that Orme come along with him to make the arrangements. It was important, he said, for Orme to see her into the ground or into ashes. Otherwise he might not get rid of her, and she could come back to haunt him.

Reynolds thought this was good reasoning, and while Barnard and Wyman got Orme out to the car, he and Boyd found a minute to talk alone.

"We've already had to replace our Sancho Panza once," Reynolds said. "I don't want to do it again at this late date if

I can help it. Besides, I'm sure it'll be the best thing for him to throw himself back into work. Do you think he'll make it?"

"I don't know. I'll stick to him the next couple of days and we'll see. He's got a lot of trooper in him; he might just pull out of it."

"He thinks the world of you. He was telling me down in Jupiter Beach what a fantastic director you are."

"Oh, is that so?"

Reynolds gave him the cowboy-trucker grin. "Told me you were too big-time for this backwater shit."

"Oh. Well."

"Listen, this is just an idea. I don't know what your schedule is. If you came on down with him for a couple of weeks . . . it'd make continuity for him and might help. I could get you on the payroll so he didn't think he was being baby-sat. We could talk about your doing a production for me. Or I could put you in touch with—I don't suppose you're interested in directing flicks?"

Boyd said that he thought he could arrange his schedule and would be very pleased to do a production at Jupiter Beach and that, yes, he would be *quite* interested in directing flicks.

Wyman and Barnard took Reynolds back to catch a plane, and Orme and Boyd went off to the funeral home.

Wendy and Shaara found themselves left behind with an afternoon to kill. They attacked Boyd's motel room, straightened the skewed covers and hung the scattered towels. They were still wary of each other, and the inanities of yesterday proliferated—Should we take the cups back? Do you think it's okay to dump the ashtrays in the toilet?—through gritted smiles. Each had seen opening night as a barrier to urgent business at the center of her life. Now that there was to be no opening the time stretched without definition, a suspended unreality. Having this sense in common, they found nothing to say to each other. They spoke of Gunilla's death with manufactured awe.

"Did you know her well?" asked Wendy.

"Not at all, really. I'm not sure she was knowable. Well, one day she seemed to be trying to make friends, but it went wrong somehow." Saying this, she was awkwardly aware that she was saying it to Wendy Soole.

"You're not blaming yourself for that, just because she died?"

"What would be the point? It's too bad, that's all."

But in fact Shaara had spent the morning jumpy, defenses at the ready, in case anyone should point out the connection between Gunilla's costume and the accident. Wendy, as she had gradually understood what went wrong in rehearsal, had also gradually understood that she was the only one who knew how the knot in the rope had disappeared, and why the prop girl had disappeared as well. Now Wendy and Shaara, shaky with lack of sleep, each guarding her partial knowledge, were judgmental of the other's ignorance.

"What an awful thing."

Shaara thought this hardly needed saying and therefore said something equally mindless.

There were scripts and scraps of paper everywhere, which they decided they had better not throw away, so they tidied them into the empty strongbox in the closet. Either could have accomplished this in five minutes; together they spent twenty. Wendy apologized that she had not had a chance to unpack, and did so; then felt her face burn as she realized that she was hanging her wardrobe up with Boyd's. She wondered if Shaara would think she was doing this on purpose, staking her claim. And Shaara was acutely conscious that Wendy was arranging her trim poplins next to the chinos that sagged and raveled whenever Boyd sat. God! she was sourly glad those popping buttons were not her responsibility. The strongbox on the closet floor put her painfully in mind of the Winn Dixie bag.

At the bottom of the suitcase Wendy found the presents she had brought—the wallet and notebook for Boyd, the dagger for Kevin, the *commedia* mask, which in a surge of purpose and goodwill she had supposed she might give to Shaara. Now she shoved it in its tissue paper swathing to the back of the closet shelf. She zipped the case—"I guess that's that"—and turned out of habit to switch on the television, where a scrubbed family sat in front of a stuccoed cake, heaping praises on the baking skills of the wife-mother who turned to wink at the camera.

Shaara made an effort. "*There's* a favorite American pastime—fooling the family." But Wendy gave her a startled look, so Shaara supposed that, oh God, Wendy couldn't cook; while Wendy swiftly fantasized how Boyd had found the time to tell Shaara that she, Wendy, habitually lied to him. Then Wendy remembered that Boyd didn't really know this yet, and

Shaara thought, what the hell, Boyd doesn't notice what he's eating anyway, and Wendy switched the television off.

Bound by the force of wanting to separate, they could not. Wendy suggested another cup of coffee at the café. Shaara said thanks, but she'd promised she'd go to Gunilla's hotel and collect her things. She was sure Wendy would be too tired to come along? Wendy said she'd be glad to help and Shaara said it was awfully nice of her but she needn't and Wendy said she'd be glad to, really, and they escaped the motel room to trap themselves in Shaara's Beetle.

It was ninety-five degrees by now and the VW had been sitting in the sun for several hours. They rolled the windows down, sweated against the vinyl, lifted one thigh and then the other as they headed toward town and Shaara tried to take a route that would salvage Georgia's reputation. All the graceful pillared homes she found to drive past seemed to have been turned into insurance companies and halfway houses. She felt personally responsible for the humidity. She detoured into the Exxon station before she remembered it was Saturday, then started to pull out again before she realized that Bud was there, was coming out and along the tarmac after her.

"Hey, Bud, are you opening weekends again?"

"No, Miz Soole. I was just doing some accounts, but I'll fill you up."

It was disorienting to sit in the smell of regular with Wendy actually there, her gamin cut against a backdrop of Atlantic-Richfield retreads. Shaara regretted, resentfully, the loss of the fantasy that they could be friends. What had possessed her? She glanced sidelong at Wendy's simple silky shirt and felt the clumsy weight of hot chains against her own neck. She slid out the credit card, then clamped the wallet closed, seeing that there was after all something perverse—insane—about carrying a picture of your former husband's second wife. How would you explain such a thing?

"I appreciate it, Bud," she said a little heartily, and handed him the card.

"Well, I was wanting to tell you, the station'll be under new management next week."

"Oh, Bud, is it that bad?"

"Well, yes and no, it's happening to a lot of independents. Exxon offered to buy me out and I don't think I better wait until I have to."

"I'm really sorry to hear it."

"We'll be all right. It's about time to retire anyways. Me and the missuz have talked about opening a curio shop down Alligator Point."

"I'll come down and buy your curios. Good luck!"

Shaara frowned for a ways, and Wendy was embarrassed to see her muttering and blinking. They pulled in under the shade of the Sheraton carport, then both were embarrassed by the fussily funereal manager, and were trapped again in the elevator with a sturdily indifferent maid who slapped her keys against her thigh, one slap per floor to the eighteenth. Each of them wondered if the maid should be tipped, then Wendy decided that it was not her business and Shaara decided she was not in the mood to offer anybody anything; and the maid, a twenty-year professional, read them better than they read each other and left them as soon as the lock clicked open.

But when Shaara had closed the door and they faced Gunilla's room they shared a reaction which, for the first time, they realized they shared. The room was dark and red and stuffy, suffused with a farrago of scents that eerily brought home the nature of their errand. Powder had been spilled on the chest of drawers and not wiped up. A lacy bra dangled from the knob of an open drawer, a silk shawl trailed across a chair arm onto the floor. On the vanity an open bottle of Perrier, flat by now, sat beside a shriveling lime of which one slice floated in a half-full glass. The plastic bucket was full of water that had been ice when Gunilla died.

Shaara breathed the expensive smells. "I haven't taken it in," she said, which may have been as banal as anything she had said that afternoon, but was for a change the truth.

"I know," Wendy said.

Shaara opened the drapes and the afternoon sunlight flooded in; she turned on the air conditioner and the perfumes began to be sucked through the ventilators toward whatever filter system would purify them out. They found two matched two-suiters of parachute quilting, a hatbox and a patent leather carry-on, and for the second time in their twenty-four-hour acquaintance they launched into enforced housekeeping.

"She didn't travel light," Wendy observed. But they emptied the closet gingerly, intruders, not commenting further on either the number or the extravagance of Gunilla's blouses, dresses, trousers, jackets, scarves. Everything lifted from the enclosure gave off another breath of Chanel or Joy or, just occasionally, human sweat. There were twenty pairs of shoes. There were five nightgowns and three robes. In their silence they became efficient. They emptied the bureau of teddies, half-slips, camisoles; they stocked the hatbox with bottles, twisting each cap against whatever journey it might have in store. Wendy took from the nightstand a wooden candlestick of curly-carved bleached birch—much more fragile than brass, and carried halfway around the world for some purpose she could only guess at—removed its burnished taper and wrapped them both in lacy scarves. Shaara bundled pins and greasepaint sticks into the hatbox.

"Look at this."

Wendy had found an oval frame of dark wood with the sepia photo of a woman. She brought it across to Shaara at the vanity. The woman wore a shantung dress plisséed across the bosom, fastened with a brooch of corkscrew bars crossed by a studded crescent moon. Shaara recognized the likeness, the high bones and rich hair that—even this was essentially familiar—was disciplined into a tight roll over the ears.

"Her mother," Shaara guessed. "Look." And picked out from the drawer a little leather box containing the original of the gold moon brooch. "Wendy, see what she kept."

A songbook, *Sjung Svensa Folk!*, bound in dark red linen. A wide-eyed wooden horse four inches long, its straps and bridles painted in childishly bright blue. They looked again at the photo of the woman who had probably been Gunilla's mother, her Protestant tight-lipped smile and the severe tuck of her handsome hair; and in Wendy's mind there appeared an image of her own mother. Neither guilt nor revelation nor forgiveness; simply an image of her mother as she had been when Wendy was a child, rich auburn wisps of hair escaping from her chignon, tugging at Wendy's Wellingtons, doing the best that she could do.

"It must be awful not to have any sort of home at all," she said.

Shaara stood and turned away.

"I'm sorry. Did I . . .?"

"No, *I'm* sorry." She buried the picture in the middle of the suitcase. But the faded photo of the dead woman, she couldn't know how long dead, did for her what the death of Gunilla had failed to do. She closed the lid on Gunilla's "effects."

Strange word that, *effects*—Gunilla had so many of them. She thought of dying alone in a strange town so that other people had to pack your underwear and the detritus of your affections, not knowing why you'd kept a songbook or a wooden toy. Hubbard was not a foreign town to her but it had always been tentative at best, and it was tainted now by Boyd's invasion and this arbitrary death. Only Gene had made it promise roots. Suddenly tired of the posturings, the self-protections, she turned back to Wendy.

"It's just that I'm in a stupid relationship that isn't going anywhere."

"Ah." Wendy packed the horse, a travel clock. "Do you want it to? I just, well, assumed you were somebody who preferred to live alone."

"One of them libbers." Shaara laughed a little shrilly. "Oh, boy. Oh, no. Oh, wouldn't it just be easy just to want to live alone."

"Do you want to talk about it?"

"I don't know. I'm trying not to think about it. No, I guess I'd rather get all this done first."

But this was not a rebuff, and Wendy didn't feel that she had been rebuffed. An awkwardness acknowledged is the end of awkwardness. Together they double-checked the drawers and closet, zipped the cases and swung them to the door, then leaned against the elevator walls exhausted.

They loaded the bags and Shaara suggested they eat somewhere. But Wendy was fretting about getting back to Boyd—why not go back to the motel first and have a drink? Disaster and a common task had bled away their unease, and no longer constrained to stay together they were in no hurry to part. At the motel they unloaded the car and Shaara slipped her shoes off by the door. She called home, and Kevin said not to rush, he and Gene were Dungeon-and-Dragoning and grilling franks. She didn't ask to speak to Gene.

There was no sign yet of Boyd, and while Shaara was on the phone Wendy filled the ice bucket, found a bottle of Southern Comfort and poured them each a drink. She opened the closet to kick off her shoes and saw the tissue bundle on the shelf. She stood undecided a moment and then—why not? She'd intended it that way—took down and unwrapped the mask, carried it to where Shaara stood staring out at the pool.

"I brought presents for everybody. This is for you."

Overcome with confusion, Shaara took the mask in her hands

and admired the beaked nose, upswept eyes, the fine mottling of blues and gold. "How could you know I'd want just that?"

"It's only papier-mâché."

"Only! My god, it's beautiful. I'm teaching a course in masks this fall. This one is for the Venetian in the *commedia dell'arte.*"

"I know."

"What are you bringing me presents for? Does Boyd know you brought me a present?"

An hour ago this would have been the wrong thing to say. Now Wendy only performed a moue—"Not yet"—sat on the bed and sipped her drink. "Can I ask you something?"

"Sure, what?"

"Do you mind if we talk?"

Shaara sat across from her and stroked the mask in her lap. "Do."

"I think I know what happened," Wendy said.

"What do you mean?"

"How the knot got taken out of the rope."

"You do?"

"I'm pretty sure. I went up to the theater last night before rehearsal. I was feeling sort of out of it and, well, I guess I thought you snubbed me."

"Oh, I did. I felt so grubby and scattered, and you looked so cool . . ."

"I thought I was in the way."

"No, I know, I'm sorry."

"Well, it doesn't matter, it's just that I went back upstairs and started talking to the props girl."

"Dora?"

"I was sitting waiting for the play to start, just feeling at loose ends, and she looked so much like she knew what she was doing that I actually envied her. I'm almost sure she did it. Well, I am sure."

"Oh, God, Dora. Yeah, clean up the set—that's exactly what Dora would do."

"The thing is—you know what you asked me?"

"What?"

"Whether I mentioned it to Boyd that I brought you a present."

"I didn't mean . . ."

"No, listen. I've been thinking about that lately. I think maybe I've got into a habit of not mentioning things to Boyd, and I'm going to break the habit because—I don't know if this is a stupid thing to say to *you*—I want to make it work."

Shaara nodded. "It's not a stupid thing to say."

"What I think is, you have to be very clear with Boyd. He has a good heart, but he isn't sensitive. That's not the kind of intelligence he has. I think you just have to be very clear with him, about what you need and what you want to do. And then it will be all right. Does that make sense?"

Out of the mouths of babes. Oh, nothing spectacular, nothing you couldn't pick up in a magazine. Shaara stroked the mask, marveling at the simplicity of the truth that had eluded her for eleven years. She thought of all the things she had wanted, that Boyd had—intellect and ambition, culture, power—and the one thing he didn't have, which it turned out was the one thing she couldn't live without. "I think it makes better sense than anything I've heard in a good long while."

"And so I've decided to be super straight with him. But do I have to tell him this?"

"About Dora."

"I'm sure she didn't mean to. She didn't know what she was doing. She was just being fussy and she got carried away."

"That would be it."

"Isn't it cleaner if it just stays a mystery? Easier on her, of course, but easier on Boyd and the rest of them too?"

"I think Dora is somebody who doesn't get away with much of anything," Shaara said. "Yeah. Just forget it, Wendy. I'll forget it too."

Once people have agreed to forget something, the barriers are pretty well down. Shaara flopped back on the bed and peered at Wendy through the mask. "I had you pegged for a, I don't know, a sort of elegant innocent."

Wendy laughed. "I am. When it comes to that, I thought you were some kind of hypercompetent superwoman."

Shaara said, "I am." She lowered the mask and flung an arm over her forehead, dragging a bare toe in the shag, looking out the window where the last stragglers pulled themselves from the pool toward supper. "Oh, I am. God help me."

"Tell me about it, Shaara."

"There isn't really much to tell. You met him. Eugene Keyes?"

"I met so many people."

"Yes, well, I'm in love and I can't have it, that's all."

"He's already married?"

"Oh, no. He's very available."

"But not the marrying kind."

"If I ever laid eyes on the marrying kind, it's Eugene Keyes!"

"Well, then?"

Shaara sipped her Southern Comfort and chewed at her lower lip. "He's a cracker. He's a skilled laborer. He's small-boned. We look like Raggedy Ann and Action Man together. He's unsocializable. He's uninterested in money and contemptuous of power. He's the least appropriate choice I could possibly make."

Wendy said, "To whom?"

Shaara glanced at her and back out the window. Georgia was redeeming itself now with a misty sunset. Vapor rose off the pool and lifted into the hanging moss, shadows dappled the azalea banks. She took the question and turned it over unrhetorically. To whom? Just who was it, exactly, that she was unable to offend by marrying Eugene Keyes? He and Kevin got on together like good ol' boys at a jamboree. Her mother would cry long-distance and send them a pot of calico flowers; her brothers would fly out. Larry McElhaney and Mike Ogburn would pump her hand—as a matter of fact, Joe Dimbleton was a justice of the peace and would probably think himself honored to do the honors. Cass Carson would send love and macramé. Una Pendleton would fall to weeping and play the wedding march. The V.P. and his Scottish wife would give them a silver salad bowl. There might be a little sibling rivalry between Bette Davis and Fibber McGee. But Jesus. She was not going to let *Boyd Soole* pick a husband for her, was she?

No, she was not. She looked at Wendy with her true eye. "I don't know. You, maybe."

"Oh, it's okay by *me*."

The simple-minded don't understand when happiness knocks on their door; that's why they cry. Soap opera at its purest, the fugleman of melodrama, Shaara howled and reached across and hugged her and hung on. She dug in her bag for the photo of Gene she'd stuck behind the photo of Wendy behind her Exxon card. She offered it across to Wendy's open palm.

"Ah," Wendy said.

ABOUT THE AUTHOR

JANET BURROWAY, born in Phoenix, Arizona, studied at Barnard College and Cambridge University, where she was a Marshall Scholar. She has been an NBC Special Fellow in Playwriting at Yale School of Drama, designed costumes for the Belgian National Theater, taught at the University of Sussex, and written plays for British television. She has also published six novels including *The Buzzards*, which was nominated for the National Book Award, *Raw Silk*, which was nominated for the Pulitzer Prize, and a textbook, *Writing Fiction*. Holder of a 1976 fellowship from the National Endowment for the Arts and Visiting Lecturer at the Iowa Writers Workshop in 1980, Ms. Burroway is professor of English literature and writing and codirector of the Writing Program at Florida State University. She lives in Tallahassee, and is the mother of two grown sons.

Look for the SUMMER IN PARADISE SWEEPSTAKES entry coupon where these bestsellers are displayed:

On May 14

JUBAL SACKETT
by Louis L'Amour
THE TWO MRS. GRENVILLES
by Dominick Dunne
SHANGHAI
by Christopher New

On June 18

IACOCCA: AN AUTOBIOGRAPHY
by Lee Iacocca and William Novak
THE CIDER HOUSE RULES
by John Irving
BEACHES
by Iris Rainer Dart

Summer in Paradise

"Burroway's hallmark is her honest, ironic portrayal of characters who fall into their own traps and are then surprised to find the simplest truths in the unlikeliest of places. And this is achieved in chapters of gem-like completeness, all of which stand on their own like short plays."
—*Kirkus Reviews*

Two novels from Janet Burroway who has been nominated for both the National Book Award and the Pulitzer Prize:

Opening Nights

In this exuberant novel, Janet Burroway explores the entwined fates of Shaara and Wendy, the first and second wives of small-time theater director Boyd Soole. The one woman never having met the other, each tries to carve out a place to hide from her unpleasant past, all the while imagining what the other wife must be like. To Shaara, Wendy represents self-possessed, youthful confidence. To Wendy, Shaara is maturity: professional, independent, and careless of what people think. Both are right ... both are dramatically wrong.

"A fine and complex novel, a comedy and then some ..."
—*The New Yorker*

Raw Silk

Nominated for the National Book Award, *Raw Silk* is the story of Virginia Marbalestier, an American in her thirties living in England. A talented textile designer, she lives with her English husband Oliver in their Tudor manor house: their six-year-old daughter rounds out the deceptive appearance of a comfortable, fulfilling life.

It is only when a weepy, catatonic girl named Frances joins her department that Virginia begins to recognize a kind of kinship with the girl's misery. The result is a series of drastic realizations and changes in Virginia's life. Her story is an astonishingly honest account of the tensions in male/female relationships and a woman's ability to live her life for herself.

"In RAW SILK, life itself seems to burst the fibers of human design."
—*The New Republic*

Coming in June 1986 from Bantam Books

BANTAM
SHOP-AT-HOME
C·A·T·A·L·O·G

Special Offer
Buy a Bantam Book
for only 50¢.

Now you can have an up-to-date listing of Bantam's hundreds of titles plus take advantage of our unique and exciting bonus book offer. A special offer which gives you the opportunity to purchase a Bantam book for only 50¢. Here's how!

By ordering any five books at the regular price per order, you can also choose any other single book listed (up to a $4.95 value) for just 50¢. Some restrictions do apply, but for further details why not send for Bantam's listing of titles today!

Just send us your name and address and we will send you a catalog!